PRAISE FOR JIM FERGUS'S
THE WILD GIRL

"Fergus makes unforgettable characters move against vivid landscapes in this laudable encore."
—*Publishers Weekly*, starred review

"A literary, but accessible tale . . . beautifully told."
—Malcom Jones, *Newsweek*

"Illuminated with the Technicolor scenery of a John Ford Western."
—*Gotham*

"*The Wild Girl* has all the hallmarks of a classic. You enter the story like a time machine and are instantly transported back to the Southwest at the true end of the 'Old West.'"
—Judith Chandler, formerly of Third Place Books

PRAISE FOR JIM FERGUS'S
ONE THOUSAND WHITE WOMEN

WINNER OF
THE MOUNTAINS AND PLAINS BOOKSELLERS AWARD

"An American western with a most unusual twist. Fergus is gifted in his ability to portray the perceptions and emotions of women. He writes with tremendous insight and sensitivity about the individual community and the political and religious issues of the time, many of which are still relevant today. This book is artistically rendered with meticulous attention to small details that bring to life the daily concerns of a group of hardy souls at a pivotal time in U.S. history."
—*Booklist*

"An impressive historical . . . terse, convincing, and affecting."
—*Kirkus Reviews*

"The best writing transports readers to another time and place, so that when they reluctantly close the book, they are astonished to find themselves returned to their daily lives. *One Thousand White Women* is such a book. Jim Fergus so skillfully envelops us in the heart and mind of the main character, May Dodd, that we weep when she mourns, we shake our fist at anyone who tries to sway her course, and our hearts pound when she's in danger."   —*Colorado Springs Gazette*

"Jim Fergus's *One Thousand White Women* is a splendid, fresh, and engaging novel. Strikingly original."   —Jim Harrison, author of *Legends of the Fall*

"A most impressive novel that melds the physical world to the spiritual. *One Thousand White Women* is engaging, entertaining, well written, and well told. It will be widely read for a long time, as will the rest of Jim Fergus's work."   —Rick Bass, author of *Where the Sea Used to Be*

"Jim Fergus knows his country in a way that's evocative of Dee Brown and all the other great writers of the American West and its native peoples. But *One Thousand White Women* is more than a chronicle of the Old West. It's a superb tale of sorrow, suspense, exultation, and triumph that leaves the reader waiting to turn the page and wonderfully wrung out at the end."
—Winston Groom, author of *Forrest Gump*

THE WILD GIRL

Also by Jim Fergus

Fiction

ONE THOUSAND WHITE WOMEN

Nonfiction

A HUNTER'S ROAD
THE SPORTING ROAD

THE WILD GIRL

The Notebooks of Ned Giles, 1932

A NOVEL BY JIM FERGUS

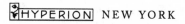 HYPERION NEW YORK

Copyright © 2005 Jim Fergus

Library of Congress Cataloging-in-Publication Data

Fergus, Jim.
    The wild girl : the notebooks of Ned Giles, 1932 : a novel / by Jim Fergus.—1st ed.
      p. cm.
    1. Americans—Mexico—Fiction. 2. Photographers—Fiction. 3. Apache women—Fiction. 4. Young men—Fiction. 5. Mexico—Fiction. I. Title.

  PS3556.E66W55 2005
  813'.54—dc22

                2004054161

Hyperion books are available for special promotions and premiums. For details contact the Harper-Collins Special Markets Department in the New York office at 212-207-7528, fax 212-207-7222, or email spsales@harpercollins.com.

FIRST TRADE PAPERBACK EDITION

TRADE PAPERBACK ISBN 978-0-7868-8865-8

10 9 8 7 6 5 4 3

SUSTAINABLE FORESTRY INITIATIVE
Certified Fiber Sourcing
www.sfiprogram.org

THIS LABEL APPLIES TO TEXT STOCK

To Guy

"I love three things. I love a dream of love I once had, I love you, and I love this patch of earth."

"And which do you love best?"

"The dream."

KNUT HAMSUN, *PAN*

If the ways of seeing in different communities are in conflict because their interpretative practices reflect incommensurable presuppositions about the human situation, can such communities understand each other? Can one culture use its own terms to say something about another culture without engaging in a hostile act of appropriation or without simply reflecting itself and not engaging the otherness of the Other? . . . Can we ever escape our provincial islands and navigate between worlds?

PAUL B. ARMSTRONG, "PLAY AND CULTURAL DIFFERENCES,"
KENYON REVIEW 13 (WINTER 1991)

Until I was about ten years old, I did not know that people died except by violence.

JAMES KAYWAYKLA, WARM SPRINGS APACHE
IN THE DAYS OF VICTORIO, EVE BALL

THE WILD GIRL

LA NIÑA BRONCA

In the beginning there was Ishtun-e-glesh, White-Painted-Woman. She had no mother or father. She was created by the power of Yusen. He sent her down to the world to live. Her home was a cave.

There was a time when White-Painted-Woman lived all alone. Longing for children, she slept with the Sun and not long after gave birth to Slayer of Monsters. Four days later, White-Painted-Woman became pregnant by water and gave birth to Child of the Water. As Slayer of Monsters and Child of the Water grew up, White-Painted-Woman instructed them on how to live. They left home and, following her advice, rid the earth of most of its evil. White-Painted-Woman never became old. When she reached an advanced age, she walked toward the east. After a while she saw herself coming toward herself. When she came together, there was only one, the young one. Then she was like a young girl all over again.

FROM THE APACHE CREATION MYTH
James L. Haley, *Apaches: A History and Cultural Portrait*
H. Henrietta Stockel, *Women of the Apache Nation*

THE GIRL HEARD THE DOGS BARKING LONG BEFORE SHE COULD SEE them, a kind of frantic, high-pitched yipping. She could not know that it was the sound hunting hounds make when they are on a fresh trail. Nor did she have any way of knowing that the trail they were on was her own, that she smelled enough like a wild animal, like the mountain lion they were supposed to be hunting, to temporarily divert them to her path. Yet in the instinctive way that all creatures sense danger in such a sound, and because the barking, though distant at first, seemed to be coming closer, the girl began to run down the arroyo.

The arroyo was dry this time of year and only ran water during the summer monsoons. On the hillsides above grew twisted mesquite trees and gnarled oaks, and above those the tall, straight pines of the high country. Down below, the broad plains were studded with prickly pear and cholla cactus, and impenetrable thickets of catclaw bushes. The arroyo ran to the river bottom, which itself was incongruously lush, a band of pale spring green with grass and ferns, giant cottonwood trees, and white-barked sycamores just beginning to leaf out. To this oasis all things aspired; the wildlife came down to water, and seek shade and cover there. The land itself—the rocky canyons and draws, the folds of land like the knuckles, fingers, and veins on the back of a man's hand—all spilled into it. Beyond and above, the high jagged peaks of the Sierra Madre rose up, hazy with dust that swirled skyward in the warm spring winds from the plains below.

The girl carried a thin cotton sack containing a few roots she had dug, the only food she had eaten in the several days she had spent wandering the hills and mountains, searching for the People. She wore a two-piece deerskin dress and high-topped moccasins with the distinctive upturned toes of Apache manufacture. The moccasins strapped above her knees, but were now almost worn through at the soles, and a thin rivulet of dried menstrual blood ran down the inside of her thighs, staining the hide of the moccasins dark all the way down to her insteps.

Only a few days before, her costume had been very beautiful, made

painstakingly over a period of weeks by her mother for her puberty ceremony, the traditional Apache celebration of a girl's menarche. The dress
was tanned soft and sewn flesh side out, dyed yellow to signify the fertility
of pollen and painted with spectacular symbols of White-Painted-Woman,
the mother of all Apaches—a rainbow, the morning star, a crescent moon,
sunbeams. It was exquisitely beaded and elaborately finished with fringes
and silver studs and tin cone-tinklers that once made a light musical tone
when she moved. But now the beads and ornamentation were mostly torn
off, the dress itself so tattered that the painted symbols hung in shredded
ribbons that fluttered as she ran, those few cone-tinklers still attached rattling desolately. And as she ran, the tatters of the dress caught on the grasping thorns of the catclaw bushes, ripping the deerskin away from her slight
frame so that she was slowly being stripped naked, her brown flesh where it
was exposed to the thorns scored by small cuts and scratches.

It had been a dry spring and scenting conditions were poor for the
dogs, which would have been to the girl's advantage, except that her men-
struation gave up the faintest scent trail of blood, permeating the desert air
like a vague perfume, further inflaming the hounds. She ran lightly, soundless as a spirit, her feet barely grazing the rocks, silent footsteps raising
small puffs of dust from the sandy arroyo, her thick dark hair unbraided
and wild, tangled and streaming behind her. She did not breathe heavily,
for even though she was exhausted and weakened by hunger she was
In'deh, Apache, and could run this pace all day.

The girl did not know what calamitous mistake had been made in her
puberty ceremony to bring this terrible disaster down upon the People.
She had not gone around with boys before her menarche, which would
have disqualified her from assuming the role of White-Painted-Woman.
Her aunt Tze-gu-juni, who served as her attendant, had bathed her before
dawn on the first morning, washing her hair with yucca root, marking her
with yellow pollen down the part of her hair and across the bridge of her
nose. Then her aunt dressed her in her puberty costume, starting with the
moccasins, then the beautiful dress, during the sewing of which the old
woman Dahteste had come to sing the proper songs so that all had been
done exactly according to ritual.

But the girl had little time to consider this now, did not think about her mother and her sister as she ran, and of the others dead in the attack upon their camp that morning, did not think about watching from her hiding place in the rocks as three Mexican vaqueros raped the women each in turn while the others watched, smoking indolently and laughing. And when they were finished, while her mother tried to comfort her sister in their disgrace, the worst fate that can befall an Apache woman, so that even death was preferable, two of the men had come up behind them with machetes and struck them each a sharp chopping blow to the back of the neck. They fell wailing together to the ground, her mother blindly trying to gather her sister in her arms to protect her from the blows. But the men continued to hack at them for a very long time with the machetes, until they lay still.

Then the men began the task of decapitating the dead with hunting knives, working with the same brutal efficiency with which they might remove heads from the carcasses of game animals. And when they had completed their grim surgery, they mounted the severed heads on sharpened mesquite sticks and rode away to claim their bounties, these *In'deh* now destined to live for eternity in the Happy Place without their heads.

But the girl did not have time to think about this now. Nor was it a good thing to dwell upon the dead, even worse to speak their names lest you call up their ghosts to bedevil the living. Still, she understood with the innate biological certainty of a species hurtling toward extinction, that Yusen, the life-giver, had abandoned the People, and that somehow she herself had brought this terrible disaster down upon them, that her power as White-Painted-Woman had failed to protect them against their ancient, hated enemies. And so weak and starving though she was, on she ran, steadily, lightly, moving like a spirit being over the rocks, the shreds of her dress fluttering like ribbons, her hair streaming wildly behind her, her soundless footsteps raising small clouds of dust in the dry arroyo.

By the time she reached the river bottom, the sound of the dogs had intensified, their yipping taking on a new resolve. Now the girl spotted the lead dog making his way down the arroyo behind her. He did not look up although he would certainly have seen her, but rather kept his nose to the ground, working a steady, if circuitous route, businesslike, inexorable. The river was low and clear, and the girl ran across on the slick rocks. But she knew that she could not outrun the dog, and partway up the slope on the opposite side, she scrambled up an oak tree and squatted there in the crotch of a branch.

The dog was only mildly confused by her crossing, working up and down the riverbank until he winded her scent and then made his way across on the same rocks. He trailed the girl to the base of the tree, looked up at her finally, in some state of canine puzzlement, growled low in his throat, not quite certain what prey this was. Then he settled himself on his haunches like compressing a spring and pushed off with surprising upward thrust, soaring skyward, as if just to have a better look, his front paws clawing for purchase at the trunk of the tree. But he fell back to the ground, sprawling and ungainly, scrabbling to his feet again, to take up a new tone, a deeper wailing song that told his fellow dogs and the hunter himself that he had brought their quarry to bay.

The hunter, Billy Flowers, had been cutting country for several hours, looking for lion sign when he heard his dogs begin to utter the short choppy bark that told him they had moved a fresh track and were trailing. Flowers knew that his dogs would never trail trash—as deer, or rabbits, or other nonpredatory animals are called by houndsmen. But he could detect a subtle difference in the pack's barking, a confused edge that suggested they might be tracking something other than a panther. Perhaps, he thought, they had moved a jaguar, although this was a bit north of that cat's traditional range. Still, it was possible that one had strayed up from the southern Sierra Madre, and he dearly hoped so, for the jaguar was one of the few species that he had not yet killed in his long and distinguished career as a hunter of predators.

Billy Flowers had answered his calling early in life, when the Voice told him to go into the wilds of his native Mississippi and slay the creatures of forest and field. Even after he had grown to manhood, married, and had three children, the Voice would not allow him to rest. And he had no choice but to obey. He finally abandoned his family (although these many years later he still sent money home to his wife and now-grown children) to hunt his way through the south, virtually exterminating single-handedly the black bear in Louisiana before moving on to the canebrakes of Texas. There, in the fall of the year 1907, in the prime of his life, he had served as Teddy Roosevelt's chief huntsman on a much-publicized two-week bear hunt. A "religious fanatic," TR had called Billy Flowers in a newspaper account of the presidential safari, simply because Flowers had refused to hunt or allow his dogs to do so on the Sabbath, even though on Monday he had gotten the president his trophy—a lean, immature she-bear, newspaper photos of which gave rise to the nation's "Teddy Bear" craze.

From Texas, Flowers kept drifting west, looking for open country to wander and varmints to hunt. He eventually settled in the Southwest, though *settled* was the wrong word. He had no home of his own and spent the better part of the year on the move, living mostly in the mountains with his dogs, only occasionally accepting temporary winter lodgings in the outbuildings of some of the ranchers to whom he contracted his services.

Thus the years had passed, and Billy Flowers became an old man, his hair and beard growing long and white, until he resembled an Old Testament prophet, and a half-crazy one at that, with his searing bright blue eyes. He tallied his kill in notebooks from which, with the hubris typical of many eccentrics, loners, and fanatics, he planned eventually to write his autobiography, under the deluded notion that people would actually be interested in reading about his solitary, violent life as an exterminator of wild creatures. Since he had arrived in the Southwest, he had killed 547 mountain lions and 143 bears. A few years before, he had killed what was very likely the last grizzly bear in the region, a huge, ancient creature, missing two toes off its left front foot, its front tusks worn to the gums. Flowers had tracked the bear for three weeks, from the New Mexico bootheel into the mountains of Sonora and Chihuahua. There he had finally trapped it in a steel-jawed leg trap, which the old grizzly dragged all the way back across the border before Billy Flowers caught up to him and dispatched him. He sent the hide and skull to the National Museum in Washington. The last grizzly bear in the Southwest.

Now, from astride his mule on the ridge above the river bottom, Billy Flowers heard his lead dog, a lanky Walker-bluetick mix named Monk, "barking treed." He turned the mule, a pale gray named John the Baptist, touched him lightly with his spurs, leaned back in the saddle, and gave him his head, letting the animal pick his own way down the steep rocky slope. John the Baptist was clever and sure-footed, stepping quickly and expertly from rock to rock, squatting low on his rear legs to slide on the loose scree. By the time they reached the bottom of the incline, Flowers heard the other dogs join Monk, taking up the same distinct baying sound that told him, whatever it was, they had the creature up a tree.

He clucked the mule into a run, splashing across the shallow river to find his dogs, all seven of them in perfect biblical symmetry, baying furiously at the base of an oak tree partway up the far slope. The dogs stood on their hind legs, scratching wildly at the tree trunk, alternately leaping and twisting in the air like performing circus dogs, all the while barking and howling their frustrations.

Flowers could not yet make out through the leafy canopy what quarry they had treed, but as he approached he could hear the creature hissing and spitting, and though he knew that it was not a lion, he had no idea what on earth it might be, for it was not a sound he had ever before heard on this earth. He reined up his mule, swung from the saddle, and slipped his rifle from the scabbard. As their master approached, the dogs' baying became even more frenzied, anticipating the moment that he shot the animal from the tree and they were rewarded for their efforts by being allowed to tear open its gut and feast upon its entrails and organs.

Although Billy Flowers was no longer young, he was still wiry and strong, and he was a man without fear of man or beast. He had wrestled alligators in the swamps of Louisiana, choked the life from rattlesnakes and water moccasins with his bare hands, killed grizzlies and lions in close combat with a knife. He believed that he had seen just about everything there was to see in the wilds, but he was entirely unprepared for the creature he beheld now in the oak tree, hissing and growling, trying to strike out at his dogs with its hands as if it had claws on the end of its slender fingers. He wondered for a moment if this might be the devil himself, come finally to test him, taking the form of this wild creature, half human, half animal, squatting nearly naked in a tree, shredded clothes falling from its slight body, hair tangled and filthy. The creature had dirty yellow stripes painted crudely on its face, framing eyes black and bottomless as time itself, and filled with a scalding rage as it growled, spat, and swiped at his dogs.

And then with a sense of relief so vague that he hardly noticed it himself, he realized that the creature was not Satan at all, only perhaps Satan's vessel, a heathen, and a spectacularly unclean one at that. Flowers had been advised when he first came down into Mexico that a small band of wild Apaches still inhabited the hidden canyons and valleys of the Sierra Madre, the high mountain country so rugged and inaccessible that few white men had ever seen it and most Mexicans were afraid to pass there. But Billy Flowers had always traveled alone and feared heathens no more than he did man or beast, of which he considered them to be simply a kind of hybrid. He could see now beneath the rags and the filth that this one was a girl, barely more than a child, and he called off his dogs, who were instantly obedient, quit their baying and began to pace around the base of the tree, panting, slavering, whining, their bony ribs heaving. The girl fell still herself, silent and watchful.

"*Thou shalt break the heathen with a rod of iron,*'" said Billy Flowers in incantation, raising his rifle to his shoulder. "*Thou shalt dash them to pieces like a potter's vessel.*'" He looked into the girl's eyes and could find there no hint of fear in her bold, strangely calm gaze, no suggestion even of a shared humanity. It was exactly like looking into the eyes of a lion or a bear, as he had done so many times before in his life in that decisive moment before he dispatched them, their eyes luminescent, impenetrable, casting back only his own reflection.

Flowers lowered his rifle, slipped it back into the scabbard that hung from his saddle, shook his head and muttered to himself in some disgust. It had been revealed to him, the face of his own fear—the vision of Satan in the person of a child, this young girl. He knew that the Mexican government had recently reinstated the bounty on Apache scalps in an attempt to rid the country once and for all of the scourge of savages that had plagued them for so many generations. Yet, though this would certainly be a legal kill, Billy Flowers had never before taken another human being's life, and he would not do so now, even one so primitive and so far from God as this one.

Flowers reached into his saddlebag and brought out a small package of waxed paper, which he unfolded to reveal a single tortilla folded around a piece of honeycomb from a beehive he had raided earlier. He carried very little food when he was hunting, eating mostly what he killed, believing that the flesh of the lion and the bear gave him and his dogs the strength of the animal. But he had a weakness for sweets and had never been able to resist honey.

Now he stepped forward again, peering up at this wild child in the tree, unwrapped the tortilla, and watched as the girl cut her eyes to it, the dogs, too, attentive to his every move. "I expect you're hungry, heathen," he said in a voice not without some measure of kindness. He pulled off a piece of the tortilla, squeezing honey onto it from the piece of hive like a sponge. "Yessir, missy," he said, taking a bite, chewing slowly, licking his fingers with great care and relish. "I expect you're mighty hungry." He pulled off another piece and reached it up toward her. "Here. Go on. Take it."

The girl watched him impassively, but made no move to accept his offering.

The old man studied her, finally nodded. "No, I don't suppose I'll get you down out of that tree until I put the dogs up, will I?" he said.

He folded the tortilla and honeycomb back up in the wax paper and slipped it into the breast pocket of his shirt. Then he turned to the mule and pulled his dog chains from a saddlebag. He led the dogs lower down the slope to a grove of mesquite saplings, where he tethered each in turn to a tree.

"All right, little missy," he said, coming back up to the girl, "come on down out of that tree. Dogs won't harm you now." He slipped the tortilla out his pocket and waved it toward her, making it clear that if she wanted it she would have to come down for it.

She looked at the tortilla, then at Flowers, then at the dogs. He held it up again. "Come, have a little bite to eat," he said, talking mainly for the comfort of hearing his own voice, in the same way that he often spoke to his dogs, who were for months at a time his only companions, addressing them just as if they were people and understood his every word. "Dogs are put up, child. I'm not going to hurt you."

Without taking her eyes from him, the girl began to climb out of the tree, dropping quiet as a spirit from the lowest limb to the ground, the tatters of her dress fluttering faintly with a sound like distant birds on the wing. Flowers couldn't help but notice the wild grace of her movement, a kind of otherworldliness, in the same way that the coyote and the wolf have a gait so distinct from that of the domestic dog.

"Won't do you any good to try to run off," he warned her. "I'll let them loose after you again, and this time they catch you they'll tear your heart out." He reached out the tortilla to the girl, but still she made no move to take it from him. "I will give you a shirt to wear, child," he said, vaguely unsettled by the unfamiliar sight of the girl's small brown breasts visible through her shredded dress. "You're practically naked. And by *God Almighty*, I am told that I'm a strongly aromatic fellow myself, having only rare opportunity to bathe, but you child, yours is an unholy scent. You stink like a beast of the wilds. It is no wonder that my dogs took you for a varmint."

The girl watched him, her eyes so dark that they appeared black, the sclera itself coffee-colored, an anatomical difference for which the "White Eyes" had gained their name. Billy Flowers had known some Apaches over the years; he had trailed game through their reservations in Arizona and New Mexico, and in general he found them to be a squalid, indolent sort, given to drink and gaming, a people for whose salvation he held out scant hope. But this child was different, untamed and of an earlier race of man altogether, a prehistoric being.

"I'm afraid that the Good Lord has his work cut out with you, young lady," Flowers said. Then he turned back toward his mule to fetch his shirt with which to cover the heathen girl's nakedness.

THE NOTEBOOKS OF NED GILES, 1932

7 DECEMBER, 1999

Albuquerque, New Mexico

A man's memory is the faultiest of instruments, vulnerable to retrospection and revisionism, altered by age and distance, skewed by heartbreak, disappointment, and vanity, tainted always by the inconsolable hope that the past was somehow different than we really knew it to be. This is why memoirs are always, by definition, false. But a photograph never lies. I think it is what attracted me to the form originally. My own memory is largely visual, the years and decades of my life defined by images, hundreds of thousands of photographs taken over the past half century, although what has become of most of them I could not say. It hardly matters anymore; I don't need to look at the images themselves in order to remember, for they live on perfectly preserved in my mind; I can see the light and composition of each, the specific expression on a subject's face, a sweep of landscape, the naked truth of an empty room, sunlight spilling across a doorway, the door itself half open, the mystery inside.

I close my eyes and see with perfect recall a dark-eyed girl of my youth running down a dry arroyo. She is slight, strong, fierce, her skin the color of a chestnut, her hair black and thick as a mane. I freeze her in my camera lens, but she moves on like a dream, refusing to be stilled. Many people believe that a photograph is an inanimate object, time stopped, frozen in place. But it is not. It is only that specific moment between what just was and what is about to come, a single moment alive and moving forever between past and future.

I no longer take photographs; I don't need to make any more memories, I have more than enough to last. My health is poor, my heart bad; I wake up in the middle of the night short of breath to feel it fluttering weakly in my chest like a dying bird. I don't have long to live.

Still, the imminence of death does not prevent me from hearing the

continual click of shutters in my dreams, or from seeing the old images passing in my mind's eye like a slide show. Quite the contrary. The old saw has it
that as you grow older you can't remember whether or not you took your
medication five minutes ago, but you can remember with total recall something that took place fifty, sixty, seventy years ago. This is appallingly true.

It was my habit for many years to keep detailed notebooks of my travels and of my work. Journals are kept largely for the benefit of the journal
keeper, in my case, as a way to chart my progress, or lack thereof, as a photographer. And if, as I believe, we define ourselves through our work, our
professions, our accomplishments, these notebooks also serve to chart my
progress, or lack thereof, as a human being, a matter which may be of little interest to anyone but myself.

I kept the following notebooks in the year 1932, the middle of the
Great Depression, not only another era, but another lifetime ago. They describe a trip I made across the United States and into the Sierra Madre of
Mexico when I was seventeen years old. It is another of my beliefs that our
characters are forged at a very young age, and although our circumstances
may certainly change dramatically in the course of our lives, our fundamen-
tal natures do not. All the self-improvement schemes, the twelve-step pro-
grams, the mood-stabilizing medications and therapies later, we are still
more or less stuck with ourselves. And while these notebooks frequently reflect the innocence, callowness, and sometimes pretensions of a seventeen-
year-old, when I read them all these years later, I am struck by how clearly I
recognize myself, how much a part of me that odd, angry, heartbroken,
hopeful, stupid boy still is. And not discounting the inevitable decay of
body and mind that has taken place in the intervening sixty-seven years, I
am struck by how little, finally, I have changed. The revelation that I go to
my grave as the boy I once was and still am, and always will be, alone makes
having preserved these notebooks all these years well worth it. In the same
way, how extraordinary to be an old man looking back upon one's youthful
self, and reading in the very first paragraph as that youthful self looks ahead
to his own old age. It is a bit like standing between two facing mirrors and
gazing down the tunnel to infinity that they create.

My original working notebooks contained photographs, sometimes loose and sometimes pasted on the page. I've lost many of these images over the years, and for practical reasons, those that have survived have not been reproduced in this manuscript, although I may have referred to them from time to time in these pages. I've also deleted many references to photographic technique and equipment, simply because they would bore all but the most serious student of photography. Finally, the reader will notice that some entries are dated, others not. I don't exactly remember the reason for these inconsistencies, but my guess is that especially during our brief time among the bronco Apaches in the Sierra Madre, I had no idea what the date was, and as we lived in an alternate reality there, it hardly seemed to matter.

Other than that, the following story is true—not as it is remembered sixty-seven years later through the gauze of time and memory, and related by an old man who might wish to aggrandize himself before his death, but exactly as it happened to a seventeen-year-old boy named Ned Giles in that long-ago year 1932.

NOTEBOOK I:

Leaving Home

5 January, 1932

Chicago, Illinois

Tomorrow morning I leave Chicago, and so tonight I begin a brand-new notebook to record my trip. All the others, the dozens that I've kept since I was a little kid, I've decided to leave behind here, along with my old life. A new notebook for a new life. It's bound to be a grand adventure, and maybe someday my children and grandchildren will want to read about it. Maybe when I'm an old man, sitting on the front porch in my rocking chair, I'll want to read about it myself. I'm excited about going, but I have to admit that I'm a little scared, too. I have butterflies in my stomach tonight and I can't sleep anyway, so I think I'll just begin by telling how it is that I came to be leaving home in the first place.

I have been living alone in our house since the deaths of my parents over three months ago. It wasn't until a week or so ago that anyone even noticed that I was alone here. I think people are a bit distracted; everyone has troubles enough of their own and what's one orphan kid compared to all the folks who have lost their homes and are living out on the street?

My mother died in Presbyterian–St. Luke's Hospital last fall. She'd been sick for over a year with the cancer. I didn't really know it at the time, but my father was already under a great deal of pressure with his business. Pop was the first Studebaker dealer in Chicago, but I guess people haven't been buying too many automobiles the past couple of years, and he got himself in a good deal of financial trouble. The last thing my mother said to me before she died was, "Take care of your father, Neddy, he'll be lost without me."

We buried my mother in the Oak Park cemetery on a cold, blustery October morning. All I really remember now about the service was the mourners all bundled up in winter overcoats, and the yellow leaves swirling on the wind. Ten days later my father put a gun in his mouth in the bathroom of our house and blew the back of his head out. I found him there when I got home from classes, sitting slumped over on the toilet. He left an envelope with my name on it propped up on the bathroom shelf. Inside there was a copy of his insurance policy and the keys and title to his new Commander Eight Roadster. There was a short note in the envelope explaining that I would be better off with the car and the money, and that he wished he could have left me more. *I'm sorry, son,* Pop said in his note, *but I just can't go on without your dear mother. You've always been a good boy. I know you love taking pictures. Why don't you buy yourself a good camera. Good luck, Ned. Love, Pop.* That was it. Pop's final advice to me. *"Why don't you buy yourself a good camera."*

I guess I sound pretty cold about it, don't I? I loved my parents but I haven't been able to cry for them yet. I guess when Mom died, I was too busy worrying about Pop. He was in pretty rough shape, drinking too much scotch and crying himself to sleep every night. But I never thought he was going to kill himself. And to tell the truth, I'm just so damn mad at him for it. What kind of father leaves his only child alone like that? I loved my father but I realize that he was a weak man. I think he had a responsibility to stay around and take care of us.

My uncle Bill, Pop's unmarried younger brother, came out from California to help with the funeral arrangements, and to settle Pop's insurance. I really don't know him very well, but he's a nice enough guy. I didn't want to go live with him out there, and I don't think he wanted me, either. So I lied and told him I was going to live with my mother's sister in Cincinnati. Uncle Bill seemed pretty relieved about that, even though my mother doesn't have a sister in Cincinnati.

"You just be sure to send me a card with your new address once you get there, kid," he said. "You know if you ever need anything, anything at all, you can always count on your old uncle Bill." He smiled as if he was kind of embarrassed about saying this, because, of course, we both knew that it was not so.

I'm a year ahead of my age in school, already one semester into my first year of undergraduate studies at the University of Chicago. And I hold a part-time job, or at least I did until just recently, at the Chicago Racquet

Club, a private men's club downtown. I've worked there in the summertime for years. I started out as a ball boy for the tennis pro, and later I worked in the clubhouse. I've done a little bit of everything at the club over the years. I've washed dishes in the kitchen, cleaned the squash courts and locker room, waited tables in the dining room. I've always been popular with the members because I've been there since I was a kid, and I'm quiet and polite, so that eventually the rich men forget I'm even there and speak as freely as if I weren't. I liked working at the club and I knew that I was lucky to have a job in these times when so many people are out of work. It's a funny thing, but most of the members don't even seem like they've been much affected by the Depression. All of Chicago's old founding families belong to the club—the Swifts, the Armours, the Cudahys, the Meers, the McCormicks—and the place is kind of like a big kids' fort for grown-ups, where the rich guys can hide out together and pretend that everything is okay, that nothing outside their walls really exists. Which I guess is the whole point of a private club. It's a whole different world in there and I feel it every time I walk through the doors. Paintings of hunting dogs and jumping horses hang on dark wood-paneled walls. The furniture is all plush leather and velvet, polished oak and mahogany. Beautiful Oriental rugs cover gleaming hardwood floors. It's hard to explain but there's a kind of comforting hush about the place that seems to mingle in the air with the rich smells of fine whiskey and Cuban cigars and choice Chicago beef searing on the grill in the kitchen. And even the sweet aftershave sweat of squash players just coming off the court seems so different from the sour sweat of workingmen gathered for an illegal pint at the neighborhood speakeasies.

If anything, the club members seem more gay than ever these days. They throw more private parties and drink more booze, and the drunker they get, the louder they defend the ruinous economic policies of their Republican hero, President Herbert Hoover. Our family is from a long line of working-class Democrats, but Pop always told me that it would probably be better if I didn't mention this at the club. Not that those men would ever ask an employee about his politics.

Some of the members had seen my father's obituary in the *Chicago Tribune* (I wrote it myself), and ever since they've been especially solicitous of me. Some of the men even slipped me envelopes of cash. It was a strange feeling to accept their gifts, as if I was being tipped for my parents' deaths. But it's been even stranger to come home after work these past weeks to our dark, empty house. Of course, it's still full of my parents' possessions, I haven't changed a thing, and it still holds their smells, as if they're just away on vacation and have left me in charge. One of my mother's nightgowns still hangs on the back of the bathroom door and my father's razor, and strap, and shaving cream mug still rest on the shelf above the sink. And I still catch myself thinking that they must have forgotten to take these things with them on their vacation. Only the faint stain left on the wall behind the toilet, and the small bullet embedded there, remind that they are not coming home after all.

After Pop killed himself, I started working more hours at the club, and I stopped going to class. I've always been a good student and academics have come easy to me, but to tell the truth, I'm really not much interested in school anymore. And so far university classes have seemed to me about like sorting through old scat to find out what the animals have been eating. All I really want to do is study photography. A few years ago, Pop bought me my first camera, a cheap box Kodak, and ever since then I've been obsessed with taking pictures. For the past two years I've belonged to an amateur camera club in the city. I'm the youngest member. We get together once a week to share ideas and technique, and to critique one another's work. I even won a prize in a club photo contest. By the way, I took Pop's deathbed advice, and after the insurance money came in, I bought myself a Deardorff 8×10 view camera, with a tripod and plate holders. It's the most beautiful piece of machinery you've ever seen.

Which brings me to my trip. On the Sunday afternoon before Christmas, I had just finished working the lunch shift in the dining room at the club. It was one of those gray, gloomy winter days in Chicago, dusk already settling in at 4 P.M., the wind whipping up off the lake, carrying a load of wet, icy snow. I was just getting ready to go home when I noticed that the manager had posted a flyer on the club bulletin board.

THE GREAT APACHE EXPEDITION

LOOKING FOR ADVENTURE?
JOIN AN EXPEDITION INTO OLD MEXICO

PURPOSE

This expedition, being organized by Douglas, Arizona, and Agua Prieta, Sonora, Mexico, business and professional men, plans to go into the Sierra Madre Mountains on the boundary between Sonora and Chihuahua, Mexico, to attempt to recover the seven-year-old son of Fernando Huerta, Bavispe, Sonora rancher, the boy having been stolen by the Apache Indians on Oct. 26, 1928, when three years old, the stealing being attended by the murder of the child's mother. It is the plan and the hope that the presence of an armed force will cause the Indians to capitulate and give up the boy, who is known to still be alive with the band.

JOIN   THE GREAT APACHE EXPEDITION   JOIN

Leaving Douglas, Arizona, April 1, 1932, for Bacerac, Sonora, and Canyon of the Caves. Inquiry of Bradstreet's or Dun's agencies will advise prospective recruits of the character of the men behind this expedition. The character of these men guarantees that the expedition will be composed of business men of as fine character as the Rough Riders and the objective will provide sufficient in thrills to make it a pleasant memory for life. It will carry those who accompany the expedition into one of the most interesting virgin forests of the western hemisphere, where few white men have been and none has explored. Excellent fishing and hunting opportunities abound. If this appeals to you, enlist and go.

JOIN   ENLIST TODAY   JOIN

VOLUNTEERS ARE ADVISED

That recruits must be self-supporting and expect no money in return. This is a mission to aid Fernando Huerta in his effort to rescue his seven-year-old kidnapped son, stolen by the Apache Indians in 1928. A daily fee of $30 will be assessed each volunteer to help defray expedition expenses. Only gentlemen of good character and strong references will be accepted. This will not be a "Soldier of Fortune" affair. The company will be a volunteer militia unit of the Mexican Army and the recruits can serve for one week or until the mission has been completed.

Well, you can just about imagine what kind of effect this notice had on me, on that gloomy winter afternoon in Chicago. *Arizona, Mexico, the Sierra Madre, Apache Indians, hunting, fishing.* I grew up in this city, and have spent almost my whole life here, but ever since I was a little kid I've been reading the outdoor magazines: *Field & Stream, Outdoor Life, Sports Afield,* as well as the Western magazines and periodicals, *Sunset,* and *Ace-High,* and *Wild West Weekly.* I love the stories of Zane Grey and Jack London, and like all boys, I read Tom Sawyer and Huck Finn. Just about my whole life I've dreamed about lighting out for the territories, seeing the country, hunting and fishing and living off the land. But the truth is that except for a few summer vacations up to Wisconsin with my parents, and once to Minnesota where Pop took me fishing, I've hardly been out of Chicago, and I've never been to the West or the Southwest. I knew it wouldn't be long before someone figured out that I was alone in my parents' house, and what better time than this for me to hit the road?

Before I went home that day, I copied every line of that flyer in one of my college notebooks. And I wrote down the address in Douglas, Arizona, where volunteers were supposed to apply. While I was doing this the club manager, a big redheaded Irishman named Frank Dulaney, stepped up beside me. None of us workers cared much for Mr. Dulaney. He treated the members with unctuous respect and took out all his secret resentments on the employees. "You might as well forget about that, Giles," he sneered. "Can't you read? It's an unpaid position; they're looking for gentlemen, men of *high* character. In case you don't understand, that means *members* of the club, not employees."

"Yes, sir, I know that, Mr. Dulaney," I answered. "But they'll need employees to take care of the gentlemen. I'm thinking about applying for a job. How about writing me a recommendation, sir?" I knew that Mr. Dulaney would only ridicule me further if I mentioned that what I really had my heart set on was getting hired on as a photographer with the expedition.

It was nearly dark by the time I walked home that afternoon. People were already lining up in front of the shelters, and at the Red Cross soup lines. They were huddled tight against the buildings, hunched up against the wind, trying to cover their faces with the collars of their coats. Others stood around barrel fires in the alleys, trying to warm themselves on the wind-stunted flames. I hurried down the street, ignoring these poor people. I only had one selfish thought in my mind, and that was of my own escape.

That night the electric power went out all over the city. I kept the furnace in the basement stoked with coal, built a fire in the fireplace, and stayed up late writing a letter to the Great Apache Expedition Committee by the light of a candle. Outside the snow drifted up against the windows and the cold wind blew through the bones of my parents' house.

It snowed over two feet that night and the *Chicago Tribune* didn't get out until late the next day. The headline read: BLIZZARD SHUTS DOWN CITY, and the paper reported that dozens of people had died on the streets during the storm. They said it was one of the worst snowstorms in the history of Chicago. I'll never forget that there was another story on the front page that day reporting a speech President Hoover had just given in Washington. The president said that intervention by the federal government in economic affairs was contrary to "American ideals and American institutions," and that the Depression must be left to run its course. The best way to respond to hunger and suffering, Hoover said, is for businessmen to take voluntary steps to maintain wages and keep people employed, and for all Americans to adopt a "spirit of charity and mutual self-help through voluntary giving." I'd like to hear the president explain that to the people who had lost their homes and were freezing to death on the street that night.

Every kid like myself who worked in every exclusive men's club in America where this notice was posted had probably applied for a job on the Great Apache Expedition. The weeks passed and I didn't hear back from the committee. In fact, I never did hear back from them.

Then a few days ago, a man and a lady from Social Services knocked on the door of our house. I knew I was in for it, and when they asked me who was taking care of me, I lied and said that my uncle Bill from California was living here, but that he was out at the moment. They looked real suspicious about this and asked if they could come in and have a look around the house. I said no, my uncle wouldn't like that, and they said next time they would come back with the police and a search warrant. They left a card and said that my uncle needed to contact them right away about filing guardianship papers. And that if they didn't hear from him in the next three days, they would come and get me and I would be sent to live in a foster home until I turned eighteen. That's when I decided it was definitely time to leave town. In another couple of months I'll be seventeen, and I've been taking care of myself for a long time now; I'm not about to go live with strangers. I've still got a few months before the expedition is scheduled to head down into Mexico, and I plan to take my time working my way south, see a little of the country, before presenting myself in person to the committee in Douglas, Arizona.

Earlier tonight I said good-bye to Annie Parsons, my sweetheart. I think she's always known that I wouldn't stick around long after my parents died. I told her I'd write, that I'd probably be home by summer, but I knew even as I was saying this that it was a lie. And I think Annie knew it, too, because the last thing she said when I took her back to her dormitory, and we kissed at the door was, "You have a nice life, Ned Giles."

I'm all packed and first thing tomorrow morning I'll load up Pop's Roadster, lock the house, and leave the key under the mat for the people at the bank, who were going to take it away anyway. (Along with all Pop's other debts, I'm leaving a stack of foreclosure notices on the table inside the front door.) Then I'll drive away from Chicago, away from my parents' house, my old life. Who knows, maybe I'll never come back. I'm awfully excited about leaving. But I've got butterflies in my stomach, too.

23 JANUARY, 1932

Kansas City, Missouri

Well, I guess I'm not such a great notebook keeper after all, because I've been almost three weeks on the road already, and I've been so busy that I haven't made a single entry. I've only made it as far as Kansas City so far. I'm trying not to spend my savings from the club, or Pop's small life insurance settlement (most of which I blew on my new camera), and so I stopped here to work for a couple of weeks in a feedlot owned by the Armour family, who are members of the Racquet Club. The only reason I got hired on in the first place is because I came with a letter of introduction from Mr. Armour himself, which I asked him to write for me before I left the club when I was planning out my route. Even so, the manager of the feedlot, a fat man named Earl Bimson, has given me the lowliest, lowest-paying job of all—mucking out corrals. I've never been afraid of hard work, and I've had jobs since I was a kid, but I've never done anything like this before. Never has my old position at the Racquet Club seemed cushier than it does after two weeks of shoveling cow manure. It's hard, dirty work and only pays a dollar a day. Still, they turn away a dozen men every day who would love to replace me.

I haven't made a single friend here. Besides making Mr. Bimson hate me, my letter of introduction seems to have alienated all the other hands, who think that I'm either a relative trying to learn the business from the ground up, or a spy for the family, or both. When I tried to tell one of them that I was just a hired man, same as him, he answered: "Yeah, well, if you really needed this job, Giles, you wouldn't be driving that fancy Studey, now would you?"

"It was a gift from my father," I answered. "It was all he had left."

Yesterday I got in a fistfight over the matter with a big Norwegian farm kid from Minnesota named Tommy Lundquist. I'm only of average size myself, but I was on the boxing squad in high school and I have a bit of a temper and a mean left hook. Tommy is a big, slow kid and I knew that the others had egged him on to give me a hard time. When he shoved me, I punched him back. He looked surprised, and then he started crying when he saw that I had bloodied his nose. I felt bad about hurting him, but I think at least the others will leave me alone now. I'm going to head out of here pretty soon, anyway.

13 FEBRUARY, 1932

Omaha, Nebraska

I have made it as far as Omaha, where my line of work has improved considerably. The owners of the *Chicago Tribune,* who are also members of the Racquet Club, gave me a letter of introduction to the owners of the *Omaha Daily Star,* and I've managed to get hired on as a temporary assistant to the staff photographer, a fellow named Jerry Mackey. It's my first real job in the business, and even though I'm just a gofer, I'm learning a lot. It sure beat the pants off shoveling cow shit all day.

Jerry Mackey is a fast-talking, wisecracking, chain-smoking, card-carrying Communist, who is not only instructing me in the craft of photojournalism but also in the politics of Marxism. He's already taken me to a couple of party meetings at the homes of some of his writer and artist comrades. They smoke and drink whiskey and rail against the ruling classes, arguing heatedly about the role of art, literature, and journalism in the "cause." Although much of what they say is way over my head, some of it makes sense. Because I'm younger than everyone else present, they don't pay much attention to me, and for my part, I keep my mouth shut and just listen. But a couple of nights ago one of Mackey's colleagues, an editorial-page columnist named Kevin Anderson, really put me on the spot.

"Young Mr. Giles," he said. "You have been very quiet at our meetings. Why don't you tell us what it is that you bring to the revolution."

I didn't really understand the question. "I don't know," I mumbled. "I guess . . . I guess I bring my camera." And everyone laughed, which only made me turn redder in the face.

"And how does your camera serve the cause?" Anderson asked.

"I'm not really sure, sir," I mumbled.

"I'm asking," Anderson said pointedly, "what in your opinion, as an aspiring photographer, is your primary responsibility in these times of social upheaval?"

"I don't know . . ." I stammered. "To be in focus, I suppose." And then everyone laughed again and Kevin Anderson slapped me on the back. "Good answer, boy," he said. "Good answer!"

19 FEBRUARY, 1932

Omaha, Nebraska

Well, that job sure didn't last long. No sooner did I get settled in a boardinghouse in town than Jerry Mackey was laid off by the newspaper, along with half a dozen other reporters. Management claims that this is a cost-cutting measure due to declining circulation and advertising revenues. Mackey is convinced that he's been canned for his Marxist sympathies, and for the fact that his photographs, not to mention his rhetoric, were becoming increasingly political.

"The greedy capitalist bastards!" he rants. "The system is corrupt and decaying and they know it; they're hanging on by their fingernails. They're desperate; they're terrified of the movement and trying to silence us. But they can't silence Jerry Mackey; they can't stop me from exposing the disease of capitalism in my photographs. Mark my words, kid, the workers of America—the hungry, the persecuted, the heroic millions who suffer quietly—will rise up and take this country back. And I'll be there in the front lines to document the revolution with my camera!"

I have a lot of respect for Jerry Mackey, and I'm grateful to him for everything he has taught me in the past few weeks. I don't know anything about revolutions, but ever since Kevin Anderson asked me that question the other night, I've been stewing over it, thinking about the answer I wish I'd given. I wish I'd said that to me the photographer's only responsibility is to tell the truth. But I guess maybe that sounds a little highfalutin', doesn't it?

Anyway, with the photographer fired, the newspaper hardly needed a photographer's assistant, and so I, too, was laid off. In a few days, I'll be hitting the road again, headed south.

29 FEBRUARY, 1932

Somewhere outside Oklahoma City

I have to admit, it's lonelier out here than I thought it was going to be, and a lot less romantic. Of course, it's wintertime, and the countryside looks pretty gloomy. It's awful cold and the trees are bare, everything brown and frozen and dead. There are a lot of people on the road, many of them obviously uprooted by the hard times, but everyone seems isolated from one another, hurrying past with averted eyes as if ashamed by their circumstances. I feel strangely dislocated myself, as if I've been cut loose from the earth, with no anchor to hold me here. After Mom and Pop died, and I lived those months in our house, surrounded by their things and comforted by their smells, I think I began to truly believe that somehow they were coming back. And not until I actually left home and have been traveling these past weeks have I come to fully understand that my parents are gone forever, and I'm never going to see them again. About all I have left are a few photographs and this automobile of Pop's. The truth is, I'm embarrassed to be driving such a fancy car. So I go out of my way to pick up hitchhikers, often entire families, their poor possessions and maybe a child or two crammed into the rumble seat of the Roadster. They eye me furtively, as if I might be the enemy, and nearly all of them have a kind of hollow-eyed look, tired and disoriented, oddly apologetic about being down-and-out as if somehow it is their fault that the bottom has fallen out of the economy, their lives cast so suddenly adrift. I think I know just how they feel, although for different reasons.

Yesterday, outside Wichita, Kansas, I stopped to give a ride to a woman traveling alone with a little girl. It was a cold, windy afternoon, and a fine dust of snow blew across the fallow winter fields. The girl was bundled in her mother's worn woolen overcoat, which was far too big for her. The woman herself was inadequately dressed in a thin cotton print dress and gray cardigan sweater with holes at the elbows. They stood on the side of the road with a single battered suitcase and two paper bags full of possessions. I got them situated in the front seat of the Roadster, gave the mother a blanket to wrap around them, and turned the heater up high. As we got under way, the little girl looked up at me with a solemn, dirt-streaked face. "Mister, we live on a farm," she said. "I have my own room. My daddy has a truck but he had to go away." Maybe they were on their way to join the little girl's father, or maybe they were going to live with relatives. I didn't ask. I've learned not to ask such questions on the road.

"Quiet, dear," her mother said. "The nice young man isn't interested in that."

"Sure I am, kid," I said. And I put the back of my hand against the little girl's ice-cold cheek. "What color is your daddy's truck?"

Then the mother leaned over her daughter on the car seat between us and whispered something in my ear that made me flush with embarrassment. Even in the privacy of my own notebooks, I cannot repeat what she said, and I saw that she was weeping herself from the shame of having to propose such a thing in order to put food in her daughter's mouth. "Oh, no, thank you, ma'am," I stammered. "But I've got a few extra dollars I could let you have. And if you and your little girl are hungry, we'll stop when we come to a café and get a bite to eat. It'll be my treat. Maybe you'd just let me take your photograph in return."

That's how it is on the road these days. It's enough to turn a young fellow into a Communist.

12 MARCH, 1932

Goodnight, Texas

I have made it all the way to Texas, where for the past two weeks I've been working on the Circle J Ranch outside Amarillo. The ranch is owned by a wealthy Scotsman named Monty McGillivray, who is in the cattle business and has a home in Chicago and is yet another member of the Racquet Club, which institution has served me so well in my travels. I saw Mr. McGillivray at the club over the holidays and he told me to stop in on my way south and he would give me a job. He's one of my favorites of the club members, a stocky, hearty fellow who dresses in tweed jackets and plus fours, sports a thick, black mustache, and wears his dark hair combed straight back. He's always cheerful, always has a kind word for the employees, one of the few members who seems genuinely interested in our lives.

I don't have much experience with horses but I figured it would help my chances to get on the Great Apache Expedition if I at least knew how to ride. So I've been trying to learn since I've been here. Knowing that I'm interested in photography, Mr. McGillivray has also had me take portraits of his family and his guests.

I like this West Texas country, the hills and plains, the striated rock canyons and vistas of grasslands. The ranch contains one of the last remnant wild herds of American bison. During the winter, wealthy sporting friends of the McGillivrays are invited to come here to hunt these animals, although the term *hunt* might be a slight overstatement. The guests are driven to the herd in well-appointed ranch vehicles, their rifles and rifle stands readied for them by gun bearers. They sight down on a buffalo bull grazing placidly in the meadow and shoot it where it stands. It seems to me about like shooting cows and I can't see a great deal of sport in it, but the herd needs to be thinned and the rich people seem to enjoy this diversion.

It is among my duties to take care of the guests, which from my years at the club is an occupation in which I've had a good deal of practice. It's also my job to photograph the sports with their trophies. I print the film myself in a makeshift darkroom off the bunkhouse and give these portraits to the guests as a memento of their visit. Mr. McGillivray seems very pleased with my work and the other day he asked me to stay on full-time at the ranch. "I've known you at the club since you were a boy, lad," he said. "You're practically like a son to me. Why don't you stay here and work for me, give up this wild Apache chase. I'll make it worth your while, Ned."

I have to admit, it was a tempting offer. "I really like it here, sir," I answered. "But just now I've got my heart set on going down to Mexico. Maybe if I don't get hired on by the expedition, I'll come back if you still need me. Or maybe after it's over, if there's still a place for me."

"There's always a place for you at the Circle J, lad," Mr. McGillivray said.

To tell the truth, as much as I like Mr. McGillivray and appreciate his kindness to me, I'm kind of tired of working for rich people. Maybe it's just from listening to Jerry Mackey and his comrades ranting about the ruling classes, or maybe it's simply from all my years at the club. Maybe it's from the past weeks of travel, and all the people I've encountered on the road who are out of work and on the move. I don't know, it's hard to explain, but I feel like everything has changed in the last few months . . . well, of course, everything *has* changed. I've been thinking a lot about Pop recently, and I realize that he made up to rich people all his life, he denied his family's politics and working-class roots in order to try to conform to some notion of being a successful Republican capitalist. His own father worked himself to death clubbing steers over the head with a sledgehammer in a meatpacking plant in the Chicago stockyards so that his son could get an education and start his own business, so that his son's son could clean his father's brains off the bathroom wall. It's a lot to think about, isn't it?

Speaking of rich people, here's a story for you . . . This week a man from Philadelphia named Tolbert Phillips, whose family made their fortune in the railroad business, came to the ranch with his son, Tolbert Jr. Tolley, as he is known, is a couple of years older than I am, a tall, gangly foppish Ivy League kid, who reminds me of all the entitled young men whose tennis balls I fetched during their summer lessons when I was a kid. Except this guy acts like a damn girl. Evidently Tolley's father is an old friend of Mr. McGillivray's and brought his son down here to shoot a bison as some sort of rich boy's rite of passage.

Young Tolley arrived for the hunt dressed head to toe in an Abercrombie & Fitch khaki safari outfit, complete with pith helmet. "Don't you just love a man in uniform?" he whispered to me, seemingly oblivious to how ridiculous he looked, even absurdly proud of it. For his part, Mr. Phillips, who is a gruff, imperious man, was clearly ashamed of his son, and after Tolley had bagged his bison, his father left him with me in the field while I set up my camera to take his portrait. As I was doing so, Tolley inspected the bull, lifting the animal's hind leg.

"What are you doing, anyway?" I asked.

"Checking out his equipment," Tolley said.

"Why the hell would you do that?"

"Comparing him to the Cape buffalo. I've been to Africa, you know?"

"No, I didn't know that," I answered.

"Father is constantly shipping me off on these sporting adventures," he said, "in the hopes that they'll make a man out of me. As you may have guessed, Giles, I like boys."

I've never heard anyone admit to such a thing before. "Ah, no, I hadn't really guessed that," I said.

"To tell the truth, I wasn't really all that interested in the big-game hunting," Tolley said. "But there are no end to the lovely young men available in Nairobi. Even on safari, I had my own tent boy."

This was much more than I cared to know about Tolbert Phillips Jr.'s predilections. "Okay," I said hurriedly. "All set. Let's shoot this portrait."

"I'm going to pose holding the bull's pizzle in my hand," Tolley announced.

"What are you talking about?"

"You heard me, old sport."

"Why would you want to do such a thing?"

"Why? To amuse my circle of close friends, of course," Tolley said. "If you understand my meaning."

"No, I really don't," I said. "I don't understand a thing about it. And I don't want to have anything to do with it."

"Oh, don't be such a prude, old sport," Tolley said. "We'll call it *The Buffalo Hunter's Reward*. God, imagine how it will infuriate Father!"

"Why would you want to make your father mad?" I asked.

Tolley looked at me with a tolerant expression. "You're rather naive, aren't you, Giles?" he said.

"I guess so."

"Well, that's all right, old sport," he said. "Because all you really need to know is that I'm the guest and you're the employee. Now let's make that portrait, shall we?"

18 March, 1932

Goodnight, Texas

Yes, well, I shot Tolley Phillips's portrait just as he requested, and for my efforts I got called into Mr. McGillivray's office this morning.

"Sit down, Ned," he said from his chair behind the desk, and I knew right away that I was in for it. "I've known you for a long time, lad. You've always been a good boy." He held out my photograph of Tolley and dropped it on the desk in front of me. "It seems quite unlike you to pull a stunt like this."

"I'm sorry, sir," I said. "But that's how Tolbert asked to have his photo taken. I think he just meant it as a joke."

"A distinctly bad joke," Mr. McGillivray said. "A sick, perverted joke."

"Yes, sir," I admitted. "I didn't think it was very funny, either."

"But you took the photograph, didn't you, Ned?"

"Yes, sir," I said. "Because Tolley asked me to. And he's your guest."

"Tolbert's father is an old and dear friend of mine," Mr. McGillivray said. "He was not in the least bit amused by your tasteless photograph of his son."

"No, sir, I don't imagine that he was," I said.

"I'm afraid that I have no choice but to let you go," Mr. McGillivray said.

"Let me go, sir?" I asked, stunned. "But I was just following the wishes of the guest."

"I think you must understand, lad, that I cannot have my employees intentionally humiliating my guests in such a manner."

I've never been fired from a job before and I could feel the blood rising to my face, not just from the shame of it, but also from anger at the casual power which the wealthy yield in dismissing others from their lives. "But I wasn't trying to humiliate anyone, Mr. McGillivray," I said. "Honest. I was only doing what the guest asked."

"You could have refused, lad," he said. "You showed very poor judgment."

"I'm just an employee, sir," I said. "I'm taught to do what my employer and his guests ask of me. That's always been my job."

"That will be all, Ned," Mr. McGillivray said. "I'd appreciate it if you'd pack your bags tonight and leave first thing in the morning. You can collect your final paycheck from Mr. Cummins before you go." Mr. McGillivray busied himself with the papers on his desk, as a sign that the interview was over.

I sat there for a moment, dazed, unable to move. And then I said: "Sir?"

Mr. McGillivray looked up as if surprised and mildly irritated to see me still there. "Yes, what is it, Ned?" he asked impatiently.

"The other day you said I was like a son to you, sir."

The man met my gaze and held it. He frowned thoughtfully and shook his head with a brisk finality. "No, lad," he answered pointedly, pushing away from his desk and standing, "I said *practically* like a son.' What you are is an employee, who has been fired."

That was a good lesson to learn. And it was almost time to move on anyway.

26 MARCH, 1932

Eastern New Mexico

From Texas I am traveling south and west, through the choppy sand-hills of eastern New Mexico—big, arid, empty country. The tiny towns are few and far between, and many of them have been abandoned, their storefronts boarded up and posted with signs that read FOR SALE, GONE BROKE, CALIFORNIA OR BUST. A cold winter wind moans through the broken windows of deserted homesteads, and in the fields, the dried stalks of last season's failed wheat and corn crops sprout brown and withered from the drought-cracked earth. It is lonely country and I am lonely in it.

I've stopped for the night in an abandoned clapboard farmhouse outside Pep, New Mexico. I don't think its previous owners will mind. Still, I can't shake the odd sense I have that they're going to come home suddenly and discover my trespass. I walk quiet as a thief through the silent, empty rooms, imagining the people who once lived here, hearing their voices and laughter. On the floors lies the detritus of their lives left behind, a child's crayon drawing . . . a bald one-armed doll . . . last year's Montgomery Ward catalog with the corners of some of the pages so hopefully turned down . . . an empty whiskey bottle . . . a foreclosure notice from the bank. Earlier, while I still had enough light, I set up my camera and tripod and made some negatives of the interior of the house, half expecting that when I print them, the family will materialize like ghosts in the photographs . . . as I once believed that my parents would magically reappear on earth.

They've left their kitchen cookstove behind, probably it was too heavy for them to transport, and as the nights are cold, I've built a fire in the grate, gathering scrap wood from the collapsed chicken coop out back and branches from a dead elm tree in the yard. I found a discarded chair on the porch and an old bench to use as a table. I tidied the place up just as if I were the new tenant, sweeping the mouse droppings away with a broken-handled broom. I spread my bedroll on the floor and lit my kerosene lantern.

I had to learn to cook a little after my mother got sick. Pop was hopeless in the kitchen and it was that or a steady diet of baloney sandwiches. I travel with a kitchen box that contains a cast-iron skillet and pot, a tin coffeepot, plate and coffee cup, basic utensils, and a few staples such as salt, sugar, flour, and coffee—everything I need. A pot of beans simmers on the stove and I bought a thin steak at a butcher shop in Portales this morning. I'll fry it up with onions and eat it with the beans and some fresh tortillas that I bought from a Mexican lady there. I have a single precious tomato that I bought in the general store and which I'll chop up over the steak. It's really not much of a tomato, small and wrinkled, but still it looks so brilliantly red against this gray winter scene.

And so I've made myself right at home here. The cookstove warms the kitchen nicely and it's kind of cozy. But I can hear the winter wind moving around through the house like another restless traveler, and outside the window the big empty country lies lonesome in the dusk.

4 APRIL, 1932

Douglas, Arizona

Today is my seventeenth birthday and I have arrived at last at my destination. I make this entry parked along the side of Main Street in Douglas, Arizona. The high desert air is cool and still, one of those limbo days that seems neither winter any longer nor quite yet spring. The sun is low on the western horizon, lighting the pale mountains to the east with soft color but without warmth. The town itself has that feeling of semiabandonment which has become so familiar to me in my travels, a scruffy, down-at-the-heels border town with empty storefronts, broken windows, and deserted streets.

It's been over two months since I left Chicago, and now that I'm here I don't think I've ever felt so lonely and homesick in my life. The desert I've been driving across these past few hundred miles seems harsh and alien. I am a stranger here in strange country. Away to the south, across the border into Mexico, I can see the high jagged peaks of the Sierra Madre Mountains, rising like monsters above the plains. In the late-afternoon light they seem a far less romantic place than I had imagined; they seem only hard and rocky and inhospitable . . .

I am scared. There, I've said it. I'm thinking about turning the Roadster right around and heading back to Chicago. But everything that is familiar to me there is gone . . . my parents, my house, my room. I have nothing to go back to. So I'm just going to sit here for a while and try to regain my courage. I don't know what's the matter with me. The sun is setting and the cold desert air seems to be falling down upon me like stones from the sky above. I wish Mom and Pop were still alive. I wish I could have stayed in Chicago, finished college, and taken a steady job. Maybe I could have gone into Pop's automobile business with him and he wouldn't have killed himself. I could have married Annie Parsons and had a family of my own . . . *Have a nice life, Ned Giles,* Annie said.

There . . . I have just finished weeping, sitting in the car parked on the side of the street in Douglas, Arizona, on my seventeenth birthday bawling like a damn baby. It's the first time I've cried for my parents . . . the first time I've cried for myself . . . and now I'm all hollowed out.

5 APRIL, 1932

Douglas, Arizona

When I read what I wrote yesterday, I'm ashamed of feeling so sorry for myself, for being such a big crybaby. So much has happened in the past twenty-four hours that everything is different now. I hardly know where to begin. If I hadn't promised to always be honest in these pages, I'd cross out my entire last entry.

After I'd had my little cry, I started the car up again and drove on into town. Because it was my birthday and because I was feeling so blue, I decided to treat myself to a hotel room, a bath, and a steak dinner. I had no trouble at all finding the Gadsden Hotel at the end of Main Street. It's a grand five-story stone building that seems completely out of place in this scruffy little border town.

It's even grander inside, and as soon as I walked in I could see that it was way beyond my means. I stood in the lobby craning my neck at the exposed balconies that spiral upward from a massive central staircase built of white Italian marble. The stairs lead to a mezzanine framed by four enormous marble columns decorated in gold leaf and spanned by a forty-two-foot-long Tiffany stained-glass mural. The lobby was full of Great Apache Expedition volunteers, milling around or sitting chatting in islands of plush velvet furniture.

The desk clerk was a slender, dapper fellow dressed in a dark suit and bow tie. I was dressed myself in dungarees and a T-shirt, and he raised his eyebrows when I walked up, sizing me up quickly and professionally as one clearly unsuited to such luxury. I know the look, and I know from my experience working at the club that the only people capable of being snootier than the rich are those who work for the rich.

"May I help you, sir?" he asked with an imperious English accent, making it clear from his tone that he probably couldn't.

"Yes, I'd like a room, please," I said, trying to appear older than my years, and somehow magically better dressed.

"Do you have a reservation, sir?"

"Not exactly."

"I beg your pardon, sir?"

"No, I don't have a reservation."

"*Ummm.* Pity." He pursed his lips and made a show of consulting the register, running a dry, papery finger swiftly down the page. "We're terribly busy, sir," he said. "You see the volunteers for the Great Apache Expedition are beginning to arrive."

"Yes, that's why I'm here myself," I said. "I read the flyer at my club in Chicago and thought I'd come down here and see about signing on."

"You're a member of a private gentlemen's club, then, are you, sir?" he asked, looking up with raised eyebrows.

"Well, not exactly a member," I admitted. "I worked at the Chicago Racquet Club. I'm hoping to get hired on in a paying position with the expedition."

The desk clerk smiled knowingly. "Ah, yes, of course you are, sir," he said, "you and everyone else in town."

"I'm a really good photographer," I said.

"Yes, sir, I'm quite sure you are," said the desk clerk. "Nevertheless, I'm afraid that I have nothing available at all tonight."

"You're completely full?"

"It would seem so, sir."

"Would you have a room for me if I was a member of a club rather than an employee?" I asked.

"Dashed unfair, I know, sir," he said. "But I have strict instructions to hold the remaining rooms for expedition volunteers."

"Instructions from whom?" I asked. "Isn't my money as good as theirs?"

"From the management, of course, sir," he said. "I only work here."

And then from behind me came a vaguely familiar voice. "Put Mr. Giles in the spare room in my suite, Mr. Browning. It has nothing in it but my polo gear."

I turned around to find Tolbert Phillips Jr., tall and gangly and tanned, dressed in natty white slacks and a polo shirt, his hair slicked back, a striped tennis sweater draped over his shoulders, as if he'd just come in off the court. He beamed affably at me, with a goofy, expectant look, as if we were the best of old friends.

"Giles, old sport!" he said. "Tolley Phillips! The Circle J Ranch, Goodnight, Texas. Remember?"

"How could I forget?" I said. "What are you doing here, Tolley?"

"Volunteering for the Apache expedition, of course," he answered. "Another of Father's schemes to make a man out of me. Which, as you can plainly see, is a losing cause. God, I wish you could have seen his face when he saw the portrait you took of me, Giles. It was absolutely delicious!"

"Yeah, well, it wasn't so delicious for me, Tolley," I said.

"I know, and I'm terribly sorry about that, really I am. Of course, I took full responsibility."

"A lot of good that did me," I said. "I got fired over your little prank."

"I know you did, Giles," Tolley said. "You took the fall for me. Isn't that what you gangsters from Chicago say? And it was damned decent of you, too. Believe me, Father would fire me as his son if he possibly could. You know he can hardly wait for another war to break out so he can ship me off to fight for democracy. 'That'll make a man out of you, Tolbert!' he likes to say. Or get me killed, which to Father would still be preferable to having a fairy for a son. Chasing wild Apaches, for God sakes! Have you ever heard of anything more absurd? But tell me, Giles, what are *you* doing here?"

"I came to apply for a job on the expedition."

"Splendid!" Tolley said. "What a wonderful coincidence that our paths should cross again. This gives me the opportunity to repay you for the trouble I've caused." He turned to the desk clerk, snapping his fingers officiously. "Put Mr. Giles on my bill, Mr. Browning. And get a bellhop down here to take his bags up to my suite."

"Very well, sir," Mr. Browning said.

"Where are your bags, old sport?" Tolley asked me.

"Look, I appreciate the offer, Tolley," I said. "But you don't owe me anything. I'll sleep in my car. I'm used to it. Thanks anyway."

"Nonsense!" Tolley said. "I won't hear another word about it. I've got a spare room in my suite, and it's all yours, Giles. And don't worry, I won't bother you, if that's what you're worried about. In fact, you're not my type at all."

"That's good, Tolley," I said. "Because I like girls."

Tolley Phillips laughed his high, whinnying laugh. "Well, of course you do, Giles. I know *that*. It's probably why I don't find you more attractive."

The desk clerk put a registration form down on the counter in front of me. Having been privy to enough private conversations at the club, and no slouch myself in the discretion department, I appreciated the man's complete mastery of the poker face; not so much as an eyebrow twitched to suggest that he had heard a single word of what Tolley had just said.

"Here you are, sir," he said to me, "if you'll just fill this out and sign at the bottom."

"You've arrived at a most propitious moment, Giles," Tolley said. "They're having a town meeting tonight in which the mayor of this charming little burg is going to lay out the details of the Great Apache Expedition. We'll go together. We'll see what we can do about getting you hired on. What do you say, Mr. Browning, will they be able to find a position for my young friend here?"

"I could not say, sir," Mr. Browning answered coolly. "However, there does appear to be a great deal of competition for a limited number of positions. And those are mostly going to the locals."

"Yes, well, we'll just see about that," Tolley said. "The name Tolbert Phillips carries a bit of weight around here, you know. Why, were it not for my family, there would be no train service to this hellhole. Now, Giles, I insist that you go on up to the room and get yourself cleaned up. Then meet me back down here in the bar." Tolley winked and looked around conspiratorially. "I have a little something that will liven up our lemonade."

And so I installed myself in Tolley Phillips's suite. I took a hot shower, changed clothes, and met him downstairs in the bar. The place was noisy, crowded with recently arrived volunteers for the expedition; a certain excited, festive atmosphere prevailed. Tolley ordered lemonades for us into which he surreptitiously poured from a pint bottle of tequila. "Picked this up across the border," he said, flashing the bottle at me. "Ever had a margarita, Giles?"

Though I've spent time with my college buddies in some of Chicago's speakeasies, drinking contraband whiskey and sundry homemade rotgut concoctions, I'd never tasted tequila before. Tolley raised his glass. "I have a hunch we're going to become the best of friends, old sport," he said. "And, of course, I mean that in a strictly platonic way. Here's to our adventure in old Mexico."

We clicked glasses and took a drink. "That's not bad," I admitted.

"Not bad? You're damn right it's not bad," Tolley said. "Now, I've been giving some serious thought to your situation, Giles. And I've decided that we should get you signed on for the expedition as my valet. Each of the volunteers is allowed to bring one servant with him."

"Your *valet*? Gee, I don't know about that, Tolley. I don't have much experience in that area. What does a valet do, exactly?"

"Oh, don't be put off by the term, old sport," Tolley said. "It's just a matter of semantics. You know I had my own valet growing up. He would lay out my clothes every morning, and help me to dress. It was the first inkling I had that I liked the touch of a man."

"I'm definitely not going to dress you, Tolley," I said. "Let's get that clear right up front."

Tolley laughed again. "Of course you aren't, Giles," he said. "Wouldn't ask you to. Quite capable of dressing myself. Perhaps we'll call you my assistant, then, rather than my valet. Does that sound better to you?"

"Not that much, really."

"You can be my man Friday, so to speak," Tolley said. "Part secretary, part valet, part groom—"

"Part groom?"

"Yes, the expedition committee encouraged volunteers to bring their own mounts with them," Tolley explained. "And so Father sent along three of his prize polo ponies for me to ride into Mexico. But I'm afraid that I had to dismiss my groom in St. Louis. Fellow had a bit of a drinking problem. Do you have any experience with horses, Giles?"

"Hardly any," I said. "Just the little I learned about them on the ranch. I grew up in Chicago, Tolley. I'm definitely not qualified to be the groom for your polo ponies. In fact, the job as your assistant is beginning to sound less and less appealing."

"I treat my people very well," said Tolley, mildly offended. "And if I may say so, Giles, you're hardly in a position to be particular. You do want to get on the expedition, don't you?"

"I'd do just about anything to get on," I admitted. "I'm just not sure that I want to be one of your *people*. I was really hoping to get hired on as a photographer."

"Oh, *please*, Giles," Tolley said mockingly. "Why on earth would they hire *you* as a photographer? Don't you think they'll have a professional covering such an important event? They're hardly going to give the job to someone who barely shaves yet."

"Well then, I'll offer to carry the photographer's camera," I said.

I left Tolley in the bar at the Gadsden and went early to the town hall. Workers were still setting up chairs and arranging the podium and speaker's table. I had brought my camera and tripod so that I might at least look the part. But I saw that another photographer was already in the process of setting up his equipment.

I went over to introduce myself. The man was an overweight, messy fellow with disheveled clothes and uncombed hair. He had a big belly hanging over his belt, and an unlit cigar butt clenched between his teeth.

"Pleased to meet you, kid," he said, holding out a hand, fingers thick as Milwaukee bratwursts. "Wade Jackson, award-winning shutterbug for the *Douglas Daily Dispatch*. Who you shooting for?"

"I'm just a freelancer, sir," I said. "I was hoping to get hired on with the expedition. But I guess you've already filled the position."

Jackson stared at me incredulously, then bellowed a loud, delighted laugh. He pulled out a Zippo lighter, flipped it open, struck it into flame, and held it up to his cigar butt, squinting his eyes and puffing until the butt glowed a bright, even orange. He exhaled an exuberant blast of cigar smoke and raised his eyes heavenward. "Thank you, God, I don't know what I've done to deserve this, but thank you." Then to me he said: "What the fuck kind of artsy-fartsy camera is that, anyway, kid?"

"It's a Deardorff," I said, confused. "Eight-by-ten view camera."

"Yeah, yeah, I *know* what it is," the big man said. "That's not what I'm asking. I'm asking why you have a camera like that?"

"I like the large format," I said.

"He *likes* the large format!" he said mockingly. "That the only piece you have, kid?"

"Yes, sir, is there something wrong with it?"

"It's a great camera for portraits and *art photography*," Jackson said with a disparaging emphasis, "when you have all the time in the world to set up and focus. But it's not exactly a spontaneous camera. What's it weigh with the tripod and plate holders, anyway, forty, fifty pounds?"

"I guess so."

"Look, kid, don't you know that no press photographer in America shoots an eight-by-ten? I tell you what I'll do. I'll loan you one of my Speed Graphics. Better yet, I'll loan you my new Leica. Ever shot one before?"

"No, sir."

"Light and fast, it'll be perfect up there."

Now I was more confused than ever. "I'm not sure I understand, sir. Up where?"

"In the Sierra Madre," he said impatiently. "Where the fuck do you think?"

"But I thought you just said you were the staff photographer for the local paper?" I asked. "Aren't you covering the expedition yourself?"

Wade Jackson opened his arms and turned his palms up. "Kid, take a good look at me," he said. "Do I look like the kind of fella who wants to chase Apaches on horseback in the fucking Sierra Madre? More to the point, do I look like the kind of guy who *could* chase Apaches on horseback in the fucking Sierra Madre, even if he wanted to?"

Well, no, as a matter of fact, he didn't, but I didn't want to be impolite about it, so I just answered: "I don't really know, sir."

"Cut the sir shit, kid," he said. "Call me Big Wade. Don't be so god-damn polite. Look, the mayor and my dumb-ass editor are insisting that I go along on this preposterous fucking expedition. They need photographs. I tell them I can't do it, I'll die up there; it's what, nine-, ten-thousand-feet elevation? I can barely breathe at sea level." Jackson took his cigar out of his mouth, looked at it sadly. "Too many of these damn things," he said. "But do they give a shit about the fragile state of my health? They do not. They say, tough shit, get yourself in shape, Big Wade, you're going. And now here you are, kid, dropping into my life like an angel sent from heaven—a fresh-faced, dewy-eyed, eager, ambitious, and possibly even talented young man, though that is somewhat beside the point. It's almost too good to be true."

"You mean I got the job?" I asked. "Just like that?"

"Not quite yet, kid," Big Wade admitted. "I have a little finagling to do. I'll have to introduce you to my editor for starters. And then I'll have to make it look like this was his idea. Fortunately, he's one of the dumbest human beings on the planet, so that shouldn't be too hard. How old are you, anyway, kid, twelve?"

"I'm seventeen."

"Okay, for our purposes you're twenty. You just look young for your age. I don't suppose you have any experience at all, do you?"

"Well, for the past couple of years I've belonged to an amateur camera club back in Chicago," I said. "Last year I won the prize for—"

Big Wade raised his hand. "Say no more, kid," he said. "Drop that part from your résumé right now. You think anyone's going to be impressed by the fact that you won a photo contest against a bunch of little old ladies with Brownies? What else you got?"

"I worked for two weeks as a gofer for the staff photographer at the *Omaha Daily Star*," I said. "They laid the guy off I was working for, so I got laid off, too."

"Now that's more like it," Big Wade said. "I can work with that. What was the guy's name?"

"Jerry Mackey."

"Mackey, Mackey, okay," Big Wade said. "Can you write?"

"Write?" I asked.

"Yeah, can you write?" Big Wade repeated impatiently. "See, they like me because I take pictures *and* write. Two for the price of one. In case you haven't seen it yet, kid, the *Douglas Daily Dispatch* is not exactly *The New York Times*. And it's not like they have a budget for a big staff of photographers and print reporters."

"Yes, I can write," I said. "I keep notebooks."

"Uh-huh, notebooks, well, that'll just have to do," Big Wade said. "Tell you what, kid, after I introduce you to my editor, you keep your mouth shut, let me do the talking, okay? You just follow my lead." He raised a fat finger in the air. "And, kid, don't ever mention the fuckin' camera club again. You're a professional now."

"Sure, okay, Big Wade."

By now a few people had begun to arrive in the hall and the committee members were taking their place at the table, chatting easily among themselves. Big Wade identified them for me and got me situated in the prime spot up front, setting up his own camera nearby.

"The chubby, cherubic-looking guy on the left is Mayor A. G. Cargill," Big Wade said as four men entered the meeting room together. "The handsome, fair-haired Spaniard next to him is Fernando Huerta, the father of the kidnapped boy. The wiry, mean-looking fella behind them, walks like he's got a rifle barrel stuck up his ass, that's Chief of Police Leslie Gatlin. And the *federale* with the mustache and the medals, looks like Valentino? That's Colonel Hermenegildo Carrillo, the commanding officer of the expedition."

"You think they'll really be able to rescue the boy, Big Wade?" I asked.

Jackson cut me a look that seemed to say I was the second dumbest human being on the planet. "You do understand that this whole thing is just a giant booster scheme, don't you, kid?"

"I'm not sure I understand what that means," I said.

"It means that everyone on the committee is a member of the Greater Douglas Area Chamber of Commerce," Jackson explained. "Señor Huerta came here looking for help in finding his son, and so the mayor and his chamber cooked up the Great Apache Expedition. But the truth is they're much more interested in promoting the town of Douglas than they are in finding the boy. Who is mostly being used as a shill. The area has been pretty hard hit by the Depression, especially since the copper mine closed down last year. The chamber is hoping to attract some big money from other parts of the country, men who can afford to invest in mining concerns, ranch land, that kind of thing. So you see the expedition is really just an elaborate excuse to take a bunch of rich guys hunting and fishing in the Sierra Madre. And maybe if they're really lucky, they'll get to take a potshot or two at a real Apache Indian."

A man carrying a reporter's notebook walked briskly into the meeting hall. "Okay, kid, get ready," Jackson said, waving the man over. "We're on."

"Hey, Bill, I got someone here I want you to meet," Big Wade said to the man as he approached us. "Ned, this is Bill Curry, distinguished editor in chief of the *Douglas Daily Dispatch*. Bill, Ned Giles. Ned apprenticed under an old friend of mine, Jerry Mackey at the *Omaha Daily Star*. Now he's stringing for the *Chicago Tribune*."

Bill Curry shook my hand. "You look mighty young to be working for a big-city newspaper, son," he said.

"*Precocious* is the word, Bill," Big Wade said. "The kid's got talent. Listen, I just found out that Ned was in the country. So I got in touch with him, asked him if he'd be willing to come down here, maybe cover for me for a few weeks while I head into Mexico with the expedition. You may not know how indispensable I am, but you're going to need someone to fill my shoes. Kid can write his ass off, too, writes all his own copy for the *Trib*. Of course, he hasn't said yes yet. But he hasn't said no, either. And we'd be damn lucky to have him, big-city reporter and all. It would sure make me feel better about being away all that time."

Bill Curry laughed. "Why in the hell would a precocious young photojournalist who's stringing for the *Chicago Tribune* want to fill in on our pissant little newspaper?" he asked me.

I've never been a very good liar but I looked steadily at the man. "Well, sir, Big Wade helped get me my first job in the business," I said. "And I feel like I owe him." I believed that while a little premature, maybe this wasn't entirely a lie.

"And you could work for us," Bill Curry asked, "at the same time that you're shooting for the *Chicago Tribune*?"

"Yes, sir, I don't see why not," I said. "I'm not on staff there yet. I'm only a freelancer." Also not entirely false. "I guess I can work for anyone I want."

Curry seemed to consider this for a moment. "Wouldn't you rather go to Mexico, young man, than fill in on the day desk in Douglas?"

"Why, yes, sir, of course, I would," I said. "But I understood that Big Wade was going with the expedition."

"Oh hell, Big Wade doesn't want to go anyway," Curry said. "He's been trying to get out of this assignment from the beginning." And to Wade he said: "Jackson, do you honestly think I'm going to let this young man cover the local school-board meetings while I send a fat, old, broken-down boozehound like you to cover the story of a lifetime?"

Although this had been the desired result of his plan all along, Big Wade seemed genuinely deflated by his editor's words, "Ah, no, Bill," he said softly, "I didn't really think that."

"Jesus Christ, this is terrific," Curry said, "just what we've been hoping for. National exposure for the Great Apache Expedition. And it couldn't have happened at a better time. I'm going to tell the mayor about it right now. He might want to announce tonight that we have a reporter here covering the expedition for the *Chicago Tribune*. We'll talk later, young man. A great pleasure to have met you."

Wade Jackson watched as his editor in chief bustled off to the speakers' table with this news for the mayor. He shook his head thoughtfully. "There, see how easy that was, kid?" he said in a subdued voice. "Now Curry thinks the whole thing was his idea . . . like I said, one of the dumbest *fuckin'* human beings on the planet."

Mayor A. G. Cargill was a cheerful-looking, roly-poly fellow with a round pink face like a baby's. He had a small mouth that seemed to be permanently pursed into an ingratiating smile. Now he worked the speakers' table, laughing and conferring confidentially with the men seated there, patting them on the back, whispering intimately in their ears, making a show of oily sympathy to Señor Huerta. The mayor was the consummate politician. Finally he took his place at the podium in the center of the table, rapped the gavel smartly, and waited for the crowd to settle.

"Ladies and gentlemen," he began. "This is an historic occasion for the great city of Douglas and for our great nation." It was warm in the packed hall, and the mayor dabbed his upper lip with a handkerchief. "Most of you know the story of poor little Geraldo Huerta," he continued, "so rudely torn at the tender age of three years from the bosom of his family by bloodthirsty Apache Indians, his mother murdered in the course of the abduction." He paused, pursed his lips tightly together.

"Seated behind me," the mayor continued, "is little Geraldo's father, Señor Fernando Huerta"—he turned and indicated the man—"who comes before us tonight to ask the brave citizens of Douglas to help him recover his beloved son." The mayor lowered his head for a moment as if in silent prayer. "Many of our older residents still remember the Apache wars in this country," he continued in a lower voice. "It wasn't really that long ago, and they remember all too well the unspeakable atrocities the godless savages committed against our fine, God-fearing citizens. But we routed them out, finally, didn't we? We whupped them good, and those who surrendered we sent to prison and to live on reservations where they belong." Now the mayor turned back toward Señor Huerta. "And so, sir, I think I speak for all of us when I say that the great city of Douglas will not stand idly by for another moment while your little boy is still held captive. We will not rest until the last bronco Apache in the Sierra Madre is dead, and your son is safe again in your arms. Isn't that right, ladies and gentlemen?" The audience began to applaud and whistle enthusiastically.

"Yes, that's right," said the mayor, pumping his hand, "that's right! The people of Douglas have spoken. Thank you very much!"

The mayor waited for the crowd to settle. Then he continued. "Tonight it is my great honor to formally announce a heroic joint Mexican-American expedition into old Mexico to rescue little Geraldo," he said. "And I predict that one day your grandchildren and great-grandchildren will read about the glories of the Great Apache Expedition in their American history books!" The mayor paused again and looked up with an expectant smile to cue the audience that it was time to applaud once more, which they dutifully did.

"Thank you, thank you all very much," he said. "Now, before I tell you more details about this exciting venture, let me first introduce to you the supreme commander of our forces, Colonel Hermenegildo Carrillo!" The mayor turned beaming to the colonel, who sat directly to his right.

Colonel Carrillo stood up to cheers from the audience and took an elaborate bow, raising his arm in a wave and sweeping it grandly across his body. He was a slender, elegant man, resplendently attired in a closely tailored dress uniform laden with medals and ribbons and gold-fringed epaulets. He wore a closely trimmed mustache and pomaded black hair, and in fact, he did look a bit like the silent film star Rudolph Valentino.

"Thank you, Colonel, thank you," said the mayor, his face flushed and perspiring. He made a little soundless clapping motion with the fingers of one hand against the palm of the other. "God be with you and your brave men.

"Now, many of you have seen our flyers around town," the mayor continued after the colonel had resumed his seat and the crowd had settled. "What you may not know is that over the past several months our personnel committee has mailed out literature to exclusive gentlemen's clubs in over twenty major cities across the United States. We have received, in response, dozens of letters and over one hundred and sixty applications for the Great Apache Expedition from prospective volunteers all across the country. If I might just read to you from one or two of the letters that typify the kind of response our mailings have elicited." The mayor cleared his throat. "This one is from a Dr. R. G. Davenport of the Denver Country Club in Denver, Colorado. 'Sirs: If you contemplate going in after those Indians soon, I should count it a very great privilege to join you. I have hunted big game in Africa and in many parts of America, but I am sure that shooting an Apache Indian would give me a greater thrill than any animal I have heretofore shot at.'" The mayor looked up with raised eyebrows, his pursed smile. "That's the spirit, Doctor," he said, punching the air with a fist. He held up another letter. "And this one is from Ellsworth Q. Drazy of Dwight, Illinois," he continued. 'Has your expedition room for a fellow who has done two hitches in the Marine Corps and one in the navy? I never fought Indians, but I have chased spics all around Haiti and Nicaragua and was in the landing and occupation at Vera Cruz. I guess I'll have the guts to chase these birds . . .'" At this, Colonel Carrillo shot the mayor a look of utter astonishment, but the mayor, so caught up in his enthusiasm, seemed entirely oblivious to the racial epithet. "Now, isn't that just wonderful?" he asked. "What a great country we live in that this poor little child's terrible plight would draw so on the heartstrings of Americans all across the land." He paused here and lowered his head as if quite overcome with emotion.

Finally he pulled himself together and continued. "Please let me assure the fine citizens of Douglas that this will be no soldier-of-fortune affair, that the men we handpick for this mission will be of the most unimpeachable character and credentials. As many of you have undoubtedly read in recent editions of the *Douglas Daily Dispatch*, we have recruited young men from some of America's most prominent families. Many of our volunteers have already begun to arrive and I'd like to take this opportunity to welcome them to our fair city." The mayor scanned the audience. "Yes, I believe that I spy Mr. Tolbert Phillips Jr. of the railroad Phillipses of Philadelphia, Pennsylvania, in the audience tonight. Mr. Phillips, won't you please stand up and take a bow?"

As if perfectly accustomed to such celebrity, Tolley Phillips, beaming goofily, stood and waved to the crowd, sweeping his arm back and forth like the pope.

"At the suggestion of the committee," continued the mayor, "Mr. Phillips, among other of our illustrious guests, has brought his string of polo ponies here with him. And Colonel Carrillo, himself an accomplished equestrian, has formed a special cavalry unit within the expedition. Despite the gravity of our mission, and the rigors of training which the men will undergo in the coming weeks, we've also arranged for some fine recreation. For example, as part of the pre-expedition activities in town, we will be organizing polo matches at the rodeo grounds between the American volunteers and the Mexican army soldiers. It should be tremendous fun and we hope you will all turn out to cheer the men on.

"Now I'm sure that everyone has noticed," said the mayor, lowering his voice to a more confidential tone, "the increased air traffic recently in the skies above our fair city. This is because some of our volunteers are arriving in Douglas via *private aeroplane*. Yes, that's right. And Colonel Carrillo has also formed a special aviation unit for those who wish to fly their own aeroplanes into Mexico."

Wade Jackson had left his camera and sidled up beside me. "God, isn't this magnificent, kid?" he whispered gleefully. "A bunch of rich guys on polo ponies chasing Apaches in the Sierra Madre! Flying their own airplanes! It's too *fuckin'* good to be true. Did you get a shot of the mayor, kid? What a hopeless windbag."

"I got the shot, Big Wade," I whispered.

"Now, another little piece of exciting news," continued the mayor, "which has just been conveyed to me by our own Mr. Bill Curry, editor in chief of the *Douglas Daily Dispatch*. We are very fortunate to have with us here tonight a young photojournalist by the name of Ned Giles, who has just arrived in Douglas on special assignment to the *Chicago Tribune!*"

"Oh no," I muttered.

"Hook, line, and sinker," whispered Big Wade.

"Ned will be accompanying our forces into the Sierra Madre as the official expedition photographer," said the mayor. "Ned Giles, won't you please make yourself known to the crowd."

"You're on, kid," Big Wade said, beginning to clap loudly. "God, I feel just like a proud papa."

I raised my hand and waved sheepishly as the crowd applauded enthusiastically. I couldn't help but look over at Tolley, who was staring at me, dumbfounded.

The meeting adjourned, and as Big Wade and I were packing up our camera gear, Mayor Cargill and some of his chamber members came over to us.

"Delighted to have you aboard, young man," the mayor said. "Let me introduce you to a few members of our committee. This is Rex Rice, director of transportation. Rex is our town's foremost real estate broker."

Rice was a trim, smiley fellow, dressed in a natty blue blazer and bow tie. "Pleasure to meet you, young man," he said. "If you have a chance to mention in one of your articles that there are some great buys to be had on ranch land in the Douglas area, I'd sure appreciate it."

A round, bespectacled fellow in suspenders stepped forward. "T. T. Schofield, here," he said, shaking my hand.

"T.T. is our director of equipment," the mayor said. "He manages our local JCPenney store."

"And this is Chief of Police Leslie Gatlin," the mayor said. "Director of personnel."

The chief of police sized me up with small, hard eyes. "You don't mind my saying so, son," he said, gripping my hand an instant longer than was really necessary, "you look awful wet behind the ears to be working for a national newspaper." It occurred to me that a single phone call to the *Chicago Tribune* would expose me as a fraud.

"I'm just a freelancer, sir," I said, holding his grip. "I don't really work for them officially."

"Even the big papers are laying off staff these days, Chief," Big Wade explained. "It's a lot cheaper to use hungry young stringers like Ned here."

Just then Tolley Phillips came over to us, and I was grateful that his presence diverted everyone's attention from me. The mayor introduced Tolley fawningly; Mr. Rice offered to show him some ranch land outside town; T. T. Schofield told him to come on down to the JCPenney store and he'd see that he was properly outfitted for the Sierra Madre. When it came the chief's turn, Gatlin looked Tolley up and down with enormous distaste. "Ready to have a go at those Apaches, are you, Mr. Phillips?"

Tolley may be a big sissy, but he's got a certain self-possession that I've noticed in other rich kids—brought up secure in the knowledge that most of the rest of the world works for them. He ignored Gatlin's obvious sarcasm and said: "As director of personnel, you're just the fellow I need to see, Chief."

"What can I do for you, Mr. Phillips?" Gatlin asked.

"I shall be requiring the services of a valet to attend to my needs in the wilderness," Tolley said. "I'd like you to arrange interviews for me with prospective candidates."

"I suppose I can do that, *sir,*" Gatlin said, clearly offended by Tolley's imperious tone. "Though I'm afraid that trained valets are in somewhat short supply in these parts."

"No experience necessary, Chief," Tolley said, smiling. "I'm quite capable of training my own help."

"Yes, well, some of our committee members are headed over the border tonight for a touch of legal libation," the mayor interjected nervously. "A little cantina called Las Primorosas. Perhaps we'll see you over there, gentlemen." He moved his entourage along.

"What'd you do that for, Tolley?" I asked.

"You heard how he spoke to me, Giles," Tolley said. "How filled with contempt he was. I was simply exercising my own leverage, which is my money and my family name. I needed to remind him that I'm his employer. A notion that drives manly men like the chief wild."

I introduced Tolley to Wade Jackson.

"If I may give you some advice, son," Big Wade said to him. "The mayor is mostly harmless. But I don't care who your father is, or how much money you have, you don't want to fuck with Chief Gatlin. He's smart, and he's mean as a snake."

"I appreciate that, Mr. Jackson," Tolley said. "And I'll keep it in mind."

"Now, if you boys will excuse me," Big Wade said, "I'm headed south of the border myself tonight. I have a date with a bottle of mescal and a pretty señorita. You come on down to the paper in the next couple of days, kid," he said to me. "I'll show you around, get you set up with that Leica."

"I like him," Tolley said as we watched Big Wade lumber off. "And as for you, old sport, haven't you certainly come up in the world! What's this about the *Chicago Tribune*? Why, not an hour ago, we were discussing the terms of your employment as my valet."

"*You* were discussing the terms of my employment as your valet, Tolley," I said. "Didn't I tell you I was going to get a job on the expedition as a photographer?"

"Indeed you did, Giles," Tolley said, "and I don't know how you did it. But this calls for a celebration. Let me buy you a drink at Las Primorosas. You do know what that means in Spanish, don't you, old sport?"

"No."

Tolley raised his eyebrows conspiratorially. "The beautiful girls!"

"I thought you didn't like girls, Tolley?"

"Wouldn't lay a finger on one," he said. "But you never know what other opportunities for love lurk in the dark shadows of old Mexico."

I realized as Tolley and I made our way down the dirt main street of Agua Prieta, that this was the first time I'd ever been out of the United States. And though we were only a hundred yards or so over the border, I already had the clear sense that truly I had entered a foreign land. It was Friday night and the street was crowded with vendors and hucksters selling food and trinkets, sex and cockfights. There were Indians dressed in brightly colored costumes, and beggars, some of them diseased or missing limbs, gaunt slinking dogs and street urchins. There were bars and cantinas and dance halls on every block, many of their doors open to the cool night air, so that tinny Mexican mariachi music and warm, smoky, perfume-and-tequila-scented air spilled into the street.

A young boy sidled up to us. "Hey, gringos," he whispered confidentially in English, "you wish to go to the whorehouse, meet pretty girls."

"Ah, not tonight, young lad," said Tolley. "Perhaps another time."

The boy tagged along behind. "You wish to see a senorita make love with a donkey?" he asked.

Tolley stopped, seemed to consider. "*Hmmmm* . . . A donkey, huh?"

The boy shrewdly sized Tolley up. "*Fifis*," he whispered. "You wish hombres?"

"Now you're talking, young lad," said Tolley.

"Speak for yourself, Tolley," I said. "I'm going to Las Primorosas."

"Alas, perhaps later, little man," Tolley said to the boy. "Right now we're in dire need of refreshment."

"For only one American dollar," the boy said, "I take you to Las Primorosas."

"We'll find it on our own, thanks, kid," I said.

"For only one American dollar, I show you the whole town," said the boy, waving his arm expansively.

"Enterprising little bugger, aren't you?" Tolley said. "I would give you a dollar just to leave us alone."

The boy held out his hand.

Tolley fished a dollar from his wallet and handed it to him.

"Follow me, señors," he said. "I take you to Las Primorosas."

"Hey, wait just a minute," Tolley protested. "I thought we made a deal."

"What's your name, kid?" I asked.

"Jesus," he said.

"Lead the way, Jesus."

A soft yellow light fell through the doorway of Las Primorosas. Inside wide plank floors were polished to a smooth scalloped patina, reflecting the flames from candles and gas lanterns. A mariachi band with strings and horns played at one end of the cantina and a few couples danced. A number of men sat up at the bar, quite a few Americans among them.

Others sat at tables drinking with the Mexican whores, who wore gaily colored off-the-shoulder dresses with low-cut bodices and bright paper flowers in their hair. I waved to Wade Jackson, who sat with a pretty Mexican woman in the dim light at the end of the bar.

We took a corner table and ordered beers and shots of mescal. When the drinks arrived, Tolley lifted his glass. "Well, Giles, here's to your new position."

"You know what else, Tolley?" I asked.

"What?"

"Today is my birthday."

"Well, damn, why didn't you say so, old sport?" Tolley said. "This calls for a real celebration! Although I have a suspicion that French champagne might be hard to come by in this establishment."

"I don't care about champagne, Tolley," I said, "but I do have a favor to ask you."

"Anything, *mi amigo.*"

"Stop calling me old sport, would you? I'm younger than you are."

"Just an expression, Giles," Tolley said with feigned hurt feelings. "Everyone uses it these days in the halls of the Ivy League. Haven't you read *Gatsby*?"

"Yeah, but Fitzgerald was using it ironically."

"Oh, for God's sake, Giles," Tolley said, "you don't need to lecture me about Fitzgerald's use of irony. I'm an English major myself, you know." He raised his glass. "Here's to you, old sport. Happy birthday and all that rot. And congratulations on your new position."

I drank the shot in one quick toss as I had learned to do with whiskey back home. It was the first time I've tasted mescal, and I could feel the raw heat of it going down my throat, spreading through my stomach like a small depth charge, burning its path to my brain. To think that several hours earlier I'd been as low as I ever had in my life, feeling so sorry for myself that I had almost given up and headed back to Chicago. Now I had my first real job as a photographer, it was my seventeenth birthday, and I was sitting at a corner table in a Mexican cantina, an exotic new world of color, light, and smell, listening to lively mariachi music, watching the musicians and the pretty girls, the couples dancing, the men laughing at the bar.

Two of the girls came over to our table and pulled chairs up beside us.

"Unless you have a brother, sweetheart," Tolley said to the girl beside him, "I'm afraid this is going to be a very short relationship."

The girl next to me was real pretty. She had a broad face and high cheekbones, smooth brown skin, and shiny black hair pulled back from her face. She had large dark eyes that seemed to shine in the candlelight. She leaned against me so that I could feel the softness of her breasts on my arm . . . she smelled like flowers. She whispered something to me in Spanish.

"I'm afraid I don't speak Spanish," I said. "But I'm going to learn."

"For five dollars I will make you very happy," the girl said in English.

I have to admit something: I've never been with a girl before . . . not that way. Annie and I talked about it plenty of times, but she wanted to wait until she was married, and so all we ever really did together was kiss, and touch each other a little. And though some of my college buddies used to go down to the red-light district in Chicago, I never really liked the idea of paying money to make love to a girl. I guess I'm kind of a prude that way. And now suddenly I got real shy. "Maybe we could just dance first," I said to the girl. I stood up quickly and offered her my hand.

I could tell right away that the dance steps I know from back home . . . like pretty much everything else from my "old" life . . . were just not going to work with this music. But I like to dance and I wanted to learn. The band members nodded and smiled at me as they played, amused by my clumsy efforts to follow the girl's steps. "Hey, I think I'm getting the hang of it," I said.

The girl laughed and rearranged my hands, drawing me closer. I could feel the fragrant heat radiating from her body like a warm spring wind, her softness. "Yeah, I definitely think I'm getting the hang of it. Don't you?"

The girl stopped dancing and I felt her grip tighten on my arm. "I am new here," she said. "If no men take me to my room, the *patrón* will turn me out. Please, would you come with me after this song? For five dollars I will make you happy."

So, at the end of the dance, I followed the girl out the back door of the cantina, which opens onto a courtyard. On the far side of the courtyard was another low adobe building, with a number of doors all painted different colors. She led me through the door painted yellow, and into a tiny room where she lit an oil lamp on a green wooden table. In the dim smoky light of the lamp I could just make out a single iron bed frame with a thin straw mattress covered by a rough woolen blanket and a lumpy pillow covered in a gunnysack. It was not exactly a romantic setting. The girl sat down on the bed and gestured for me to sit beside her.

"I don't even know your name," I said.

"Magdalena."

"That's real pretty. I'm Ned."

"You must give me five dollars now, Ned," she said. "And I must go to give it to the *patrón,* and then I will come back."

"All right." I handed her a five-dollar bill and she left the room and I sat alone on the bed. When she came back, I stood up and she reached behind her back and began to unhook her dress. I guess I got shy because I put my hand on her arm. "No, that's all right," I said. "Let's just sit here and talk for a minute. Then maybe we'll go back in and dance some more."

"You do not find me pretty?" she asked.

"Sure, I do, I think you're real pretty," I said. "But I just thought we could talk first for a few minutes. How is it that you speak such good English, Magdalena?"

And so we sat side by side on the bed and began to talk. And soon the girl was just a girl again instead of a whore. And I was just a fellow instead of a customer. And then we were just a couple of kids talking. She told me that she had grown up outside the small village of Bavispe in Sonora. She told me that her family were peons on a hacienda whose *hacendados* spent most of their time in Paris, which, she explained solemnly, was a city very far away across the sea. The *hacendados* had survived Pancho Villa's sacking of their hacienda in 1913 because they were out of the country for the duration of the revolution and President Obregón had restored their property to them in 1920, although their land holdings had been greatly reduced in size by the new laws of the government. But they were still very important ranchers in the state and their lands had steadily increased again since the end of the revolution. The current *hacendado* was a son who had come back from Paris to live in the hacienda with his French wife and run the family ranching operations. All this the girl told me, and that she had three brothers and four sisters. She said that her father worked as a blacksmith in the village and her mother as a domestic in the *hacendados'* house. That from the time she was a very small girl she had worked with her mother in the house, and that there, due to the kindness of the *hacendado's* wife, she had learned to speak both French and English. There was not always work on the hacienda for all the children of the peons, and when they reached a certain age, the girls were encouraged to marry or to move into the cities or border towns to find work. One day the padre came to the hacienda and the girl's parents told her to pack her bags, the padre had found work for her. The priest took her away, brought her here to Las Primorosas. Money changed hands. Of course, her parents did not know what kind of work she was doing in the border town, and the girl would never tell them. In this way, the priest had brought a number of village girls here over the years, their shame assuring their silence. Magdalena told me that she had only been here a few weeks, and she was afraid that the proprietor was going to put her out because she did not do as much business as some of the other, more experienced girls.

"Oh, I bet you'll get the hang of it," I said, and then I realized how stupid this sounded, as if we were still discussing my dancing. "You're real pretty."

She blew out the lantern and kissed me on the cheek. "Thank you," she said. "Are you certain that you do not wish to lay down with me?"

"No, that's all right. Maybe another time." And I gave her five dollars more to keep for herself.

"Don't think I didn't see you slip out the back door with the little *puta*," Tolley said when I got back to the table. "Damn, Giles, you don't waste any time."

"She's not a whore," I said. "She's a nice kid. And we were just talking."

"Not a whore?" Tolley said, incredulous. "Just talking? Good God, old sport, don't tell me you didn't do the dirty deed?" He laughed. "Why, you're even more naive than I thought. And I'll bet you paid her anyway."

"As a matter of fact, I did," I said. "Double. You know, Tolley, you're a rich kid, you've always had everything you've ever wanted. It's probably never occurred to you that some people are forced to do things against their will in order to make a living."

"Oh, isn't that sweet?" Tolley said mockingly. "Young master Giles to the rescue of the damsel in distress. But please, spare me the class lecture, would you? We all have our crosses to bear, old sport, even rich kids such as myself."

We had a couple more shots of mescal, and then I left Tolley in the cantina and headed back over to Douglas. It had been a long day, and I was tired and suddenly quite drunk. Outside the night air was cold and a waning moon rose late over the mountains, flooding the plains so that the sparse greasewood bushes and mesquite trees cast thin shadows across the desert. As I left the yellow lights of Agua Prieta behind me, the coyotes took up their moon song, a high warbling pitch that seemed to accompany the tinny cacophony of music from the cantinas.

I walked unsteadily back to the hotel with the strange, giddy, exhilarating, drunken sensation that the door from my childhood had swung closed forever behind me tonight, and that nothing would ever be the same again.

LA NIÑA BRONCA

BILLY FLOWERS TURNED TO PULL A SHIRT FROM HIS SADDLEBAGS IN order to cover the heathen girl's nakedness, and when he turned again to see what had so suddenly agitated his dogs, who had begun whining and barking and straining at their chains, she was gone. He could not see or hear her running, no rustle of her tattered dress, for it lay now in a pile on the ground as if she had simply vanished within it.

He thought, but only for the most fleeting moment, that perhaps she had, after all, been some kind of spirit being. But Billy Flowers was no great believer in supernatural manifestations, preferring to believe that both God and Satan worked more quietly in the souls of men.

Flowers knew instantly from the dogs' posture what direction the girl had taken. He quickly scanned the surrounding country, catching just the slightest movement in the rocks above the river bottom, a movement so fleeting that it was little more than the memory of a movement. But it was enough. He considered but quickly rejected the notion of releasing the dogs, for he knew that if they caught her, they would certainly kill her, and that knowledge would as surely make of him a murderer. Instead, he un-hooked a small liver-spotted bitch named Queenie and secured her chain to his own belt. Then he picked up the girl's ragged dress, which stank of her wildness, and he rubbed it in the dog's nose. "Now, Queenie, you are going to trail this heathen girl," he said. He picked the dog up by the col-lar and with a rattle of chain swung her up onto the pommel of his saddle, where she balanced herself deftly. Accustomed to having dogs as passen-gers, John the Baptist did not flinch. Flowers climbed up behind.

He knew that with her head start, the girl could easily outrun him on foot. Nor did he attempt to ride into the steep rocks where she had fled, for it would clearly be impassable to the mule. Instead he followed the river bot-tom, until they came to the first dry arroyo that spilled down out of the hills, and up this he rode.

John the Baptist was the best mule Billy Flowers had ever owned, seemed to know where they were going even before his rider, as well as the best way to get there. He was an athletic animal and understood his limits, pushed himself as far and fast as he knew he could safely go, some-times farther and faster than Billy Flowers would ever have expected or attempted himself. And he let his rider know, in no uncertain terms, when he could go no farther. Flowers respected the animal's courage and judgment and had never asked him to do anything that he said he could not do.

The arroyo was so steep where it topped out on the ridge that the mule took the last few steps as a series of grunting lunges, trying to keep for-ward momentum in order to avoid sliding back down on the slick rock. Flowers leaned forward in the saddle, holding the dog splayed tight around the mule's withers, trying to keep their weight as neutral as possi-ble. "That's my boy, John," he whispered like an entreating lover in the mule's ear, "that's my good John, almost there now, yes, my John."

With a final lunge, dog chain rattling like the mail-clad mount of a medieval knight, John the Baptist gained the level ground of the ridgetop, trotted a few paces, snorted, his sides heaving. "Well done, John," Billy Flowers said, patting the mule's lathered neck. "We'll leave you here now." He dropped the dog Queenie to the ground and dis-mounted behind her, hobbled the mule's front legs, and from behind the saddle untied the thongs that held his lariat on one side, and his coiled bullwhip on the other. "You wait right here for us, John, and we'll be back shortly with the heathen child." Caught up now in the excitement of the hunt, a thrill that had not paled for him in better than sixty years, Billy Flowers had not yet even stopped to ask himself why it was so important that he capture the girl.

Flowers knew that he was above her now, and that she would probably move laterally in the rocks, looking for a crevice or a cave in which to hide. He did not think that she'd come right away to the top, but would first find a place to lay up, a place where she'd feel safe from the dogs, and where she could stop and listen to see if they pursued her. Prey does not run unless chased—a central law of the hunt. Had he pursued her from below, or had she heard the dogs trailing her again, she would almost certainly have kept climbing. As it was, Billy Flowers believed that he had preempted her next move, forced her to seek a secure hiding place, the natural instinct of animals. She would wait until after dark before she traveled again, which gave him nearly two hours of daylight still to find her.

The girl lay crouched in a shallow cave in the rocks, listening. She could hear the dogs barking distantly where they must still be chained, for the sound did not come closer or change direction. She heard the clattering hooves of the mule climbing the arroyo, striking rock, reverberating through the earth all the way down to her hiding place, and from there entering her bones. She heard the chain rattling, a sound which she would forever after associate with dogs. And she knew from all this that the old White Eyes was after her, had ridden up the canyon to the top of the ridge, was now on foot himself above her and that he must have at least one dog with him.

She was naked now, but for her moccasins and a breechclout that covered her sex. She had lost her small ration of roots. She knew that she could survive the night here; it was a small enough space and well protected, although it would be very cold. She did not think that the old White Eyes would find her, at least not before dark. The rocks themselves did not betray footprints and she had been careful to sweep away the little bit of sand and pebbles that she had disturbed at the entrance to the cave. But the dog would eventually find her, and if she waited until dark to move, she would be exposed to the night cold with no way of covering herself. All this she considered.

The cave smelled faintly of cat urine and she found beside her in the dark a small piece of dried scat, so that she knew a she-lion must have denned up here to give birth, the scat left by one of her kittens. The girl hoped that the lion wasn't coming back here tonight, although she was far less afraid of that right now than she was of the old White Eyes. She lay curled in the cave, exhausted now beyond the point of simple tiredness. She slept.

It had been the one they called Indio Juan who had brought the Mexicans down upon the People once and for all. He who had been bitten in the face by a rattlesnake when he was a boy, so that he had the snake sickness, the madness, his face grotesquely disfigured. It was Indio Juan who would ride boldly with his warriors in full daylight into the tiny mountain villages and announce from astride his horse, "*Yo Indio Juan.*" And he would laugh as the villagers in the street fled screaming in all directions, and he and his men would kill them all, entire towns thus depopulated.

It had been Indio Juan's idea to steal the Huerta boy, although the girl's grandfather, the white Apache named Charley, tried to talk him out of it. The Huertas were a powerful ranching family and Charley knew that such an act would do nothing but further enrage the Mexicans. He and Juan quarreled over this, but Juan was loco and no one could tell him what to do, and the more Charley told him not to steal the boy, the more determined Indio Juan became to do so. Knowing the trouble this would cause the People, Charley finally took his own small band and moved farther south, to another *ranchería* deeper into the Blue Mountains.

The girl was sorry to see her grandfather leave and she wished that she could go with him. Her own father had been killed by Mexican soldiers some years before and her mother, Beshad-e, had married Indio Juan's cousin. And because her sister was married to Indio Juan, she had no choice but to stay with his band. So it was among the People.

They had taken up their positions in the hills above the Huerta ranch, waiting patiently, as is the Apache way, watching for weeks until they knew the daily habits and rhythms of the ranch, knew all who lived there, who came and went. They knew on what day the family went to church in the village, at what hour they departed, knew that Geraldo's mother always drove the one-horse buggy with the boy on the seat beside her, that his father always rode his horse alongside, carrying their infant daughter on the saddle in front of him. They knew that where the trail narrowed in a small pass between the rocks, the man had to drop back to allow the buggy to pass first. And it was in this place that Indio Juan planned to abduct the boy.

Because she was nimble and small enough to operate in the close confines of the buggy, Indio Juan gave the girl the job of taking charge of the reins and the boy, while he himself cut the woman's throat. The two of them crouched together on the rocks above the pass, waiting for their moment, while the others stayed with the horses farther up the trail. And as the buggy passed beneath, they fell upon it, dropped soundlessly from the sky with nothing but the faintest rush of displaced air to warn the hapless churchgoers. Maria Huerta looked up in that instant and it must have seemed as if enormous birds of prey were stooping upon her from the heavens, blocking out the sun. Her eyes were wide with terror as Indio Juan fell onto her back, took hold of her hair, snapped her head backward, and drew the knife across her throat. In the same instant, the girl dropped onto the buggy seat beside her and gently took the reins from the woman's yielding hands as if Maria Huerta were herself complicit in the abduction. She remembered how the Mexican woman had looked at her in that moment, the surprise and terror in her eyes, how she had tried to cry out for her son, but nothing came forth but a final rush of escaping breath from her severed windpipe to which she raised a futile hand to stem the geyser of warm blood that spilled flowing down her breast. The girl had seen a great deal of violence and death already in her short life, and she had been brought up to consider all Mexicans her enemies. Yet as she looked in the woman's dying eyes all she saw was the heartbreak of a mother taken from her child.

As the woman tumbled lifelessly from the buggy like a limp child's doll in her Sunday dress, Indio Juan climbed onto the back of the buggy horse and cut the traces of the harness. The girl gathered up the screaming boy, holding him tight, and leaped nimbly on the horse behind Juan, and they rode off down the trail to join the others. Behind them, the husband and father, Fernando Huerta, bellowed in rage and anguish, but as they had counted on, he did not dare ride forward in pursuit, for he still held his baby daughter in his arms.

She did not sleep long, and when she awoke in the cave she was fully alert and lay listening for several minutes. She peered cautiously through the opening of the cave, unable to see the ridgetop from her hiding place. If she stayed low and moved carefully, she could conceal her movements behind the rocks. She would certainly hear the old man if he was nearby, for the rattling of the dog's chain would betray him. Unlike the People, who had moved through this country for centuries as soundlessly as a breath of wind, both the Mexicans and the White Eyes were clumsy and made a great deal of noise when they traveled.

She slipped from the cave and began working her way toward the arroyo up which the old White Eyes had himself ridden. He would be searching for her in the rocks or keeping to the ridge hoping to intercept her if she came over the top. He would not expect her to double back and pick up his old trail up the arroyo.

When she reached it, she made her way quickly to the top, running lightly over the rocks, her feet barely seeming to graze the ground as she ran. At the head of the draw she peered carefully over the top, hoping to spot the White Eyes' mule. And there it stood, dozing in the afternoon sun, head hanging low, eyes hooded, ears laid back, one hobbled front hoof cocked in repose. But in the same moment that she spotted him, the mule sensed her presence, perhaps he smelled her, for he raised his head and pricked his ears forward, his eyes opening wide. He nickered softly in alarm.

Before giving the mule any more time to worry over the matter, the girl revealed herself to him. She had a great deal of experience with horses, mules and burros, had helped steal them from the Mexicans since the time that she could walk and was one of the best horse thieves in the band. Now she approached the animal quickly and confidently, speaking soothingly to him, as if she had every business being here. He remained vigilant, but relaxed somewhat once he identified the unknown danger as something specific, recognizable—a creature that walked upright on two legs.

When the girl reached him she took hold of the reins just behind the bit, stroked his chin, and continued speaking in a language unknown to the mule, but in a tone he understood. She held him by the chin, and he raised his head slightly, his nostrils flared as he took in her scent, and then he nuzzled her chest and exhaled a warm humid breath onto her bare skin. Her peace thus made with the mule, she quickly unfastened the hobble, let it fall to the ground, picked up the reins from behind the saddle horn, and in one graceful bound was on his back.

It was said that Billy Flowers's bullwhip was at least thirty feet long, and as thick around as a man's forearm, that the crack of the popper at its end sounded like a clap of thunder, like the voice of God Himself, a sound that drove terror into the hearts of men and beasts alike. And now, before they had taken two steps, it froze the mule, John the Baptist, in place. The second stroke came in what seemed the very next instant, and did not crack like the first, for this one curled over the girl's shoulder, the force of it pulling her backward off the mule as if plucked from the saddle by a single marionette string. She tumbled to the ground, and before she could regain her feet, Flowers was atop her, his rope in hand to bind her.

Billy Flowers was unprepared for the girl's strength and ferocity. She squirmed like a wild panther, biting, scratching, and striking him, her quick slender limbs eluding his grasp. Yet despite his age, Flowers was all muscle and sinew himself. Still, though he had wrestled real panthers, and engaged in hand-to-hand combat with grizzlies, in those cases, he generally had a rifle in hand with which to administer the coup de grâce, or at the very least a knife to plunge into their black hearts. He had never tried to tie one up before.

The girl struggled ferociously, drawing blood with her bites and scratches, but she was finally no match for the old man, who managed first to bind her arms and then to loop the rope around her head, pulling it tight across her mouth, neutralizing at last the weapon of her teeth. Lastly, he ran the rope down her back, tied her legs, and cinched them up tight. The bound girl lay on her side, breathing heavily, and looking at him with eyes wild and less impassive now, the eyes of a terrified, trapped animal.

"I do hope you're not rabid, girl," Billy Flowers said as he inspected his wounds, his own breathing labored. He considered that he had been lucky the girl's teeth had not found their way to his throat. "You know, you almost made it," he added with a grudging respect. "Another few seconds and you'd have been gone. And I'd have been afoot, having lost my best mule. The only reason I caught you was that I got to thinking that I'd made a mistake leaving old John the Baptist all by himself up here. I've trailed a lot of varmints across the country over the years, missy, but I'm unaccustomed to following one that could double back and steal my mule. The only mistake you made was not getting here a moment sooner."

Billy Flowers picked up his old sweat-stained felt hat, dusted it off on his thigh, and put it back on his head. "And you, John," he said to the mule. "Shame on you, son. Letting yourself be seduced by this naked heathen child. 'Put on the whole armor of God, that ye may be able to stand against the wiles of the devil.' He works in cunning ways and you almost crossed over with him to the dark side. I've heard tell that the heathens ride their mounts until they drop from exhaustion beneath them, then cut their throats, carve steaks from their hindquarters, roast them on the fire and feast upon their flesh right then and there. That would have been your fate, John, had I not come back when I did. That's where Satan was leading you. Straight into the fires of damnation."

Now Billy Flowers stood regarding the girl, hog-tied on the ground. He had caught her, that much was certainly true, but the real point of the exercise, he realized now that his blood was settling again, had been the hunt itself. And now he wondered, finally, what in the world he was going to do with her.

THE NOTEBOOKS OF NED GILES, 1932
NOTEBOOK II:
The Great Apache Expedition

We have always known about the existence of the *In'deh* in Mexico. It is believed by some that they are the spirits of former warriors and for this reason they are called the ghost people. Those on the reservation are afraid of them. In the old days, young men would sometimes slip away to join them, and they would never be heard from again. And from time to time women or children would disappear. They would vanish in the night; it was said that they had been stolen by the ghost people and taken back down into old Mexico. But no one ever really knew if this was true or not, for no one ever saw these people. They were like ghosts who came and went among us and all feared them.

FROM AN INTERVIEW WITH JOSEPH VALOR,
CHIRICAHUA APACHE (24 APRIL, 1932)
Douglas Daily Dispatch, Ned Giles

18 APRIL, 1932

Douglas, Arizona

Almost two weeks gone by without an entry. Busy with work and preparations for departure . . . some play . . . much to report . . .

Volunteers for the Great Apache Expedition have continued to flood into Douglas: wealthy men from all over the country, arriving by private motorcar, or in private train cars, bringing, like Tolley Phillips, their strings of polo ponies, their bamboo fly rods, their English double shotguns. Others fly into town in private airplanes. The publicity campaign for the expedition has been successful beyond anyone's wildest expectations, the committee so inundated with applications that they've had to post notices all over town stating that no more volunteers are being accepted. As it is, the town is filled to capacity with a broad cross section of humanity: There are veterans of the Great War, others who served under Pershing during the Mexican revolution, soldiers of fortune, adventurers, cowboys, mule packers, professional hunting guides, and cooks and the less savory element of petty criminals, prostitutes, and sundry border riffraff. There is even a pair of Apache Indian scouts, recruited from the Mescalero Apache reservation in New Mexico, who have been hired to guide the expedition into the Sierra Madre. One is a very old man reported to have scouted for General George Crook in 1883.

A bustling Hooverville has sprung up on the rodeo grounds east of town to accommodate all the new arrivals. This is keeping Chief Gatlin and his deputies busy, as nearly every night there is some kind of disturbance— reports of thefts, fistfights, drunken brawls, gunfire.

In the afternoons, polo matches are held at the rodeo grounds between the Mexican army regulars and the American volunteers, followed by training sessions in which Colonel Carrillo drills his troops. Tolley plays in these scrimmages, and although he's not much of a polo player, he's got good horses and takes great pride in being the best dressed of the competitors.

He's decked out in white leather riding breeches and gleaming brown boots, which he has polished every day at the hotel.

For my part, I've been spending my time learning to shoot the Leica that Wade Jackson has lent me. What a wonderful little camera, light and fast, although of course, I get nothing like the depth and definition with it that I do with my 8×10. Still it's dandy for newspaper work, and my photographs of the polo matches and expedition preparations are appearing regularly in the *Daily Dispatch*. Big Wade has been a big help to me. It's true that he drinks too much, but when he's sober he's a real pro. Critical of what he calls "tricked-up art photography" and "photography with a political agenda," he preaches simplicity in his craft and refers to himself as strictly a "meat-and-potatoes shooter." Although he is way better than that.

"How did you ever end up in Douglas, anyway, Big Wade?" I asked him one afternoon when we were drinking a beer together across the border at Las Primorosas.

"I've bounced all over the country, kid," he said. "I was at the *New York Daily News* for a few years, the *Miami Herald*, the *Phoenix Gazette* . . . with a few stops in between. It's been a long bumpy downhill road to the *Dog-ass Daily News*."

"I don't understand," I said. "With that kind of résumé, you could shoot for anyone."

"Could *have*," he said. "Could have once shot for anyone. Not anymore, kid . . . my reputation in the business is shit now." He held up his Mexican beer bottle to the light, peered through the clear glass. "Couldn't keep away from the hooch. Finally gave up trying and came down here, where a man can walk across the border and have a legal drink." Jackson signaled for the waiter. "*Dos mescals, Miguel, mi amigo, por favor.*" And when the shots arrived, he held his glass up to me and said, "Let me serve as a cautionary tale to you, kid," he said. "It's the most valuable thing an old rummy can do for a young fellow photog. Take a good look at me. This is not how, or where, you want to end up twenty, thirty years from now. Trust me on that." And then he downed his shot. "But the best thing about working on the *Dog-ass Daily Star*," he said, "other than its proximity to Mexico, is that even a washed-up old drunk like me can do the job."

I feel bad for Big Wade and I'm grateful to him for everything he's done for me. Lucky for him, he has a pretty Mexican girlfriend named Maria, who takes care of him. I don't know what's in it for her but she seems to really care about him; she sees that he gets home from the bars every night and that he gets his work done when he needs to, not that the demands of the job are so great.

With Big Wade's help, I've also been writing short articles about the activities going on in town, and profiles of some of the volunteers. Or at least, I do the research and write the first draft and Wade rewrites it. To tell the truth, I think he's taking a little advantage of me, having me do a lot of his own work. But I don't mind.

One morning last week, the official expedition director of aviation, Spider King, came over to my table in the hotel dining room during breakfast. King is a trick flier who has flown in fairs and air shows all over the country and was brought in especially by the committee to lead the expedition "air force." He's a brash, flamboyant fellow who sports aviator goggles and a long flowing white scarf.

"I have orders to take you up today, Giles," he said. "I was supposed to take Big Wade, but he begged off, said he was afraid he'd toss his cookies in my plane. Said I should take you instead. Just as well, because I think the big fella might put me over my weight limit. We're flying down into old Mexico. Meet me at the airfield in an hour. And bring your camera. I have something to show you, and the newspaper is definitely going to want photographs of it."

It was a clear, windless morning and we flew due south out of Douglas. It's the first time I've ever been in an airplane, and I have to admit I was a little nervous. But King is one of those fellows whose natural self-confidence inspires trust in others. We flew across the plains of northern Sonora, gaining altitude as we approached the foothills of the Sierra Madre. The overlapping mountain ranges in the distance were hazy with a light morning fog and appeared to run to infinity, stretching south and west as far as the eye could see. Timbered in tall pine, the massive peaks, jagged hogbacks, and steep-tilted rock formations are cut by a labyrinth of canyons and river valleys, a magical land that seems from the air to be pristine, untouched, somehow prehistoric. Spider leaned over to me, grinning, and said, "Now you know how God must have felt when He looked around at what He had made."

A bit later, King said, "Hang on," and the airplane suddenly banked and fell away beneath me, leaving my stomach in the air. We dropped down into a canyon and flew a winding slalom course down the river, so close that you could see the shadows of the airplane cast upon the steep canyon walls; I felt that I could reach out and touch them.

"Look at that, Ned," King said, pointing to a series of caves connected by elaborate man-made rock structures at different elevations in the canyon walls, almost like an apartment building. "Those are pre-Columbian cave dwellings, built by an ancient civilization that inhabited this country over a thousand years ago. This is where the expedition is headed. The Mexicans think that the Apaches use them as hideouts. Look carefully and you can see the remains of recent fires in some of them, and what looks like cooking utensils and blankets. I'll make another pass and get us closer." King crested the canyon wall, banked the plane sharply, and dropped back down into the canyon. As he did so, I was looking out my side of the plane when I thought I saw something move, a figure in the rocks, and then clearly, just for a flashing moment, I recognized that it was a human being. I felt goose bumps and the hair stood up on the back of my neck. But in the next instant the figure was gone, like an afterimage.

"Did you see that, Spider?" I said excitedly. "Did you see it?"

"See what?"

"I think I saw someone."

"Where?"

"Right back there."

"Let's have a look."

Spider banked the plane again and made another pass, but this time we saw nothing, and I began to doubt my own eyes. "Maybe I just imagined it," I said, "but I could have sworn I saw someone."

"You didn't imagine it," Spider said. "They're here."

King made a number of passes from different angles so that I could photograph the caves. Having never shot from an airplane before, I found the exposures and focusing tricky, but under the circumstances, some of the images turned out surprisingly well. They had a slightly grainy, mysterious quality, and in one of them, what might have been the figure of a human being crouched in the rocks was visible. The next day, the *Daily Dispatch* ran this image on the front page, under the headline EXPEDITION LOCATES APACHE HIDEOUT.

Besides Spider, we have had a few other additions to the staff, including a young woman named Margaret Hawkins, a doctoral student in anthropology at the University of Arizona. Margaret is writing her dissertation on the bronco Apaches, and through the auspices of her department has managed to talk her way into a position as the unofficial expedition anthropologist. "Letting Margaret come along was a shrewd move on the part of the committee," says Wade Jackson with his typical cynicism. "In case the rich guys actually get a chance to wipe out some Apaches, it allows them the illusion that they are doing so as part of an important scientific study."

Margaret herself is a tall, long-limbed, graceful woman in her midtwenties. She has short blond hair, a fine athletic figure, a deep rich laugh, and one of those brilliant smiles that makes everyone upon whom it shines feel graced, as if they are the most special person on earth. A number of the men, both among the volunteers and the staff alike, have already fallen in love with her. I interviewed and photographed her for the newspaper when she first arrived and she and I became friends right off in that easy, uncomplicated way that sometimes happens.

As often as I am able, I cross the border and expose film in Mexico. What a vibrant country, full of life, energy, and color. The street urchin, Jesus, whom Tolley and I met on our first night in Agua Prieta, has become my unofficial guide, assistant, and translator. I've even begun to pick up a little Spanish. The first time I drove my Roadster into Agua Prieta, the boy looked at it wide-eyed, ran his hand reverently over the finish. "You must be very rich, Señor Ned," he said.

I'm still staying in the spare room in Tolley's suite at the Gadsden, and he refuses any payment for it, which is certainly a good deal for me. In the evenings, we frequently cross the border together to drink and dance in the cantinas in Agua Prieta. Tolley may be a sissy but he loves to dance with the whores. He teases them and adjusts their hair and dresses, and makes them laugh, and because he wants nothing more from them than that, they treat him just like "one of the girls," as he himself puts it. Las Primorosas has become the unofficial expedition watering hole and gathering place for both staff members and volunteers. Although he's probably richer than any of the others, Tolley's a bit of a black sheep among the volunteers, and he seems more comfortable hanging around with the "help." Often Margaret joins us in the bar, and for her part seems completely uninterested in the other men who vie for her favors. She prefers to sit with Tolley and me and turns down all other offers to dance. She seems to be a competent, confident woman, and yet I sense in her some kind of sadness.

"Tell me, darling," Tolley asked her the other night, "are you a Sapphist?"

Margaret laughed. "God, no, Tolley, I'm not," she said. "Whatever gave you that idea?"

"Because you seem so inured to the advances of all the men who are panting after you," Tolley said.

"That's because I'm working," Margaret explained. "And it's always a mistake to mix business with pleasure. The only thing more distracting than a love affair in the field is a love affair gone bad in the field."

"You say that as if you speak from experience, Mag," I said.

Margaret smiled wryly. "Let's just say that I've learned to choose my friends carefully," she said. "In this case, I think it's safe to say that Tolbert and I are not going to become romantically involved."

"Safe?" Tolley said. "Bookmakers are offering ten-million-to-one odds on that one, darling."

"And as for you, little brother," Margaret said, patting my hand, "I'm too old for you. Besides, you're already in love. Don't think we haven't noticed how love-struck you are when you gaze at that little señorita."

"God, I know, isn't he a bore?" Tolley said. "Mooning over the first whore he meets in a Mexican cantina. It's so pathetic!"

"I think it's sweet," Margaret said.

"Oh, *please*," Tolley said, "the boy's a walking cliché of adolescent romantic yearnings. And what's worse, he's not even getting laid."

"That's even sweeter," Margaret said.

"I just don't want to be one of her customers," I said. "If I did that, I'd be just like all the others. She's a nice girl and I want to get to know her first."

"He wants to get to know her first!" Tolley said. "While half a dozen other men hump her every night. What a romantic! What a hopeless chump!"

"Shut up, Tolley," I warned. "You know if you weren't such a big sissy, I'd punch you right in the nose."

"That's what I like about you, old sport," Tolley said. "Most of the men here want to punch me in the nose because I *am* such a big sissy."

"Well, I think you're perfectly darling, Neddy," Margaret said. "The world could use a little more romance and chivalry."

"Shall we dance, Mag?" I asked.

"I thought you'd never ask, sweetie."

I've learned the steps to the Mexican dances, and if I do say so myself, I've become a favorite partner of the cantina girls. Everyone knows I'm sweet on Magdalena, but because the *patrón* frowns on the girls entering into personal relationships with customers, I can't dance with her very often. So I dance with all of them.

"I think your girlfriend's jealous," Margaret said after we took to the floor. It was a slow evening and Magdalena was sitting at a table with two other girls. "She's watching me with daggers in her eyes."

"You think so?" I asked.

Just then Chief Gatlin walked out on the floor and tapped me on the shoulder. "I'm cutting in on you, son," he said.

"You'll have to ask the lady about that, Chief," I said. Gatlin hasn't liked me from the start, I guess because I hang around with Tolley. Guilt by association.

"I've noticed that you only dance with queers, Miss Hawkins," Gatlin said now. "I thought you might want to try a real man on for size."

Margaret laughed. "Thanks anyway, Chief," she said, "but I *like* queers."

"Hey," I protested. "I'm not a queer."

"All right, ma'am," he said, ignoring me, tipping his hat to Margaret. "Whatever you say. But if you change your mind, all you have to do is ask." Gatlin went over to the table where the girls were sitting and held his hand out to Magdalena. She looked at him nervously, finally stood reluctantly and walked out on the dance floor with him.

"Thanks a lot, Mag," I said. I noticed that Margaret was watching the chief with a strange, pensive look on her face.

"What for, sweetie?" she asked. "For failing to defend you against the charges of being queer, or for driving the chief into your girlfriend's arms?"

I considered this for a moment. "Both, I guess," I said.

"You know, he's not entirely unattractive," Margaret said.

"Jesus, you don't *like* him, do you, Mag?"

Margaret shrugged. "I think he reminds me of my father," she said.

"Your father must have been a real dick."

She laughed. "Yeah, he was."

"Magdalena's afraid of him," I said.

Margaret was silent for a long time. "Yes," she said finally. "She probably should be."

24 APRIL, 1932

This morning I went out to photograph the Apache scouts for the newspaper. It was supposed to be Big Wade's assignment, but he was hungover as usual and sent me instead. The Apaches are camped off by themselves in a grove of sycamore trees up a little canyon outside town. Evidently they walked all the way down here from the Mescalero reservation in New Mexico, at least three hundred miles, and one of them is a very old man.

I drove out to their camp and was just getting my camera gear out of the automobile when the younger of them approached me, his eyes flashing angrily.

"What do you want?" the man asked. He looked to be in his midtwenties, with a strong, broad face and dark skin. I don't know what I expected . . . war paint and tomahawk, I suppose . . . but I have to admit that from a photographic point of view I was a bit disappointed to see that he was dressed in regular clothing—a work shirt, dungarees, and cowboy boots—and his dark hair was cut short like a white man's.

"I'm with the *Douglas Daily Dispatch*," I answered. "They sent me out here to take your photograph."

"That's the trouble with you White Eyes," he said. "You have no manners. You come uninvited and you take without asking."

"You don't have to be unfriendly about it," I said. "You haven't even given me a chance to ask permission, yet." But at the same time I was thinking about Big Wade's instructions to me on the subject. "Never, ever, ask someone if you can take their picture, kid," he told me. "That's the first rule of photojournalism. If you're going to be a pro, you have to take the position that it's your God-given right to photograph anyone, anywhere, anytime."

"All right, go ahead and ask, then," the man said.

I stuck my hand out. "My name is Ned Giles," I said. "I'm with the *Douglas Daily Dispatch*. I'd like to take your photograph."

The man got up very close to me. "No," he said. "And if you don't leave here now, I will smash that camera."

"If you were to try to do that," I said, "I'd have to punch you in the nose."

The Indian stared at me for a moment, then he laughed.

"What's so funny?" I asked.

"In the old days, we made a point of killing White Eyes if they showed fear," he said. "We enjoyed torturing them and killing them very slowly in order to prolong their suffering. But you are lucky. You are too stupid to be afraid of me."

"Why should I be afraid of you?"

"You don't know much, do you, White Eyes?" he said.

"I guess I don't," I admitted. "I'm from Chicago."

"Please forgive my grandson," the old man said, approaching us. He was a small, spry, broad-chested old fellow, more photogenic than the younger man, his face the color and texture of old cracked leather, his white hair long and braided into a ponytail that hung halfway down his back, beneath a large, round, wide-brimmed straw hat that tied under his chin and looked somewhat like a Japanese farmer's hat. He was dressed in patched blue jeans rolled up at the ankles, and a faded blue work shirt buttoned up to the neck. From his belt hung a rawhide pouch, and around his neck a large silver medallion on a chain. On his feet he wore rawhide moccasins with upturned toes, which gave him a kind of elfin look, and he walked with a funny, rolling, bowlegged, pigeon-toed gait. "He is an angry young man," explained the old Apache. "It comes from being sent away to the Indian school when he was a boy. And now that he is back on the reservation, he doesn't have enough to do there besides hate white people. But no matter what he says, he's never actually killed one before." He held his hand out to me. "I am Joseph Valor. This is my grandson, Albert."

"I'm very pleased to meet you, sir," I said. "The newspaper sent me out here to take your photograph and to interview you. They say you scouted for General George Crook."

"I have had my photograph taken many times before," the old man said with pride in his voice. He opened the pouch at his waist and extracted a piece of folded paper, which he opened carefully. It appeared to be a page torn out of a book, yellowed and cracked, and on it was the much-faded image of an old daguerreotype photograph. In the photograph General Crook and several other soldiers were seated on the ground with some Indians. "This photograph was taken in Mexico in the White Eyes year 1883," Joseph Valor said, "the first time Geronimo surrendered to the *nantan lupan*. That is what we called your General Crook." He pointed at one of the figures. "This is me, here. Goso was my name in the old days. This is the *nantan lupan*. And this is Geronimo."

"You mind if I borrow this?" I asked. "We could run it in the newspaper. I promise I'll bring it back to you."

But the old man was already carefully folding the page back up. "No, that is not possible," he said, putting it back in the pouch.

Albert laughed derisively. "My grandfather is very proud of that picture," he said. "Even though it is only torn out of a book. Show the White Eyes your medal now, Grandfather. That is the other thing of which he is so proud."

"I have been to Washington, D.C., to meet with your president," said the old man.

"Herbert Hoover?" I asked.

"Grover Cleveland."

"What year was that, sir?"

"Eighteen eighty-six," said Joseph Valor. "The Great White Father gave me this peace medal." He held out the medal for me to admire. It had faint engraving on it, worn away by fifty years of handling, and it was stamped with the president's image. But unless I had my American presidents all mixed up, it wasn't Grover Cleveland on the medal.

"Isn't this Chester A. Arthur?" I asked.

"Yes, it is," Joseph Valor said. "He was the Great White Father before President Cleveland."

Albert laughed again. "It must have just been lying around in the White House," he said. "They were too cheap to make new ones. You know, they slaughter the savages, steal their homeland, imprison the survivors. And give them a nice leftover presidential medal for their troubles."

"My grandson is full of hate," the old man said.

I set my camera up and made a portrait of Joseph Valor. Afterward we sat around their campfire drinking coffee while I interviewed the old man.

"I am *ch'uk'aende*," he began in the curiously oratorical way he has of speaking, "the band of the great Chief Cochise, who was my uncle. We considered ourselves to be the only true Chiricahua. The White Eyes try to put us all together as one people, *Apache*, but this is not at all how it is with us. We are many different bands, even among those the White Eyes call Chiricahua, we are several different bands. We lived apart in those days, in a different country, although we sometimes came together for celebrations or just to visit. Or to raid and wage war. And we often married among each other. Later I married a N'dendaa girl, which was Chief Juh's band, and also the band to which Geronimo belonged, although despite what the White Eyes believe, Geronimo was never a chief, but a *di-yin*, a shaman. I lived for some years among the N'dendaa in Mexico. I have had four wives altogether and many children, and grandchildren. Those who are still living are scattered across the earth like grass seed on the wind."

"The readers of the *Douglas Daily Dispatch* would be interested in knowing how you became a scout for the whites," I said.

"After we surrendered to the *nantan lupan*," said the old man, "we were taken to live at the agency in San Carlos. It was a terrible place. We all hated that country. It was hot and dry and there was no game, and the rations that were promised us by your government never came. Many of us became scouts. The *nantan lupan* took good care of us. And it was the only way we had to be men, to be warriors. It was all we knew how to do. We were allowed to have weapons and we were allowed to leave the agency with the soldiers, to go back up into the mountains, to the country we loved."

"To hunt down their own people," Albert said bitterly. I had not wanted to say it, and I felt sorry for the old man for the disrespect his grandson showed him, but I was wondering about that myself.

Joseph Valor looked hard at the younger man. "You do not know what it was like in the old days," he said in a low voice.

"I know that Geronimo never scouted for the White Eyes," Albert said.

"My grandson believes that I am a traitor," Joseph Valor said. "As do many others on the reservation. He believes that Geronimo was a great man, a great hero of the People. But others believe that Geronimo caused nothing but trouble for us. He was an untruthful man and many believe that his lying and drinking, and his breakouts from the agency, only made things worse for everyone. It was for this reason that many of us became scouts. The *nantan lupan* told us that if we helped him to bring in Geronimo and the others who were still out, things would go easier for all Apaches, and the Chiricahuas would be given our own agency."

"Yes, and tell the White Eyes how you were repaid for your loyal services as a scout to the United States Army, Grandfather," Albert said. He gestured with his hand toward my notebook. "Maybe he will write it in his article for the newspaper."

Joseph looked steadily at Albert and shook his head sadly. "My grandson is so poisoned by hate," he said finally, "that he even hates his own grandfather."

And it was true that I could feel the anger and hatred coming off Albert Valor like heat vapors.

"When they sent my grandfather and some of the other scouts to Washington in 1886," Albert said, "the *Great White Father*"—he spoke this last in a voice heavy with sarcasm—"promised them a big reservation of their own. But instead of sending them home, the president put them on a train to Florida. They were imprisoned in an army fort near St. Augustine. Later that fall, after Geronimo surrendered for the final time to General Miles, he and his followers were also sent there. Of course, they all despised my grandfather and the others who had served as scouts, and they treated them as traitors. My grandfather was held with Geronimo and the other Chiricahuas as a prisoner of war for twenty-seven years, first in Florida, then at another fort in Alabama, and then finally in Oklahoma. He lived as an outcast among his own people. It wasn't until 1913 that some of the Chiricahuas were allowed to go back to their home country. And even then we were not given our own reservation, as we had been promised, but were sent to live with the Mescalero Apaches. That is how the White Eyes repaid my grandfather for his loyal service as a scout. And yet he still wears the medal that the *Great White Father* gave him. And still he is an outcast among his people."

My last question was an obvious one. "What made you come down here to scout again, Mr. Valor?" I asked. "And you, Albert? If you hate the whites so much, why have you agreed to help them now?"

"I did not come to help the White Eyes," Albert said. "I came because my mother asked me to look after my grandfather."

Joseph smiled. "I do not need to be looked after," he said, "by a boy who grew up on the reservation."

"This winter some White Eyes from Douglas came up to Mescalero," Albert said. "They posted a notice on the bulletin board in the community center asking for Apache scouts to guide an expedition into old Mexico. They made inquiries around the reservation to see if any of the old-timers were still alive. There are a few old women left who once lived in the Sierra Madre—the Blue Mountains, we call them. And there remain a few people who had been children and infants there when we surrendered. But my grandfather is the last of the old scouts. He insisted on coming. We could not talk him out of it. And he won't even tell us why."

I looked at the old man. He gazed off to the south. He had clearly finished speaking.

30 APRIL, 1932

On the plain outside Agua Prieta, Sonora

I write this from my cot on our first night's bivouac in the plains just beyond Agua Prieta. The Great Apache Expedition officially departed Douglas, Arizona, this morning with a downtown parade of no small fanfare. A bandstand had been set up in front of the JCPenney store, from which the mayor, surrounded by his committee members, and with his typical bombast, gave a rousing speech. I had my camera set up on a tripod in the corner of the bandstand to record the scene for posterity.

A marching band from the local high school led the parade down Main Street, which was lined with cheering well-wishers, waving flags and throwing confetti. The band was followed by the company of mounted Mexican cavalrymen, in full dress uniform, headed by the dashing Colonel Carrillo, who rode a prancing white horse and waved eloquently to the crowd. Overhead, Spider King performed daring aerial stunts in his plane, towering dives and loop-de-loops, buzzing low, waggling his wings and generally thrilling the spectators. Next came the company of paying volunteers, nearly fifty strong, led by a wealthy young man from the East named Winston Hughes, whose family is in the steel business, and who proudly bore the American flag. Some of the men were dressed in quasi-military attire—their old uniforms from the Great War, or Teddy Roosevelt–inspired Rough Rider outfits. Yet others sported brand-new Western wear purchased from the Douglas Dry Goods store—snap-button shirts and chaps, cowboy boots and spurs, and spanking-new cowboy hats. Always the clotheshorse, and never one to try to blend in with the crowd, Tolbert Phillips Jr. wore his crisply pressed Abercrombie & Fitch khaki safari outfit, complete with pith helmet, as if he were off to the African bush. He blew magnanimous kisses to the crowd as he passed.

Behind the volunteers came the staff, about thirty people altogether, which included muleteers, cowboys, guides, cooks and sundry attendants, riding horses, mules, and donkeys. Harold Browning, the British desk clerk from the Gadsden Hotel, has been pressed into service as Tolley's valet. Clearly not much of an equestrian, Mr. Browning bounced uncomfortably down the street on a little white burro, his feet nearly grazing the ground.

The Apache scouts, Joseph and Albert Valor, brought up the rear, mounted on mules. They sported red bandannas around their heads, the traditional accessory of the scout, worn in the old days to identify them from the hostile Indians they were chasing. The crowd had a curious reaction to the appearance of the scouts; there were scattered catcalls and boos as they passed, expressions of the deep antipathy that many in the Southwest still feel toward the Apaches. Joseph ignored them, staring straight ahead, expressionless, but Albert glared menacingly back at the spectators. He looked up at me on the bandstand, pulled a rifle from his scabbard, and raised it overhead, shaking it and uttering a fierce Indian war cry, which actually brought a collective expression of alarm from the crowd. Then he laughed.

The grand send-off from Douglas was largely ceremonial. After the parade, everyone dismounted and we were loaded into buses and driven into Mexico, while the stock, equipment, and provisions were trucked across the border. It took the better part of the day for the expedition to clear Mexican customs. To overcome the obvious political problem of an armed force of Americans entering their country, the president of Mexico, Ortiz Rubio, issued special hunting permits to each member of the expedition, allowing volunteers to carry sporting arms only into the country—shotguns and deer rifles.

A comfortable camp was set up in advance in the plains just outside Agua Prieta, and after our arrival here, the Mexicans put on an enormous dinner feast under a huge tent. Tables were laden with all manner of food-stuffs, and white-jacketed waiters served cocktails, while a mariachi band played and the volunteers danced by the light of kerosene torches with the girls who had been bused out from town along with other dignitaries.

Mayor Cargill and his committee members and their wives had also come out to the camp for the evening festivities and were joined there by the mayor of Agua Prieta, Presidente Rogerio Loreto, and the governor of the state of Sonora himself, Fausto Topete. I was stunned to see Wade Jackson descend from one of the late-arriving buses toting a duffel bag, in addition to his camera gear.

"What in the world are you doing here, Big Wade?" I asked him.

"You're not going to believe it, kid," he said disgustedly. "But I'm bunk-ing with you. Turns out my asshole editor is making me go on the expedi-tion, after all. Says we need two photographers to cover it in case something happens to one of us . . . yeah, like, for instance, I drop dead of a *fucking* heart attack . . ."

Magdalena was one of the girls from the cantinas who had been driven out for the evening, and I spotted her now standing by one of the tents, talking with Chief Gatlin. With all the preparations for departure, I had barely been able to see her this past week and had not even said good-bye. I went over to her.

"I didn't think I'd see you again, Magdalena," I said to her.

She kept her eyes downcast and looked as if she'd been crying.

"Are you okay?"

"She's fine," Gatlin said impatiently. "What can I do for you, boy? The young lady and I are discussing business."

"What kind of business?" I asked.

"The kind that's none of yours."

"They are taking some of us along to Bavispe, Ned," Magdalena said to me. "It is the town where my family lives. I do not wish to go."

"Why are you bringing the girls?" I asked the chief.

Gatlin smiled a thin, ugly smile. "Because it is among my duties as director of personnel to see to the entertainment of our distinguished volunteers."

It came out of my mouth before I could stop myself: "Doesn't that make you a pimp, Chief?"

Before I even saw it coming, Gatlin had clamped his hand around my throat. He put his face up inches from mine so that I could smell his breath. "Who do you think you are, you little pissant?" he said, spitting his words at me. "Do you think you're a tough guy?"

I do not think I'm a tough guy, but I was unable to answer because Gatlin was squeezing my throat so hard that I couldn't speak.

"Well, do you?" Gatlin asked.

I managed to shake my head.

"That's right," Gatlin said. "You're not tough at all. You're just a smart-aleck city boy. And if you ever speak to me that way again, I'll kill you. Do you understand me?"

I nodded.

"I don't want you bothering this girl again," Gatlin said. "We're not in the cantina now. We're in the field. And you are here at the pleasure of the Great Apache Expedition; you are here at *my* pleasure. There will be no more mooning around like a lovesick puppy dog. Do you understand what I'm telling you, boy?"

Margaret Hawkins walked up then. "What's going on here?" she demanded.

"Just teaching young Mr. Giles some field protocol, Margaret," Chief Gatlin said. "That's all."

"Let go of him, Leslie," Margaret said. "You're hurting him. He's just a kid."

"Yes, ma'am, that's exactly what I was explaining to the boy myself," said the chief, releasing his grip. "There we are, son. The lady comes to your rescue. But I think we understand each other now, don't we?"

I rubbed my throat.

Gatlin tipped his hat to Margaret. "Always a pleasure to see you,

Margaret," he said. "Right now I'm just getting the staff settled, but I'd love to take a turn with you on the dance floor later." He took Magdalena by the arm and led her off.

"Are you all right, Ned?" Margaret asked.

"I'm okay."

"What did you say to him?"

"I called him a pimp."

"I don't think Chief Gatlin is a man you want for an enemy," Margaret said.

"It's a bit late for that, Mag," I said. "And besides, he is a pimp. That girl is not here of her own free will. She never chose this life. And now he's making her come with us. To service his volunteers. It's slavery."

"Okay, Neddy," Margaret said. "I'll speak to him myself about it."

"I didn't realize you two were on a first-name basis."

Just then one of the waiters walked past, half carrying, half dragging the boy Jesus by the scruff of his neck. "Señor Ned!" he called out, struggling to escape the waiter's clutches. "I have been looking for you!"

The waiter stopped and spoke rapidly to me in Spanish while pointing and gesturing at the boy.

"The part I understood," I said to Jesus, "is that you're a thief and the son of a whore. Is that true?"

The boy shrugged. "I do not know my mother."

"What did you steal?"

"The Americans do not miss a few quarters from their pockets," the boy said. "Please tell him I come with you, Señor Ned."

"You're not coming with me."

"Yes, I am coming," Jesus insisted. "I am working for you. I am carrying your camera, I am teaching you to speak Spanish. I am very helpful. Please."

"Esta bien," I said to the waiter in my rudimentary Spanish. "Usted puede dejar al chico." Grudgingly the waiter released Jesus, but not without first cuffing the boy sharply on the back of the head. The boy hollered.

"Si yo le agarro robando otra vez, yo cortaré la mano," said the waiter, making a little chopping gesture with one hand on the wrist of the other.

I cuffed the boy on the back of the head myself, which made Jesus holler again, but which seemed to placate the waiter somewhat. "I'll cut his hand off myself if I catch him stealing," I said.

"If I work for you, Señor Ned, I will not have to steal," Jesus said, rubbing his head.

"You'll have to talk to Big Wade about that, kid," I said. "I don't have the authority to hire you and I'm not exactly on the best of terms with the director of personnel."

Now I lie in my cot in the canvas wall tent I'm sharing with Wade Jackson, who passed out earlier and is snoring like thunder. The boy, Jesus, is wrapped in a blanket on the floor of the tent, sound asleep himself. It's well past midnight, but I'm all keyed up. I don't see how anyone could sleep through all this racket, anyway. Not only Big Wade's snoring, but a number of the men are still up drinking and dancing. A few minutes ago it sounded like a fight broke out, with shouting and cursing in both Spanish and English. Shots have been fired . . .

A moment after I made that last entry, the flap to our tent opened and someone slipped in.

"Who's there?" I asked.

"It's just me, Neddy, Margaret."

"What are you doing here, Mag?"

"I got spooked," she said. "Did you hear the gunshots? Can I stay here with you?" Not waiting for an answer, Margaret climbed into my cot. She was fully clothed.

"Don't get any ideas, little brother," she whispered. "I'm just feeling a little vulnerable. It was you or Tolley, and I thought you might offer me a bit more protection."

"Gee, thanks, Mag," I said. "I'm flattered."

"Plus you never know who might already *be* in Tolley's bed," Margaret added.

"I guess you could have tried Chief Gatlin's," I said. "I saw you dancing with him tonight."

"From the sounds of things, I imagine the chief is busy with law enforcement duties tonight," Margaret said.

"Oh, so were it not for that, you would have gone to his tent?"

"I didn't say that."

"You implied it," I said. "Jesus, I really can't believe you like that asshole, Mag."

"I'm sorry, sweetie, really I am," she said. "I have terrible taste in men. That's why I try to stay away from them."

"What happened to you, Mag?" I asked. "Some man must have treated you really badly."

"Yeah, I guess you could say that, Neddy," Margaret said. "But I don't want to talk about it now."

"Okay."

So we lay quiet for a while. I could feel the soft weight of Margaret's breast grazing my arm, her heart beating, the warmth of her body next to mine. I could feel myself becoming aroused.

"It's a little tight in here, isn't it?" I said, trying to shift my body and accidentally brushing up against her.

She obviously felt me because she said: "Maybe I'd be safer in Tolley's bed, after all. Don't disappoint me, Neddy. I need you to be my friend."

"I'm sorry, Mag," I said. "I am your friend. I didn't do it on purpose. I'm only human."

She laughed. "You're a darling boy. If I was five, *ummm*, maybe ten years younger, I'd fall in love with you. Then you could break my heart."

"I'd never do that, Mag."

And so we lay still. I tried to think about other things, concentrating on the drunken brawl outside. There was more shouting and scuffling, and finally we heard Colonel Carrillo's troops being called out to quell the disturbance. "God, they're all going to kill each other before we even get started," Margaret said. "I'm glad your roommates are such sound sleepers. I don't know what's worse, the noise out there, or Big Wade's snoring."

It was at least an hour before the camp settled down. I felt the tenseness gradually leave Margaret's body as she relaxed against me, her breathing becoming slow and even as she drifted off to sleep. I couldn't sleep myself, and so I lit the candle and rolled over on my side to make these entries.

1 MAY, 1932

On the Sonoran Road

Ignoring Chief Gatlin's warning, I went early this morning to the tent in which the prostitutes are housed to check on Magdalena. There the other girls told me that rather than face the disgrace of returning to her village with the expedition, she had run away in the night. They had no idea where she had gone. Perhaps she had made her way back to town. Or had she just wandered off into the plains? After I discovered that she was missing, I went to see Gatlin, to find out if he had sent out a search party for her.

He chuckled and shook his head. "She's just a whore, boy," he said. "Not worth bothering about. I was getting a little tired of her bellyaching anyway."

"She didn't ask to be a whore," I said.

"She was lucky to have the work," Gatlin said. "Why, she probably walked back to town and set up shop somewhere on a street corner."

"Yeah, Chief," I said, "she was a real lucky girl."

"I guess you could go look for her yourself, son, if she's so important to you," he said. He looked out across the plains. "'Course it's mighty big country out there, and in case you didn't get back before we left, you'd miss out on the expedition altogether."

And so I hurried back to our tent and got Jesus, who, ever resourceful, talked one of the drivers from town who had spent the night at the camp into giving us a ride to Agua Prieta. There was clearly no sense in searching the plains for Magdalena, and I could only hope that she had had the sense to walk back to town, although even there, I had no idea where I would look for her. She could certainly not return to the cantina.

"You have any suggestions where she might be, kid?" I asked Jesus, after the driver dropped us off.

"If she came back to town," he said, "there is only one place that she could go."

Jesus crossed himself as we entered the church on one end of the town plaza. We stood in the back examining the few people who sat in the pews.

"I think she is there," Jesus said, pointing to a figure huddled at the end of a pew near the front of the church.

I approached the figure, whose head was shrouded with a shawl, and not until I had slipped into the pew beside her, and looked directly into her face, did I see that the boy had been right; it was Magdalena. She looked frightened to see me.

"What are you doing here, Ned?" she asked, and I thought for a moment that she was going to bolt.

"I came looking for you," I answered. "What are you doing here, Magdalena?"

"Are you going to make me go back?" she asked.

"No, of course I'm not," I said. "Not if you don't want to."

"I cannot go home, Ned."

"I understand," I said. "But what are you going to do now?"

"I do not know," she said. "I will wait for the expedition to leave here, and then perhaps I will return to the cantina. And if they will not take me back, I will go to another."

"Maybe you could find some other kind of work, Magdalena," I suggested.

"What kind of work, Ned?" she asked.

"I don't know . . . anything . . . anything at all." I dug in my back pocket, pulled out my billfold, and removed some bills. "Here, use this money until you get on your feet. I'll come back when this is all over and find you."

She accepted the bills, and I noticed that she held rosary beads in her hands. She smiled gratefully. "Thank you," she said. "You have been very kind to me, Ned."

"I have to go back now," I said. "I just wanted to see if you were safe."

She nodded. "I am safe."

I turned once more at the large carved wood doors of the church to look back at Magdelena, a dark hooded figure huddled on the pew. I wondered if I would ever see her again.

Jesus and I got back to camp in plenty of time. There we learned that a Mexican vaquero had been killed in last night's brawl, and three others, including two American wranglers, seriously wounded. Those held responsible, both Mexican and American, had been escorted this morning by some of Carrillo's soldiers and turned over to the sheriff in Agua Prieta, which had delayed the start of the expedition. It was nearly noon before the buses were finally loaded and under way, a considerably less festive departure than yesterday. Everyone is subdued today, and a number of the men are sick with hangovers.

I'm riding in one of the staff buses with Big Wade, Margaret, and Jesus, among others. Wade managed to secure permission to bring Jesus along, after all. Between us we have a lot of gear and he has already proved himself useful.

The Sonoran roads are rough, in places little more than faint two-tracks, the going slow, bumpy, and dusty. In the first hour, one of last night's revelers vomited inside our bus, and the stink of it mingles sickeningly with the smell of diesel fumes. Big Wade finally lit a cigar to cover the stench, but I don't know what's worse. Then two hours later, as the bus was climbing a steep grade, the engine overheated and the radiator boiled over and we were all asked to get out and walk to the summit.

Jesus managed to find a man in one of the other buses willing, for a price, to give his place up to Big Wade.

"It was a stroke of pure genius to bring the boy along," Jackson said to me. "I owe you big-time for this one, kid." And to Margaret he said: "I know that a gentleman is supposed to offer his seat to a lady. But you're young and in shape, and I hope that under the circumstances, you will forgive me."

"No problem, Big Wade," said Margaret. "I'd just as soon walk, anyway, as smell this revolting stew of puke, diesel fumes, and cigar smoke."

So we walked to the summit, mostly in silence, and are now back on the bus. I diverted myself by making some negatives of the countryside with my 8×10 before we loaded back up. The landscape looks rather different at ground level than it did from Spider King's airplane and has risen quickly from treeless plains to rolling hills covered in pale green spring grass and bright wildflowers. The hills are studded with oak trees and mountain cedars, and in the lush river and creek bottoms we ford, mature cottonwoods and sycamores grow.

The bus motor is so noisy that it's difficult even to make conversation. I don't feel much like talking anyway, and besides my camera I'm glad I have my notebook to distract me, even if these entries do look like they've been written by a drunkard.

Well after dark . . . a long, rough, dusty day of travel . . . breakdowns and flat tires . . . our ungainly convoy has finally reached the expedition base camp outside the village of Bavispe on the river of the same name. Camp has been set up in advance of our arrival and dinner was waiting for us. Everyone is whipped. We ate quickly, with little conversation, and have retired early to our assigned tents. All is quiet, but for Big Wade's snoring, but I don't think even that will disturb my sleep tonight. Too dark by the time we arrived here to see much of our surroundings. I was thinking today on the bus that I should find Magdalena's parents and tell them what happened to their daughter. But it occurs to me that I never even learned her last name. And anyway, what could I possibly say to them?

7 MAY, 1932

Bavispe, Sonora

A busy week, spent planning and preparing for our first foray into the Sierra Madre. We've been making short day trips into the foothills, in order to acclimate both man and stock to the terrain. A dirt airstrip, marked by oil lanterns and a wind sock, has been carved out above the river and the expedition "air force," which consists of five planes, including that of Spider

King, makes daily reconnaissance flights into the mountains, looking for signs of the bronco, or "lost" Apaches, as they are called.

I've been assigned to a sorrel mule named Buster, a gentle, sure-footed beast who is patiently forgiving of my lack of equestrian skills. Jesus has been given a donkey, which also carries our photographic gear. He trails along behind me a bit like Sancho Panza. Big Wade rides a stout bay gelding and mutters expletives to himself and anyone else within earshot. *"Fucking madness,"* he gripes. "Has anyone else noticed that neither our mayor, nor any of his illustrious committee members, are along for the expedition? No, instead they send an overweight, middle-aged rummy photographer in lousy health to bring back vacation photos for them."

Indeed, so far the expedition resembles nothing so much as a leisurely idyll through interesting new country, very much as Big Wade originally described it: "an excuse to take a bunch of rich guys hunting and fishing in the Sierra Madre." The guides have begun taking some of the volunteers out to hunt deer and quail, and to fish for trout in the mountain streams around Bavispe. So far our main responsibility has been to take photographs of the beaming sports with their game and catch. The film is then flown back to Douglas and the photos run each day in the *Daily Dispatch* with stories that we both write. The pilot returns the following day with the newspapers so that the volunteers can see their photos, with captions such as: *Mr. Dudley Chalmers, of Greenwich, Connecticut, with a 14-inch Apache trout taken on a dry fly in Santa Maria Creek, a small tributary of the Bavispe River.* Or, *Mr. Charles McFarlane and his English pointer, Brewster, with a brace of masked bobwhite quail.* No one seems to be in any great rush to engage the dreaded Apache Indians.

In the evenings, communal dinners are held in the mess tent during which volunteers and staff mingle. In keeping with the general tone of the expedition thus far, these are not exactly spartan military camp meals, so much as well-catered social events. Besides what was trucked and flown here from Douglas, the cooks secure all manner of produce and other foodstuffs from the village, and with the bounty of fresh fish and game supplied by the sporting members of the party, we are eating quite well.

Even though there is a certain democratic spirit inherent in the fact that we all share the same mess tent, it's interesting to note how everyone divides up into their little cliques during meals. The wranglers tend to sit at tables together, as do the mule packers, as do the former military men, as do the wealthy young scions. For their part, Joseph and Albert Valor have pitched camp along the river at the edge of the village. They keep entirely to themselves and prepare their own meals.

Our own little dinner clique consists, with some variation, of Margaret, Big Wade, Spider King, Mr. Browning, and yours truly. Often Tolley sits with us. It occurs to me that we are perhaps less judgmental of his . . . *peculiarities.* Some of his wealthy young peers and some of the military men seem almost afraid to associate with him, as if he might be contagious. They make little effort to conceal their disdain, and some of them ridicule him openly.

I'll say this for Tolley: He may be a big sissy, but he has a certain strength of character; he is forthright and entirely unapologetic about his own nature. For the most part, he ignores the insults and snubs of the others, even sometimes encouraging them. One fellow who particularly enjoys needling him is the steel magnate's son, Winston Hughes. He's a stolid, dim-witted Yale boy, with close-set eyes and a smugly amused look on his face, as if his little mind is forever cooking up some fraternity prank or other. Last night in the dining room he was mimicking Tolley's effeminate mannerisms to the snickers of his tablemates, when Tolley walked up behind him, put his hand affectionately on his shoulder, leaned down, and said in a stage whisper, "Winty, you simply *must* stop being so swishy, or everyone will guess that we're lovers."

Hughes leaped up from his seat. "Jesus Christ, Phillips," he said, red-faced and flustered. "Keep your faggot hands off me or I'll beat the stuffing out of you!"

"See you later in my tent, big guy," Tolley said, pursing his lips in a kiss.

Tolley sat down at our table. "God, what a moron," he said. "It's shocking that he actually got into Yale. His father must have built them a new science laboratory."

"You know one of these days, sweetheart," Margaret said, "Winston really is going to beat the stuffing out of you."

"Margaret's right," I said. "Why do you provoke everyone so much, Tolley? You're just asking for it."

"What would you two have me do," Tolley asked, "pretend to be something I'm not? Swagger around like some kind of macho cowboy?" He leaned over toward Margaret and in deep voice said, *"Hey there, little lady, how 'bout a little tumble in the old hay?"*

Margaret giggled. "Okay, sure, Tolley," she said. "Anytime."

"Yeah, that's much better, Tolley," I said. "You just have to behave a little less like a . . ."

"Like a what, Giles?" Tolley asked. "A faggot? A fairy? A fruitcake?"

"Yeah, like that," I said. "Like a homo. That's what some of the kids in college called people like you. But I guess you're right, Tolley. You should just be yourself, and damn the consequences. In fact, as weird as I sometimes think you are, one of the qualities I admire about you is that you're exactly who you are."

"A *homo*?" Tolley said. "God, is that the best you can come up with, Giles? How deeply unoriginal." He turned toward Mr. Browning. "Mr. Browning, tell us, what do they call fellows like me in your country?"

Being very much of the old school, Mr. Browning does not approve of servants dining with their employers, so that when Tolley joins us he generally retires discreetly to a different table. But tonight, much to his chagrin, we had prevailed upon him to sit with us.

"I beg your pardon, sir?" he said now, as if he hadn't heard a word of our conversation.

"I appreciate your discretion, Mr. Browning," Tolley said, "but you're not deaf."

"In my profession, sir," Mr. Browning said with the faintest smile, "there is a very fine line between discretion and deafness."

"The question again, Mr. Browning," Tolley asked. "In your country, what do they call fellows like me?"

"Why, we call them young gentlemen, of course, sir," answered Mr. Browning.

"Ha! Damned tactful of you, man," Tolley said. "However, not a genuine answer to my question."

"Truly, sir, we have as many terms for your . . . predilection . . . as the Eskimos have for ice," said Mr. Browning. "But may I just say, sir, that I, personally, have never been one to categorize people in this fashion, to put them in a box, as it were. Indeed, that strikes me as a very American characteristic. We in Britain, and I believe in Europe in general, find such notions to be rather provincial. Even small-minded."

"Well said, Mr. Browning," Tolley said. "Couldn't agree with you more. Although you have still managed to avoid answering my question. Out with it now."

"Nancy boy, sir," said Mr. Browning. "That would certainly be the most common euphemism in my country."

"Ah, yes, nancy boy," said Tolley. "Excellent! And what else?"

"Poufter, sir. Or sometimes people will simply say 'poof.' As in, 'he's a bit of a *poof*,'" Mr. Browning said, flashing open his fingers like a small sunburst.

At this Margaret dissolved on the table in a fit of helpless laughter.

"Are you all right, miss?" Mr. Browning asked.

Margaret lifted her head from the crook of her arm. "I'm not laughing *at* you, Mr. Browning," she managed to say through her tears. "Really, it's just that your delivery is so charming." And then she fell apart again. "I'm not laughing at you, either, Tolley," she managed to say through her tears. "Honestly."

"I do hope that I have not offended you, sir," Mr. Browning said.

"Not in the least, Mr. Browning," Tolley said. "Indeed, it's one of the best descriptions I've ever heard of myself. 'That Tolley Phillips is a nice enough fellow, but he's a bit of a *poof*.'"

By now all of us had been infected by Margaret's laughter, and Tolley's outrageousness, including Tolley himself. Other tables were eyeing us curiously as we giggled and guffawed.

And so we amuse ourselves, not always so childishly, but it's true that there is something about the expedition so far that feels a bit like summer camp.

.   .   .

On a more serious note, I've tried as much as possible to stay away from Chief Gatlin these past days, to concentrate on just doing my job. But I have a sinking feeling from the looks he and Margaret exchange that she may secretly be seeing him. I hope this is not the case, and I cannot bear even to ask her about it. What darkness in her heart could possibly cause her to give herself to a man like Gatlin? I'm running out of space in this notebook. Tomorrow I'll start a new one.

LA NIÑA BRONCA

BILLY FLOWERS RODE DOWN THE DUSTY MAIN STREET INTO THE
nearest village, Bavispe, Sonora, trailing the Apache girl on a length of
dog chain. The girl's hands were bound with rope, the chain fastened
around her waist and a bandanna knotted across her mouth to keep her
from biting. Flowers had fixed a pair of mule hobbles between her ankles
so that she had to take short, quick steps in order to keep up. He had not
liked having to bind her like this, but she had tried repeatedly to escape
and it was the only way that he could manage to bring her into town.

The girl was dressed in one of Flowers's shirts that hung past her
knees, and she still wore her high moccasins, the insides of them all the
way down to her instep stained dark with dried menstrual blood, so that
she was not only terrified and exhausted, but humiliated.

Curious townsfolk came out of their *jacales* to watch the procession,
and they questioned Flowers about what kind of prisoner she was, and
when he answered, simply, "Apache," the dreaded name of their ancient
enemy ran through the crowd like a wind. *"Apache."* The crowd grew, and
the more brazen boys among them ran up to touch the girl, as if counting
coup, so that they could boast that they had touched a real Apache. They
laughed and mocked her. *"Hediendo a chica apache,"* the boys hissed, *"la hija
del diablo, la salvaja mugrienta."* The girl kept her eyes cast to the ground.
She understood enough Spanish to know what insults the boys were
speaking to her but she could not elude their grasping fingers, for it required all of her attention to keep up with the mule and to avoid falling
down. Half a dozen thin, mangy town dogs slunk behind her, raising their
noses to sniff her scent on the air. Now and then one of them made a
quick feint forward to snap at her heels, as a dog chases a car tire without
actually engaging it, then falling proudly back with his confederates.

Billy Flowers rode directly into the town square, ignoring the growing
crowd who followed behind. He dismounted and fastened the end of the
girl's chain to the hitching post, where she fell to her knees, exhausted.

Flowers spoke sharply in fluent Spanish to those who crowded around
her. *"No la desate,"* he warned the spectators. *"La pagano muerde como un*

perro." He rolled his sleeve back and held up his arm as proof; it was lacerated with teeth marks.

Flowers found the sheriff sitting behind his desk in the jailhouse, his feet up, his chair tilted back. He was a heavyset, indolent man with sleepy, hooded eyes; in fact, he may have been asleep. Flowers explained that he had caught an Apache girl up in the mountains and was now delivering her into the sheriff's custody because she was completely wild and he did not know what else to do with her.

The sheriff sat looking dumbly back at him, blinking somewhat vacantly, as if he didn't fully comprehend what had just been said to him. Finally, he took his feet off the desk and tilted heavily forward. "Is this Apache girl guilty of a crime?" he asked.

"None that I know of," Flowers said. "Other than the crime against God of living in heathen darkness."

"That is a sin, señor," said the sheriff, "not a crime. And I'm afraid that God has no jurisdiction in my jail. Perhaps you should consult the padre about taking the girl in at the church."

"What about the reward for Apaches?" Flowers asked.

"The reward is for Apache scalps," the sheriff said. "One hundred pesos for the scalp of a man, fifty pesos for that of a woman, and twenty-five pesos for a child's hair. Is the girl a child or a woman?"

"Somewhere about in between," Billy Flowers said. "What shall I do then, scalp her?"

The sheriff shrugged as if he didn't particularly care. "She is without monetary value alive," he said.

Before Flowers could respond, a great commotion arose outside, a thin, terrified screaming and much excited hollering among the people. The sheriff pushed back from his desk and he and Flowers went outside.

Despite Billy Flowers's warning, some kind townsperson had tried to give the girl a drink of water, and in so doing had untied her hands and removed the gag from her mouth, and now she lay atop one of the boys who had been tormenting her, her teeth clamped on his neck, shaking her head like a dog. The boy screamed and screamed, a high-pitched wailing that sounded something like the cry of a terrified rabbit in the jaws of a predator.

His friends and some of the women were trying to pull the girl off, but she held on to him so savagely that they could not be separated.

"*¿Qué piensa usted ahora, alguacil?*" Billy Flowers asked the sheriff over the commotion. "Would you consider now that you've apprehended the heathen in the act of committing a crime?" Flowers took hold of the girl's hair, wrapped it once around his fist, and with one quick yank snatched her off the boy, in the same decisive way that he sometimes broke up fights among his dogs. The boy, wild-eyed, clutched his bloody throat, still screaming and sobbing hysterically, crabbing backward away from the girl, which Flowers took to be a positive sign that his wounds were not fatal.

Now he held the girl by the hair at arm's length. She did not even attempt to struggle against him, knowing the futility of it all too well. "I have to say I'm getting mightily tired of you, missy," he said. "I'll be glad to be free of you." When he released his grip, she sank back to her knees.

"I'm leaving her right here, Sheriff," Billy Flowers said, mounting his mule. "I caught her, now you may do with her as you will. Let her go if you like. It's all the same to me. But I would caution you to watch out for her. As you have witnessed, like any other wild creature, she will kill when cornered." Flowers took one last look at the girl where she knelt in the dirt, her head downcast. He was not a sentimental man but he felt a certain grudging respect for her, just as he respected the lions and bears that he hunted. And he felt, just for a moment, as he occasionally did with these animals, a pang of something like pity for her. He turned the mule and spurred him into a quick trot back down the street the way he had come.

THE NOTEBOOKS OF NED GILES, 1932
NOTEBOOK III:

La Niña Bronca

HEATHEN SUN GOD RESTORES LIFE TO DYING GIRL

12 May, 1932

Bavispe, Sonora

How quickly the "summer camp" atmosphere has come to an end, and after the terrible events of this day, I'm embarrassed by the flippancy of my last entry. Where to begin . . .

I woke early this morning, as I have every day since our arrival here, to the sound of roosters crowing in the village. I decided that I would walk into town and make some photographs.

I dressed and loaded film in the Leica, and stepped over Jesus, who lay wrapped in a blanket on his sleeping pad by the tent opening.

He sat up. "I come with you, Señor Ned."

"No, it's early, go back to sleep, kid. I'm just going to take a little walk. I won't be long."

It was cool outside and smoke from the chimneys in the village had settled like a low fog over the valley floor, the hills above the river a pearly gray, not yet colored by sunlight, a sheen of dew coating the grass in the river bottom so that everything seemed sheathed in a pale icy silver.

Our camp is pitched on a broad grassy bench and is like a small village itself, with crisp white canvas tents of various sizes neatly laid out in separate neighborhoods for volunteers, staff, and commissary. Smoke curled from the morning cook fires in the mess tents, and the stock grazed on the lush meadow grasses, whorled by dew.

Bavispe is a typically poor Mexican village of dirt streets lined by mud adobe *jacales*. Chickens pecked in the yards, dogs barked, and people peered out at me through drawn curtains and shuttered windows. Although the residents are accustomed by now to seeing me around town with my camera, they remain guarded. A pretty girl swept a doorway on the edge of the plaza, but ducked shyly back inside when she spotted me.

Indian men dressed in serapes, the women in colorful dresses and

shawls, were setting up tables around the plaza, unloading baskets of produce from donkeys and mules. I realized that it was Saturday and they
were setting up the market. I exposed some film of the scene, and for the
most part, the merchants were friendly and cooperative, although one old
woman waved her cane threateningly when I pointed my camera at her.

An enormous, incongruously ornate adobe brick church dominates
the plaza. Built in the past century by Franciscan missionaries, or rather
by the Indian slave labor they employed, it seems to loom threateningly
over the little village. Inside, it was cool and dark, lit only by candles and
wall sconces. I could hear the priest saying morning mass from the altar,
but I could barely make him out in the dimness. I had not yet seen this
man who sent village girls off to a life of prostitution in the border towns
and I sat down in a pew in the rear of the church, waiting for my eyes to
adjust. But there was something hypnotic about the low, echoing incantations of the mass, the dim candlelight, and I think I must have dozed off
sitting there. The next thing I knew someone slipped into the pew beside
me. It was Jesus, breathing heavily.

"You must come with me, Señor Ned," he whispered urgently.

"What's going on, kid?"

"They caught an Apache. A real wild Apache."

I followed the boy out of the church. A crowd had formed on the
other side of the plaza and we pushed our way through it. There I witnessed a sight such as I have never before seen. An Indian girl, maybe thirteen or fourteen years old, was tethered by a rope to a hitching post in
front of the jailhouse. She sat on her haunches in the dirt, peering out at
the crowd through fiercely tangled hair. An overturned bucket lay beside
her, and several uneaten tamales that had been thrown to her, as to a dog.
The girl was filthy, streaked with dirt, sweat, and blood, dressed in a soiled
man's shirt and high moccasins. Even from a distance I could smell her.

"You see, Señor Ned?" Jesus said in a low voice of wonder. "A wild
Apache. A *real* wild Apache Indian. A gringo lion hunter caught her with
his dogs in the mountains."

"Why do they have her tied to the hitching post?" I asked.

"Because she is so dangerous," said the boy.

"She's just a girl, for Christ's sake."

"She bit one of the village boys," Jesus insisted. "She nearly killed him. You must take her photograph."

The boy's words snapped me out of my state of shock. "Yeah, you're right, kid."

It is both disturbing and at the same time comforting, the sense of detachment that overcomes me when I look through my camera lens. Suddenly I was all business and the girl became a subject now, fodder for the camera, a photographic problem to be solved rather than a suffering human being to be pitied. I shot her from several different angles and then I moved in closer. The crowd buzzed excitedly.

"Be careful, Señor Ned!" Jesus said. "Do not go too close. She is very dangerous."

The girl's eyes followed me from beneath the tangle of hair, and from her throat issued a low warning sound like a growl.

"It's all right," I said. "I'm not going to hurt you."

Now the crowd parted again and the sheriff, a heavyset man with a thick black mustache, approached. Behind him followed the town doctor, a small thin man in a closely tailored black suit. He carried a black medical bag.

"What are you doing here, young man?" the sheriff asked me.

"Taking photographs, sir," I answered. "I'm with the expedition."

"I must ask you to stand back," he said. "This girl is dangerous. She bites like a wild animal."

"Yes, sir, so I understand."

Someone fetched the padre from the church. He was a younger man than I had expected, plump in his black priest robe, and very dark-skinned. Squinting in the sudden bright light of the plaza, he joined the doctor and the sheriff to confer over the girl. They kept their distance. I exposed some film of the scene: three grown men, all in positions of authority, afraid of this one small Indian girl crouched in the dirt.

Finally the padre approached the girl, crossed himself, and held his palm up as if in benediction, praying as he did so, presumably summoning divine protection. But clearly his faith wavered, for the young priest's posture was tentative, and when he reached down and put his hand on the girl's head, she snarled and, quick as a dog snapping, latched her teeth onto the fleshy underside of his arm.

"*Aieeeeeeee,*" cried the padre, grabbing the girl by the hair and trying to pull his arm away. "*Aieeeeeeeee.*"

The crowd erupted in excitement, and someone actually laughed inappropriately at the young priest's nearly girlish distress. But no one went to his aid. For my part, I was glad that she was biting him and all I could think was, *Good, I guess you won't be taking this one off to the whorehouse in Agua Prieta.*

The sheriff rushed into the jailhouse and came out again carrying a blanket. The padre had finally managed to disengage himself from the girl's teeth and now he staggered back holding his arm, which was bleeding profusely. "*¡Ayúdeme!*" cried the padre. "*¡Alguien me ayuda! ¡Ella me mordió!*" The doctor stepped forward to minister to the priest's wounds as the sheriff called out for someone in the crowd. The crowd parted and a stocky fellow with short, massively thick arms, and wearing a blacksmith's apron, stepped forward. The sheriff handed the blanket to the man, who approached the girl, waving the blanket ahead of him like a graceless bullfighter. Meanwhile the sheriff circled to the side; clearly the plan was to throw the blanket over the girl as one does to subdue vicious dogs.

The crowd watched spellbound, occasionally calling out encouragement to the blacksmith. But they were soon disappointed, for when he threw the blanket over the girl, and both he and the sheriff pounced upon her, she was so exhausted and weak that she barely struggled; like a bird in a covered cage, she lay still. The two large men looked suddenly quite foolish lying atop her on the ground.

Now the blacksmith picked the girl up, still wrapped in the blanket, and carried her into the jailhouse, the sheriff closing the door behind them.

Jesus and I went back up to camp and loaded my 8×10, tripod, plate holders, and a set of lights on the burro. I sent the boy to find Margaret, and I woke up Wade Jackson. "You have to come into town with me, Big Wade. They caught an Apache girl."

As he did most mornings, Big Wade looked like hell. "It's your story, kid," he said. "You go ahead and cover it. I'm feeling a tad *punky* today." He smiled painfully. "In case you haven't noticed, I'm not really a morning person."

"It's nearly ten o'clock," I said, but Big Wade had already rolled over.

Jesus returned to say that Margaret had gone up in the airplane with Spider King. And so we went back down to the village alone and tied the burro to the hitching post to which the girl had been tethered. The plaza was even more crowded now, people arriving for the Saturday market, only to find that there was yet another attraction in town today. A line had formed in front of the *jugzado,* and an old woman waiting at the end of it told us that they had put *la niña bronca* in a cell and that for five pesos each the sheriff was allowing people to enter to view her. We went to the head of the line and asked the man guarding the door if we could speak to the sheriff.

"Tell him we're with the expedition," I said, "that I'm a reporter for the newspaper in Douglas."

The man retreated into the dark jailhouse and came back a moment later with the sheriff.

"What do you wish now, young man?" the sheriff asked me impatiently.

"I wish to photograph the Apache girl."

"You have already done so."

"I want to photograph her in the jail."

"For what reason?"

"Because it's a good story for my newspaper," I said. "'Wild Apache Girl Jailed in Bavispe.'"

"You wish to make us look cruel and barbaric," the sheriff said.

"I don't care about making you look one way or another. I just want to take the girl's photograph."

"She is in our jail only because we have nowhere else to put her," said the sheriff. "You saw for yourself how wild she is."

"Yes, I did."

"And your newspaper is willing to pay for the privilege of photographing her?"

"Of course."

The sheriff seemed to calculate for a moment. "One hundred pesos," he said, "and I will close the viewing down for one hour. In your newspaper article you will write my name. Sheriff Enrique Cardenas. You will say that the girl is being well treated, and that she has been examined by our doctor."

"Okay, I can do that. Just one other thing: I'll need a generator to run my lights."

It took two men to carry the generator into the cell area in the back of the *jugzado*. The sheriff led us there by the light of a kerosene lantern. The cell area had one high barred window through which a few desultory rays of sunlight fell, overwhelmed by the dimness and squalor of the cell, the heavy smell of human waste, the faint acrid undercurrent of disinfectant. The girl was the sole prisoner. They had removed the shirt she had been wearing and her moccasins, and covered her with a woolen blanket, but now she lay naked in a fetal position on the stone floor of the cell, the blanket bunched up beside her. Jesus stepped up to the bars, crossed himself, and whispered something under his breath.

"Shouldn't this girl be in a hospital?" I asked the sheriff. "Why is she curled up like that?"

"We are a poor village, young man," the sheriff said. "We do not have a hospital here. The girl refuses food and water. *El doctor* says there is nothing more that can be done for her."

"Couldn't you clean her up a little?" I asked. "Couldn't you put some clothes on her?"

"After the doctor examined her, we covered her with the blanket," said the sheriff. "She threw it off. Do you wish to make your photograph, or not?"

"I want to shoot inside the cell," I said.

"That is not possible," the sheriff said. "It is too dangerous."

"She doesn't look so dangerous anymore, does she?" I said. "In fact, she looks like she's unconscious."

"You have one hour, young man," the sheriff said, and he left us alone in the cell area.

I set up the camera on the tripod, rigged the lights, then cranked up the generator; it sputtered into life, making a terrible racket and belching black exhaust smoke. Even with the window and the door left open behind us, I knew I didn't have long to work before we would be overcome by the gas fumes. I hit the light switch, flooding the cell in a lurid white light.

I took a meter reading, stopped my lens down to f8, to give myself a little more depth of field, and carefully focused, bringing the lines of the girl from a soft, indistinct blur into sharp clarity.

Big Wade says that the camera never lies, only the person behind the camera, and that the photographer's sole responsibility is to let the truth be revealed. I had retreated into the safety of my viewfinder, the space that allows me a kind of perfect objectivity, where my sole concern is the composition of the image I am trying to make, and where all becomes a photographic problem, rather than a human one. I re-aimed the lights, moved my tripod slightly, and refocused. In my complete absorption, even the sound of the generator seemed to recede. I made several negatives, repositioned the camera and lights, and shot from a different angle. Finally satisfied that I had what I wanted, I stepped back and hit the cutoff switch on the generator. It ground to a halt, the lights fading slowly.

My job done, the truth recorded, it was only then, in the dim light, and the sudden absence of noise, that I was able to truly look at the girl. It was only then that the nausea began to rise from my stomach, and the sweat broke out on my forehead.

"*Good God,*" I muttered. And to Jesus, I said: "Go tell the sheriff I need to see him. Then go find a bucket of water, soap, a sponge, and a couple of towels." I pulled some peso notes out of my wallet and handed them to him. "And see if you can buy some kind of nightshirt. Something to cover her with . . . and a hairbrush."

The sheriff came back into the cell area. "Your time is nearly up, young man," he said.

I understood that the sheriff was not going to help the girl for any humanitarian reasons, but I thought that I might still be able to appeal to his economic instincts.

"My newspaper will not be able to run these photographs, after all, Sheriff," I said. "You see, the girl is naked, and my editor will say that they are too lurid for his readers. And you're right, they will only make you look cruel and barbaric. So I wish to pay you for another hour to photograph her again. But I need first to clean her up and cover her."

The sheriff considered this. "If I let you in the cell, you understand that you enter at your own risk?"

"Yes."

After Jesus returned, the sheriff unlocked the door to the cell and swung it open. He stepped back. I carried the bucket of water in and knelt down beside the girl. Jesus refused to enter the cell. "Do not touch her, Señor Ned," he begged me. "Please."

"Don't be ridiculous, Jesus," I said. "Can't you see that she's unconscious?" I spoke then to the girl, though I knew she wouldn't hear or understand me. "I'm just going to clean you up a little," I said. I turned her over onto her back. She did not resist, and though her eyes were open, she didn't appear to see me. I squeezed a little water from the sponge onto her lips, but she did not respond. I cannot describe her odor . . . beyond the filth, something else, a deeper scent.

I rubbed soap onto the sponge and washed the girl, periodically wringing the sponge out in the bucket and resoaping it. I washed her thoroughly from head to toe, washing caked dirt and what looked like dried menstrual blood from her legs and feet, washing between her legs and under her arms, washing her back and her breasts. I had never touched another person, least of all a girl, so intimately before in my life, but, oddly, despite my generally shy nature, I was not embarrassed. Rather I had the strange sense of ministering to a wounded animal rather than to a girl, and all the while I spoke softly to her, as one might speak to an animal, knowing that she could not understand.

The water became quickly dirty and I had Jesus empty it outside and bring me a fresh bucket. And then a third, with which I washed the girl's hair. I dried her with towels, wiped the floor, and pulled the muslin nightshirt over her. I combed her hair, carefully loosening the tangles until it lay straight and shiny; it was actually quite beautiful, black and coarse as a horse's mane.

I was still brushing the girl's hair when the light began to come back into her eyes, some kind of recognition of her surroundings, and as it did a strange, chilling noise rose from her throat, a kind of low moan that carried with it such a depth of despair and suffering that it raised gooseflesh on me. Behind me I heard Jesus whisper in terrified Spanish, and the sheriff spoke to warn me. Now suddenly the girl looked me fully in the eyes and her moan turned to a hiss, a kind of snarl, and she sprang away from me with remarkable strength, crabbing backward into the corner of the cell, where she squatted and peered out at me through her hair like a trapped animal. She began to speak then in her own language, a low, guttural ancient tongue that sounded like the mutterings of the earth.

"*La chica está loca,*" Jesus whispered.

"It's all right," I said to her. "I'm not going to hurt you."

"Do not touch her, Señor Ned," Jesus said. "Please. She will bite you. She is crazy."

"You must come out of the cell now," the sheriff said.

"I'm not going to hurt you," I repeated, ignoring them. I held the blanket out to the girl. "I just want to put this blanket around you so you don't catch cold. Here, see? Take it. It's all right."

The girl was still speaking in her low voice, a kind of incantation, and as I moved closer to her, she crouched lower. Suddenly she lunged snarling at me.

Jesus cried out in terror, but the girl's lunge was only a warning, and she sank back into her corner again, a low growl issuing from her throat.

"Jesus Christ, Jesus!" I said. "Will you please shut the fuck up? You scared me more than she did. What's the matter with you?"

"I am sorry, Señor Ned," he said. "I thought she was going to bite you."

"She's just a girl, Jesus," I said. "Look at her. She's just a scared kid."

"She is a wild Apache Indian," he insisted. *"Ella está loca."*

"I'm going to put this blanket around you now," I said to the girl. "Jesus, tell her that in Spanish. Maybe she'll understand."

Jesus stepped tentatively up to the bars.

"Tell her I just want to help her. That no one's going to hurt her."

"El gringo dice que él desea ayudarla," the boy said in an oddly formal tone of voice. *"No la va a danar."*

"You sound like a damn bill collector, Jesus," I said. "Can't you try to be a little friendlier?"

"El desea ser su amigo, y para ayudarla," said the boy. *"El no la va a danar."*

I couldn't tell if the girl understood him or not, but very slowly and deliberately I reached the blanket out to her again, and again the sound arose from her chest, a low warning growl. But this time she allowed me to drape the blanket over her shoulder.

"Keep talking, kid," I said. "I think maybe she understands you."

"The Apaches have always lived in our country," the sheriff said. "They steal our women and babies. In this way, many of them have learned our language."

As the boy spoke, I slid the blanket around her shoulder. "There, see? Nothing to be afraid of."

Now the girl huddled under the blanket in the corner of the cell, but her eyes seemed to be losing their focus again.

"Crank the generator up," I said to Jesus. And then I made another negative of the girl, the one I think the newspaper will run under my headline:

WILD APACHE GIRL CAPTURED!

BAVISPE SONORA, May 13—Conclusive proof of the existence of the bronco Apaches in Mexico's remote Sierra Madre was produced yesterday when a wild Apache girl was captured in the mountains near Bavispe, Sonora.

The Apache girl, age approximately 14 years, was taken prisoner by an American contract predator hunter named Billy Flowers. Flowers said that he was tracking a mountain lion when his hound dogs treed the girl. The American brought her into the town of Bavispe on Saturday morning. However, before she could be turned over to the custody of Sheriff Enrique Cardenas, she attacked and wounded a local boy, 12-year-old Jorge Ibarra. The Ibarra boy suffered severe bite wounds to his neck and shoulders. He is being treated for his injuries by the town physician, Dr. Hector Ramirez.

In a separate incident, the Apache girl bit the village priest, Father Raul Aguilar, whose wounds also required medical care.

Dr. Ramirez examined the Apache girl, whose name remains unknown, and found her to be suffering from dehydration and starvation. For her own protection and for the protection of town residents, she is presently being cared for in the Bavispe town jail. "She is very wild," said Sheriff Cardenas. "She is like a dangerous wild animal. However, we are doing everything possible to make her comfortable."

And now it is well past midnight. I have stayed up late to print several of my negatives, and to record this long, disturbing day. The prints are fine; one of the girl, in particular, is excellent. (Not the cleansed and blanketed version, either, the negative of which has already been flown to Douglas, along with the piece I wrote, which will both satisfy the readers of the *Daily Dispatch* as well as ingratiate me with the sheriff, who will be pleased to see his name so respectfully in print; I may need his goodwill again.) But here in this one perfect print is the naked truth only the camera is capable of telling. As I look at it, I see the girl as vividly as I did earlier in the flesh, perhaps, oddly, even more vividly, as if the depth and focus and definition provided by the camera lens and the lights are somehow more real, more specific than real life. *La niña bronca,* this slight starving creature curled in a fetal position on the stone floor of the Mexican jail cell, the shadows of the iron bars falling like a convict's striped uniform across her naked body. I cannot get the girl out of my mind; when I close my eyes the image of her continues to haunt me. I understand that this is how she will die, that my camera cannot save her, that all it can do is to record this awful truth.

The doctor gives her five days to live if she does not eat or drink. What good then is a photograph if it cannot save a girl's life? And what good then is the truth?

14 MAY, 1932

In the foothills of the Sierra Madre

It wasn't exactly a jailbreak, but we have "sprung" *la niña bronca,* as they say in Chicago gangster parlance, and I make this entry from our first night's camp at a spring in the foothills of the Sierra Madre.

Early the next morning after my session with the girl, I went to Margaret's tent to show her my prints. Her reaction to the images and to my story about the girl's imprisonment was equal parts horror and anger, some of which she took out on me.

"*Goddammit,* Ned," she said. "This is monstrous. This child needs help. Why didn't you tell me about her? Why didn't you take me with you?"

"I tried to, Mag," I said. "I sent Jesus for you, but you'd already gone up with Spider."

"So why didn't you come see me when I got back?" she asked. "Where were you during dinner?"

"I was busy writing my piece," I said, "and then I was up late printing."

"What do you think this is, Neddy," she said, flicking the print with the back of her fingers, "a fucking journalistic exercise? This is a human being. She needs help."

"Calm down, will you, Mag?" I said. "Do you think I don't know that? I saw her, remember? I did what I could."

"I want to see her myself," she said. "And I want to talk to the sheriff. We need to get this girl to a hospital."

"Before we go back there, let me make a suggestion," I offered. "Why don't we take Joseph Valor with us? He could communicate with the girl."

This seemed to calm Margaret a bit. "Yeah, okay, that's a good idea. At least Joseph can speak her language. I'm sorry to holler at you, Neddy, but *good God . . .*" She looked at the photograph again, tears welling up in her eyes. "How were you even able to *take* this picture?"

"It's my job, Mag," I said.

A low fog, not yet burned off by the sun, clung to the river as Margaret and I walked down to the Apaches' camp. Other than to lead Colonel Carrillo and his men on their daily forays into the mountains, Joseph and Albert had kept very much to themselves since the arrival of the expedition in Bavispe. Because of the Mexicans' instinctive fear and hatred of the Apaches, the scouts had been forbidden even from going into the village alone. I'd hardly seen them myself, and Margaret had probably spent more time with them than anyone else. She had been down to their camp several times to interview the old man about traditional Apache culture for her doctoral thesis, and this time when we arrived, Joseph greeted her warmly. I couldn't help but notice that even Albert's aversion to the White Eyes seemed to be somewhat pacified in Margaret's presence. It was obvious to me that like all the other men, they had both fallen in love with her.

"Being locked up in a jail is not a thing understood by the People," Joseph said when we showed him the photograph. "If the girl chooses to die, there is nothing that can be done for her."

"We can get her to a hospital," Margaret said. "We could fly her to Douglas."

"You say she is afraid now," said the old man. "Think how she would feel about flying in your airplane. Nor will your hospital save her life. She wishes only to go home."

"At least come down to the jail with us, Joseph," Margaret said. "Just to hear someone speaking her own language might give her hope."

"Hope of what?" asked Albert.

"Hope of living," Margaret answered.

It was Sunday and churchgoers were coming in from the outlying villages and ranches for mass. But word of the capture of *la niña bronca* had clearly already spread through the Bavispe River valley, and traffic on the main road to town was particularly heavy that morning; a steady stream of people, most on foot, others on horses, mules, and burros, some in buggies and wagons, *hacendados* and peons alike, entire families, as if on a pilgrimage. Margaret says that the Apaches have been the bogeymen of northern Sonoran culture for generations, that in the old days the villagers here believed Geronimo to be the devil, come to punish them for their sins. More recently he has been replaced in their legends by the bronco Apache known as Indio Juan. It was Indio Juan, the Mexicans say, who was responsible for the Huerta boy's kidnapping, and who continues to terrorize the region. And now that they had a real live Apache in their possession, everyone wished to see her.

The plaza was already crowded and an even longer line had formed again in front of the *jugzado*. Nervous glances were cast at Joseph and Albert as we walked by; the locals knew about the Apache scouts camped on the river outside town, and now there was finger-pointing and whispering and some of the older people crossed themselves.

"Look at that," I said, astonished that anyone could fear this elfin little old man. "They're afraid of you."

"In the old days we used to joke that Yusen put the Mexicans on earth for the convenience of the People," Joseph said. "To raise horses, mules, and cattle for us, to provide wives for our warriors and slaves for our wives. It is true that I killed many Mexicans when I was young." The old man turned his palms up. "They can still see the blood of their ancestors on my hands."

This time when we went to the door of the *jugzado*, the sheriff refused us entry. "You must wait in line like everyone else," he said curtly.

"I demand to see that girl right now," Margaret said.

"Mag, I don't really think that's the right approach here," I warned.

The sheriff looked hard at Margaret. "You Americans always think that you can come into Mexico and make demands," said the sheriff. "But I am not your servant, señorita. You are a guest in my country, in my village, and in my jail. You will wait your turn in line."

"Sheriff, let's say we offered you a larger contribution to the town jail fund," I said. "Could you possibly let us in now to see the girl?"

The sheriff smiled benevolently. "Ah, you are a very polite young man," he said, nodding. "For you I will make such a special arrangement."

"Thank you."

"However as you can see for yourself," the sheriff continued, "we have many people who have come here today to view *la niña bronca,* and some have come from very far away. Thus you will not be allowed to go inside the cell today. And you may only stay to view her for the same period of time allotted everyone else."

"Understood."

The deputy led us back to the cell area. He raised his lantern up to the bars to cast a faint yellow light on the girl. As when I had left her the day before, she lay still in the corner of the cell, curled again in a fetal position.

"Oh my God," Margaret whispered. "Talk to her Joseph. *Please."*

Joseph began speaking to the girl in his low, chanting voice, and as he did so, he squatted on his haunches and from the pouch he wore at his waist, he extracted a pinch of fine yellow powder, which he held through the bars and sprinkled over her.

"Es prohibido acercarse a la celda," the deputy said sharply.

"What is that?" I asked.

"Hoddentin," Albert answered. "The powder of the tule plant. It's a sacred substance to Apaches."

Now from his pouch the old man removed a small object that I could not make out, and he reached again through the bars and pressed it into the girl's closed fist.

"Sal de aquí, viejo," ordered the deputy, and he grabbed Joseph by the collar and yanked him roughly away from the cell.

Albert stepped up threateningly to the deputy. "Leave my grandfather alone," he said. "He's an old man."

"It's all right, Albert," I said, taking his arm. "We don't need any trouble."

"El tiempo ya paso," said the deputy. *"Ustedes deben salir ahora."*

"But we just got here," Margaret protested.

"Ustedes deben salir ahora," the man repeated, herding us back out.

"That girl is dying," Margaret said angrily, "and they're selling admission tickets to see her."

"Keep your mouth shut, Mag," I said. "You're not going to help her by pissing off the sheriff."

Outside again, the morning sun had burned off the last of the night fog over the river and seemed harshly unforgiving after the dank light of the *jugzado*. A strangely discordant atmosphere of festivity prevailed in the plaza. Vendors had set up stands and were doing a brisk business in food and refreshments. The church bells rang, announcing the second morning mass.

"Do you think she heard you, Joseph?" Margaret asked the old man.

"She will be dead in four days and four nights," said the old man. "There is nothing I can do for her."

"What was that you put into her hand?" I asked.

"Something to take with her to the Happy Place," he said.

"What's the Happy Place?" I asked.

"What you White Eyes call heaven," Joseph said.

That same afternoon, Mayor Cargill, with several of his committee members, was flown into Bavispe from Douglas in order to check on the progress of the expedition. The airplanes carrying this contingent brought with them copies of the Sunday *Daily Dispatch* with my photograph and piece about the girl on the front page. Evidently her capture had caused quite a sensation in town, and the mayor wished to see her for himself. By then, many members of the expedition had themselves been down to the village to see *la niña bronca*.

Hoping that she could convince Mayor Cargill to take the girl back to the hospital in Douglas when he returned the next morning, Margaret arranged a meeting in Colonel Carrillo's quarters before dinner. Big Wade and I came along to offer moral support; it was early enough in the evening that he wasn't too drunk yet. Chief Gatlin was also present.

As befits his own personal stylishness, Carrillo's spacious wall tent is elegantly appointed with Persian rugs on the floor, an ornately carved

Spanish colonial writing desk and leather campaign chairs. As the guard ushered us in and greetings were being made, the colonel kissed Margaret's hand, and Big Wade whispered to me: "This is why they fought the Mexican revolution, kid. A lot of good it did, huh?"

"I've always considered it bad luck to have a woman along on a military campaign," Carrillo was saying to Margaret. "Especially a beautiful woman. But for you, Miss Hawkins, I make an exception."

"I would be flattered, Colonel," said Margaret, "had I not noticed that the exception had also been extended to half a dozen prostitutes."

The colonel swept this notion away with a precise little backhanded motion of his arm. "Who are certainly not attached to the Mexican army, I can assure you," he said, deftly deflecting the subject. "May I offer you an aperitif, señorita?"

"We didn't really come here to socialize, Colonel," Margaret said. "We came to ask Mayor Cargill to take the Apache girl back to Douglas. She needs to be in a hospital."

The mayor raised his hands in a politic gesture of helplessness, pursed his lips into his ingratiating little smile. "Miss Hawkins," he said. "Surely you must understand that I have no jurisdiction here. The girl is a matter for the local authorities. And she has become such a valuable tourist attraction, I think it highly unlikely that they would let her go. Even if they did, there are numerous legal impediments to taking her across the border. For one thing she has no documents."

Margaret nodded. "Yes, so I thought you would answer, Mayor," she said. "Therefore I have an alternate proposal. Colonel Carrillo, you do have the authority to have the girl released into your custody, don't you?"

Carrillo answered carefully. "Possibly, yes," he said. "But why would I wish to do so, señorita?"

"Because you could use her to trade for the Huerta boy," Margaret said. "Of course, if you let her die, she'll be useless to you."

"I am listening, señorita," said the colonel.

"I propose that you let the Apache scouts take the girl back up into the Sierra Madre," Margaret said. "The expedition would follow at a reasonable distance behind. When contact with her people is made, a trade could be effected, the girl for the Huerta boy."

"We've all seen the girl, Margaret," Gatlin said. "She hardly appears to be in any condition to travel."

"If she's left in that jail cell, she's going to die anyway," Margaret answered. "But if we get her out of there right now, and back up into her own country, maybe she still has a chance."

"The girl's survival is hardly our concern," Gatlin said.

It was all I could do to be in the same room with Chief Gatlin, and I bit my tongue. Even Margaret looked at him now with genuine loathing in her eyes. "If you can use her to get the Huerta boy back, what do you have to lose, Leslie?"

Big Wade spoke up then. "Margaret, hasn't it occurred to you that maybe the Douglas area Chamber of Commerce doesn't really care about rescuing the Huerta boy? That maybe they're just taking a bunch of rich guys hunting and fishing in Mexico?"

"What would you know about that, rummy?" Gatlin said. "You haven't covered a chamber meeting sober in five years."

"Who could bear to, Chief?" said Big Wade. "And you know, the thing about being a rummy is that you can wake up one morning and decide not to be one anymore. You, on the other hand, you're pretty much stuck with being an asshole every day for the rest of your life."

"That is enough, gentlemen," Colonel Carrillo commanded. "Let me assure you, Mr. Jackson, that President Ortiz did not attach his troops to this venture in order to serve the interests of your Chamber of Commerce. Recovering the Huerta boy is of the utmost importance to the Mexican government."

"That's where your interests are mutual," Margaret said. "Think about it, Mayor, if you actually did rescue the Huerta boy, you'd put Douglas on the map. Every newspaper in the country would cover the story."

"How do we know we can trust the scouts?" said Gatlin. "They're Indians, after all. What's to prevent them from letting the girl go? Or joining the bronco Apaches themselves?"

"Simple," Margaret said. "You send someone with them to report back to the expedition. Ned and I can go along. I'm sure the newspaper would love to cover it."

"And how do we know you wouldn't let her go?" Gatlin asked.

"Because we want to get the boy back as much as you do, Leslie," Margaret said. "Probably more."

This was the first I'd heard of Margaret's plan myself, but she'd clearly given it some thought. And it made sense—a way to save the girl and recover the Huerta boy.

"Well, of course, it goes without saying," said Mayor Cargill, never one to miss a political opportunity, "that the matter is entirely up to the discretion of Colonel Carrillo. However, I myself can't think of a single objection."

Carrillo stood erect with his hands behind his back. Now he inclined his head in a slight bow to Margaret. "I will speak to the sheriff tonight myself," he said, "and arrange for the girl's release. By all accounts she does not have long to live. If this plan has any hope of succeeding, you must be prepared to depart first thing in the morning."

"Good God, Margaret!" Tolley said, over dinner that evening in the mess tent. "Have you completely lost your mind? It's one thing to use the girl as bait, but why do *you* have to go?"

"Because I want to, Tolley," Margaret answered. "It's the professional opportunity of a lifetime. If we actually make contact with the bronco Apaches, it will be the anthropological scoop of the century."

"Right, sweetheart," Tolley said. "You can measure their skulls before they roast you over the fire."

"I'm afraid you're confusing my scientific discipline, Tolbert," Margaret said. "I'm a cultural anthropologist. I study cultures and languages, not skulls."

Tolley waved this distinction away with a flutter of his hand. "You're both absolutely hopeless," he said. "The big question is: Who are they sending along to babysit the two of you?"

"Me!" said the boy Jesus, who had snuck up behind me. "I come with you, Señor Ned. I carry your camera."

"No way, boy," Big Wade said. "You're staying right here with me. I need you more than he does."

"I'm traveling light, Jesus," I said. "I'm just going to take the Leica. I'm not even packing a tripod. Besides, you're terrified of *los Apaches*, remember? You're even afraid of that girl."

"I am not afraid," said the boy with bravado.

"Why don't you come with us, Tolley?" Margaret said. "You're a paying volunteer. You could come if you wanted. All you have to do is tell Gatlin. He'd probably be happy to be rid of you."

"Oh, *please*, darling," Tolley said. "If you think I'm giving up the creature comforts of this delightfully cushy expedition in order to sleep on the ground and dine on jerky and wild roots with a bunch of savages, you've really lost your mind. Plus"—Tolley looked around confidentially—"just between us, in case you've wondered where I've been spending my evenings of late, I'm seeing a lovely Mexican soldier boy. Very much frowned on by army regulation; he'd be executed by firing squad if our liaison were discovered. Which only makes it all the more exciting."

"You're a sick guy, Tolley," I said.

I was so keyed up that I barely slept all night and rose before first light. I walked over to Margaret's tent and woke her, and together we walked silently down to the stock corral.

The cold night air had settled into the river valley, so cold that the horses and mules blew plumes of steam from their nostrils. A few of them nickered softly at our arrival. It's a lucky thing we weren't horse thieves, because the wrangler on night watch, a skinny young fellow named Jimmy, had fallen asleep with his chair tilted back against the rails of the corral, his rifle lying across his lap, and even the stirring of the stock didn't disturb him. Afraid that when we woke him he would fall off his chair and accidentally discharge his rifle, I put one hand on the barrel of the rifle itself while Margaret took hold of Jimmy's shoulder very gently. He woke up as calmly as can be, just his eyes opening, not moving a muscle.

"Jimmy, it's Margaret Hawkins," she said. "We came to get our mules."

Jimmy tilted forward in his chair. "I must have fell asleep," he said. "Don't tell no one on me, all right, Miss Hawkins?"

I collected my jack mule, Buster, and Margaret her gray jenny, whose name is Matilda, and Jimmy helped us saddle them. To each he fixed two pairs of saddlebags for our personal effects, one in front and one behind the saddle. A third mule to serve as our pack animal was outfitted with panniers, which were half loaded with tents, food, cooking utensils, etc.

"The *injuns* already come and got their animals," Jimmy said.

"When?"

"'Bout an hour ago. I got a rifle scabbard here for you, too, Ned."

"I won't be needing that, Jimmy. The only thing I know how to shoot is my camera."

"By golly, you *are* a city boy, ain't you, Ned?" Jimmy said with wonder in his voice. "You can't go into Apache country without a firearm. The chief has a rifle for you along with the rest of your gear down at the jail-house."

Margaret and I split up again, leading our mules back to our respective tents to load our personal effects. We arranged to meet on the road at the edge of town in thirty minutes. At the tent I packed my saddlebags, trying not to disturb Big Wade, who, as usual, was snoring like a freight train. Just as I was about to leave, he snorted awake and sat up on one elbow. He looked at me vacantly for a moment with red, mescal-sodden eyes. He cleared his throat, a long, ugly process, and rubbed his hand across his face.

"So you're really going through with this, huh, kid?" Big Wade said at last. "Jesus, I hope you know what you're doing." He shook his head. "And the scary thing is, I know that you don't have a fucking clue."

"I'll be okay, Big Wade."

"Yeah, that's what you kids always think, isn't it?" he said. "Because youth has an underdeveloped sense of mortality. It's why the old fucks always send young men off to fight their wars for them."

"I wouldn't exactly say we're going off to war."

"Oh, you wouldn't, would you, kid?" Big Wade said. "I guess you're right . . . you're more like sacrificial lambs than you are warriors. I can hardly believe Carrillo is letting you go. But I suppose to him the lives of a couple of naive gringo kids is worth the risk if you can help him locate the Apaches."

"You got any last-minute professional advice for me before I leave, Big Wade?"

Jackson considered this for a moment. "Yeah, as a matter of fact, I do, kid," he said. "And I want you to pay close attention."

"Okay."

"Your camera is not a shield."

"What does that mean?" I asked.

"It's not a lucky charm. Or a weapon."

"I don't get it."

"It means your camera does not protect you from harm," said Big Wade. "It *just* takes pictures. Photographers can get themselves in a whole world of trouble because they seem to believe that in the face of danger, they can hide behind their camera and somehow it makes them bulletproof, or invisible. It doesn't. Trust me on that one, Ned."

"Okay. Listen, I'd better be going." I held my hand out. "Good-bye, Big Wade. I'll see you soon."

"So long, kid, good luck to you," he said. "Hey, before you go, hand me that cigar butt and the bottle of mescal at the foot of the bed, will you? Time to restart this old heart for another day."

I led Buster and the pack mule down to the scouts' camp. It was daylight now, but the sun had not yet crested the bluffs above the river. Joseph and Albert sat cross-legged by the fire drinking coffee. Knowing better than to try to hurry them, I sat down myself and Albert filled a tin cup for me from the pot. "Coffee is the best invention of the White Eyes," he said.

They already had their mules saddled, and a burro loaded with packs. Behind the burro they'd rigged up a travois to carry the girl—a stretcher-like affair that consisted of a piece of canvas lashed to pine poles.

We met Margaret as planned, and all rode into town together. Word had gotten out about our mission and a small group of townspeople had already gathered in the plaza. Chief Gatlin, Colonel Carrillo, and Mayor Cargill were waiting for us in front of the jail. With them was Billy Flowers, the old lion hunter who had caught the girl. He is a tall, gaunt, white-bearded man with fanatical blue eyes, who looks like he has wandered right out of the Old Testament.

"Mr. Flowers will be trailing your party into the Sierra Madre," Chief Gatlin explained after all the introductions had been made. "He will provide our contact with you. He knows the country and will report back to the expedition."

"Does the old savage speak English?" Flowers asked, nodding toward Joseph, who had stayed back with the animals.

"His name is Joseph Valor," Albert said. "He is my grandfather. He was a prisoner of war of the American government for seventeen years. Which was sufficient time to learn your language. Even for an ignorant savage."

"And is your grandfather now a Christian?" Flowers asked.

"He was baptized into the Dutch Reform Church at Fort Sill, Oklahoma, in 1903," said Albert.

"That's fine," Flowers said, nodding.

"But only because he enjoyed the church social activities," Albert added. "He accepted your God so that he could play Saturday-night bingo."

Flowers looked hard at Albert. "And what about you, son?" he asked.

"I was educated by your reverends at Carlisle Indian School in Pennsylvania," said Albert. "They took us away from our families, cut our hair, and dressed us in white-man clothing. They beat us if we were caught speaking our own language, and they taught us about your God." Albert smiled. "Why I'm almost as white as you, old man."

"And did the reverends teach you to accept the Lord Jesus as your only true savior?"

"What is this, Mr. Flowers?" interjected Margaret. "Are we all going to be interrogated about our religious affiliations? Or just the Apaches?"

"I like to know who I can trust, young lady," Billy Flowers said.

Gatlin had sent a truck down from camp, loaded with the rest of our gear and food supplies, and two men now transferred this into the panniers on our pack animal. They slid rifles into scabbards on my, Albert's, and Joseph's mules.

A few minutes later the sheriff came out of the jailhouse, carrying the girl, still curled in a fetal position and wrapped in a blanket. He was followed by the town doctor.

They laid her on the travois, securing her there with leather thongs. Joseph knelt beside her and began to speak in a low, chanting voice. He opened his medicine pouch, took a pinch of powder from it, and sprinkled it over her.

"Does this man have any medical experience?" asked *el doctor* in perfectly enunciated English.

"Yes," Albert answered, "he's an Apache medicine man. Fully accredited by the tribal medical board."

The doctor didn't appear to have much of a sense of humor. "Aboriginal quackery is not medicine," he said severely, "and will not cure this girl."

"Yes, well, it doesn't look like your medicine has helped her much, either, does it?" said Albert.

Just then the sun crested the river bluffs, flooding the plaza with clear morning light, and in that precise moment, as the sun illuminated her face, *la niña bronca* opened her eyes. It was surely nothing more than a coincidence, perhaps simply a result of her having been moved outside, the sunlight striking her face after the darkness of the jail cell. But at the time it seemed to all present that Joseph's magic powder and his strange guttural incantations had not only resurrected the girl, but had brought the sun itself forth. There arose an appreciative murmuring from those in the plaza who had witnessed this miracle. *El doctor* scowled disagreeably at their effrontery, as if in a kind of professional snit.

Albert laughed and raised a fist in the air. "Aboriginal quackery strikes again!" he said. "There's your newspaper headline, White Eyes," he said to me. "'Heathen Sun God Restores Life to Dying Girl.'"

"I like it, Albert," I said.

The girl looked around her, panic beginning to flood her eyes. She stretched out of her fetal position, straining against the leather thongs. But Joseph took her by the shoulders and spoke firmly to her and held her until she relaxed and closed her eyes again.

It was clear that in her weakened condition, the girl could not survive a long journey. And so it was decided that we would take her east into the foothills, just far enough from town to find a suitable place to camp. There we would rest a few days, trying to nurse her back to health. Billy Flowers would follow us, keeping far enough behind that his presence would not be obtrusive.

"If the girl is still alive, and sufficiently recovered to travel," said Colonel Carrillo, "we will send you on ahead with her to attempt to make contact with the bronco Apaches. If she does not survive, you will rejoin the expedition."

"She will be dead within three days," the doctor pronounced solemnly. "She is already severely dehydrated."

"You almost sound like you want her to die, Doctor," Margaret said. "So that you're not upstaged by an Apache medicine man."

"Just remember," Billy Flowers said, "in the off chance that she recovers, the first thing she's going to do is run off."

"Maybe not," Margaret said. "Maybe she'll find that she's among friends."

"Either way, Miss Hawkins," Flowers said. "I caught her once, I can catch her again."

Margaret laughed. "And you, Mr. Flowers," she said, "sound like you almost want her to run off. So that you can chase her again. It's amazing the power this one poor child exercises over grown men."

We were just preparing to ride out when a commotion arose on the far end of the plaza, a clattering of shod hooves on brick and a high, familiar voice crying *"Hiiiiii-yooooo."* Everyone looked up to see Tolbert Phillips Jr., mounted on one of his prize polo ponies, gallop grandly into the plaza. He reined up, his horse stopping on a dime and whinnying as if on cue; Tolley took his pith helmet off and waved it in the air. Behind him, trotting clumsily on his mule, and leading another pack mule, outfitted with panniers stuffed to capacity, came Harold Browning. Now Tolley spurred his mount on again, galloping toward us.

Margaret started laughing. "God, isn't he a terrific horse's ass?" she said.

Tolley reined his horse up short in front of us, kicking up a cloud of dust. "Good morning, gentlemen," Tolley said. "Ladies. As you can see, I've decided to cast my lot with the advance guard. Terribly sorry to be late. Had a bit of trouble getting out of bed this morning. Damned chilly, wasn't it? And I was up half the night trying to decide how to pack for our little mountain idyll."

"Traveling light, are you, Tolley?" I said.

"Just because we're entering the heart of darkness," he said, "doesn't mean we have to be barbarians ourselves."

"Mr. Phillips," said the mayor, "I don't see how the expedition can possibly spare you, sir. Nor could we guarantee your safety were you to leave us. Your father would have our hide if anything happened to you."

"Nonsense," Tolley said. "My father would love nothing more than for me to be captured by the Apaches. Tortured? Staked to an anthill? I can just hear him now: 'That'll make a man out of you, Tolbert.' And don't worry, Mayor, even if I vanish without a trace in the Sierra Madre, you'll still get your thirty dollars a day. My father is good for it."

The mayor laughed nervously. "Well, of course he is, son. Never any doubt in my mind about that."

By now poor Harold Browning had reached us, huffing and puffing and bouncing painfully in the saddle.

"How nice to have you join us, Mr. Browning," Margaret said.

"The pleasure is entirely mine, miss," he said gamely.

"Gentlemen," Tolley said. "Just so that we have our chain of command straight, may I assume that as the sole *paying* member of your volunteer army in the present company, I shall be in charge of this mission?"

"Why, yes, Mr. Phillips," said the mayor, looking for confirmation from Gatlin and Carrillo. "I would assume so. Chief? Colonel?"

Gatlin chuckled deeply. "Well, let's see," he said, looking us over, "we've got a woman, a city boy, pair a' *injuns*, a dying savage girl, and an English butler. Hell, if the pervert wants to be in charge of this little troop, I have no objections. You, Colonel?"

The colonel smiled sardonically. "Captain Phillips," he said with a brisk salute, "I appoint you commanding officer of this company."

"Splendid!" Tolley said. "Let's be under way, then, shall we? We have an important mission to accomplish. And by the way, Chief Gatlin, speaking of perversion, I've gotten to know a few of the girls in your pimp stable, and I think that the mayor and the good citizens of Douglas will be interested in learning what their chief of police has been up to . . . south of the border . . . if you understand my meaning. Wouldn't do the expedition a bit of good, if that were to get out in the newspapers. It's a conversation we must all have upon our return."

Gatlin's face darkened and he did not respond.

"Company, move out!" Tolley called. "Look sharp, there, men! Woman!"

"Oh brother, Tolley," I muttered. "We're happy to have you along, but you're dreaming if you think anyone's going to take orders from you."

"You heard the colonel, Giles," Tolley said. "That will be Captain Phillips to you from now on. And don't make me cite you for insubordination before we're even under way."

And so we started off down the street, the scouts Albert and Joseph leading the way, the travois with the girl bouncing lightly behind their pack mule. Behind them, Margaret and I rode on either side of Tolley, with Mr. Browning leading his pack mule bringing up the rear. Some of the crowd began to follow us, but quietly this time, even the boys and the town dogs keeping a respectful distance. It was as if the girl had become a kind of town mascot, and they were sorry to see her leave. They dropped off one by one as we reached the edge of the village.

We were just about to cross the wooden bridge over the river, when I heard, *"Señor, Señor Ned, wait, wait for me!"* and turned to see Jesus riding toward us on a burro. The burro trotted along at a brisk, rough gait, the boy kicking his flanks and swatting the animal on the rump with a leafy branch. *"Wait for me, Señor Ned, I come with you."*

"What are you doing here, kid?" I asked when he caught up to us. "Didn't I tell you to stay with Big Wade?"

"I come with you," he said.

"Where did you get the donkey?"

"I borrow him from the corral."

"You mean you stole him."

"I borrow," he insisted. "I give him back when we return."

"You're not coming with us, Jesus," I said.

"Yes, I come with you," he said.

"I mean it, kid, I want you to go back."

"You cannot make me," the boy said. "I come with you."

"Get lost."

The boy dropped back and continued to follow us at some distance behind. I turned in the saddle and waved him away crossly, but he only looked back at me obstinately.

We crossed the bridge and followed the dirt road until it dwindled down to a trail, which rose winding into the hills, and as it gained elevation, dwindled to an even fainter game trail. As we quit the lush river bottom, the landscape changed quickly. We rode through scrub oak and mesquite thickets, across rocky hillsides studded with yucca and agave plants, the improbably green valley of the Bavispe snaking away below us. In the faint middle distance ahead, the massive, steep-tilted broken masses of rock and serrated hogbacks of the Sierra Madre proper rose up above.

Where the trail became too rough for the travois, we stopped and Albert Smith and I dismounted, unrigged the poles from the mule, and put them over our shoulders to bear the Apache girl aloft like an Egyptian queen; she seemed nearly weightless.

We didn't travel far, coming up over a ridgetop and down into a small valley formed by a tributary of the big river, where we stopped to make camp on the edge of a grassy meadow. The meadow is watered by a spring trickling out of the rocks at one end, and forming a series of pools spilling one into the next. At our approach, a flock of great blue herons flushed off the pools, a half dozen of the gangly, leggy birds, their wingbeats heavy, their strange warbling cries.

"The girl must have water," said Joseph. "The Mexican doctor is right. She will die if she does not drink." He gathered the girl up in his arms and carried her to the largest of the pools, squatted down, and laid her on her back in the water. Her eyes were open but she did not appear to see. Joseph held her there, speaking to her softly, and then he simply released her in the water. For a moment she floated there on her back as if weightless. And then she began to sink beneath the surface.

"What in the world are you doing?" Margaret said, moving toward the girl. "She's going to drown."

Albert took hold of her elbow. "No, leave her," he said softly.

I, too, began to reach out for the girl, but Joseph took hold of my arm with a surprisingly strong grip. He shook his head. I had the strange sensation of being in a dream, all of us watching, paralyzed, as the girl's black hair fanned out in the water, her eyes dead as a corpse staring up at us as she sank downward into the darkness of the pool. Air bubbles escaped from her parted lips, and at just that moment you could see consciousness flooding back into her eyes. Then she was clawing at the surface of the pool with her hands. She lunged up out of the water, gasping for breath and choking, and scrambled to the side of the pool, where she held on to the rocks and began to cough violently. When she had quieted at last, she turned and peered out at us and at the surrounding country as if seeing the world for the first time, as if reborn in the water. Joseph spoke to her in a low voice and you could see that she was listening to his words.

"What's he saying?" Margaret asked Albert.

"He says that he is from the *ch'uk'aende* band," Albert said, "that his mother was a sister of the great chief Cochise. He says that he once lived in this country himself. That he is taking her home."

"She's listening," Margaret said. "She understands him. I can see it in her eyes."

"Yes, of course, she understands," said Albert. "She is *In'deh,* as we call ourselves. One of the 'People.'"

Now the girl scooped a handful of water into her mouth, and then another. She coughed again but less violently.

"That's a hell of a way to get someone to take a drink," I said.

"She was leaving this world," said Joseph. "I had to bring her back through the water."

The girl spoke then, softly but firmly, and for some reason the sound of her voice sent a chill up my spine. Joseph and Albert laughed.

"What did she say?" Margaret asked.

"She said," Albert translated: "'Grandfather, if you are *ch'uk'aende,* why do you ride with White Eyes?'"

Joseph answered her and the girl nodded as if satisfied.

"And what did you tell her?" Margaret asked.

"I told her that you are my slaves," he said.

We pitched camp, put up our tents, and collected firewood for dinner. Joseph and Albert constructed a small wickiup for the girl, made of bent branches covered with canvas. As we worked, the girl fell asleep and woke and fell asleep again. Whenever she was awake Joseph spoke to her, talking on and on in a steady hypnotic current of language like a river, so that all of us listened spellbound, carried away down it, though, of course, we couldn't understand a word he said. As he spoke to her, the girl watched him intently, nodding and smiling faintly from time to time, drifting off to sleep again to the soothing sound of his voice.

As we were cooking dinner and dusk was settling over the land, the boy Jesus crept into camp, leading his little burro, which he turned out in the meadow with our own animals. He did not say a word and would not look me in the eye, but simply took a seat by the fire, watching *la niña bronca* warily. When it was time to eat, I handed him a plate of food, which he took with a grateful smile. It was too late to send him back now.

Joseph made the girl drink a little broth made from meat and wild herbs, and then she crawled on her hands and knees into the wickiup. He spread his own bedroll near the opening in case she woke during the night.

The rest of us sat up by the fire for a while, drinking coffee and smoking. Tolley brought out a bottle of French brandy that he had brought among his many provisions, which also included an entire case of wine. "I'm all for camping out," he said, "but I learned on safari in Africa that you don't have to give up all the creature comforts."

"Yeah, especially when you have your own butler," I observed.

Tolley passed the bottle around.

"Not for me," Albert said, when it reached him. "I gave it up five years ago." He smiled wryly. "Like many of my people, I'm not a good drinker."

Mr. Browning, who was still bustling around the camp, tidying up, also declined the bottle.

"Are you a teetotaler as well, Mr. Browning?" Margaret asked.

"Not at all, miss," he said. "I enjoy a nightcap myself from time to time. But never while on duty."

"Let the poor man off for the evening, *Captain* Phillips," Margaret said. "He's been working like a dog all day."

"By all means, Mr. Browning," Tolley said. "You're officially off the clock. Sit down with us. And let me pour you a brandy."

"Very kind of you, sir, thank you," Mr. Browning said. "I've already turned your bed down for the night, and if I can be of no further assistance to you, perhaps I will have a wee splash."

"You know, Tolley," said Margaret, "it's possible that you're the only person in history to go into the Sierra Madre of Mexico with French cognac and an English butler."

"I wouldn't be so sure of that, darling," Tolley said. "There's always Maximilian."

Mr. Browning settled himself by the fire. Now that I've gotten to know him a bit better, I've decided that he's not such a snob, after all. He just has an acutely developed sense of discretion. He's really a fine fellow, perhaps in his midforties, always neat and impeccably attired, even in the field. Slender, with an erect bearing and an elegant way of moving, he's as quick and efficient as a magician. As inscrutable as he often seems, I notice from time to time a certain sadness around his eyes that suggests another life about which the rest of us know nothing.

"If you will forgive me for suggesting so, sir," said Mr. Browning, "I don't believe that the Emperor Maximilian ever made it this far north. And in any case, I suspect that his valet would have been either Austrian or French, rather than British."

"Ah, see how impertinent the butler becomes," said Tolley with mock offense, "when one relaxes the social barriers?" He handed Mr. Browning a cup and raised his own. "To your health, Mr. Browning. You're a wise fellow, indeed. In addition to being an excellent valet."

"Thank you very much, sir," Mr. Browning said, with a slight incline of his head. "I endeavor to give satisfaction."

"Tell us, Mr. Browning," asked Margaret, "how you came to be in this country? You're a long way from home."

"Indeed, I am, miss," he said. "You see I came to Douglas several years ago in the service of a gentleman by the name of Lord Crowley. His Lordship was one of the Phelps-Dodge Mining Corporation's principal British investors."

"And what became of your lord, Mr. Browning?" she asked.

"I'm afraid that when the copper mine closed down last year, miss," Mr. Browning replied, "Lord Crowley lost a substantial amount of money. He was forced to dismiss me and returned alone to England."

"You didn't want to go home yourself?" Margaret asked.

"Oh, yes, miss, I most certainly did," he said. "But I'm afraid that I did not have sufficient funds to make the passage."

"Wait a minute," I said. "You mean, His Lordship brought you over here with him, and then abandoned you in Douglas, Arizona? Left you behind because he was too damn cheap to pay your fare home?"

"In all fairness to Lord Crowley," said Mr. Browning, "he suffered a considerable financial setback with the closing of the mine. He was very much in the soup with his accountants. I'm told that he lost over a million pounds sterling. It's only natural that he should feel the need to economize."

"And you don't think the bastard hired another butler as soon as he got back to England?" I asked.

Mr. Browning considered this question for a moment. "It is not unlikely, sir," he said, entirely without rancor.

"Isn't that typical of how the rich economize when they're feeling broke, Mr. Browning?" I said. "Stiff the help?"

"Is that a rhetorical question, sir?"

"No, it's a real question."

"In that case," Mr. Browning said with his poker face. "I would prefer to express no opinion, sir,"

"Bully for you, Mr. Browning!" Tolley said: "Exceedingly discreet. I value that quality highly in a valet. Let's not allow the Communist agitators among us to undermine the time-honored servant-gentleman relationship. Why bite the hand that feeds you?"

"Precisely, sir," Mr. Browning said.

"God, I didn't know you were such a snob, Tolley," Margaret said.

"It's not a question of snobbery," Tolley said. "Mr. Browning and I simply understand the necessity of maintaining a certain . . . shall we say . . . *etiquette,* between a valet and the gentleman whom he serves. Is that not so, Mr. Browning?"

"Very much so, sir."

Tolley beamed with self-satisfaction. "Splendid!"

"I'd just like to say, Mr. Browning," said Margaret, "that around this campfire, everyone is equal. You don't have to call anyone 'sir' or anyone 'miss,' unless of course, you want to. You don't have to wait to be asked a question in order to speak. And you're allowed to express any opinion you wish on any subject whatsoever. Understood?"

"Perfectly," said Mr. Browning. "Thank you very much, miss. In that case, I'd be fascinated to know how you became interested in the study of anthropology. I was somewhat of an amateur ethnographer myself while in Africa with Lord Crowley."

"I guess it runs in the family," Margaret answered. "My father was an anthropologist. He specialized in South American Indian tribes, particularly the Yanomami, who live in Brazil along the Orinoco River near the border of Venezuela. My mother died when I was a young child and so Father had to take me with him into the field. I spent much of my childhood down there. Inevitably, I developed an interest in native peoples myself."

"That's fascinating, miss," said Mr. Browning.

And so the evening was passed, sitting around the fire, smoking, drinking coffee and brandy, laughing and telling our respective stories. We have gained considerable elevation today, the night air even cooler than it was in Bavispe, and we kept the fire stoked high. Above the tall flames a trillion stars sprayed like sparks across the black night sky. Despite the vast differences in our backgrounds and circumstances, in age, sex, race, and nationality, we seem closer now that we have *la niña bronca* in our charge. When we witnessed earlier her rebirth in water, a kind of baptismal ceremony, it was as if we became her adoptive family. I try to imagine the wild, ancient life she leads with her people in the hidden depths of these forbidding mountains to which we are returning her. And in so doing I am overcome with the uneasy sense that this holiday idyll, this "pretend" expedition that we have been on so far, is drawing to an end.

I make this final entry of the day from my bed in the canvas wall tent I share with Tolley and Mr. Browning, or I should say that they share with me. Speaking of creature comforts, the place is fit for Emperor Maximilian himself, with canvas cots and fine linens, a collapsible table, leather folding chairs and kerosene lanterns, by the light of which I make these notes. The others are asleep already, snoring lightly. All is quiet. Except that the girl must be having a nightmare, because from her wickiup comes a kind of eerie ululation, a chilling, heartbreaking lamentation, an ancient song in an ancient tongue. It's been a long, exhausting day, and I must sleep.

LA NIÑA BRONCA

DAALK'IDA 'AGUUDZAA. IT HAPPENED LONG AGO. SHE DREAMS THAT her aunt Tze-gu-juni is washing her for her puberty ceremony, and as she does so she sings the puberty songs to the girl, in a low, soft voice. *White-Painted-Woman, mother of all Apaches. Five thousand years and two hundred generations ago, you are already among us as both man and woman, child and elder, hunter and suckler of babies, dressed in the heavy skins of mastodons, as we make our way in a blizzard across the frozen Siberian plains.*

Her aunt washes her feet, her calves and thighs, gently between her legs, washing away the blood that has begun to flow. The girl tries hard to push the bad thoughts away, to concentrate on the songs, to do everything correctly so that she will not bring misfortune down upon the People. But she is worried. Her sister's husband, Indio Juan, has announced that after the end of the traditional four-day recovery period following the cere-mony, he will take her as his second wife. It is true that there are few men left in the band suitable to be her husband; the Mexicans have been killing them off one by one, so that almost all who remain are boys and a few old men. But she does not wish to marry Juan; he is crazy and beats her sister, and all are afraid of his madness. But her mother says that the People need babies, and as the last of the girls coming into menarche, she is White-Painted-Woman now, the future of the People depends upon her and she will have to overcome her objections to Indio Juan. She tries hard not to think about these things. The water is cold but her aunt's hands are gentle and sure, and after she finishes washing her body, she dries her and then she washes her hair with yucca root, and combs it out and dresses her in her beautifully beaded puberty dress, and combs her hair again, and the girl, so grateful for these kind and loving attentions, looks up into her aunt's eyes. But it is no longer her aunt who combs her hair and the girl does not know where she is, or who this is into whose eyes she looks. She isn't even sure who she is; she is no longer White-Painted-Woman, her en-tire world has vanished, and all those she knows in it are gone as well, and all who inhabit this new world are strangers and enemies. She is caged in a cold dark place and she is alone. She has only her own ancient self now to protect her, the hard kernel of her wildness, a memory of freedom. *Duu ghat' iida. Do not touch me, White Eyes, stay away, keep back, ba'naag'uuya, I will bite you, I will kill you, I will die defending myself, you may not touch me, I will kill you, I will kill you, I wish to die now, do not touch me, I warn you, keep back, I will bite you, I will kill you.*

"The gringo asks me to tell you that he is not going to hurt you. He just wants to put the blanket around you. *El quiere ayudarlo. El no lo dolerá. ¿Me entiende usted?*" *He wants to help you. He will not hurt you. Do you understand me?*

"*I will die before I allow anyone to touch me. Ishxash. I will bite you, I will kill you, do not touch me, I wish to die.*"

Now the White Eyes puts the blanket around her and she huddles under it, peering out at him. Who are these people? There is a Mexican boy speaking to her and another man, and when the hot white sun strikes her inside this cold dark hole in the ground, blinding her, she knows that she has indeed fallen through the old world and into another, and she wonders if she is already dead.

She curls up again on the cold floor and lies perfectly still, closing up into herself, and she dreams this life of the People from beginning to end. *Daalk'ida 'aguudzaa. Three thousand years ago the People crossed the frozen Bering Sea to Alaska, and you are again among them as both man and woman, child and elder, hunter and suckler of babies. White-Painted-Woman, mother of all Apaches.*

She dreams of sunlight flooding her face, and of an old man speaking to her in her own tongue. She opens her eyes and looks up into his ancient, furrowed face, and she thinks that this must be Yusen himself, that she has gone at last to the Happy Place. But then she looks around her and she sees all the Mexicans and the White Eyes staring at her and she knows this is not the Happy Place at all, and she begins to cry out, to struggle, and the old man takes her by the shoulders and speaks softly to her. "*Duu hajit'iida. Lie still, child, and I will take you home.*"

After they stole Geraldo Huerta, Indio Juan led the band back to one of their old *rancherías*. They rode on stolen mules and burros and others walked, through nearly impassable mountain passes into secret *cañóns* watered by unnamed rivers, where no Mexican dared follow. It was the same country to which those who had refused to surrender to the American army had fled fifty years ago, and had lived ever since. There was still game in the valleys, which were well protected by the mountains, and they were able to grow some crops. Whatever else they had needed, including women and children to supplement their dwindling bloodlines, they had stolen in stealthy, middle-of-night raiding forays upon the Mexican mountain villages and the isolated ranches, so that none could even say for certain that it had been the bronco Apaches who had preyed upon them.

More recently, the ranchers had been expanding their range, their cattle and vaqueros penetrating the People's country. The vaqueros were hard, cruel men, and well armed, and ever since Indio Juan had begun his bold daytime predations, they killed on sight every Apache they happened upon in the high country, man, woman, or child, beheading or scalping them in order to collect their bounty. And so the People's numbers were being steadily reduced, the survivors driven farther south, ever deeper into the mountains.

The Huerta boy cried throughout the first day's travel, and most of the next day, and Indio Juan finally told the women that if they had not quieted him by nightfall, he would kill the child. He knew that Fernando Huerta had surely formed a posse by now and that the boy's cries would give them away. So the women and girls of the band cooed and cuddled and fussed over the boy, as if he were the most important person on earth; they rode with him on their warm laps, holding him in their pungent brown arms; they gave him precious chunks of sugar to suck and they spoke to him in Spanish as well as Apache.

Little Geraldo was grateful for their attentions and their kindnesses and soon they even encouraged from him an exhausted smile and by the evening of the second day he had stopped crying, and he did not cry again. Within a week he was speaking Apache and within a month he remembered his old family mostly in dreams from which he awoke disturbed, disoriented, in that strange shadow limbo between his new life and the old.

She dreams that the People are traveling and she is an infant riding in a cradleboard strapped to her mother's back. It is springtime and the motion of her mother's walking stride bounces and jostles her gently and she sleeps peacefully, waking from time to time to look up at the trees and the clouds moving across the sky, to hear the birds singing. And she sleeps again.

They come to a stop for the day, and her mother lifts her out of the cradleboard to bathe her, dips her into the warm water and holds her there, floating on the surface, secure in her mother's sure gentle hands. She dreams that she is back in her mother's womb, surrounded by water, floating, warm and safe. *Daalk'ida 'aguudzaa. It happened long ago. And you are again among us as both man and woman, child and elder, hunter and suckler of babies as we make our way up the Yukon to Canada following the caribou herds into the upper Mackenzie drainage, from there over the millennia down the eastern edge of the Rockies and out onto the Great Plains, where we follow the great herds of bison.*

Over the centuries, we drift south, to take up residence in the southern plains, where another tribe of fierce enemies, the Comanches, themselves driven out by the even more numerous Sioux, come down upon us from the north, pushing us west into the mountains and deserts that are to become our new homeland. And you among us as both man and woman, suckler of babies and slayer of enemies. White-Painted-Woman, mother of all Apaches.

She opens her eyes and looks up to see the old man peering down at her; it must be Yusen, the life-giver, and she is being born again onto the earth, how many times now in this endless cycle of birth and death? And although she does not wish to give up the comfort and safety of her mother's womb, suddenly she has no air, her lungs ache to breathe, she struggles clawing for the light, thrusting violently from the water, fully awake now and trying to draw breath, gagging and choking.

She knows this place where she is now, recognizes this spring; many times the People have stopped here to water. And suddenly she is overcome with a terrible thirst. She drinks water from her cupped hand but it makes her cough again.

"Do not drink too much water, too quickly, child," says the old man, "for it will make you sick."

"Who are you, Grandfather?" she asks.

"My name is Goso," says the old man. "I am *ch'uk'aende*. My mother was a sister of the great chief Cochise. I once lived in this country myself. I am taking you home to the People. I am taking myself home to the People."

"If you are really *ch'uk'aende*, Grandfather," she answers, "why do you ride with White Eyes?"

"My *tsuye* and I," the old man says, "have taken these White Eyes captive. They are our slaves."

She leaves the water and dries herself in the sun as the old man and the others set up camp. She sleeps and wakes and sleeps again, and all the while the old man talks to her. He tells her of his own people, and of those with whom he rode; he speaks names and places she recognizes from the old stories. She understands that the old man is a *di-yin*, that he has Power, that somehow he has rescued her from the Mexicans. And that he is taking her home. She drinks a little broth, but she is so tired and she must sleep again. She crawls into the wickiup they have built for her, warm and snug on the sleeping place they made of soft pine boughs covered in blankets. She sleeps, and as she sleeps she dreams this life of the People from beginning to end. *Daalk'ida 'aguudzaa. It happened long ago.*

Now the Spaniards come up from the south, thousands of them in their suits of armor, they slaughter and enslave the People, sending them to dig holes in the center of the earth, or to Mexico City to work as servants in their homes. And she among them, howling in the darkness.

Those who survive have hardened into a nation of raiders and warriors; they attack the missions and presidios, mercilessly slaughtering the soldiers and the Black Robes, stealing their stock, making captives of the women and children; in this way they drive the Spanish, finally, from their land. And thus for a time the People rule the country others called Apachería. And she among them as both man and woman, child and elder, suckler of babies and slayer of enemies. White-Painted-Woman, mother of all Apaches.

And she is again among them after the Spanish became the Mexicans, the People's hatred of them undiminished. As both man and woman, child and elder, warrior and bearer of children, she rides with the raiders as they plunder villages in Chihuahua and Sonora, stealing stock and murdering the townspeople, taking prisoners of the women and children. Then the scalp hunters come to claim their bounties—one hundred pesos for the scalp of an Apache warrior, fifty pesos for that of a woman, twenty-five pesos for the hair of a child, and many of the People, and she among them, go to the Happy Place without their hair.

Some of the scalp hunters are a strange new race of man with pale skin and white eyes, and soon from all directions more come into their country, trappers and miners, soldiers and ranchers, and there is more war and more butchery. She rides with the various bands of the chiefs known as Chuchilla Negro, Juan José, Mangas Coloradas, Cochise, following a long trail of blood and death, of killing, dying, running. The People murder and are murdered in kind, pushed deeper into the twisted canyons of the Chiricahua, the Mogollon, the Dragoon, the Huechos, the Sierra Madre, raiding on both sides of the border, stealing stock and killing the hated Mexicans, killing, too, the hated White Eyes and taking their children to make of them Apaches. Nana, Chato, Loco, Geronimo, Victorio, Juh, with their bands she rides as both man and woman, warrior and mother; she runs from their pursuers through the night, a cradleboard strapped to her back.

But so many of the People are exhausted now from the endless wars, the constant flight, and they surrender, finally, to the White Eyes and are taken to live on the reservations. Others are sent by train to the iron house in Florida, hated place with the air hot and thick as wet wool, and many die there of disease, heartbreak and madness, die in the sweltering dark of their stone cells. And she among them, howling in the blackness.

Now there is nothing more that can be done to her or that she can do to her enemies, no more tortures or murders or suffering that she has not already endured, has not already inflicted in the brutality of centuries she has dreamed. She is curled up in warm blankets atop soft pine boughs in a wickiup in the foothills of the Blue Mountains, and she sleeps, dreaming this life of the People from beginning to end. White-Painted-Woman, mother of all Apaches.

THE NOTEBOOKS OF NED GILES, 1932
NOTEBOOK IV:

Into the Sierra Madre

19 May, 1932

From our camp in the foothills of the Sierra Madre

For all the dire premonitions of my last entry, the past days have been nothing if not an idyll, the easiest, laziest, most carefree time we have yet spent. A small river courses down the valley just below our campsite. The water is perfectly clear, running over a freestone base, with deep pools and riffles and full of fat trout. Tolley has given me the loan of one of his bamboo fly rods and I go out early every morning, or in the evening just before sunset, to fish for an hour or two. It's nothing in that time to catch a couple dozen trout. I save a few for breakfast, rolled in flour and fried in bacon grease, or for dinner variously prepared by whoever is cooking that night. Strangely, the Apaches will not eat fish as they consider it to be unclean. Although they remain very closemouthed about revealing anything to us "White Eyes" concerning their religious or cultural practices, with some delicate prodding from our resident anthropologist, the old man finally admitted that they consider fish to be the spirits of wicked women.

During our first night here, we heard a pitiful wailing issuing from the girl's wickiup, a sound of such pure, primeval grief that it raised gooseflesh on me as I lay in my bunk. In the morning she emerged from the wickiup with her hair hacked off at the shoulders. When we asked Joseph about it, he would only say that she had borrowed his knife for the job, and that it was the Apache custom for women and children to cut their hair upon the death of a close family member.

"Who died?" Margaret asked.

"We do not ask such questions," Joseph said. "It is not a good thing to speak of the dead."

"Now that she's back among the living," Tolley asked, "do we have to worry about her running off?"

"She won't run off," Joseph said. "She has no place to go yet. And she has heard Billy Flowers's dogs barking."

In the few days that we have been here, the girl is making an astonishing recovery. At the beginning, she spent most of her time in the wickiup or squatting by the fire, silently watching us. Now, day by day, she seems to be coming back to life, as if she takes her sustenance from the country itself, from the mountains and fresh air and sunlight as much as she does from food and water. She is a pretty girl, even with her crude haircut. Slender, lithe and fine-boned, with small, perfectly formed hands and feet, she has an an extraordinary way of moving that is difficult to explain in physical terms, a kind of grace that seems almost otherworldly. Margaret obtained some clothes in Bavispe for the girl to wear—a skirt and blouse of brightly colored Mexican fabric—and Joseph has made her a pair of traditional Apache moccasins, and a breechclout to wear for riding. Already it's hard to remember the filthy, naked, hissing creature crouched in the corner of the dank jail cell.

She is still shy with us . . . by *us* I mean especially the white people . . . unable even to look us in the eye, though I have the oddest sense that she recognizes me, for she seems even shyer in my presence, and I catch her watching me furtively from time to time. I think she remembers that I washed her in the jail cell and is ashamed of such an intimate act being performed by a stranger, a man and a White Eyes at that.

She seems fascinated, too, by Margaret and yesterday before dinner actually approached her, reaching out to touch her blond hair with a kind of timid wonder. Margaret stayed perfectly still, the way you might do to avoid frightening a wild animal, and then very slowly she reached out herself and touched the girl's cheek. "There," she said. "Now that wasn't so bad, was it?" And she smiled at her and the girl smiled back.

"What is this young lady's name, Joseph?" Margaret asked.

"She does not have a name," he answered.

"What do you mean by that?"

"It is the old way to change the name of women and children upon the death of a close family member," he said. "To protect them from the deceased's ghost. Thus the girl has given up her name and will not speak it."

"What do you call her, then?" Margaret asked.

"It is not necessary to call her anything," Joseph said. "In the old way, Apaches do not greet each other by name, for it is impolite to call a person's name to his face."

"And so is it impolite of me to call you by name?" Margaret asked the old man.

"I am a civilized man," he said with a smile, "baptized in your church."

"She has to have a name," Margaret said.

"Right now she is *la niña bronca*," Joseph said. "That is sufficient. Later on something may occur that will cause people to call her another way, and then she will be given a new name that will fit her."

"You let us know when that happens."

We have been making short exploratory rides every day in the vicinity of our camp. Joseph serves as our guide. He knows all this country and has already shown us some extraordinary sights: the pueblos of the ones he refers to as *ilk'idande,* the "ancient people," with the remains of small stone dwellings thousands of years old; there are pottery fragments scattered all over the ground and dozens of *metates,* the large stones, cupped in the center, that were used to grind corn. Many of the hillsides are elaborately terraced with rock walls, so that they resemble giant natural amphitheaters. Margaret herself has studied these earlier civilizations in her university classes and tells us that the walls are called *trincheras* and were constructed by the ancient people for agricultural purposes.

La niña bronca rides one of the pack burros on these outings and by the third day had already regained sufficient strength to put on a performance worthy of a professional trick rider. Suddenly she swung off the burro, trotted alongside it, swung back on, twirled around on the animal's back, dismounted on the other side, moved to the burro's rear and catapulted herself onto its rump, stood up and walked to its shoulder, spun around and walked back, moving with her strange and indescribable grace. All the while she laughed with pure joy and abandon, the first time we've heard laughter from her, a lovely trilling sound.

"Apaches are the finest horsemen in the world," said Joseph, who watched her performance as proudly as a grandparent. "In the old way of living, children learn to ride before they can walk. But now the young people on the reservation are losing these skills."

The girl has started talking more frequently to Joseph, and to a lesser extent to Albert. It's frustrating for the rest of us not to be able to understand their conversations and Joseph and Albert are taciturn about revealing much of what is said. And so we're all trying to learn Apache, although the language seems nearly impenetrable to our ears and tongues. Only Margaret, because she has already studied the southern Athapascan languages, seems to be making some progress. The girl also clearly understands Spanish because whenever Jesus speaks in his own language, she appears to be listening to him, although she has not yet spoken it herself. Joseph, too, speaks Spanish and says that all the Sierra Madre Apaches have learned the language due to the fact they have had contact with the Mexicans, and before them the Spanish for at least a couple of centuries. "In the old days, many of us took Mexican women as captives," he said. "I myself once had a Mexican captive. Her name was La Luna. She became just like an Apache."

We tease Jesus mercilessly because he is still terrified of the girl; he watches her warily and always keeps a certain distance from her. He is so afraid she will slit his throat in the night that he has set out booby traps around his sleeping place to alert him to her approach, a kind of necklace of tin cans which he has strung together in a circle around his bedroll and tied to his neck so that the noise they make if she violates his inner sanctum will wake him. As it is, we hear the cans rattling every time the boy shifts position, and so it is mostly our sleep being disturbed.

Other than that, thanks largely to the provisions Tolley brought with him, we've been eating and drinking rather well, although Tolley informs us that his wine supply is already running low and he's thinking of sending the boy back to Bavispe to collect his last case.

We take turns cooking, although some are more skilled in that department than others. After a day of exploring and a dip in the springs, "cocktail hour" and dinner are festive times. We had all begun to notice of late that Albert, so generally outspoken, has become tongue-tied and shy when he's ever around Margaret, and she herself seems uncharacteristically quiet and self-conscious in his presence. A couple of nights ago Tolley embarrassed them both by suddenly announcing: "Okay, I saw that, you two are making *goo-goo* eyes at each other, aren't you?"

"Shut up, Tolley," Margaret said.

"I thought you said that you didn't believe in having love affairs in the field, darling," Tolley asked.

"We're not having a love affair," Margaret said.

"It won't do you any good to deny it," Tolley said. "We've all noticed. And I've heard you sneaking around in the night. You're among friends, darling, why not just get it out in the open and move into the big *injun's* tepee?"

"I said, shut up, Tolley," Margaret said. "You're just jealous because you can't have him."

"That's true," Tolley admitted. "I've always wanted to have a fling with a *real* savage. And I mean that in the nicest possible way, Albert."

"I must tell you, Tolley," Margaret said, "one thing I've learned in my studies is that the Apache culture, unlike that of many other Native American tribes, is not in the least bit tolerant of sexual deviations."

"That is true," Albert said, nodding. "In the old days homosexuals were considered to be witches and were usually put to death."

"Well, then you see, our cultures aren't so terribly different, after all," said Tolley. "So if your people are so intolerant of sexual deviations, does that mean you confine yourselves to the missionary position?"

"No, Tolley," said Albert, smiling. "As a matter of fact, in our worldview the missionary position is a deviation."

21 MAY, 1932

From our camp in the foothills

Billy Flowers came calling today, strode into our camp like the day of reckoning itself. At the sight of him, the girl cried out, terrified, and looked as if she was going to run away, but Joseph took hold of her and led her into the wickiup.

We offered Flowers a cup of coffee. He sat down, fixing us with his bright blue eyes that seem to bore holes into whomever he is looking at. He told us that he had been watching us, and that now that the girl had recovered, our time here was nearly up. The expedition was scheduled to leave Bavispe in three days, and we must prepare to move deeper into the mountains.

"We shall need to resupply before we depart, Mr. Flowers," Tolley said. "The cupboard is nearly bare."

"Run out of French wine already, have you, Mr. Phillips?"

"You should have made yourself known," Tolley said, "rather than spying on us. We'd have invited you to share a glass."

"The elixir of the devil, sir," said Flowers. "'Look not upon the wine when it is red,'" he quoted, "'when it giveth his colour in the cup . . . At the last it biteth like a serpent and stingeth like an adder.'"

"Oh, nonsense, Mr. Flowers," Tolley said with one of his little dismissive flutters of his fingers. "Those biblical people you're always quoting were swilling wine at every opportunity. When they ran out during the wedding feast of Galilee in Cana, didn't Jesus Himself help out by turning water into wine? 'Wine is as good as life to a man, if it be drunk moderately,'" he quoted, amazing us all. "'What life is then to a man that is without wine? For it was made to make men glad.' Ecclesiasticus."

Flowers, too, seemed suitably impressed at Tolley's knowledge of Scripture.

"One of my father's most notably unsuccessful schemes to save me," Tolley explained. "As a boy he insisted I become an honor acolyte in our church. I went to confession every week.

"'Forgive me, Father, for I have sinned,' I would confess to kindly old Father McClellan, a dear family friend.

"'And what sins have you committed, my son?'

"'I have had impure thoughts, Father.'

"'And did you touch yourself while you had these thoughts, my son?'

"'Yes, Father.'

"'Are you touching yourself now, my son?'

"'Would you like me to, Father?'"

Billy Flowers's face registered a look of growing astonishment and disgust at Tolley's absurd performance. Margaret and I made the mistake of looking at each other in that moment, and, like children, we both dissolved into a fit of involuntary laughter, until tears ran from our eyes and snot spewed from our nostrils.

"Blasphemers!" Billy Flowers hissed in a low voice. *"Satan's spawn."* Which only made us laugh more convulsively.

"Well, it's hardly my fault that so many of the clergy are pederasts, Mr. Flowers," said Tolley. "Indeed, I was only a child, an innocent victim of the old buggerer."

Without another word, Billy Flowers rose and left our camp the way he had come. Later that day we heard the haunting tones of his horn in the distance and we knew that he must have taken his dogs out for a hunt.

23 MAY, 1932

From our camp in the foothills

And so just when we thought we had seen the last of Billy Flowers for a while, he was back in our camp again today, but in a considerably less comic appearance this time. It has become chillingly clear to us that not only is he an eccentric and a religious fanatic, but quite possibly insane.

He carried an enormous bullwhip coiled in his hand, a braided leather instrument as thick at the handle as a man's wrist. He told us that we must leave here tomorrow, and then he made a strange request. He invited us back to his camp in order "to attend the trial of the dog named Tom."

"Ah, a sporting-dog trial," said Tolley. "A demonstration of tracking skills, perhaps? Splendid, Mr. Flowers! And a fine gesture of reconciliation on your part. Why, we'd love to come."

"No, Mr. Phillips," said Billy Flowers. "Not a sporting trial. A jury trial."

Intrigued, Tolley, Albert, Margaret, and I followed Billy Flowers back to his camp while Joseph, Jesus, and Mr. Browning stayed with the girl. As we went, Flowers explained that the other day after being in our camp, and in order to "cleanse himself of our filth," as he put it, he had taken his dogs out for a hunt. He "cut country" for a full day and all through that night, looking for a "varmint trail," when he came upon the sign of a young black bear. It was fresh sign and Flowers and his dogs tracked that bear for nearly six hours. They were just closing in on him when the lead dog, the dog named Tom, up and quit the trail. "Just like that he lost his heart and stopped hunting," Flowers said sadly. "It is the law of the pack to conduct a trial to determine the appropriate punishment for such an offense."

At our approach, Flowers's hound dogs began barking and straining at their chains, but at one word from their master—"*Silence!*"—they all stopped instantly, flattening themselves against the ground, their bony ribs heaving.

The accused, the dog called Tom, was tied to a twisted oak tree off by himself. He stood with his head hanging, his tail tucked tightly between his legs as if his guilt had already been established.

Flowers directed us to sit, and then he went over and stood before the dog. He cleared his throat. "Ladies and gentlemen of the jury . . ." he began. His dogs watched him attentively as if they had attended such proceedings before. "We have before us a hunter who yesterday failed miserably in the performance of his duties, who gave up on a trail, betrayer to his species, to his other fellows in the hunt, a coward and a slacker. I believe that this crime of sabotaging the work of good dogs—of you his fellows in the hunt—demands the death penalty and I ask you to see justice in this sentence."

"The death penalty?" Margaret said. "What in the world are you talking about?"

"Silence!" Flowers commanded.

Now he turned to the condemned dog and spoke to him in an oddly gentle tone, with no trace of anger in his voice. "I trained you myself, Tom," he said, "brought you up from a little pup, taught you the path of godliness and hard work. You are like a son to me." He lowered his head, genuinely saddened. "Oh, you have disappointed me mightily, Tom." Now Billy Flowers uncoiled his whip, and with a flick of his wrist laid its length out, over twenty feet; it landed in a perfectly straight line on the ground ahead of him with a little *whuumfp* sound and a slight raising of dust. "'Whatsoever a man soweth,'" he said softly, "'that shall he also reap.'"

"*Whooooaaaaa,*" whispered Tolley under his breath. "This is very *strange.*"

"Wait just a minute." Margaret spoke up. "Who said he was guilty? I thought this was a jury trial. Aren't we supposed to vote now?"

Billy Flowers turned and stared at her, as if Margaret had breached some cardinal rule of courtroom protocol. "The verdict has been reached, young lady," he said. "A jury of his peers has convicted the accused and voted unanimously for the death penalty."

"But we didn't vote," Margaret said.

"Because you are not members of the jury," Billy Flowers said. "You were invited here as witnesses. And if you cannot be silent during the carrying out of sentencing, I shall have to ask that you remove yourself from the courtroom."

"Quiet, Margaret," Tolley whispered. "Can't you see that the man is insane?"

Flowers turned back to the dog, raised his whip, and with another smooth levering of wrist and elbow, a nearly supernatural strength, he had it in the air; like false-casting a fly line, it shot backward, unfurling with a sinuous, hypnotic grace. Then he brought it forward and cracked the popper at its tip an inch above the dog's head, a report like a clap of thunder, like the voice of God himself, that caused the dog to whimper pathetically and drop to his haunches, his eyes averted, as though, if he were not watching, this would not happen. "'WHATSOEVER A MAN SOWETH,'" Billy Flowers repeated now in a louder, evangelical voice, "'THAT SHALL HE ALSO REAP.'" The whip was still aloft, shooting backward again, hissing as it cut the dry air, accelerating, and Margaret muttered, "*Oh, goddammit,* the crazy bastard," and she turned her head away, unable to watch. But the rest of us sat as if paralyzed, unable to avert our eyes as the next forward cast came down upon the dog, wrapped neatly around his throat, slicing like wire through hide, muscle, and vein so that the poor beast had only time for a mercifully short squeal of pain as he was lifted off the ground and jerked violently backward, his windpipe and jugular severed with a spray of bright red blood and a hiss of escaping air; he collapsed in a heap, twitching and convulsing in his death throes.

Without a word, Margaret left Flowers's camp ahead of us, and when we caught up to her, she turned on us angrily. "You big, brave men," she said. "Not one of you so much as opened your mouth to intervene in that *horror.*"

"It wasn't our business, Mag," I said lamely.

"Yeah, plus he scares the shit out of me," Tolley said. "Did you see what he could do with that damn whip?"

"My grandfather says that Billy Flowers is a *di-yin,*" said Albert. "That he has big Power. That all creatures fear him."

We sent Jesus down to Bavispe this afternoon to pick up some supplies before we head for the higher country. We expect him back in the morning and plan to depart as soon as he arrives. We will all be happy to be under way again.

31 MAY, 1932

A week of hard travel in increasingly rough country, climbing, climbing, climbing. The steep mountainsides are gashed with deep arroyos, and precipitous gorges. The horses, mules, and burros clatter and scramble over the rocks, slipping and sliding, the trail so narrow in places that we frequently have to dismount and walk them through the passes. Yesterday we had an accident involving Tolley's pack mule, which was more heavily loaded than the others. The panniers bounced against a boulder in one of these tight spots, and the mule lost his balance, the weight of the load tipping him over off the trail like a top-heavy cabinet. Down he rolled, over and over down the hill with increasing speed, cargo spilling from the packs as he went; the mule must have fallen two hundred feet before his descent was checked finally by a large tree. We thought surely that the animal could not survive such a fall, at least would have broken a leg and need to be destroyed. But after he came to a halt at the base of the tree, the mule struggled back to his feet, and other than scrapes and abrasions to his hide, he was not seriously injured. Of course, Tolley was mostly worried about his precious wine supply, but miraculously only one bottle was broken. Still, it cost us most of the day to recover the spilled goods, and to get the mule back up on the trail and repacked.

From thickets of scrub oak and scattered pines we have finally gained the true pine forest of the Sierra, a region so quiet and pristine that we have the sense of being the first human beings ever to set foot in it. We fall silent ourselves in its midst, as if conversation in a place of such primeval solitude would be like talking in church. Deer fade into the timber like ghosts at our approach and I think we each secretly wonder if they might be Apaches.

Everything seems exotic and oversize in this country. Many of the trees are over a hundred feet tall and pale gray squirrels the size of cats chatter at us from the branches above. A strange giant woodpecker, nearly two feet long, drums on the tree trunks, creating an eerie echo through the forest that joins up with others of its kind to form a kind of somber percussion orchestra. Large flocks of enormous gray pigeons as big as hawks flush from their roosts in the trees as we ride beneath, startling us with their noisy wingbeats.

We have seen bear sign, great mounds of scat, and although we have had no further contact with him since our departure, we know that Billy Flowers is still trailing us, and we worry for the bears.

After all these years, Joseph Valor seems still to have an infallible sense of the country, and he picks our route through this vast and rugged terrain as surely as if he had been here last week rather than nearly a half century ago. When I ask him how he can navigate without a map, he answers: "Only White Eyes need paper maps." He taps his chest with a finger. "We carry maps in our hearts."

The girl herself has become more and more animated and attentive as we move deeper into her homeland. I've made a number of negatives of her as we go, and although I have no way of developing these out here, I hope that when I do, they will seem like a kind of time exposure; the images I have in mind will show her opening up in posture and demeanor like a blooming flower. She seems to become prettier all the time as she regains her strength, her tawny skin and deep brown eyes taking on a new luster. Oddly, the farther away we get from civilization, and the deeper we enter this strange, wild country, the less wild *la niña bronca* begins to seem, as if she is a natural and essential element of the landscape. Perhaps because I've spent more time with her taking her photograph, I feel that she and I have formed a particular bond in the past days. Although communication remains difficult, I'm more than ever certain that she has a memory of my being with her in the jail, because there is between us a kind of unspoken familiarity.

Even Jesus has now lost his fear of the girl and they converse easily in Spanish. She speaks a bit to all of us now, a few words of Spanish, a few of Apache, and now even a little English, which Mr. Browning is teaching her. "The young lady may as well learn the King's English," he sniffs, "rather than the adulterated American version." And, in fact, it's amusing to hear the girl speak her broken English with a British accent. Without the slightest provocation she will utter a string of non sequiturs: *"right-o, toodle-oo, cheerio."* And she will parrot Mr. Browning by saying such things as *"Very good, sir."* And, *"I beg your pardon, sir."*

For his part Mr. Browning, who calls her "little miss," dotes on the girl as if she is his long-lost daughter. "Could I make the little miss some breakfast this morning?" he will say cheerily each day.

For all our nosy prying while we're sitting around the campfire at night, we have still not learned a great deal about Harold Browning, other than the fact that Tolley considers him to be an excellent valet, and we all agree that he's the best camp cook among us. Despite both Margaret's and my best interview techniques, the man remains famously taciturn, always managing to deflect any personal questions.

"You'd make a good Apache, Harold," Albert observed one night when we were being especially relentless. "We find most White Eyes to be very impolite, the way they're always asking questions, always wanting to know about our religion, our culture, our ceremonies, our history, our family relations. What business is it of theirs anyway? We Apaches have learned to answer with silence."

"Yes, sir," Mr. Browning said, smiling slyly, "that's an old butler's trick as well."

And it occurred to me then that for all Margaret's questioning of others, and mine, too, for that matter, neither one of us has been very forthcoming about our pasts, either. I have never told the others about my parents' deaths, for instance. I suppose that somehow I am ashamed of the way Pop died. "What about you, Mag?" I now asked. "You mentioned your father the anthropologist, and the fact that your mother died. Is your father still alive? Do you have any other family?"

"No, I'm an only child," she said. "And as far as I know, my father is still alive."

"What does that mean?"

"It means that I don't have any contact with him any longer," she said coolly. "Last I heard he was still alive." And then she quickly changed the subject.

Margaret, too, is taking extensive notes now. "It would be interesting to compare our notebooks, wouldn't it, Neddy?" she said one evening around the fire. "One from the point of view of an artist, the other from that of a scientist."

"I'm not an artist, Mag," I said. "I'm a journalist. A workingman, as Big Wade puts it. My photographs and my notebooks just tell what happens."

We had found level ground on the summit of a *cordón* and there we were camped for the night, with a view out over the closely timbered mountains, superimposed one upon the next, pine-covered hills and plateaus, the sharp, serrated rock crests of the sierras, looming overhead now, as if they might fall down and crush us.

"Just out of curiosity, Mag," I asked, "are your notes all scientific data? Or do you make personal observations?"

She thumbed through her notebook. "Not unless you consider notes on verb morphology to be personal, sweetheart," she said.

"God, *give* me that," Tolley said, pretending to lunge for her notebook. "Verb morphology is my passion."

Margaret ignored him. "I'm mostly trying to learn enough Apache from the girl and from Joseph to understand how the language and the culture have evolved differently among this isolated band than among the reservation Apaches over the past half century," she said. "I'm hoping to make that the subject of my doctoral thesis."

"Oh, *please*, Margaret," Tolley said. "Do you expect us to believe that you haven't made a single entry about your lover boy here? 'Dear Diary,'" he said, adopting his most mincing tone, "'It's official, I'm in love with A.V. . . .' We always use initials in our diaries," Tolley said in an aside, "in case our parents ever read them. 'He is such a darling boy. I just get all squishy inside when I'm around him.'"

Margaret smiled with tolerant amusement. "These are my professional notebooks," she said. "I keep them separate from my personal life."

"Oh, who are you kidding, darling?" Tolley said. "You're supposed to be studying the Apaches, not doing it doggy style with one."

"Maybe Albert is just one of my research subjects," Margaret said, "and I'm observing him, and it's not personal at all. Didn't that ever occur to you?"

"Well, I suppose that's possible," Tolley said. "It's true that both you and Giles are rather similar that way. Both observers rather than participants. He sees the world through a camera lens. You see it through the impartial eyes of a scientist. But you're both on the outside looking in and neither of you sees it as it *really* is."

"Oh? And how is it, really, Tolley?" I asked. "For someone on the inside like yourself."

"A lot bigger than can ever be contained in your viewfinder, *mi amigo*," Tolley said. "And bigger than can be contained in the morphological study of verbs, darling. Big, messy, and complicated."

"What do you know about the 'real' world, anyway, Tolley?" I asked. "You're a rich kid. Look, you can't even come into the Sierra Madre without bringing a valet to protect you from it."

"That's where you're wrong, old sport," Tolley said. "When you're as *different* as I am, nothing can protect you from the realities of the world.

Not money. Not even a butler. Do you know that I've been arrested three times already, just for frequenting clubs where my 'kind' congregate? Some of my friends have gone to prison simply for being themselves. *That's* living on the front lines, not hiding behind a camera like you, or being an objective observer of other people's cultural practices, like Margaret. You're both really glorified voyeurs."

"So how come you didn't go to prison with your friends, Tolley?" I asked.

He smiled. "In order to avoid the disgrace it would cause the family name," he said, "Father makes a generous contribution every year to the greater Philadelphia Police Benevolent Association."

"I rest my case," I said. "Let's face it, we're all outsiders looking in, you included, Tolley. We're just looking at different things."

4 JUNE, 1932

Today we came upon our first sign of the Apaches. We rode into a clearing on the crest of a hillside, and there we found several crude rock pillars, built of stones stacked on top of one another, three feet or so high and spaced about twenty yards apart. Joseph dismounted and knelt by one of them, examining it. He spoke to the girl.

"What are those?" I asked Albert.

"We are in Apache country," he said.

"You mean they're some kind of boundary markers?"

"Apaches do not make boundaries," he said. "White Eyes make boundaries. These are used for another purpose."

We have camped for the night in the clearing not far from these stone monuments. There is a distinct chill in the high mountain air, and a certain sense of foreboding among us, as if the markers themselves have the power to create climate and mood. And perhaps this, then, is their purpose, to warn off intruders. There was even some discussion about whether or not we should avoid making a fire tonight for fear of giving away our location, until it was pointed out that we are *trying* to make contact with the Apaches, not avoid it. In any case, Joseph now tells us that he has seen signs of the

Apaches for the past two days, and that they have known of our presence for at least that long, that they know exactly how many we are and that we are traveling with the girl.

"How do you know all this, Joseph?" I asked. "Why didn't you tell us before?"

"The signs were there for you to see," he said.

This information put us even more on edge, and that night around the campfire we decided that we should begin posting a guard at night.

"And what will you White Eyes do," Albert asked, "if a wild Apache sneaks into our camp while you're on guard duty?"

"I don't know, Albert," I admitted. "I'd probably ask him to pose for a photograph."

"Yeah, and I'd want to interview him for my thesis," Margaret said.

"What about you, Mr. Browning?" Albert asked.

"I am not a violent man by nature, sir," Mr. Browning said. "I would probably try diplomacy. Perhaps I'd offer him a spot of tea. When I was in Kenya with my former master, Lord Crowley, I found that a cup of tea provided a wonderful icebreaker with the natives."

"We're a dangerous bunch, all right," Margaret said. "What would you do, Tolley? Try to have a peek under his breechcloth?"

"Very funny, darling," Tolley said. "As a matter of fact, I would raise my hand in the sign of peace to show the fellow that we are here in a spirit of goodwill. And I would say"—Tolley drew himself up—*"Chuu ilts'ee'a."*

Margaret started giggling, and even Albert laughed. "He would either kill you where you stood, Tolley," Albert said, "or he would roll on the ground in laughter."

"I'm hoping for the latter," Tolley said. "Because it's the only thing I know how to say in Apache. I made your grandfather teach it to me so that when I go home I can amuse my friends with my command of the Apache tongue."

"Okay, let the rest of us in on the joke," I said. "What does that mean?"

"Roughly translated," Margaret said, "it means, 'My penis is stiff.'"

And so, as usual we leave it to Tolley to provide the comic relief for our collective tensions. But the fact is, we're all on edge. Throughout this conversation, Jesus had remained quiet and thoughtful and had not joined in the laughter. "And you, boy?" Albert asked him now. "Speak up. What would you do if an Apache warrior snuck into our camp tonight?"

"I would be very, very afraid," Jesus answered in a small, deathly serious voice.

I drew the first watch tonight and so I sit by the fire passing time with my notebook, trying to keep my eyes open . . .

5 JUNE, 1932

The girl is gone. She left in the night. We don't know on whose watch she slipped away . . . it hardly matters.

"Do you know where she went, Joseph?" I asked the old man.

"She has returned to her people," he answered.

"And you didn't hear her go?"

"Do you not see that *la niña bronca* moves like a spirit?" Joseph asked, and we all know what he means. "It is the way the People once lived, a Power we once had, but have lost in your world. It does not exist any longer on the reservation except among a very few old ones. But the People here still possess the Power. You will see. If they choose to reveal themselves to us, we will not hear them come, they will simply appear before us."

Jesus crossed himself and whispered a small invocation. Such talk only confirms the folk superstitions upon which he was raised, the notion that the Apaches are supernatural bogeymen.

"Why don't we just go right to them," Margaret said, "rather than waiting for them to come to us?"

"Why would we want to do that?" Tolley asked. "Without the girl in our possession, we have no bargaining power whatsoever. Our orders now are to notify Billy Flowers of her escape. And then get the hell out of here. This place is beginning to give me the willies."

"Are you really willing to turn Flowers and his dogs loose on her, Tolley?" Margaret asked.

Even Mr. Browning, alarmed at this notion, spoke up then. "I should not advise it, sir," he said, "really I shouldn't."

"Joseph, you can track the girl, can't you?" I asked.

"It is better that you turn back now," Joseph said. "If the girl has found her people, they will not allow you to follow them."

"But how can you know she's already found them?" I asked. "Flowers's dogs could run her down in hours. I say we keep moving."

"You seem to forget, Giles," Tolley said, "that I am the commanding officer of this little detachment. I give the orders, not you."

"Look, Tolley," Margaret said. "We can't take a chance on letting Flowers catch her. You know what his dogs would do to her. I'm with Ned."

"This is mutiny," Tolley said. "I could have you all court-martialed."

"Okay, sweetheart, consider us under house arrest," Margaret said. "We'll turn ourselves in when we get back to the expedition. In the meantime, let's get moving. We're wasting time."

We didn't get far. We had only traveled a few hours, and had stopped to eat a bite, when we heard the ghostly rattling of chains announcing Billy Flowers and his dogs. A moment later the hunter rode up on his white mule, the chained dogs, lean and muscled, trailing behind him.

He did not dismount, but sat his mule, looking down upon us like Moses atop Mount Sinai, the shadowed sun streaming through the timber above, backlighting his long white hair and beard, his eyes burning bright. "You have let the heathen girl go," said Billy Flowers.

"She ran off in the night," Margaret answered. "How did you know?"

"Where you dismount to walk, her prints are missing," Flowers said. "It took me longer to notice than it should have. Why did you not notify me?"

"Because we're going to find her ourselves," I said.

"I warned you that she would run off. Now my dogs will find her, while her trail is still fresh." The old man's hunting blood was clearly up, and we all had the sense that he had just been waiting for this opportunity to put his dogs down and run the girl to ground again.

"You will return to notify the expedition immediately, Mr. Flowers," Tolley said, striking his most imperious pose. "You will guide them back here while we will go after the girl."

Flowers looked down at Tolley with an expression of enormous contempt. "Are you *giving* me orders, Mr. Phillips?" he asked.

"Captain Phillips to you, sir," said Tolley, and despite the gravity of the situation, and the terrible weight of Flowers's presence, we all had to work hard not to bust out laughing. "And I am in command here. Didn't Colonel Carrillo make that perfectly clear?"

"Tolley does have a point, Mr. Flowers," Margaret said. "If you go chasing off after the girl now, how will the expedition ever find us?"

"Because you will go back for them yourself," Flowers said, "and the old Indian will lead them here. They are only a day's ride behind us."

"No," Margaret said, shaking her head. "That's what we're trying to tell you. We've come this far and we're not turning back."

Billy Flowers considered this for a moment. "You're a foolish young woman, Miss Hawkins," he said. "You think this is a university field trip, don't you? And that the noble savages are going to take you into their world, embrace you, let you study them like museum specimens." He turned to Joseph. "Why don't you tell these folks what your people are really like, old-timer?" he said. "Tell them about the darkness in your own heart before you were civilized yourself, before you were baptized in the name of Jesus Christ. Go ahead, tell them what they might expect if they meet up with the bronco Apaches. 'The enemies of the cross of Christ: Whose end is destruction, whose god is their belly. Whose glory is their shame. Strangers from the covenants of promise, having no hope, and without God in their world.'"

Seated cross-legged on the ground, Joseph seemed tiny and frail in comparison to Billy Flowers, mounted on his mule above. He did not respond but neither did he turn away from Flowers's searing gaze.

"What do you know about our people, anyway, you crazy old bastard?" Albert asked.

Flowers reined his mule around. "All right," he said. "If that's how it's going to be, I will go back for the expedition myself. But you best hope I return with them before you learn for yourselves what I know about the godless."

It is an odd thing, and I don't know whether the others felt it or not, but watching Billy Flowers ride away in that moment, his dog chains rattling desolately, I suddenly experienced a terrible chill of vulnerability. He may be a zealot and half insane, but at the same time there has been something strangely comforting about having the old man trailing us all this time, as if God Himself has been watching out for us, keeping us safe. And suddenly we are all alone, in the heart of another God's country.

LA NIÑA BRONCA

THE GIRL LAY AWAKE, HUDDLED UNDER HER BLANKET, LISTENING to the owl calling in the forest, a sound that terrified her. It was the worst possible sign, and she knew that someone was going to die. She knew that Indio Juan had been watching them for several days now, and that he would come into their camp in the night and kill these people who had saved her. She thought to talk to the old man about it, but even before they came upon the rock pillars, she sensed that he, too, was aware of the presence of the People. She thought that Indio Juan might spare the woman and the boy to make captives of them, but he would surely kill the men, including the old man and his grandson. They had all been kind to her and she did not wish for them to die; neither did she wish for the woman and the boy to be taken captive, for she knew what terrible things would befall them.

And so she lay awake under her blanket, trying to gain her courage, listening to the hooting of the owl, the messenger of death. She was afraid of traveling in the night, especially with the owl abroad, for if she saw the owl in addition to hearing it, if she walked up on it or if it flew across her path, then it was she who would die. And yet she knew she could not stay here any longer, and that if she did, Indio Juan would come for her and cut the throats of these kind people in the night.

When she thought they were all asleep, she slipped from her place without making a sound and moved past them, quiet as a ghost. The girl-boy, as she thought of the one they called Tolley, was on guard duty by the fire but he had fallen asleep and the fire had burned down to embers. He would have been the first to die. As she passed by the old man, she looked down at him and saw that he was awake and that he was watching her. They looked in each other's eyes, but they did not speak, and she knew that the old man understood and would not stop her from leaving. *Good-bye, Grand-father,* she said, using her hands to make the sign talk. *I will come with you, child,* he answered with his hands. *No, you must go back,* she signed. *You must take the others back.*

A three-quarter moon had risen to light her way and the trees cast dark shadows across the forest floor. The owl hooted rhythmically, his voice filling the forest, and she tried to identify where the sound was coming from so that she could avoid walking close to it, but it seemed to be coming from all around and from no particular direction. She was afraid and she began to run in a light jog, her feet barely grazing the ground.

She knew this country well and knew the spring by which Indio Juan would be camped. But before she reached it, she saw the outlines of the people moving toward her through the forest, moving in and out of the shadows ahead, and then one of them stepped out in front of her and her breath caught in her throat, but she did not cry out. It was Indio Juan. He took hold of her arm and put his face up close to hers. "I was coming for you," he said, smiling crookedly. In the moonlight the dead side of his face, paralyzed in childhood by the snake venom, had a faint waxy sheen, the corner of his eye and mouth downturned.

"Yes," she said. "I know. And so I have come to you."

"You ride with White Eyes and Mexicans now," he said.

"And *In'deh*," she added.

"Reservation Apaches are not *In'deh*," he said.

"The old one is *ch'uk'aende*," she said. "He knows this country."

"He scouts for the White Eyes and the Mexicans."

"He brought me home," she said. "I was captured because you left me behind; you left my mother and my sister and the others behind to be killed by the Mexicans. The old one took me away from them and brought me home."

"They have fine horses and mules and many provisions," Indio Juan said.

"Yes, that is so."

"We will make a raid upon their camp tonight."

"No," she said. "In the morning they will leave this country. I do not wish them to be harmed."

Indio Juan laughed scornfully. "You do not wish them to be harmed?" he mocked.

"We will travel south to the *ranchería* of my grandfather," the girl said. "I will tell him that his daughter, my mother, and his granddaughter, my sister, are dead because you left us behind for the Mexicans. I will tell him that these people rescued me and brought me home and I promised them that they would not be harmed. And if you kill them now, my grandfather will be very angry."

"I do not fear your grandfather," said Indio Juan boastfully.

"Yes, you do," said the girl. The others had faded out of the shadows now and gathered quietly behind, listening, half a dozen young men hardly older than boys, and two women, one a Mexican captive named Francesca, taken many years ago as a child, and now as Apache as any of the others, the other the hawk-faced one they called *Gent,tuuyu,* the "ugly one," all that was left of Indio Juan's band.

"Let us leave them alone tonight," said Francesca, who was carrying Indio Juan's child. "And if they turn back in the morning, we will let them go. But if they try to follow us, we will take their fine horses and mules, and we will do as we wish with those who ride them."

This compromise seemed to satisfy Indio Juan. It was true that he had the snake sickness and was always unpredictable, but he also feared her grandfather. "Agreed?" he asked the girl.

She nodded.

She returned with them to their camp, trying to avoid Indio Juan, trying to avoid even looking at him. She wondered now that she was back how long it would be before he claimed her as his wife. She went off to sleep beside the woman, *Gent,tuuyu,* the others oddly shy and uncertain with her, as if they feared that in her time among the White Eyes and the Mexicans, she had been tainted.

She lay awake, unable still to sleep. From the forest came the deep reverberating hooting of the owl.

THE NOTEBOOKS OF NED GILES, 1932
NOTEBOOK V:
Captured

Joseph was right, we never heard or saw them coming, they were simply there, above and behind us. Ahead of us. Atop us. We were riding single file up the face of a steep canyon wall. On the other side was a nearly sheer drop-off into a river gorge hundreds of feet below, so far down that although we could see the churning, rushing white water, we could not hear it. Tolley was riding ahead of me, and I saw the figure leap upon him from the rocks above, but before I could even cry out to warn him, I felt one of them drop onto my own back, light as a cat pouncing. And then I felt the knife blade at my throat, the slightest pressure, and I smelled her unmistakable scent, her wildness, and I knew in that instant that I was going to die at the hand of *la niña bronca*. Tolley fell from the saddle uttering a small surprised cry, the Apache on his back like a small troll, the two of them rolling on the ground, the nimble troll coming up on top, picking up a rock to smash in Tolley's skull. His now-riderless horse panicked, reared, and whinnied, one hoof coming down to strike a glancing blow to the Apache's shoulder, entirely by accident, knocking him off Tolley, who scrambled to his feet and tried to grab hold of the reins. But the horse, wild-eyed, reared again, lost his footing, and teetered backward, falling off the trail, landing on his back on the rocks, then flipping over, and falling, falling off the sheer face of the canyon wall, falling into the gorge, falling and screaming as he fell twisting through the air. How will we ever forget the sound of Tolley's horse screaming all the way down to the rocks below?

Then came the distinctive ratcheting of rifles being cocked, and several others were ahead of us on the trail, above us in the rocks, and behind us. Tolley had raised his arms in surrender to the man who had knocked him from his horse . . . except now I saw that it was actually a woman, dressed in high-topped moccasins, and a breechcloth. I was able to turn my head just enough to see that a young man sat behind Albert on his horse, holding a knife to his throat, and a young boy behind Joseph, also with a knife at his throat. Margaret, Mr. Browning, and Jesus remained unguarded, but none of them had weapons, a fact the Apaches must already have known. In any case, there was nowhere for them to run.

Jesus began to whimper softly, captured by *los Apaches*, his worst nightmare come true. He spoke in blubbering Spanish: *"Salvamos tu vida,"* he said. "We saved your life, we took you away from the jail where you were dying, *nosotros te cuidamos bien*, we took care of you. Why do you do this to us now?"

From behind me came the answer, and I knew for certain what I had already known, that it was the girl herself holding the knife at my throat. *"Si no dejas de llorar, mexicano cobarde, te mataremos,"* she answered without pity. "If you do not stop crying, Mexican coward, we will kill you." And Jesus stopped crying.

The others came forward now; moving as soundlessly as dream people, they slid the rifles and shotguns from the scabbards on our saddles. The girl took the knife from my throat and slid off the back of the mule, as did the boy behind Joseph and the young man behind Albert.

A short barrel-chested man, carrying an old Winchester repeating rifle, swaggered to the front. One side of his face was horribly disfigured; the cheek and jaw scarred and missing flesh, one eyelid drooping lifelessly.

"Yo Indio Juan," the man said, with a crooked smile, and Jesus uttered a kind of involuntary choking sound. The man laughed at the boy's terror.

Indio Juan approached Margaret on her mule, grabbed her by the arm, and dragged her out of the saddle. He took a handful of her hair in his fist and pulled her close to him as if to study her with his good eye.

"Good Gad!" Mr. Browning shouted, dismounting clumsily and moving toward the man. "Unhand the young lady immediately, sir!" But before Mr. Browning could take three steps, another of the Apaches moved up behind him and clubbed him over the head with a rock. Mr. Browning collapsed in a heap. Margaret cried out. The girl lowered her knife, and I jumped off my mule and went to him; he was unconscious but still breathing, blood welling up through the hair on the back of his head. I pointed at her. "This man fed you," I said. "He cared for you when you were sick. He saved your life. And this is how you repay him? Tell her that, Joseph!"

"And this woman, too," I said, pointing to Margaret. "We are your friends. We did not come to hurt you. *Somos sus amigos.* Tell him to let her go."

"It's all right, Ned," Margaret said, staring defiantly at Indio Juan, who still held her by the hair. "I'm all right. It's not the girl's fault. She can't do anything. This one is in charge."

Joseph spoke then, in a low, calm voice; he spoke in his strange oratorical way, and as he did so, the one called Indio Juan released his grip on Margaret and all listened to the old man. And after a moment, Albert began translating for us:

"'I am *ch'uk'aende*, the only true Chiricahua. In the old days I lived in this country with the People. My name is Goso and I was married to the one called Siki and I had three children with her in these mountains. Later I surrendered with old Nana, to the *nantan lupan*. Surely, the old people among you still tell the stories of those days, of the *nantan lupan* and Geronimo, Mangus, and Nana. Surely I have relatives here still among you who will remember the warrior named Goso. Now I have come back to die in these mountains where I was born. You may kill me right now if you wish. I am an old man and I have lived too long already; I have outlived four wives and most of my children and many of my grandchildren. I am not afraid to die. But why kill these White Eyes and this Mexican boy, and my grandson, who is also *In'deh*? They have done nothing but come here with me. They have done nothing but save the life of this girl, who was dying in a Mexican jail. They have done nothing but bring her home to the People. For that, rather than hitting them over the heads with stones, you should hold a feast in their honor.'"

Indio Juan laughed derisively then and approached the old man.

"'A feast you say, old one? For the White Eyes and the Mexican boy, and this reservation *In'deh*? Yes, this is a fine idea. And if you have not lived so long among the White Eyes yourself that you have forgotten the ways of the People, you will remember that our women will dance all night with the men we take prisoner. And in the morning when all are weary of dancing, they will kill them. We will keep the boy, and if he stops crying and seems useful to us, we will allow him to live with us. As the Huerta boy lives with us. I myself will keep this White Eyes woman as my slave, and she will bear my Apache children, in the same way that your Mexican slave woman bore your children. For the ways of the People have not changed. And we are few now and fewer all the time. We always need women and children. As for you, old man, we will see if any of our old people remember you. And what stories they have to tell of you.'"

They helped themselves to some of our food first, then mounted our mules and donkeys and herded us along on foot. We had managed to revive Mr. Browning, but he was weak and disoriented and had difficulty keeping up. Joseph told us that the Apaches would kill him if he held us up, and so Albert, Tolley, and I took turns helping him down the trail. "I'll be quite all right, sirs," he said gamely. "Just need to get my legs back under me. Oh dear, I'm afraid that I have rather a knot on the back of the old noggin."

"That was very chivalrous of you to come to my defense, Mr. Browning," Margaret said. "I noticed that none of the other men did. Thank you."

"Perhaps you didn't notice the knives they were holding to our throats, darling," said Tolley.

"The very least I could do, miss," Mr. Browning said. "I've never been able to tolerate the abuse of women, children, or animals. I'm terribly sorry about your horse, by the way, sir."

"Yes, thank you, Mr. Browning," Tolley said. "He was the finest polo pony in Father's string. I'll be catching hell for that . . . Such a ghastly sound he made plunging to his death, wasn't it?"

"Catching hell from your father is the least of your worries, Tolley," I said.

"True," he said. "Albert, if I correctly understood your translation of the swaggering little toad, this evening we are to be the guests of honor at a feast, at which we gentlemen will dance the night away with our charming hostesses . . ."

"It's an old Apache tradition," Albert explained. "Captive men are made to dance all night. And in the morning the women kill them. In this way, they will take their revenge for the attack on their camp in which the girl's mother and sister were killed."

"How did you know her mother and sister were killed?" Margaret asked. "Why didn't you tell us that?"

"We heard the girl talking in her sleep," Albert answered. "We didn't tell you because it is not your business."

"Perhaps when they see what a perfectly delightful dinner companion I am," Tolley mused, "they'll reconsider the part about killing me in the morning."

"Tolley, will you please, for once, just shut up?" Margaret asked.

"And you, of course, darling," Tolley continued, "will be allowed to live—as the slave bride of our dashing captor, Indio Juan. Doting mother to his children . . . a whole brood of little brown babes . . ."

"You know, Tolley, if for some reason they don't kill you," Margaret said, "I promise you that I will."

"I hate to say I told you so, people," said Tolley. "But if you'd only listened to your *captain*, we wouldn't be in this predicament in the first place. We'd be safely back with the expedition by now."

"Shut up, Tolley," I said.

It was a long, grueling day of travel, south through increasingly steep, rugged country. We stopped only once and were each given barely a mouthful of water. Mr. Browning's condition continued to deteriorate and it was necessary for two of us to take turns supporting him between us. We had tried to bandage his head with a torn-up shirt but the blood had soaked through. He asked us several times to leave him by the side of the trail.

"Nonsense, Mr. Browning," Tolley said. "If you think I'm going among the wild Apaches for what may well be my last dinner dance without my valet to dress me, you are sorely mistaken, my good man."

"Yes, very well, sir," poor Mr. Browning mumbled. "I am at your service, sir."

We traversed several *cordones* and traveled up another very steep *cañón*, through a pass that dropped back down on the other side into a small fertile river valley, surrounded by forests of pine, oak, and cedar. Clearly some signal must have been given to announce our approach because a group of children met us down the trail, half a dozen lithe brown beings, who themselves seemed to fade out of the trees like wildlife, so that one minute we saw nothing and the next they had appeared in exactly the same place. They followed along silently, somberly, and not until we approached the outskirts of the *ranchería* itself did they become bolder, running up to inspect us from a closer vantage point and beginning to chatter excitedly, a few of them leaping up behind the riders of the mules and burros . . . such an odd, otherworldly way they have of moving, like spirit beings.

There appear to be fewer than three dozen people in residence in the *ranchería*, which is set on the north side of a small brook, spilling into the main river. Behind the *ranchería* the valley narrows into a canyon, the walls of which are striated with ledges and pockmarked with the cave dwellings of the "first people." There is an eclectic hodgepodge of lodgings, everything from what look like old canvas army tents much patched with various fabrics, to brush wickiups, to crude mud huts with thatched roofs. From all of these structures people now ventured forth to hail the returning party. They were dressed in equally diverse clothing—shirts and dresses of calico and various brightly colored Indian fabrics; some of the old men and boys wore Mexican or American army jackets; some wore trousers, others breechcloths; some wore Mexican riding boots, others high-topped moccasins; hats and bandannas; most of the women wore jewelry—silver medallions and strings of beads around their necks, bangles and bracelets on their wrists and rings on their fingers. Beyond the sheer color and spectacle of the moment, I couldn't help but notice how few of these people were young men; they seemed to be mostly women, a few old men, and a number of children of various ages. The handful of warrior-aged men and older boys seemed to be concentrated in the band that had captured us, who now led us triumphantly into the *ranchería*.

There arose from those coming out of their lodgings a strange ululation sound to welcome the returning war party, a sound that seemed to issue from deep within their chests, rising from their throats like a bird's warbling, echoing off the canyon walls, a sound so primeval that it sent chills up our spines.

"God, isn't it incredible?" Margaret marveled. "It looks like an encampment of gypsies, doesn't it?"

"It looks like an Hieronymus Bosch painting of hell to me," said Tolley.

Jesus began to weep softly, overwhelmed by fear and fatigue, by the sheer strangeness of this place and of these people, such as none of us had ever witnessed before. Now Albert knelt down in front of him. "Listen to me, boy," he said, taking him gently by the shoulders. "There is nothing that Apaches despise more than crybabies. If you do not stop now, they are going to kill you. And they will torture you first. Do you hear me?"

Jesus nodded his head, choking back sobs.

A number of the Apaches approached closer now to inspect us. They were particularly fascinated by Margaret's blond hair and there seemed to be some squabbling over the rightful ownership of Jesus. Two old women held a spirited exchange, until one of them spoke to him in Spanish. *"Usted vendrá a vivir conmigo en mi choza, chico,"* she said. "You will come to live in my hut, child."

"Sí, señora," Jesus answered politely, nearly gratefully. As the old woman led him away, the boy looked back over his shoulder at us plaintively. "Señor Ned . . ." he said, raising his hand in a small, uncertain wave.

"You'll be okay, kid," I called after him. "Don't worry. I'll find you."

Indio Juan approached now to claim Margaret, but before he could do so, *la niña bronca* came toward us through the crowd. Walking beside her was the strangest Apache we had seen yet.

"Good Christ!" whispered Tolley. "Who in the hell is this big drink of water?"

The man was dressed like the others, in moccasins, leggings, a breechcloth, and a loose-fitting gingham shirt. He wore a faded blue bandanna tied on his head. But compared to the others he was a giant, well over six feet tall. But this still wasn't the thing that set him most apart from the others. No, the strangest thing about him was that he was a white man. He had long reddish blond hair that spilled down his back and over his shoulders, and a long red beard that hung nearly to his waist and was just beginning to be tinged with white. He was not a young man by any means, perhaps in his fifties, his naturally fair skin ruddy and weather-beaten from a lifetime of exposure to the elements.

The giant redheaded white man approached Indio Juan, towering over him, and spoke to him in a deep voice. Indio Juan spoke angrily back to him.

"The white Apache says he is taking Margaret for himself," Albert translated. "Indio Juan answers that it was his raid and that by rights she belongs to him."

"Aren't you the lucky one, darling?" Tolley said. "All the men squabbling over you. But the real question is, what is a white man *doing* here?"

"He is not a white man, Tolley," Albert said. "He is a white Apache. Probably taken captive as a child. Look at the others. Do you not see that there are also those with Mexican blood among them?"

Joseph spoke up then: "He is called Charley," he said.

"How do you know that?" I asked.

"Because I caught him myself when he was a boy," said the old man.

Albert continued to translate for us. "'It is my granddaughter's wish that the White Eyes woman comes to live with us as our slave,'" the white Apache said to Indio Juan. "'It was her raid as much as yours. It was she who led you to them. Therefore she claims this woman as her captive.'"

Indio Juan regarded the white Apache with murderous eyes. The big man stared down upon him. There was clearly bad blood between them.

"'I have spoken,'" the white Apache said.

Now Tolley cleared his throat. "Excuse me, my good fellow," he said, approaching the white Apache. "Permit me to introduce myself." He thrust his hand out. "Tolbert Phillips Jr. here. Of the railroad Phillipses of Philadelphia."

"What the hell are you doing, Tolley?" I asked.

The white Apache looked at Tolley with contempt and said something in Apache.

Tolley laughed his high whinnying horse's-ass laugh. He was clearly very nervous and jabbered away ridiculously. "Oh well, I'm all for 'when in Rome,'" he said, "but I'm afraid I don't speak a word of the language. Well, that's not entirely true, I do know one phrase . . ."

"Don't even think about it, Tolley," I warned.

"Tolley, you fool," said Margaret, "don't you understand that he doesn't speak English?"

"But he's as white as we are," Tolley said. "Why, he looks like an Irishman to me." He looked expectantly at the man. "I'll wager you have Irish blood, sir," he said.

"What do you think this is, Tolley, the Princeton campus?" I said.

"I'm simply trying to have a civilized conversation with this gentleman who appears to have some influence here."

The white Apache spoke again. And this time the girl answered him.

"He wants to know," Albert translated, "why they brought White Eyes men into the *ranchería* instead of killing them."

Now Joseph stepped forward. He was so tiny that he looked like a child standing next to the giant man.

"'I am the warrior once known as Goso. Many years ago I captured a boy named Charley, who was traveling in a buggy with his mother and father on the road from the White Eyes' mining town of Silver City. That boy lived with me and my wife, Siki, and our children, and he became like my own son. When the American soldiers came into Mexico and attacked our *ranchería*, I was away with Mangus and Geronimo raiding against the Mexicans. When we returned, many of the People were dead, and many others had surrendered. We held a council and decided to surrender ourselves, and when we came into the *nantan lupan's* camp carrying our white flag, I believed that I would find my wife and children and the boy Charley already there. But I did not. I never saw them again. *Daalk'ida 'aguudzaa.* This was long ago.'"

The white Apache looked for a long time at Joseph. "'I remember the warrior Goso. But in my memory he was a large man, a man with big Power, and I feared him.'"

"'That is because you were only a small boy. And because I am an old man now. As we grow old we become smaller and smaller, and our Power seeps back into the earth whence it arose until there is nothing left and then the wind blows us away.'"

"'Now perhaps the warrior fears the boy,'" said Charley, looming over the old man.

Joseph smiled. "'No, no more than he fears the wind. But perhaps the boy still fears the warrior.'"

The white Apache laughed with disdain. "'I do not see a warrior standing before me. I see an old man who has lived so long among the White Eyes that he is nearly a White Eyes himself.'"

The old man nodded. "'Yes, that is so. And I see a White Eyes who has lived so long among the Apaches that he is nearly an Apache himself.'"

"'He is more Apache than the old man. Why have you come back to us now? Why do you travel with White Eyes?'"

"'I return this girl to you. Did she not tell you that we rescued her from a Mexican jail?'"

"'Yes, and it is only for this reason that you are still alive.'"

"'We bring you your granddaughter and we ask that you give us the Mexican boy in return.'"

"'Have you not sufficiently betrayed the People? Now you lead the White Eyes and the Mexicans to us again?'"

"'They only want the boy back.'"

"'Do you understand that no one who comes here is ever allowed to leave again? Why should we give up the Huerta boy? He belongs to us now. The Mexican ranchers are our enemies. They kill us on sight. And except for this woman and the Mexican boy, who may be useful to us, these White Eyes you bring among us will all die in the morning.'" Charley looked now at Albert, who had continued to translate this conversation for us. "'Including this one, who speaks our language but looks and dresses like a White Eyes himself. As for you, old man, I remember the warrior Goso. I remember him as a large, strong, brave man. Then we heard that he had surrendered to the *nantan lupan* and became a scout for the White Eyes. I will let the old woman Siki decide if you are really the warrior Goso and what is to be done with you.'"

"'She is still alive?'"

"'You will come with me, old man.'"

Charley gave an order, then abruptly took hold of Margaret's arm and began to lead her away. Margaret tried to shake loose from him. "Hey, you don't have to rough up the girls to prove that you're a big man," she said. She turned and smiled at us bravely. "I'll be all right. Take care of Mr. Browning."

Tolley gave a wave. "We'll see you later at the dinner dance, darling," he said with bravado.

Joseph and the girl followed them. Indio Juan watched them go with an expression of loathing on his face.

Albert, Tolley, Mr. Browning, and I have been lodged in one of the caves at the base of the canyon. A boy with a rifle has been posted in front to guard us. All of our possessions have been taken from us, along with our mules and burros. I have only the notebook that I carry in the pocket of my jacket, and a pencil. Mr. Browning sleeps.

"I must say, I'm terribly disappointed in the big white man," said Tolley. "I felt certain he would feel some racial loyalty to us."

"It doesn't work that way, Tolley," Albert said. "He is as Apache now as if he had been born among them. The others don't even think of him as being a White Eyes any longer."

"Oh, they don't notice the fair hair and beard, the pale skin and the fact that he's a foot taller than anyone else?" Tolley asked.

"He doesn't even speak English anymore," I said. "But don't you think there must be some buried part of him that remembers his old life, his white parents, his first language?"

"That's the part I'd like to get in touch with," said Tolley. "The part that doesn't believe all white men need to be murdered. "'Hello in there,'" Tolley mimed, his hand cupped to his mouth. "'Come out, little Charley, wherever you are.'"

Exhausted from the day's travel, we dozed off, to be woken just as darkness fell by the monotonous beating of a single drum, then a second and third. We peered out from our cave to see flames rising from several fires in the center of the *ranchería*. As if ignited by the flames themselves, an enormous orange moon blistered up behind the high savage peaks of the sierras. The scent of roasting meat carried to us on a faint breeze, reminding us that we had not eaten since morning. Mr. Browning still slept fitfully. We tried to make him as comfortable as possible.

Two other Apaches came then to join the boy who guarded us, and they led Tolley, Albert, and me down from the cave, poking us along with the barrels of their rifles, laughing and mocking us as we went.

Now to the music were added the plucked notes of a string instrument that sounded like something between a banjo and a guitar, then the rattling of shaken gourds, the tones of a high haunting flute, the ringing of bells, a harmonica—all creating a strangely discordant but somehow hypnotic music.

Some of the women tended to the fires, stirring cooking pots and turning the meats which were impaled on long sticks supported over the fire by rocks. Two whole deer carcasses were suspended from a cross pole over another fire. Everyone was beginning to congregate now for the feast, and some of the children had already begun to dance.

Margaret was standing with the girl in front of the central fire. She was dressed in a billowing brightly colored skirt and loosely fitting blouse, with several strings of beads around her neck, and a large silver medallion on a chain. She was flushed and seemed strangely excited by all the activity.

"Well, it didn't take you long to go native, did it, darling?" Tolley said.

"They gave me these clothes to wear for the dance," Margaret said. "I learned in the Amazon that the sooner you adopt the native customs and attire, the quicker they accept you."

"Are you all right, Margaret?" Albert asked her. "Have they hurt you?"

"I'm okay, Albert," she answered. "No one has hurt me. How is Mr. Browning?"

"He's sleeping, Mag," I said. "But he doesn't look so good."

"It's fascinating, isn't it?" she asked, looking out again at the assemblage, her cheeks glowing in the firelight. "How this isolated population has become a cultural island, a specific, one-of-a-kind mélange of cultures. Can you hear the Mexican influence in the music? Look at their clothes and the fabrics. Almost everything they own has been stolen over the years in raids on Mexican villages and ranches, and probably from time to time over the border as well. At least three or four of the women here are Mexicans, and there are several women from the Tarahumure tribe as well, a tribe that lives farther south with whom the Apaches trade. But you know what's most interesting to me from an anthropological point of view? How uniformly Apache all the children look. It's as if their genetic structure is so strong that it completely overpowers the other races. Look at this girl, for instance," she said, tenderly cupping *la niña bronca*'s cheek in her hand. "She's a little taller than most of the others, but other than that, would you ever guess that her grandfather was a redheaded white man?"

"Darling, aren't you having rather too much *fun?*" Tolley asked. "Have you forgotten that your friends are scheduled to be executed in the morning?"

"I'm sorry," Margaret said. "It's something else my father taught me about fieldwork. When you feel threatened or afraid, take refuge in your work. Be professional, because it's all you have, your last illusion of control. I guess I'm trying to pretend that this is all an anthropological exercise."

"I know what you mean, Mag," I said. "I'd do exactly the same thing if I could get my hands on my damn camera bag. God, I hope they didn't destroy it. All my film . . . my notebooks . . ."

"Good *Christ,*" said Tolley. "*What* is wrong with you two? Our lives are in jeopardy and you're talking about your jobs. As if any of that matters now."

Just at that moment one of the Apache men strutted proudly by dressed in Tolley's white leather riding breeches and silk smoking jacket. "Scoundrel!" Tolley cried after him. "Thief! Those are my clothes!"

"I have your knapsack with your camera in it, Neddy," Margaret said, "and your notebooks. They're still going through our possessions, discarding anything that has no practical value to them. They're dividing up our clothes, food, tools, utensils. They fought like dogs over Tolley's wardrobe, but no one was in the least bit interested in your camera. This is not exactly a machinery-oriented culture."

"Will you take care of it for me, Mag?"

"Who cares about your *fucking* camera?" Tolley hollered. He suddenly seemed near tears. "Are you all insane? They're going to *kill* us in the morning."

"Calm down, Tolley," Albert cautioned. "If you fall apart now, they'll kill you before morning."

"Maybe we should make a run for it," Tolley said in a panicked voice. "Look, no one's paying any attention to us. We could just slip away."

"We wouldn't get a hundred yards," Albert said. "They'd send the boys after us with sticks and rocks to kill us like rabbits."

"Oh, *God*," Tolley whimpered. "Why does everybody want to kill us? What have we done?"

"Look, Tolley." I said, "I'm going to worry about my camera, Margaret's going to worry about cultural anthropology, and you can worry about getting your clothes back. That'll give us all something to live for."

"Okay, okay, you're quite right, old sport," Tolley said, collecting himself. "I'm sorry. I had a brief moment of weakness there. I'm a little on edge."

"Who isn't, sweetheart?" said Margaret.

"What do you have to worry about, darling?" Tolley asked. "You're going to be the bride of the big white chief. I'd trade your fate for ours in a heartbeat. In fact, though he's a bit old for me, I find him rather attractive in a brutish sort of way."

"I'm not going to be anyone's bride," Margaret said.

"You do understand, don't you, Margaret," said Albert, "why the Apaches always kill the men they capture and keep the women and children?"

"Of course," she answered. "Because like most seminomadic indigenous people, they don't have a structured penal system. And no practical way to imprison male captives for any length of time. Thus as long as they're alive, men from other tribes pose a threat. So it's more practical just to kill them. Whereas women and children are more docile and more easily assimilated."

"And also useful for breeding purposes," Albert added. "To broaden the genetic pool."

"Oh God, I think he's jealous," Tolley said. He waved his hand in front of us, as if to get our attention. "Can we please concentrate on our most immediate problem? Which, as Giles points out, is the fact that my wardrobe has been plundered."

We had to laugh; as desperate as was our situation, we were relieved to see that Tolley had at least recovered his sense of humor.

"Look, there's one of them right there in my Abercrombie & Fitch safari jacket," he said, pointing. "And there's another in my pith helmet. The
brutes!" he added. "They don't even know any better than not to break up
the outfit."

It was true that the Apaches wore bizarre combinations of clothing.
The men sported all manner of headgear, everything from narrow-
brimmed straw hats, to Mexican sombreros, to their most recent additions
of pith helmet and Mr. Browning's bowler hat. Others wore brightly colored cloths wrapped around their heads like Indian turbans. Some were
dressed in variously styled vests and jackets, others had blankets tied around
their waists almost like Scottish kilts. The women were equally colorful in
their bright calico dresses and skirts and as much jewelry as they could fit
on their persons.

More of the Apaches had begun dancing. It was unlike anything we'd
ever seen before, a kind of stuttered prancing, a nearly spastic, out-of-sync
movement that seemed nevertheless in perfect keeping with the strange, dis-
sonant music, the blazing bonfires, the full orange moon . . . I knew then
that when we had first crested that final tortuous pass in the rocks and
dropped down into this valley, we had crossed a threshold into another
world, a world with its own sun and moon, and its own separate race of man.

We were seated on blankets and hides spread on the ground in the
place of honor in front of the central fire. The white Apache Charley had
arrived with Joseph and they had taken their seats beside us. With them
was a woman whom we took to be Charley's wife, and another very old
woman, who appeared to be blind. We were fed two different kinds of
roasted meat, perhaps beef pilfered from the Mexican ranchers, or maybe
horse, as well as venison. With this they served sweet mescal, the succulent
crown of the agave plant, which had been steamed all day beneath the
coals, and according to Albert is both an Apache staple as well as a delicacy.
The women had also baked a flat unleavened bread for the feast that must
have had its origins in Mexican tortillas. The food was delicious and we
were ravenous; we ate with a strange abandon, the notion unspoken but
palpable between us that this might, after all, be our last meal and we
might as well enjoy it. Never has anything tasted better. Before she would

eat herself, Margaret wrapped some food up in a cloth and sent the girl with it to Mr. Browning. But when she returned she said that he was still sleeping and so she had left the food in the cave beside him.

Now the dancers were each singing in turn as they danced, a kind of chanting. One of them suddenly made a chilling screaming sound that faded away like an echo and that raised gooseflesh on our arms . . . it was the exact sound of Tolley's horse falling into the abyss.

"Good God," Margaret whispered.

"They're telling the story of our capture," Albert explained, ". . . with some . . . elaboration."

Each Apache who had participated in the event took their turn singing and dancing their exploits. When it came Indio Juan's turn, his dancing was even wilder and more exaggerated than the others, his singing edged with a distinct madness. "This one is not right in the head," Albert said. "Look at the others. You can see that even they fear him . . . Listen, now he is telling of claiming Margaret as his slave, and the fact that she is his rightful property, not Charley's. It is a great breach of etiquette to make such a claim at a dance in front of the rest of the tribe." I sneaked a look at Charley, who sat stone-faced and expressionless.

When Indio Juan was finished, it was *la niña bronca's* turn, and she stood gracefully and walked to the center, and began to dance. I recognized in her stylized movements the act of falling onto my back, swooping down like a bird of prey, holding the knife to my throat, all performed with a strange, evocative grace. As much as she had blossomed when she was with us, now that she was back among her own people, she seemed restored to the full bloom of her young womanhood, full of confidence and joy. Gone is any trace of the terrified wild creature I first saw those weeks ago, squatting naked on the stone floor of the jail cell. Here is a dark, supple, lovely young woman, dancing in the flames, dancing under the moonlight; I could not take my eyes off her.

Several small groups of women sat by the fire, gossiping and watching the dancers, periodically looking over at us and giggling.

"Oh God, here they come," Tolley said as several of the women stood and made their way toward us. "Our executioners. Never have I wanted to be a wallflower more than I do at this moment."

"The ceremonial dancing is over," Albert said. "This is the beginning of the social dancing."

"Just don't let anyone know that you're a *poufter*, Tolley," I said. "It might go even worse for you. Remember what Albert said."

"Oh, thank you, Giles," Tolley said sarcastically. "I'll try to avoid asking the boys to dance."

Now the women urged us to our feet and led us out among the dancers. We felt enormous and ungainly beside them. The Apaches are a small, compact people, the men with broad shoulders, deep chests and lithe, athletic limbs, the women, equally well formed, hardy and strong, with fine features, clear dark eyes and skin and small hands and feet. We felt like pale clumsy giants among them.

Everyone made great fun of Tolley and my first tentative steps, a general hilarity that had some of the spectators and dancers alike literally rolling on the ground in laughter. However, they were all suitably impressed with Albert's dancing skills. Although the ceremonial dances had been outlawed for many years on the reservation and in the white-run boarding school which he had attended as a boy, Albert, like many Apache youths, had surreptitiously learned the forbidden steps.

Margaret, too, was led into the dance circle now. She was tall, slender, and far more graceful than we, and her own efforts less slavishly imitative. Perhaps as a child among the South American tribes, she had learned something about native dances, for she seemed not to care particularly whether she performed the steps with exact correctness, imposing instead her own sense of rhythm on the music, so smooth and sinewy, that it was hard for all not to watch and admire her.

Now a curious thing began to happen. As exhausted as we were by the ordeals of the day, the strangeness of this new land, the terrifying uncertainty of our predicament, we all became caught up in the hypnotic music, the arrhythmic dancing, the otherworldly atmosphere of the place. And we gave ourselves up to it, letting the beat of the drums reach into that primal part of our beings that knows instinctively how to dance, that remembers the steps. Margaret says that dance was the first form of human communication, the first art form, the first entertainment, that from the beginning of the species, *Homo sapiens* danced to celebrate love and war, and everything in between; it is the one activity universal to every culture on earth. And now caught up in the music and the dance, we forgot all else; we even managed to forget in this brief respite of mad pulsing gaiety that our lives were in jeopardy. It seemed impossible to believe that these same smiling, laughing people with whom we whirled and pranced and cavorted by the flickering light of the fires intended to murder us in the morning, to chase us about the camp and beat us to death with rocks and sticks, to run us through with knives and lances. This was the Apache way, Joseph said; the killing of male captives was business left to the women and children, for it was not fitting occupation for a warrior.

And so we danced under the full moon, the flames of the fires blazing high. And now we knew the steps to each of the different dances, one in a line, one in a circle, one with partners dancing back and forth, another with changing partners . . . within this trance state we lost all track of time and all of life in that moment became simply the dance; all else was forgotten, past and future, nothing mattered but the immediacy of the dance, the dance absorbed us into its being . . . and within the sanctuary of the dance we were no longer afraid.

Hours passed; the moon rose high and white, moving across the sky in a splendid arc. Joseph had told us that sometimes these dances went on for three or four days, that some people danced the entire time. There was more cooking and feasting and the drinking of a mild homemade beerlike beverage called *tiswin*, made from fermented corn. One was able to drink a great deal of it before becoming drunk.

Earlier in the evening I had caught a brief glimpse of Jesus with his new "family." He gave me a small, tentative wave and looked so sad, but also somehow resigned to his fate. I think that they were keeping him intentionally separated from us in order to hasten the process of assimilation and I was not allowed to go to him. A bit later I saw another Mexican boy, a slender, fair-skinned child, whom I knew must be little Geraldo Huerta.

He played with some other boys, completely at ease, clearly fully assimilated into the tribe after three years of captivity.

Joseph was still seated in front of the fire with Charley and his wife, and the old blind woman Siki. We had barely been able to speak to the old man and had not yet learned what fate had been decided for him. I wondered how it was for him to come back to this world all these years later, wondered if he found everything altered from what it had once been in his long-ago days of freedom, or if he felt that he himself was altered by the time he had spent among the White Eyes and on the reservation. To look at him now, he seemed, as always, inscrutable, unflappable, fearless; he watched the dancers and spoke from time to time to the old woman.

At some point the girl claimed me as her dancing partner. She was taller than the other women and danced so lightly that her feet seemed barely to touch the ground. And then she began to dance a different step with me, one that was somehow more intimate than the others, a step that was specifically ours, and which clearly interested the people, as there was suddenly much attention paid to us by all who watched. Now the high clear tones of the flute rose above the other instruments and the other dancers began to drop out of the dance circle. As he went, Albert came past me and said: "Congratulations, White Eyes. You've been saved."

"What does that mean?" I asked.

"The girl is doing the marriage dance," he said. "They cannot kill you if she chooses you as her husband."

The drums and other instruments fell silent one by one until only the flute still played, clear and haunting, its rich, vibrant tones rising on the flames into the cool mountain air. The girl did not look directly at me as she danced; in fact it struck me in that moment that she had never looked me directly in the eye but always seemed to be gazing at a point just beyond me. She danced as if floating off the ground, her thick dark hair glossy in the moonlight, the flames of the fire glittering in her dark eyes, her tawny skin glowing. She made a gesture with her hands as she danced, a kind of offering, her small slender fingers drawing to her hips and then opening out to me like a flower. And I was flooded in that moment with such a feeling of tenderness and gratitude . . . and something else . . . desire.

But the spell was broken in the next instant. Indio Juan staggered into the dance circle, clearly drunk. He spoke harshly to the girl, took hold of her wrist, and tried to lead her away. Sounds of disapproval rose from the spectators, a kind of half-hissing, half-hooting noise against this terrible breach of dance etiquette. The girl spoke angrily and shook loose from him, but he grabbed her again. Without even thinking about it, I stepped forward and jabbed him twice sharply in the temple. Indio Juan dropped to his knees and shook his head, dazed for a moment. Then he struggled back to his feet.

There is no boxing tradition among the Apaches. Indeed, Joseph told us that they do not use their fists in such a way, although they enjoy competitive wrestling. Stupidly, I was still in my boxing posture, turned slightly sideways, my hands raised to protect my face. But Indio Juan simply smiled and pulled his knife, and said: *Vas a morir ahora, ojos blancos.* You will die now, White Eyes."

I saw no point in matching my fists against a man armed with a knife, and I opened my hands in a supplicating gesture, as if to say that maybe we could discuss this like gentlemen. I have to admit, I was afraid of Indio Juan.

But from the sidelines, Albert called: "You must fight him, Ned. If you back down now, they will all turn on you. Better to die like a man than to be beaten to death like a dog."

And so I assumed my boxing position again, hands held high, feeling both powerless as well as ridiculous, not to mentioned terrified.

"Protect your body, old sport," Tolley called out. "Think of Tunney versus Dempsey in '27. The thinking man over the brute. You can do it."

If there was any equalizer at all, it was simply that Indio Juan was drunk and perhaps slightly dazed from my jabs. But he did not seem much intimidated by my boxing stance and he advanced upon me, if a bit unsteadily, his knife carving the air, glinting in the firelight. He was smiling on one side of his face, the other, disfigured side locked in its grotesque perpetual grimace of dead flesh, muscle, and nerve like a half-melted mask.

"Jab and move, Giles," Tolley said. "Stay out of his way."

"Tolley, please shut up," I said.

"No, I will not," Tolley said. "I can help you, Giles. Did I tell you that I was lightweight boxing champion at Princeton?"

"You're so full of shit, Tolley." Flat-footed and terrified, I shuffled backward from Indio Juan's approach. I noticed that, unlike the noisy hooting crowd at a white man's fight, not a sound issued from the spectators, who seemed to watch impassively, as if they didn't particularly care who prevailed.

"*No, no, no,* old sport," Tolley said. "Get on your toes, don't let him get you moving backward like that."

"He has a knife, Tolley," I pointed out.

"Which is going to be in your gut if you do not take the offensive," Tolley said. "On your toes, old sport. Jab and move."

And so I took Tolley's advice and stepped forward, jabbing Indio Juan twice in the face. The move caught him off guard and the punches stunned him, but he still managed to cut my arm with his knife.

I dropped back again and circled him, blood running down my arm.

"Well done, Giles!" Tolley said. "Keep it up, man. But you've got to hurt him quickly now. Two lefts and a finishing right this time. Throw the money punch, old sport; you've got one shot and you must give it everything you've got."

I moved in again, but this time Indio Juan was ready and he thrust at me, stabbing me in the side before I was even able to land a punch. But in the heat of the moment, though I knew I'd been cut, I barely felt the knife blade, and I jabbed him twice more, rocking him, and then I stepped in again and threw the right for all I was worth, putting my full weight behind the punch and connecting on the side of his head. Indio Juan went down. And this time he stayed down.

"*Yes!*" Tolley cried out. "*KO!*" He ran to me and raised my arm in the air, dancing around like a madman. "Well done, old sport! Of course, you couldn't have done it without my expert coaching." And for once I had to admit that Tolley was right.

Margaret and Albert had also come over to me. "You're bleeding, Neddy," Margaret said. "We need to have a look at that."

"I'm all right."

There was no cheering exactly from the spectators, but now there came a great deal of animated conversation among them. No one went over to see to Indio Juan.

"They want you to kill him now," Albert said.

"What?"

"You heard me."

"Why?"

"Because he's crazy, and he brings trouble down upon the People. You must kill him."

"He's unconscious, for Christ sake," I said. "What am I supposed to do?"

"Go to him now," Albert said. "Take his knife, and slit his throat with it."

And so I approached Indio Juan where he lay, and I took the knife from his hand, and I placed the blade against his throat.

"Go on, Ned," Albert said. "Do it. It will go better for all of us."

I pressed the blade harder against his throat, but my hand had started to tremble, and finally I dropped the knife. "I'm sorry, Jesus Christ," I said, "I'm sorry, I just can't. Not like this." Of course, I knew even then that I should kill Indio Juan while I had the chance. But I did not. I could not. It is not such an easy thing to kill a man in cold blood, even a bad man. "Why don't you do it, Albert?" I asked.

"Because he is not mine to kill," he answered, "and it will make you look even weaker if you ask another to do it for you."

"I don't think you could do it, either," I said. "You want to be a wild Apache like these people, but you're a civilized man just like me."

When it was clear that I was not going to finish Indio Juan off, two of the Apaches took hold of his legs and dragged him out of the dance circle and left him on the edge of the *ranchería* to sleep it off. The music and dancing resumed as if nothing had happened.

Margaret led me back to the wickiup where she had been lodged. In addition to my camera bag, among the items she had managed to salvage from our plundered goods was the first-aid kit. The knife wound in my side was not deep and she cleaned and bandaged it, but the slash on my

arm required stitches, and this Margaret did herself, neatly and professionally, though I admit I whimpered like a baby throughout the procedure.

"God, you men are such sissies," she said.

"I'm sorry, Mag," I said, "but that damn needle hurts worse than the
knife wound."

"You do understand, Neddy," she said, "that in her dance the girl announced to all that she's marrying you? That's why Indio Juan went off like
that; he wants her for himself."

"Shouldn't we date first?"

"Very funny, sweetheart."

"When's the marriage?" I asked.

"It's more or less already been," said Margaret. "The Apaches don't really
have a formal ceremony. You just move in and begin living together as man
and wife."

"I'm only seventeen years old, Mag," I said. "And she's even younger
than I am. I hadn't really planned on settling down just yet. And especially
not here."

"I wouldn't complain too much if I were you, little brother," Margaret
said. "She saved your life."

"And she almost got me killed," I pointed out. "Either way, it doesn't
do Tolley and Albert much good, does it?" I said. "Or Mr. Browning. We
have to get out of here before dawn, Mag."

"Why don't you sleep, Neddy?" Margaret said. "You can barely keep
your eyes open. I'm going to check on Mr. Browning. Maybe I'll sit with
him for a while."

The pulsing music still played, seemed to vibrate through the ground
beneath me like the heartbeat of the earth itself. I must have dozed off while
Margaret was still bandaging my arm. I began a dream that I was making
love to the girl, that she had come to me in my sleep, and opened my pants,
and pulled me out and mounted me. I remember the wet warmth and snug-
ness of her, a reality so unlike any dream I had ever had, so much more real,
and I remember thinking in my dream that this was not at all the way I had
imagined losing my virginity, I wanted to be awake, I wanted to participate.
I woke up then to find her straddling me like a small, fierce animal, her thick

coarse hair spilled across my face and chest as she raised and lowered herself upon me to the cadence of the drums. This coupling seemed far less an act of love or even passion, as it did one of elemental mating. I had the sense that in this way the girl was protecting her sacred womb, a kind of preemptive breeding which would ensure that no matter what happened to me, she would not have to carry Indio Juan's child. I put my arms around her and held her and whispered, *"Está bien."* I felt her relax against me, felt the hard urgency leave her body as she settled into a slower, softer rhythm, something that felt a bit more like lovemaking. *"There,"* I said, *"there."*

I took her by the shoulders and lifted her from my chest, pushed the hair from her face and looked in her eyes, which still would not meet mine. I took her face in my hands and turned it toward me until she was forced to look at me, her dark bottomless eyes impenetrable. *"I don't even know you,"* I whispered. *"Yo no sé nada acerca de ti.* I don't even know your name."

"Chideh," the girl said, and she lay back down on my chest and began to move upon me again. "Chideh."

I must have fallen asleep afterward, because I was suddenly awakened by a terrible, high-pitched scream. The girl was gone. I pushed aside the blanket over the opening of the wickiup and looked outside; the moon had moved all the way across the sky but it was still night. The musicians still played but the music had taken on a new raw edge, even more disjointed, and the sounds that came from the dance were no longer of celebration, but of anger and contention. The scream came again, and I knew whose it was. I ran toward the sound.

The Apaches had discovered Tolley's stash of wine, seven or eight bottles' worth, and three bottles of mescal, which he had cushioned in two of the packs that had been filled with grain for the stock in case grass became scarce on our journey. Because the bottles had been concealed in this way, they must have escaped initial detection by our captors, but now someone had uncovered them and brought them to the dance. The Apaches had pried the corks out with their knives and swilled the wine down as fast as they could. They drank the mescal in somewhat more modest gulps, passing the bottle among themselves. A number of them were already very drunk. Some people still danced, but they stumbled and bumped into one another and fell to the ground, laughing or quarreling, wrestling one another drunkenly, so that you could hardly tell if they were making love or fighting. The music itself had degenerated into a mad, rhythmless cacophony, the music that one might expect to hear from an orchestra of madmen. Or in hell.

As I came into the light of the fire, I heard Tolley's terrified scream again and I saw the silhouettes of two bodies hanging by their feet from the crossbar where the deer carcasses upon which we had feasted earlier had hung. I pushed through the small drunken crowd that had gathered to watch. Tolley and Albert were suspended from the crossbeam, their hands tied behind their backs, their heads suspended a couple of feet off the ground. A boy was raking hot coals from the fire into small piles under each of their heads. Joseph had told us of this torture, in which the Apaches slow-cook a captive's head until his brain explodes. Albert remained stoically silent, but Tolley screamed and blubbered pitifully.

"Oh, please, God no, please don't do this, I beg you, oh God, please, I'll do anything, please no . . . oh God, it's so hot, please let me down."

Those who were watching passed a mescal bottle around, laughing and mimicking Tolley's terrified cries. I stepped forward and slapped the boy across the back of his head, sending him sprawling into the ashes, and kicked the piles of coals out from under Tolley and Albert's heads.

"Oh God, Giles, is it you, thank God, cut me down, please, get me down from here, please. It's so hot."

Three of the Apache men who had been watching approached threateningly. But by now they were already so drunk that they could barely walk, let alone fight, and I easily knocked them down. The others watching seemed to find this inordinately amusing and they laughed at their friends until they were rolling around on the ground in drunken hilarity. They seemed to have lost all focus and paid no more attention to me.

I untied Albert's hands first. The ropes by which they had been hoisted up the crossbar were secured to the poles on either side of it and I lowered him to the ground. *"What the hell's taking you so long?"* Tolley said, *"Good God, get me down, Giles, please."*

We untied Tolley's rope and lowered him. "It's all right, Tolley," Albert said. "You're all right, you're okay. It's over."

But Tolley was weeping now, in great heaving sobs. *"Oh God . . . please, get me out of this nightmare . . . please, I want to go home now . . . oh God . . . they're savages, they're insane."*

"Where are Joseph and Margaret?" I asked Albert.

"Margaret went to check on Mr. Browning some time ago," he answered, "before the drinking began. My grandfather got drunk with Charley and passed out. He has not had a drink of alcohol in ten years."

"And Jesus?"

"I haven't seen the boy."

We moved farther away from the fires, fading into the shadows beyond the dance circle. Most of the Apaches were by now completely incapacitated by the alcohol, the music and dancing had come to an abrupt halt, and many had passed out where they stood, in a twisted jumble of bodies, like some strange scene of war carnage. Others sat on the ground staring vacantly in drunken stupors. We knew that this was our chance to escape. Encouraged by that possibility, Tolley managed to pull himself together, and we all hurried back up to the cave.

We found Margaret there, sitting with Mr. Browning, who was conscious now, but still very weak. Down below, the *ranchería* had fallen suddenly and strangely silent, and the fires had burned down to glowing coals.

"Gentlemen, I am so very relieved to see that you are safe," said Mr. Browning weakly.

"What happened down there?" Margaret asked. "It sounds like a madhouse."

"They found Tolley's stash of wine," Albert said.

"We can get out of here," I said. "No one is even guarding us anymore. We can slip down, take some mules, and leave. By the time they wake up from their binge, we'll be long gone. How are you feeling, Mr. Browning? Can you travel?"

"You must go without me, sir," he said. "I will only slow you up."

"Unlike your ignominious Lord Crowley, Mr. Browning," said Tolley, "I do not abandon my staff in the wilderness."

"And I am not leaving without my grandfather," Albert said.

"What about Jesus?" asked Margaret. "We don't even know where he is."

"If I may be permitted to offer an opinion on the subject?" said Mr. Browning.

"Of course you may, Mr. Browning," Margaret said.

"Even with a head start," he said, "if we all try to leave together, they will track us down again, long before we reach the expedition. We have witnessed with what great facility they are able to move in this country. We wouldn't have a prayer of outrunning them, especially with me holding you up."

"We're not leaving you, Mr. Browning," I said.

"I'm afraid that you shall have to, sir," he said. "I'm afraid that I'm quite incapable of traveling."

"He's right, Ned," Margaret said. "Our best chance is for you, Tolley, and Albert to go. I'll stay here with Mr. Browning. We know they're not going to kill me, or the boy, and I might be able to help protect them."

"I'm married into the tribe now, remember, Mag?" I said. "I'll be safe here, too. You go with Albert and Tolley. I'll stay with Mr. Browning."

"Don't be a fool, Neddy," she said. "As long as Indio Juan is alive, you're not safe. You wouldn't last another day here."

"What about my grandfather?" Albert asked.

"If your grandfather has passed out, Albert," said Margaret, "he's hardly going to be able to travel. And Joseph, too, can take care of himself here."

"I must insist that you not stay here on my account, miss," Mr. Browning said. "Nor you, sir. I, too, am quite capable of looking after myself."

"I'm staying, and that's all there is to it," Margaret said. "I'll be all right. Get out of here now, Ned. All of you. It's our only chance and you're wasting valuable time."

Tolley, Albert, and I looked at one another. It was an impossible decision to make. Were we cowards for running, abandoning our friends, and in Albert's case, his grandfather, in order to save our own skins? Was I so afraid of Indio Juan that I would let Margaret stay here in my place? Did we all feel some flicker of relief that we were the ones chosen to leave? Yes . . . probably so.

"I'm sure that I shall be quite recovered when you return with the cavalry, gentlemen," Mr. Browning said bravely. "And ready to resume my full duties, sir."

"Take care of the lady, will you, Mr. Browning?" I said.

"Of course I will, sir," he said.

We each shook Mr. Browning's hand and hugged Margaret good-bye. "We'll be back for you, Mag," I said. "I promise you that."

"I know you will, sweetie," she said. "You're doing the right thing, the only thing. Don't worry about me. I'll be fine."

We didn't want to risk walking through the *ranchería* again and so Tolley, Albert, and I took a circuitous route around it to reach the edge of the meadow where the stock had been turned out for the night. It was so quiet that you could hear the sounds of the animals grazing, ripping grass from the ground, and an occasional contented sigh as they chewed. The moon was lower in the sky now, but still provided enough silvery light that the grazing animals were each perfectly defined, casting their thin shadows across the meadow.

We rested for a moment on the edge of the meadow. We were filthy and bloody from the trials of the past twenty-four hours, our clothes torn, Tolley and Albert's faces streaked with black soot, their hair singed. And we were as exhausted as any of us had ever been in our lives. Were it not for the fear that fueled us, we could have curled up right here in the cool grass among the peacefully grazing stock and slept. But now there was just the faintest streak of dawn on the eastern horizon, and we knew that we must keep moving.

A single boy guarded the herd. He sat cross-legged on the ground, wrapped closely in a blanket against the cool mountain air. We stood watching him for a moment, trying to decide what to do next. We assumed that there must be a few in the *ranchería* who had not indulged in the alcohol and who had gone back to their lodgings when the drinking began, and that one shout from the boy would bring them running. "We're going to have to take him with us," Albert said finally. "It might even be useful to us later to have a hostage. But one of us is going to have to sneak up on him, get a hand over his mouth and a gag on him before he can alert the others."

We moved around through the trees into position behind the boy. I crawled on my stomach toward him through the cool grass, moving very slowly, certain that he would hear me. But he never moved and I wondered if he might have dozed off in his sitting position. When I was directly behind him, I rose quickly to my knees, clamped one arm across his chest and with the other hand covered his mouth and pulled him over backward onto the ground. I held him tightly there, and after his initial panicked struggle, he lay perfectly still, rigid. Tolley and Albert came to us. Albert slipped a bandanna in place and pulled it tight across the boy's mouth as I removed my hand. He tied the boy's hands behind his back, and we rolled him over to have a look at him in the moonlight. It was Jesus.

The boy's eyes welled up with tears of relief as I removed the gag. "What the hell are you doing here, kid? Why did they let you guard the stock?"

"I am not guarding the stock," he said. "The Apaches who take me are *borracho*. They forget to tie me up. I am going to run away but I do not know where to go. I do not know where to find you, Señor Ned. So I come here. I think maybe if you can run away, you come here, too, to get mules."

"You think right, kid. Let's get the hell out of here."

We caught several of our old mules who were hobbled with the others and even managed to recover some of our tack, which had been piled on the edge of the meadow. As I was saddling my mule, I felt a light touch on my arm and turned to see *la niña bronca* standing before me. She smiled shyly. "*¿Ya te vas, marido mio?*" she said. "You are leaving me, my husband."

"I'm sorry, I have to go," I said. "*Tengo que irme, lo siento.*"

"*¿Regresarás?*"

"Yes, I'll be back."

She nodded. "You will bring the Mexican soldiers and the White Eyes with you."

"I only want my friends back," I said. "I don't want to hurt you."

Then she did a strange thing. She put a hand on her belly and she said: *"Dzaltsa. Estoy embarazada de tu bebé."*

"That's not possible. How can you know that already?"

"Sí. Tu bebé."

"I have to go now," I said. *"Tengo que salir ahora."*

The girl hugged me then, holding on tight, and I hugged her back, feeling her hard, slender body fitting itself against me, her breasts against my chest, her strange earthy scent that was part of me now.

"I'll come back to you, Chideh," I whispered to her.

"Sí, mi marido," she whispered. And then she was gone.

It was nearly dawn by the time we mounted and rode away from the *ranchería*. Our only hope was that the Apaches would be sleeping it off for at least a few more hours, and that by the time they finally woke up, they would be too sick to follow us. Our next greatest hope was that the expedition wasn't too far behind and that we would be able to find them.

"Do you really think you know the way out of here, Albert?" Tolley asked after we had set out.

"I may have grown up on the reservation and in the White Eyes Indian schools," Albert said. "But I still have an infallible sense of direction. It's in our blood, passed down by a hundred generations of wanderers."

"I saw for myself how Apache you still are," said Tolley.

"Not Apache enough," said Albert. "Neither a White Eyes, nor a real Apache. My own people tried to put me to death."

"When they dangled us from the spit, you didn't utter a sound," Tolley said. "How much more Apache can you get than that?"

"They wanted to see us suffer, Tolley. They wanted to hear us scream and beg for our lives. I did not wish to give them the satisfaction."

"Well, they got their money's worth out of me, didn't they?" said Tolley.

Dawn was coming on fast now, the moon not yet set behind the peaks of the sierras, nor the sun yet risen, that brief spectral time between day and night, moonlight and sunlight. The air was cool and dead still, which seemed to amplify the clattering of the mules' hooves as we climbed the pass. Every now and then one of the animals would dislodge a rock off the trail and send it tumbling down into the canyon below; you could hear it bouncing, echoing hollowly all the way to the bottom, and it seemed that the sound must be audible to the whole world.

But for the steady clack of hooves and creak of saddles, we traveled silently under the cold morning moon and I think we must have all been thinking the same thing as we looked out over the endless sierras lying like a rough dark sea in all directions. How could we ever expect to find the expedition out here? What could we possibly have been thinking? What fools we had been, and were. How long would it take the Apaches to track us down? What a lonely place to die. We had left Margaret, Mr. Browning, and Joseph behind in that terrifying world on the other side of this one, a world that seemed already like a dream, peopled by dream people. We wondered if we would ever see our friends again or would they simply fade gradually away in our memories as is the way of dreams, until the specific details became only a vague feeling and then the feeling itself is gone.

The sun rose before the moon set, two enormous twin orbs on either side of the horizon. I remembered with a pang of heartsickness the already indistinct image I had of the girl, her rich, loamy scent, her brown skin and sleek, hard limbs, her dark impenetrable eyes, the way she moved like a spirit. I tried to bring her back into sharp focus as one focuses a camera lens, but I could not. I understood that we did not inhabit the same earth, could not live in each other's worlds; in mine she curled up in a fetal position and starved herself to death, and in hers I was stoned to death by savage women at dawn.

"Albert," I asked, breaking the silence, "does the word *chideh* mean anything in Apache?"

"It means 'blackbird,'" he said.

"That's her name," I said.

"Whose name?"

"The girl. My wife. Her name is Chideh. Blackbird. That's pretty, isn't it?"

Now, as we rode through this limbo space between the setting moon and the rising sun, amid all this wild country that lay around us, nothing looked even remotely familiar to me. Only Albert seemed to know the way back, and so we followed him blindly, as dumb and trusting as cattle trailing the lead cow.

And, in fact, after several hours we reached the place of our original abduction, and here we stopped and dismounted, and walked the narrow trail above the canyon, leading our mules in single file.

"Right down there," Albert said, pointing to the bottom. "There's your poor damn horse, Tolley." And we all heard again the terrible screaming of the horse falling into the abyss.

The sun was high enough now that the world looked a bit less foreign and frightening. We were beyond being tired, aware of how exposed we were in the daylight, but simply too exhausted to care. We imagined the Apaches waking up, discovering our flight, perhaps already in hot pursuit. How long would it take them on fresh mounts, moving like the wind across these peaks, to find us? Not long.

"We're going to have to rest for a while," Albert said. "Maybe sleep for a few hours."

"I say we push on," I said. "I'll bet they're after us already."

"Easy for you to say, Giles," Tolley said. "You probably had a little nap last night, didn't you, after you consummated your marriage? While Albert and I dangled from the spit?" He took off his hat. "Look at the top of my head; it's sunburned."

"It could have been worse, Tolley," I said.

"Indeed it could have, old sport," Tolley said. "I haven't even thanked you properly for saving my life. I don't know how I can ever repay you."

"You already have, Tolley," I said. "Remember your boxing instruction? By the way, I haven't had a chance to ask you, were you really lightweight champ at Princeton?"

"Not exactly," he admitted. "But I *was* in the boxing club. And I could tell with one look at you that you were a lousy high school palooka."

"We'll compromise," Albert said. "We rest for one hour."

"I'll stand guard," I offered. "You're right, I did get a little sleep last night."

We found a small clearing by a spring, watered and hobbled the mules.

The others collapsed on the ground and fell instantly asleep. I sat with my back against a tree. I had realized earlier that when I ran from the wickiup toward Tolley's screams, I left behind my camera, which Margaret had recovered, in its bag with all my film and all but the one notebook I still had in my pocket. I hadn't dared go back for it before we left the *ranchería*. If we ever get out of here, I'm going to catch hell from Big Wade for losing his Leica, that much is sure.

NOTEBOOK VI:

Among the Sierra Madre Apaches
(by Margaret Hawkins, filling in for Ned Giles)

INTERESTING READING, LITTLE BROTHER, ALTHOUGH I'M SORRY TO tell you that you're deeply misguided on several scores. For one thing, you clearly know nothing whatsoever about women—me, *la niña bronca*, or any others for that matter—but then again, what man, let alone a seventeen-year-old pipsqueak such as yourself, really does? At the same time, I find amusing the modern conceit of photographers that they are somehow amateur ethnographers, able to capture the essence of a culture in individual "snapshots." But really, how severely inadequate, not to mention unscientific, such an approach is.

So you see, in addition to trying to keep your notebooks (not to mention your precious camera and film) safe for you, I've now appropriated them and I'm going to make a few entries of my own in your absence. Chances are these are going to be destroyed before this is all over, anyway, and assuming that you ever even make it back here, you may still never get to read what I have to say. So far I've managed to convince my Apache hosts that these notebooks are BIG medicine, not to be tampered with unless they are willing to risk some very, very bad fortune, indeed. Among the many practical lessons I learned living among the Yanomami in Brazil is that most aboriginal people have in common a certain superstitious reverence for the written word. Because theirs are spoken rather than written languages, they tend to ascribe all kinds of magical properties to books and to those who make them. Which is one reason the Bible has always been a relatively easy sell for missionaries to native peoples, who tend to be unduly impressed that all those stories and lives can exist within that single bound and printed space. What could that be, after all, but magic?

Let me get a few things clear first, Neddy. In your entries about me, you seem rather overly concerned with my romantic (or maybe just my sexual) life, which strikes me as a particularly "male" point of view on your part. I must remind you that the reason I came along on this expedition in the first place was for the rare opportunity to do ethnographic fieldwork, access to which women in my profession have traditionally been denied. We (women, that is) have been largely relegated to doing our research in the libraries and universities, interpreting the fieldwork of our allegedly stronger, heartier, more adventurous male colleagues. Having grown up in the field, albeit very much in the shadow of my father (in more ways than one), when I decided to enter the profession myself, I had no intention of doing so as a glorified secretary serving the men. And so now I'm right where I dreamed of being—as deep in the field as one can get—among the lost Apaches themselves. Any anthropologist in America, male or female, would surely view this as an unparalleled professional opportunity.

And yet, speaking of conceit, I have to admit that under the circumstances of the past forty-eight hours, it's hard to look at my present situation as a good career move. At the same time, it seems both ironic, and a bit unfair, that whereas a male anthropologist would surely be praised for getting "close" to his subject in the best Malinowskian tradition of direct observation, I'm sure that as a woman, I shall be accused of having compromised my professional objectivity . . . and possibly much worse. Although I'm not at all convinced that American anthropology has adequately addressed the question of where one draws the line in ethnographic fieldwork between being an observer and a participant, one thing for certain is that becoming the slave woman of an infamous Apache warrior is sure to be considered a quantum leap over the line.

In any case, little brother, you are clearly not much interested in anthropological methodology, so I will try to confine my comments here to telling my side of the story that you have begun, the part that you are missing right now, and a bit of the history that you cannot know. I suppose that the very least of our worries at this moment is whether or not these notebooks will survive, when the much larger question is whether or not any of us will survive. Still there is something rather comforting about writing in these pages, isn't there? They give the notebook keeper a certain illusion of immortality, in the same way that terminally ill people like to make plans for the future in the misguided belief that they can't possibly die if they have a train reservation.

Here then are some of the things you need to know, Neddy, both those that have happened to me and those that I have pieced together since I have been here. It is a story that does not fit in your viewfinder, that cannot be told in photographs, or in simple notebook entries describing the events of our days. Tolley is quite right about that.

After you, Albert, and Tolley left, my first order of business was to try to keep poor Mr. Browning alive, and as comfortable as possible under the circumstances. It was quiet below in the *rancheria*, the fires burned all the way down to smoldering embers. When Mr. Browning dozed off again, I slipped down from the cave. What a scene there to behold. The area in which the dance had been held looked like a battlefield littered with living corpses, or as if some terrible plague had struck, bodies lying in twisted heaps, the acrid mingling odors of smoke, gunpowder, and vomit. The revelers slept fitfully in the predawn stillness, some breathing heavily and snoring, others moaning sickly or mumbling insensibly in their drunken repose. A feeble hand reached out and grabbed my ankle as I passed, but I kicked it away and hurried on.

With some difficulty I finally located the wickiup where I had patched you up, and there I changed back into my own clothes—my boots, riding breeches, and jacket. I took a woolen blanket and retrieved your satchel with your camera gear and these notebooks, and I found some strips of dried jerky and a piece of flatbread to take back for Mr. Browning, even though he had not yet eaten what the girl had brought to him last night. I went down to the creek and filled an earthen jug with water. The water was clear and cold and in the breaking light of dawn sparkled off the riffled surface of the creek in a way that in different circumstances might have seemed cheerful.

Mr. Browning woke with a start when I got back to the cave. He seemed groggy and disoriented, and even paler than before. I asked him how he was feeling.

"A little foggy, miss, the truth be told," he said. "I've a terrible headache."

"Drink a little of this water," I said, holding the jug to his lips. "I've brought you a little something to eat."

He drank. "Ah yes, that's lovely, miss, very kind of you," he said. "But really I don't have much of an appetite."

"We're all alone here now, Mr. Browning," I said. "Just you and me. Don't you think you could call me Margaret? And I'll call you Harold."

"Very well, Margaret."

"Yes, that's much better, isn't it, Harold?"

"Indeed," he said, and he smiled . . . dear, sweet Mr. Browning . . . what a fine gentle soul. "What do you think will happen, miss . . . oh, terribly sorry . . . what do you think will happen, *Margaret,* when they discover that the others have departed?"

"I don't know, Harold. My guess is that they'll go after them."

"Yes, I would expect so," he said. He chewed a little of the jerky and tried to take a bite of the flatbread. "Oh dear, a bit hard, that, isn't it?" he said. "Liable to break a tooth on that, one is."

"You should probably try to get a little more sleep," I said.

"I am rather tired. Can't seem to keep my eyes open."

"I'm tired, too," I said. "I brought us a blanket. I hope you won't mind my asking, but would it be all right if I curled up next to you, Harold? It's a little chilly, isn't it?"

"I wouldn't mind at all, Margaret," Mr. Browning said. "Indeed, it would be a great comfort to me."

So I curled up behind Mr. Browning and covered us with the blanket, and I put my arm around him and held him. "Before we fall asleep, tell me something about your life, Harold," I said. "Just anything at all . . . You never told me if you'd ever been married. Or if you had a family."

"My employers have always been my family, miss," he said.

"Haven't you ever been in love, Harold?"

"Yes, Margaret, I have. Once."

"Tell me about her."

"All right, Margaret," he said. "Have I told you that I spent several years in Africa with my former employer, Lord Crowley? Yes, in Kenya. You see, the lord was involved in gold-mining operations there. We first went over in . . . in . . . twenty-one, I believe it was. Spent the better part of the decade on the continent . . . a fascinating time really . . ."

And so Mr. Browning began to tell me the story of the woman he had fallen in love with. "Ours was a forbidden love, Margaret," he said. "She was

African, a member of the Kikuyu tribe, and the servant of one of Lord Crowley's business colleagues. She was so stunningly beautiful . . ." Mr. Browning talked on softly, remembering his forbidden love, the only love of his life, until his voice trailed away, and he drifted off to sleep. And I, too, slept, curled beside him, my arm around him. When I woke again, the moon was low on the horizon and dawn was coming on, and I knew from the cold, still feel of his body against me that Mr. Browning was dead.

I sat for a while in the cave with him, just to keep him company, and because I couldn't bear to leave him alone. I spoke to him, and told him things that I have never told before. And I wept for dear, sweet Mr. Browning. The *ranchería* lay silent below in the deathly quiet of daybreak. I thought about how simple it would be for me just to walk away from here. Except, of course, that I had nowhere to go. I wouldn't last a day out there alone, and in any case, they'd only find me and bring me back. Oddly, despite my grief over his passing, with Mr. Browning gone, I was suddenly less afraid, I felt a certain relief, for now I had only myself to worry about. I decided that I would put my professional hat squarely on again, and in the same way that you, Neddy, hide behind your camera, I would thus be able to maintain the illusion of safety. Another lesson I had learned in the Amazon was that one must never allow the natives even a glimpse of one's fear, for to display weakness is to invite attack.

I walked back down to the *ranchería*. As the sun rose, a number of last night's revelers crawled off to their wickiups; others were just waking up, so sick and hungover that they barely seemed to notice me. I had in mind to find the girl, and if I could, Jesus, to see that he was safe. I didn't know where to begin my search and so I started peering randomly inside the huts and wickiups. But before I could find either of them, I ran directly into Indio Juan.

He was sitting on the ground in front of one of the wickiups and appeared to have just woken up himself. He seemed dazed and half drunk still, and when he saw me he looked at me murderously and struggled to his feet. I should have run right then, but instead, stupidly, stubbornly, I stood my ground. I blamed him for Mr. Browning's death and my anger and grief overcame any fear I had of him in that moment. He staggered toward me; I could smell the stench coming off him—the sweet-sour odor of alcohol, the acrid stink of vomit that stained the front of his shirt, and a deeper, rotten scent that I think is simply the smell of his evil. He held his arms out to me.

"*Has vuelto con Indio Juan, mi esclava bonito,*" he said. "You have come back to Indio Juan, my pretty slave girl."

"Fuck you, you filthy swine," and I slapped him as hard as I could.

Even in his half-drunken stupor, Indio Juan's next movements were so brutally fast and rough that I was completely overwhelmed. He grabbed me by the hair, yanked me to the ground, and fell atop me. He is not a large man, shorter than I, but I was astonished by his sheer brute strength. I tried to bite him and he struck me savagely across the face. He held me by the throat, cutting off my wind, tore open my blouse, and pried my legs apart. Unable to negotiate the complexities of my riding breeches, he drew his knife, intending simply to cut himself access. I knew then that I was going to die and I experienced a peculiar sense of detachment. I remember thinking, *Ah, yes, of course, now I remember why women aren't given ethnographic fieldwork assignments* . . . In the next instant I heard a hollow ringing sound, and the breaking of glass, and Indio Juan went limp atop me. I looked up to see *la niña bronca* standing over us, holding one of Tolley's empty wine bottles by the neck.

"I hope you killed the bastard," I said.

The girl and I sat cross-legged together in the wickiup. I had cleaned up at the creek and changed my torn shirt. The side of my face was swollen from where Indio Juan had struck me and it was painful to talk. The girl had built a small fire in front of the wickiup and put a tin coffeepot on to boil.

"Where did you go last night?" I asked her in Spanish.

"I took some of the young girls to hide in the caves," she said. "When it is like that, no one is safe, bad things happen."

"Do you know where Joseph is?" I asked.

She nodded.

"Jesus?"

"He has run away with the others."

"You know that Ned and the others are gone?"

"Yes, I saw them before they left."

"Did you know that Mr. Browning is dead?"

The girl looked away from me with a sudden frightened look in her eyes. I remembered that the Apaches are terrified of death; to even mention the word is enough to conjure up the dead person's ghost. I should have said that Mr. Browning was "gone."

I took her face in my hand and turned it toward me and made her look me in the eye. "Mr. Browning is *dead*. Your people killed him when they hit him over the head with the rock. Do you understand me? He was your friend. He was kind to you. He was a good, gentle man. And now he is *dead. Murdered*. For no reason."

The girl nodded and tears welled up in her eyes. "My mother, too, is dead," she whispered. "And my sister . . ."

"That's right, sweetheart," I said. "And they, too, were murdered by bad men for no reason. Ned and the others are going to bring the Mexican soldiers and the Americans back here. They just want the boy, Geraldo. If you do not give him up, more of your people will die. Please, I must speak to your grandfather."

A woman tended the fire in front of the white Apache's wickiup. A cradleboard in which was strapped a cheerful smiling baby was propped up beside her. The girl spoke to the woman, who answered crossly, and gestured for us to enter the wickiup, as if she was completely disgusted with its occupants and wanted nothing to do with them herself.

The air was dim and rank inside, and as our eyes adjusted I saw that Joseph and the white Apache, Charley, both lay asleep, sprawled atop the blankets. A not quite empty bottle of mescal lay on its side between them. Seated cross-legged in the rear of the wickiup was the old blind woman Siki; she stared straight ahead out of milky eyes. The girl spoke to her softly and the old woman smiled and returned the girl's greeting.

I gently shook Joseph's shoulder until he opened his eyes. He looked at me blankly for a long time, as if trying to place me in his memory. Finally he dragged himself into a seated position, his eyes hollow and sick. "Where is my grandson?" he asked.

"He is safe for now," I said. "But while you were drunk last night, they strung him up over the fire. If it hadn't been for Ned, they'd have cooked his brains."

"I have not had a drink of alcohol since the last time my friend Harley Rope and I got drunk at his shack in White Tail," Joseph said. "That night Harley went outside to take a piss and when he finished he walked out to the highway and lay down and fell asleep. He was run over by a truck just before dawn. Harley was my last friend from the old days. We had ridden together and scouted together and had been in Florida, Alabama, and Oklahoma together. Once a week, I walked to his shack, or he to mine, and we got drunk together. But after Harley died, I decided that I would not drink alcohol anymore."

"What made you drink last night, Joseph?" I asked.

He didn't answer for a long time, just stared hollowly into space. Finally he nodded and said, "I was feeling pretty bad."

"How are you feeling now?"

He smiled wanly. "Not too good."

"What were you feeling bad about?"

"It was a very long time ago . . ."

"Tell me."

He looked at the white Apache, who still slept heavily. "This man's name is Charley," Joseph said. "Charley McComas. I caught him when he was a boy."

"Yes, I heard you say so yesterday," I said. "I've read about little Charley McComas. Kidnapped by the Apaches outside Silver City, New Mexico, when he was six years old. His parents were killed during the abduction. The boy was never found."

"That's because he is here," Joseph said.

"And you're sure it's really him?"

"Of course," Joseph said. "I caught him. I killed his mother."

Here then, Neddy, is the story that I have cobbled together about little Charley McComas, both from that which Joseph has told me about that long-ago day of his abduction, and what Charley himself, his Apache mother, the old woman Siki, and the girl, his granddaughter, your wife, Chideh, have all related to me in bits and pieces during my days here. Of course, like so many native cultures theirs is a strictly oral history, the stories passed down through the generations, subtly altered and elaborated upon in the retellings until it's hard to say exactly where the truth leaves off and the legend begins. Further adding to this difficulty is the fact that I myself have taken some creative license in order to fill in the blanks, which, to be sure, is poor science, but I hope at least makes for interesting reading for you. And although I would be drummed out of my profession if I ever admitted it to any of my colleagues, in the little time that I have spent among these people, I am increasingly of the opinion that one can more accurately describe them with an act of imagination than with the strict facts. Therefore, without further ado . . .

Little Charley McComas and his parents were traveling in a buckboard wagon on the way to Lordsburg from their home in Silver City. It was late March of the year 1883, and the McComases had stopped to have a picnic under a walnut tree. For dessert they were having a cherry pie that had been baked by the nice woman at whose inn in Mountain Home they had stayed the night before, and with whose children Charley had played. The pie had still been warm when they left Mountain Home that morning and Charley had been able to smell it in the wagon all morning long.

They had stopped to eat their picnic under a walnut tree. It was a lovely spring day and his mother had taken the picnic basket out of the back of the wagon and laid all the food out on a red-checked tablecloth that she had spread on the ground under the tree. They sat cross-legged on the tablecloth, just like Indians, Charley remembered thinking, and they ate cold fried chicken and hard-boiled eggs and fresh bread that Mrs. Dennis had also baked for them. Charley's father was a judge, a stern, severe man of whom Charley was a bit afraid. His mother was pretty and gay, vivacious, a good tonic to her sometimes dour husband. They were having a fine time at their picnic. The cherry pie was set out under a white cloth napkin. Charley could hardly wait to eat a piece for dessert. He'd been looking forward to that pie all morning.

But Charley McComas never got to eat his pie. Because at that moment a hole tore open in the universe and his old world began to rush out of it, like water swirling down a drainpipe. The horses in their traces suddenly raised their heads and nickered softly and Charley and his parents looked up to see the Apaches thundering up the arroyo toward them, like some terrible vision from hell, riding hard and yipping in a way that would eventually become very familiar to Charley, but at the time sounded so strange and savage.

A cloud of dust roiled up from the Apaches' horses' hooves, which made it appear as if they were riding out of a misty dream, and Charley wasn't so much afraid at first as he was fascinated at this spectacle of *real* Indians riding down upon them.

His father said: "Get in the wagon. *Now!*" And his mother snatched Charley to his feet, her own terror washing over him like a stink; she ran with him, stumbling, to the back of the buckboard, where she half lifted, half threw the boy in. She screamed at him in a high thin voice he had never before heard, ordering him to lie down. His father picked up his Winchester repeating rifle, and both his mother and father climbed into the front seat of the wagon. His father took the reins and slapped the horses' rumps with them, hollering them into motion. Why did his father think that he could outrun mounted Apaches in a buckboard wagon? Later, after Charley grew up and became an accomplished Apache warrior in his own right and the People told the story of his abduction, he would think less of this White Eyes man who had been his father for this terrible lapse of judgment. It would have been far better to release the horses from their traces, to cut them out if necessary, or even to shoot them where they stood and take cover behind the wagon. His father could have held the Apaches off for a long time with his Winchester, and with his Colt pistol, at least killing a few of them, and possibly aborting the attack or at least slowing it, buying time until help came.

Before they had gone fifty yards in the wagon, the first bullet struck his father in the arm. He cried out and handed the reins over to Charley's mother, taking the Winchester from her. "*Go!*" he said. It was the last word

Charley would ever hear his father speak. *"Go!"* and his father leaped from the wagon to the ground and began running toward the approaching Apaches, firing his rifle. Whether he had initially panicked or not, it was a courageous, if futile move on Judge McComas's part, to try to divert the Apaches while his wife and son escaped. Charley watched solemnly, trance-like, from the back of the wagon as more bullets struck his father until finally he stopped running and fell to his knees, still jacking shells into his rifle and firing, even as he was dying. In their retelling of the story, the People always said that Judge McComas had been a brave man and had died honorably, and for that they did not scalp him or mutilate his body.

Charley and his mother did not make it far. A bullet struck one of the horses and it fell dead in its harness and the wagon came to an abrupt halt. The Apaches approached on their horses, surrounding them, yipping and waving their rifles overhead in triumph. His mother leaped from her side of the wagon and tried to come to Charley, who sat up now in the back of the wagon, but they blocked her way and one of them, the man called Goso, struck her mercilessly in the face with his rifle butt, knocking her to the ground. Charley hollered and tried to jump from the back of the wagon and go to his mother's aid, but one of them stepped off his horse onto the back of the wagon and held the boy there. He struggled fiercely against the man, which caused the others to laugh at the boy's feistiness— there was nothing that the Apaches admired more than the display of courage—but he was only six years old, after all, and the man easily subdued him.

His mother's face was bleeding from the blow of the rifle butt, and she was unconscious, and the Apaches stripped the dress from her body, careful not to tear it. The warrior Goso would give that dress to his young wife, Siki, who would wear it, with some modifications, for years to come. And for a long time, the boy Charley would think of his White Eyes mother every time he saw Siki wearing that dress, until eventually the memory of her faded, and the dress had no more significance than any other which his Apache mother wore.

Wielding their knives as precisely as surgeons, the Apaches cut the shoes from his mother's feet, cut the stockings from her legs, cut the corset from her torso; these articles they did not care about preserving because no women among the People would wear such things. Because he was the leader of the raid, Goso took Charley's mother by the hair and raised his breechcloth and, laughing, mounted her from behind the way that Charley had seen dogs do, although he did not yet understand why exactly they did this. His mother had begun to regain consciousness and she uttered a terrible moan that made the other Apaches laugh. Goso was finished with her in a very short time, and the next man mounted her, and the next. And when they had all finished with her, his mother weeping softly, begging for mercy, begging not for herself but for her son's life, the man named Goso struck her two sharp blows to the back of her head with his rifle butt, crushing her skull, a heavy dull cracking sound like a gourd splitting open. All of this Charley watched as the Apache held him on the back of the wagon. He did not cry.

The warriors now turned their attention to the boy. The one holding Charley and the man named Goso began to quarrel. The one holding him pulled his knife and held it to Charley's throat. Charley was not afraid. He himself had rushed out the hole that had opened in the universe and through which his old life was pouring and it seemed now as if he was floating in space, detached, light as a feather, weightless.

Later, when the story was told, it was always said that the boy Charley never cried; even when the warrior held the knife to his throat, he did not cry, he showed no fear. The Apache intended to cut the boy's head off; by prior agreement, no captives were being taken on this raid of vengeance through White Eyes country. So far they had killed every man, woman, and child they had encountered at the isolated ranches and in the small settlements through which they had swept, stealing stock, stealing guns and ammunition, stealing whatever they could carry off and burning the buildings behind them. As the fires blazed, they had ridden off yipping like coyotes, carrying off the infant babies of the White Eyes they had killed, swinging them overhead by one leg, like twirling a lariat, flinging them away, to spin through the air and crash to their deaths on the hard, rocky ground. All this the Apache raiders had done to avenge the wrongs done the People by the White Eyes in a world gone mad with vengeance.

The boy Charley was not afraid. He looked in the eyes of the man who held the knife to his throat and he did not cry, he did not beg, he did not whimper. He looked straight in the warrior's eyes and he did not make a sound. Charley had the Power. The warrior named Goso spoke sharply again to the man, who finally lowered his knife.

The Apaches plundered the McComases' wagon, taking everything that was of value to them. They stripped the clothes from the judge's body, and collected his Winchester rifle, the Colt revolver, and a good supply of cartridges for both weapons. Then they finished off the abandoned picnic. Charley remembered watching them dip into the cherry pie with their fingers, pushing bright red gobs of it into their mouths, laughing, cherry juice all over their faces. Charley remembered that he never got to taste that cherry pie; they never offered him a bite, even though it had been his pie and his parents' pie, baked especially for them that same morning by nice Mrs. Dennis.

When they had completed their plunder, the Apaches remounted and the man named Goso walked his horse up to Charley on the back of the wagon. He leaned down and took hold of the boy by the scruff of his neck, as one picks up a puppy. Though Charley was only six years old, he was large for his age, weighed nearly seventy-five pounds already, but the man lifted him effortlessly and swung him up behind him on the horse.

"You belong to Goso now, White Eyes," the Apache said in English. "Hang on to me." And as they rode away from the wagon under the walnut tree in Thompson Canyon, away from the stripped, lifeless, violated bodies of little Charley McComas's white parents, away from the first six years of Charley's life, the last bit of his old world drained out through the hole in the universe, and just as suddenly as it had opened up, so did the tear close seamlessly behind him.

And that, Neddy, is how the white Apache they still call Charley came to be here. Now I watched warily as the man himself came awake in the wickiup; he groaned and squinted his eyes with the pain of a burning mescal hangover. He grunted something to the girl, and she answered him back. He sat up, seeming to suddenly fill the wickiup with his bulk, a giant wild-bearded redhead in this world of small brown people.

How odd to think that but for a single twist of fate, being in the wrong place at the wrong time on that March morning in 1883, Charley McComas would surely have grown up to be an upstanding, God-fearing citizen of the white world, a pillar of the community, perhaps, like his father, a judge himself.

Charley looked at Joseph and then he peered at me for a very long time. I wondered when the last time had been that he had seen a white woman, and if he still held some racial memory that identified in the slightest way with white people. Did he think of us as in any way similar? Did he see my blond hair and fair complexion as something we had in common? It occurred to me that our arrival yesterday might have been the first contact he had had with white people since he was six years old, and that his antipathy for the White Eyes might simply be a cultural response learned over the years from the tribal stories.

"¿Cual es su nombre?" I asked. "What is your name?" He did not answer, just looked at me. "I know you speak Spanish, Charley. Why won't you answer me?"

"Because it is considered impolite for a woman to question a man in this manner," said Joseph. "Especially a captive woman."

"Ah, of course, the etiquette of captivity," I said. "How careless of me."

"You must show respect to him," Joseph said.

"I'm not a captive," I said. "I came here of my own free will. As a scientist."

"He does not know what a scientist is," Joseph said. "You are his captive. You must serve and obey him. You must obey his wife."

The white Apache spoke at last, addressing Joseph.

"He wishes to know where the other captives are."

"Mr. Browning is dead in the cave," I said. "Murdered by Indio Juan and his men. I want him properly buried."

"I am sorry," Joseph said. "Mr. Browning was a good man."

"Yes, he was."

"And the others?" Joseph asked. "Tell me where my grandson is."

"I don't know."

"What does that mean? You said that he was safe."

"As far as I know, he is safe," I said. "Safer than he was here at least."

"They have escaped?"

"Does he understand English?" I asked.

"I don't know," Joseph said. "Maybe."

"What do you know?"

And so from Joseph's account, I continue little Charley McComas's story.

Forty-nine years ago, Goso led his raiding party from the murder scene in Thompson Canyon, south across the Burro Mountains, to the Pyramid Mountains, traveling at night across the broad open grasslands of the Animas Valley and finally crossing the border into Mexico. The Apaches knew that they were being pursued, both by army troops and civilian posses, and they kept up a punishing pace, traveling up to seventy-five miles a day, running their horses to exhaustion and replacing them with fresh mounts stolen from the ranches and settlements through which they swept. They slaughtered the spent animals and ate their organs raw so as not to give away their location by making fires.

The warriors were impressed with Charley's endurance, so unlike the other White Eyes captives they had known. The boy was hearty and strong, kept quiet, and did not complain. Where usually they found it necessary to force raw meat down captives' throats in order to make them eat, the first time Goso handed Charley a piece of horse heart, he ate it without hesitation. After the second day, he stopped tethering the boy to his waist, and a day later he gave him his own horse to ride.

On the evening of the seventh day, deep in these mountains, the raiding party rode a perilous canyon trail so narrow in places that they had to ride single file, the horses picking their way carefully through the boulders. A river roiled at the base of the canyon far below, and high above hawks circled the thermals, shrieking. The trail climbed through a natural archway in the rocks and up onto a high grassy bench, where the stolen stock fanned out to graze on the bright green spring grass. From the bench the trail fell away into a small river valley where lay the *ranchería* of the People, Charley McComas's new home.

Already alerted by sentries to the arrival of the raiding party, the women had come out of their wickiups to greet the returning warriors, making their high trilling sound, and the children ran to them, chattering and laughing. They surrounded little Charley, touching him, snatching at his pant legs, shrieking in delight. The boy kept his composure, swatting some of the more aggressive children away, which made everyone laugh.

Perhaps Charley had been destined for this strange new world of noise and color and smell, for he was not afraid. Already the memory of his old life had begun to recede in the same way that even the most vivid dream is eventually overwhelmed by the relentless actuality of the present. So Charley began to forget.

It had been a successful raid and the warriors had brought back many head of stock, and all manner of plunder. That first night a great feast and dance was held in their honor, as had always been the People's way, and the men danced their triumphs before a huge bonfire, where they displayed their war trophies and chanted their tales of the raid. There were drum players and flute players and fiddle players, playing a strange, pulsating music such as little Charley had never heard before.

Goso himself recounted the story of Charley's capture and the boy himself was pushed to his feet and made to dance, which he began to do shyly at first. But all encouraged him and they showed him the steps and soon Charley was dancing with greater and greater abandon, a child caught up in the music and the chanted tales, and though he could not understand the words, he felt the music and the stories deep in his bones, and he danced.

But suddenly the boy stopped dancing and he looked at these people, the women wearing their finest dresses, and the sparkling new jewelry presented them by the returning raiders, the men in their best breechcloths, leggings, and moccasins, others dressed in the boots, shirts, vests, jackets, and hats taken from their victims. From his young eyes, which had already witnessed such unspeakable atrocity, Charley looked out at this magic world, inhabited by these magic people, and he did not hold the horror against them. He was only a child, full of forgiveness and purity and the need to love and be loved. Charley looked out at them and then he did something that the People would always remember, that would enter their legends and be told time and time again when they recounted the old stories. He beat his little chest with his fist, and he cried out: *"I am Charley!"* They were the very first words he had uttered since his abduction, a simple declaration of identity. *"I am Charley!"* He was staking his territory in this new world, and his own name was all he had left to take with him from the old. The musicians stopped playing, the flute players and string players and drummers, the music dissipating into the thin mountain air. The People stopped dancing and all strained to hear what the boy was saying. *"I am Charley!"* he cried again, pounding his chest. *"Charley! Charley!"*

Some of the People, Goso among them, had already spent enough time among the White Eyes that they spoke a little English.

"The captive boy wishes the People to know that his name is Charley," said Goso. The murmuring of the name ran through the crowd. *"Charley."* The Apaches liked the sound of it. *"Charley,"* they repeated, and some of them laughed delightedly at the way the word rolled off their tongues. *"Charley, Charley, Charley."*

The musicians started playing again, the dancers taking up their steps. And little Charley McComas, too, began to dance, a small, stocky, flush-faced, fair-haired boy, dancing before the blazing fire in the hidden Apache *rancheria* in the heart of the Sierra Madre, dancing amidst this dark, wild, ancient race of man, dancing under the stars.

The white Apache's wife entered the wickiup and spoke sternly to me in a harsh, scolding voice. She was a strongly built, large-breasted woman with a broad face, high cheekbones, deep brown eyes, and a certain haughty demeanor.

"What does she want?" I asked Joseph.

"She wishes for the white slave woman to gather firewood for her," Joseph said.

"Tell her I have a name," I said. "It's Margaret. And that I'm not her slave."

"Your name is of no interest to her," Joseph said. "And perhaps you would prefer to be the slave of Indio Juan."

"Is that how it is, then?"

"That is how it is," Joseph said. "The only reason Charley protects you is because his granddaughter requests it. But if you displease him, or his wife, they will cast you out. You will become the property of whoever else wishes to take you in. And if it is Indio Juan, Charley will not interfere again on your behalf."

"I see," I said. It wasn't a terribly difficult choice to make. "I guess I'll go gather firewood, then."

I followed the woman out of the wickiup, the girl behind me. I stopped by the cradleboard to tickle the baby's face; he was an astonishingly handsome, good-natured little creature. He smiled broadly and cooed at me, which seemed to soften somewhat his mother's harsh manner.

"If your mother was Charley's daughter," I asked the girl, "who is this woman? She does not seem old enough to be your grandmother."

"She is Charley's third wife," she answered. "There are so few men left that Charley and the others must take as many wives as they can in order to make more *In'deh* babies." The girl seemed completely unaware of any irony in the fact that this white man was the primary brood stock for the production of Apache babies.

I think that *la niña bronca* was sent along with me to gather wood, not so much because they feared that I would try to escape, but simply to teach me the finer points of the chore. This involved bundling the sticks and branches together and tying them up with leather thongs. On the other end of the thongs was a kind of harness affair that slipped over the forehead, thus distributing the weight onto the neck and shoulders, allowing the bearer to carry heavier and larger loads . . . So much for my role as a professional ethnographer; I had become, in very short order, a slave and beast of burden. It was exhausting work and I was already thoroughly spent from the trials of the past twenty-four hours.

Charley's wife, whose name I have since learned is Ishton, was roasting a piece of meat over the fire and stirring a pot when we returned with our loads of firewood. Joseph and Charley had been down to the creek and had washed off some of their hangover stink and were seated by the fire, as was the old woman Siki. We sat down ourselves. Ishton served everyone a portion of meat and some sort of root vegetable on a tin plate—everyone, that is, but me. The others began eating, ignoring me altogether.

"Wives do not serve slaves," Joseph explained. "You must wait and serve yourself after everyone else has finished . . . if there is any left."

The girl, however, took pity on me, filling a plate with food and handing it to me. As we were eating, another man came to the fire. He clearly had news but waited politely until he was invited to sit and had been served a portion himself. Then he began speaking.

"What's going on, Joseph?" I asked.

"They have discovered that my grandson and the others have escaped," he said.

"Tell Charley that a large expedition of Americans and Mexican soldiers is headed this way," I said. "All they want is the Huerta boy. He could meet them halfway and turn the boy over to them. The expedition will never even have to come here."

I saw that Charley was watching me intently as I spoke and I wondered again if perhaps he understood some of what I said. After Joseph had finished translating, Charley spoke to the girl, who rose and hurried away.

I addressed Charley in Spanish. "The boy's father wants his son back," I said. "That's all. Young boys should be with their families. Do you remember what it was like? *¿Recuerda usted como era?*" I turned to Joseph. "What happened to this boy, Joseph?"

"He became just like one of us. You can see for yourself."

"But he's not one of you." I took Charley by the wrist and turned his arm over to expose the pale flesh underneath. He scowled at me. I put my other arm next to his. "Look, you're one of us. *Usted es como yo. Usted es un hombre blanco.* You're just like me. You're a white man."

"The color of his skin is not important," Joseph said. "He is *In'deh.*"

And so, little brother, I give you the rest of Charley and Joseph's story, which I have pieced together in these last strange days among the bronco Apaches. Thank God for these notebooks, and for my self-appointed role as substitute notebook keeper, which, more than anything, has kept me sane here.

Because he had been claimed by Goso, little Charley went to live with the warrior's family—his wife, Siki; their baby daughter; and a son of about four. The Apaches love children, dote on them and spoil them, and Siki accepted the boy as if he were one of her own, bestowing a freer and more natural affection upon him than he had ever known before. In his first days in the *ranchería*, she let him sleep under the robes with her, cuddling him when he awoke with nightmares of all that he had witnessed and only faintly understood. She whispered to him in her strange, guttural tongue, which he did not yet understand but which soothed him, until he burrowed his face into her warm, brown pungent breasts, and he slept again.

Speculation about the fate of little Charley McComas was rampant in the American newspapers of the day, and angry outrage voiced against the government and the U.S. Army for their inability to protect the citizenry from the terrible depredations of the devil Apaches. Less than two months after his abduction, the American soldiers under George Crook, the *nantan lupan*, entered Mexico under the new agreement between the two countries that allowed either army to cross the border, in "hot pursuit" of their savage common enemy. General Crook had with him a large force of Apache scouts from the San Carlos reservation; they knew the location of the secret *rancherías* and led the army directly to them.

Goso and many of the other warriors were off raiding in the state of Chihuahua on the morning that Crook's forces surrounded the *ranchería*, and there were mostly women, children, and elderly people in residence. Charley remembered that he was playing a game of hoop and stick with some of the other children when the scouts and the army regulars burst into camp, firing their weapons. No one could understand why they were being attacked by some of their own people, and there was great chaos and screaming as the fleeing women and children were cut down by the soldiers' bullets. Siki gathered Charley and her children and ran into the bushes as an old woman named Dahteste tried to help some of the younger people escape. The old woman had been very kind to Charley since he had been there, and when he saw her collapse, struck in the back by a bullet, he tried to run out to her. He was a brave boy, even then. But before he could reach her, a soldier grabbed hold of him. "I've got the boy!" the soldier hollered. "I've got the McComas boy!" But Charley did not feel like he was being rescued. On the contrary, he thought that the white soldiers were his enemies and that they wished to hurt him and his new family. Charley bit the soldier on the arm; the man cried out in pain and loosened his grip, and Charley slipped away, dashing back into the underbrush. "Hey, boy, come back here!" the soldier called after him. "Where are you going? What's the matter with you? I'm trying to rescue you. Damn, I had him and he run off!"

Goso and the other warriors returned from their raiding three days later to find the *ranchería* destroyed and their families gone. By then most of the Apaches had already surrendered to Crook, the women and children who had not been killed or captured during the attack straggling into the soldiers' camp in small groups. Goso did not know what had become of his wife and children, did not know whether they had been killed in the attack or had turned themselves in. He and several other chiefs and warriors, Chato, Chihuahua, and old Nana among them, decided to surrender themselves and they rode into Crook's camp carrying a white flag. Even Geronimo, who had brought so much trouble down upon the People, brought his band in, to plead with the *nantan lupan* to return them to the San Carlos reservation, where he promised to live in peace.

Of each person who surrendered, Crook demanded information about little Charley McComas, but none could say for certain what had become of the boy. Some said that he had fled into the bushes, others that he had been killed by the soldiers' bullets, though his body had not been found. But now that they were in the custody of the army, all of the Apaches feared reprisal and punishment for Charley's kidnapping and the murder of his parents, and none wished to accept responsibility, least of all Goso himself. And so in perfect Apache fashion, they closed up around the secret as tightly as a covey of quail bedding down for the night, like spokes on a wheel, each facing vigilantly outward. They never spoke of Charley McComas again.

Goso never learned what became of his wife, Siki, and his children, or the boy Charley. He was returned to the San Carlos reservation, and eventually, like so many of the other Apache men, he became a scout for the army and joined the reservation "police force." It was something to do to combat the endless hours of boredom and inactivity, a last chance to use the only skills they owned, to do the one thing they knew how to do, to be warriors, to be men. He took another wife at San Carlos, a young widow named Huera, and she gave birth to their first child there. Although employment for monetary remuneration was not a concept understood by the Apaches, Goso worked for the United States government now, and in return for his services as a scout, he earned meager rations for his family, barely enough to live, but better than nothing. He knew that the old days were gone forever, and that only by cooperating with the White Eyes and learning to live in their world could the People hope to survive.

Two years later, May of the White Eyes year 1885, a number of the discontented Apache chiefs and warriors, Geronimo, Chihuahua, Mangus, Naiche, Loco, and Nana among them, got drunk on *tiswin* one night and broke out of San Carlos again, splintering off into their respective bands and fleeing for old Mexico, raiding and killing as they went.

By now Goso was chief of his own scouting force of a hundred men, and he and his warriors set out in advance of the regular army troops, in hot pursuit of the renegades. Early one morning two weeks later, he trailed Chihuahua's band into a ranch yard near Silver City, New Mexico. It was a fine spring day, clear and cool. But for the incongruous singing of the birds, the ranch yard possessed that specific deathly quiet that immediately follows a raid, the emptiness that fills the void left by chaos and death. The raiders had departed only minutes before, their dust barely settled, and as Goso rode in, he had the sense of being a ghost reliving his own past. Later he would come to think of this as the dividing moment between his old life and his new.

The gates of the corrals were open, the horses and stock gone, the discarded possessions of the house scattered in the yard. The rancher lay dead by the front door, scalped and stripped of his boots and clothes. His wife, too, dead, naked, violated inside the house, a small boy decapitated beside her, his head on the kitchen table.

Goso found the little girl hanging from a meat hook on the barn wall behind the house. She was still alive, the hook buried in the base of her skull. She must have thought when she saw him ride up to her that the Apaches had come back to finish her off, to torture her further. She looked him straight in the eye, and Goso imagined that he was the man who had hung her here, saw himself lifting her slight body by one powerful arm, slamming her against the barn wall, impaling her on the hook.

Goso would never for the rest of his life forget the way the little girl looked at him on that morning, hanging from the meat hook on the barn wall, the birds singing so joyfully in the cool spring still of the day; this child who had seen coalesced into the final brutal moments of her short life all the horror of these centuries-long wars between the races, between their unspeakably depraved gods, who permit men to slaughter the children of their enemies. Her gaze was calm and steady, and she looked into Goso's eyes with . . . *pity*. With forgiveness. And she smiled, as if apologetically, and reached out her arms for him to take her down. Goso lifted the little girl up off the hook and brought her toward him on his horse, and as he did so she wrapped her frail arms tenderly around his neck, and she died.

Goso and his scouts pursued the renegades south across the border into Mexico, leading the army troops into the old country of his birth and youth, across the high plains and grasslands, into the foothills of the Blue Mountains, the Sierra Madre, the hard massive rock formations that erupted so violently from the earth, lacerated by canyons and arroyos, and dark shadowed valleys, this vast quiescent country that ran on forever, like the crests of waves on a storm-driven sea.

While he was in Mexico, Goso heard faint rumors from the renegades as they trickled into the soldiers' camp to surrender one by one that some of the People had fled into the mountains farther to the south, that some of those who had not surrendered three years before were still living there, having made their new *rancherías* in places unknown to Goso and the other scouts, in the country of the peaceful Taramuhare Indians, a strange lush land, where enormous green birds spoke the language of men. He heard vague murmurings to the effect that his old wife, Siki, and his two children had been seen there, and that she had taken a new husband. He even heard that little Charley McComas was still alive. But for all his inquiries, Goso could never confirm these rumors, and because the renegades so hated the scouts, he thought this was probably nothing more than the malicious talk of vengeful men who wished him to imagine his family living free and wild without him.

And the rest of the story you already know, Neddy. Shortly thereafter, the summer of 1886, the scout Goso traveled to Washington, D.C., with the contingent of Chiricahua and Warm Springs Apaches to meet with the Great White Father, ostensibly to negotiate a reservation for the People in their homeland. But instead he and the others were sent to Fort Marion in St. Augustine, Florida, where they were held as prisoners of war with Geronimo and his people, and a number of other Chiricahuas—men, women, and children—who had been shipped there from the San Carlos reservation in Arizona. Less than a year later, in the spring of 1887, the government shipped the Apaches to Mount Vernon Barracks, Alabama, an abandoned army fort in the swamps of Mobile Bay. But these were a people of the mountains and deserts and they could not tolerate the hot, damp climate of Florida and Alabama. Babies died from mosquito bites, and by 1894, nearly half of the Chiricahuas had succumbed to malaria, dysentery, or tuberculosis. Others had simply died of homesickness and broken hearts. That year the government finally transferred Goso and the rest of the survivors to Fort Sill, Oklahoma, a military reservation which housed the Wichita, Kiowa, and Comanche Indians, and where the Chiricahuas were given their own allotment of land upon which to live. But not until 1913, twenty-seven years after his initial incarceration, was Joseph Valor, as he had been renamed by his captors, allowed to return to his home country, or at least close to it—the Mescalero Apache reservation in New Mexico.

The girl came back to the fire in front of the white Apache's wickiup leading a young boy. I did not have to be told that it was Geraldo Huerta. He was a slender, willowy child with fair hair, light skin, and fine features.

Charley spoke to him in Apache and the boy answered. Of course the irony of an American man speaking to a Mexican boy in their common tongue, Apache, was not lost on the cultural anthropologist in me.

And to me in Spanish, Charley said: "He does not wish to return to the Mexicans. *Es uno de nosotros. Es Apache ahora.* He is one of us now. Ask him yourself if you like."

"Hello, Geraldo," I said. "*He encontrado a tu padre.* He misses you very much. I'm going to take you home to him."

The boy looked uncertainly at Charley. "He does not remember his Mexican father," the white Apache said. "This"—he gestured with his arm to take in the *ranchería*—"this is all he knows."

"Let him go," I said to Charley. "Give him the chance you never had. To live the life he was born to live. The life that you stole from him. The life that Goso stole from you."

"I did not capture the boy," Charley said. "He is not mine to give back."

"If you give him up, you may be allowed to continue to live here as you have been living all these years," I said. "If you don't, you and the rest of your people will be destroyed. That's your choice."

Charley looked at me for a long time. His pale blue eyes were weathered and deep-set, shadowed by a prominent brow, and long, delicate blond eyelashes that lent his face a certain sensitivity. There was intelligence in those eyes, that much was sure; I could see him evaluating me with a certain shrewdness. And I also saw the antipathy in his gaze, the disgust, even hatred. A white Apache brought up to hate white people.

"Once we are discovered here, we will not be allowed to live free," he said. "Even if we give up the boy. This much we know."

"How do you know?"

"We have lived peacefully here for a long time," he said. "But now the Mexican government has reinstated a bounty on Apache scalps. The bounty hunters are so greedy to collect their reward that they kill and scalp our neighbors to the south, the Taramuhare, who are a peaceful people without weapons. The Mexicans can't tell the difference between Apache hair and Taramuhare hair. Some of them even kill and scalp their own people, as long as the hair of the victim is long and dark." Charley smiled slyly. "In the villages you will see that the Mexican men all wear their hair very short now, in order not to tempt their neighbors." He took his own long red locks in his hand. "But I do not have to worry about losing my scalp, as who would pay a bounty for hair of this color?"

I smiled myself. It appeared that Charley McComas had a sense of humor. "You should never have taken the boy," I said. "You must know that the Huertas are a powerful ranching family. You brought this upon yourselves."

"There are those among us who I do not control," he said. And, of course, I knew that he was speaking of Indio Juan.

"Your only chance is to give the boy up."

"No one who comes here is ever allowed to go back," Charley said. "Our warriors are already in pursuit of your men who escaped. We will catch them. The only reason we did not kill them before is because you saved my granddaughter's life. But now that favor has been repaid."

"That's how you repay a favor?" I asked. "You send a madman to attack us on the trail? You hold knives to our throats? You bash a dear, gentle man's skull in with a rock? You hang the others over a fire to explode their heads?"

Charley spoke angrily to Joseph in Apache.

"What did he say?" I asked.

"He says that the white slave woman has very bad manners."

"Very bad manners?" I said.

"Be careful, Margaret," Joseph said. "He says that you need a beating in order to learn your place here."

And then I made a serious cultural misjudgment, and one about which I should have known better. Not wishing to appear weak, or afraid of Charley, I challenged him. "Well, go ahead, then, big boy," I said, speaking to him in Spanish. "Go ahead and beat up a girl if that will make you feel like a man."

Charley looked at me coldly and then he stood calmly and came over to me. He reached down, took hold of my hair, and wrapped it around his enormous fist, and he dragged me, kicking and hollering, behind the wickiup. There, out of their sight but not out of their hearing, he beat me, methodically and passionlessly, the way a man whips a dog simply to teach him a lesson, slapping me about the head with his open hands, until my ears rang, and I could feel my face swelling, the warm blood running. I fell to the ground and curled up and tried to cover my head with my arms.

I do not remember how I got back there, but I woke up in the other wickiup with the girl dabbing my face with a wet cloth. My eyes were swollen so that I could barely see her and every inch of my body ached, particularly my face, which felt like it had been overinflated with air and was about to explode. "Oh God, I hurt," I muttered. And in Spanish I said to the girl, "Why did your grandfather do that to me? What is the matter with you people that everything must be addressed with violence? With murder, torture, and beating?"

"He did it to teach you respect," she said, "and because he had to do it. You insulted him in front of others and the chief cannot lose face in that way. To do so is to weaken his position."

Of course, I should have known this, indeed, I did know; it is a common law of native tribal societies that the chief must not be challenged, particularly in front of others. But I had stupidly let my own professional hubris get in the way of my instincts for self-preservation.

"And he did it to protect you from Indio Juan," the girl added. "By beating you, he claimed you once and for all as his slave. If another ever touches you again, he can kill him."

So this, once again, little brother, is what women are reduced to in both the civilized and savage worlds—seeking protection from men, a position that I have been trying to escape my entire life. And in order to satisfy your curiosity, I will tell you a little something about that life now. My mother died of malaria in Brazil when I was ten years old. My father was a difficult, demanding man, for whom his profession was everything, and after her death, I largely took over the household duties that had been my mother's responsibility. We were living in the jungle in very primitive conditions, and there was always a great deal of work to be done. I became somewhat of an indentured servant myself, working for room and board, and the education my father gave me himself, as, of course, there were no schools in the Amazon. I was daughter, student, housekeeper, cook, laundress, gardener, and when I reached puberty, my father had me assume the rest of my mother's duties—as his wife. A man has needs, my father explained, and he did not care for the native women; he said they were dirty, that they stank of the mud they rubbed upon themselves. He preferred blond women, like my mother, like myself.

There was never any question of saying no to my father, about that or anything else. Indeed, our life there was so isolated that it wasn't until some years later, after we had returned to the United States, that I even realized how deeply wrong this had been, how deeply, and irrevocably, my father's despotism had scarred me.

Does that explain some things to you, little brother? The law of the jungle which I learned at a young age, and have been trying to escape ever since, is that we do what we must to survive.

NOTEBOOK VII:
The Rescue

"Mr. Giles," Billy Flowers intoned in his deep Old Testament voice. "You have lost three of your party and all of your outfit."

I had fallen asleep, after all, sitting up against the tree, writing in my notebook, and I thought for just a moment that I must be dead, that I had gone to meet my Maker, that here He stood before me. For when I opened my eyes all I could see against the deep blue morning sky was the outline of his craggy head, his long white hair and beard, his intensely blue eyes boring into me. I scrambled to my feet.

"We were ambushed," I said, "not far up the trail." The others, too, had come abruptly awake to the sound of Flowers's voice.

"Yes, I know," Flowers said. "I've seen the place where it happened. I saw Mr. Phillips's prize polo pony dead at the bottom of the canyon. They were eight altogether in number who set upon you, including *la niña bronca* herself, who aided them in your capture. I identified her track. So much for the savage's sentimental attachment to her new white friends."

"If it hadn't been for her, they would have killed us right then and there," I said. "We've been to their *ranchería*. We escaped last night."

"And left Mr. Browning and the woman behind?" Flowers asked. "And the old heathen? Or are they dead? Someone was badly injured by a rock during the attack, that much was clear in the sign I saw."

"They're alive, they're all still alive but we had to leave them."

"You left a white woman in the clutches of the savages?" Flowers said. "Shame on you. You know what they do to them, don't you?"

"We had no choice," I said. "Mr. Browning was hurt too badly to travel and Margaret insisted on staying with him. How far behind is the expedition?"

"Less than a half day's ride," Flowers said. "I came ahead to scout the route."

"We have to get to them before the Apaches find us again," I said. "We can lead them back to the *ranchería*."

"I am quite capable of finding the *ranchería* myself, young man," Flowers said. "Just by following your trail."

Tolley spoke up then. "You don't want to do that, Mr. Flowers. Not alone, in any case. The *ranchería* is well protected. We need reinforcements."

Flowers smiled. "Ah, yes, so you have finally discovered, *Captain* Phillips."

"I never thought I'd say this," said Tolley in a small voice, "but I'm happy to see you, Mr. Flowers."

Flowers set a grueling pace. We followed him, traveling with one eye cast back over our shoulders, half expecting that at any moment the Apaches would fall upon us again. Someone once told me that chickens and game birds never learn to look up into the air, which is what makes them so vulnerable to avian predators, but for our part we had learned our lesson and at every rocky pass through which we traveled, and every canyon wall beneath which we rode, we looked skyward, remembering the shadows descending upon us from above. And I think we all had the same eerie sense that even though we had not seen them yet, they were following us, watching and biding their time.

The summer monsoon season was just getting under way, and the heat and humidity built all day, dark storm clouds piling on the southwest horizon, wicking their cargo of moisture up out of the Gulf of California. In the afternoon, the winds picked up and bent the tops of the tall pine trees, pushing huge black cumulonimbus clouds over the distant mountains. We watched them coming gradually closer, roiling and rumbling and flashing with lightning, and we could smell the rain long before it reached us, its pure fresh scent delivered on the warm wind. We watched as the gray undulating sheets obscured the far peaks and the wind came cooler, the temperature dropping precipitously, until it was suddenly quite cold and enormous ice-cold silver-dollar-size drops began to fall, just a few at first splattering off the mules' backs, and then harder and harder. We rode into the expedition base camp just at dusk and just as the rains came in a sudden vicious deluge.

Two wranglers came out in their raingear to tend to our nervous mounts, the roar of the rain so loud that we had to shout to be heard over it. Now the thunder seemed overhead, great erupting bursts and cracks of it, and the camp was lit by brilliant flashes of lightning. Billy Flowers went off to tend to his dogs and the rest of us were led to the mess tent, where people were just beginning to congregate for dinner.

"Hey, kid!" Big Wade called out from one of the tables. "Jesus Christ, you look like a *fuckin'* drowned rat." He rose and came over and gave me a big bear hug. "Damn, am I ever glad to see you. We figured the Apaches had gotten you."

"Yeah, they did," I said.

"Where's the rest of your bunch? Margaret and Mr. Browning. Are they okay? And goddammit, Jesus, where the hell have you been? You were supposed to stay with me, boy. I've had to pack my own damn gear."

"Margaret and Mr. Browning are still with the Apaches," I said. "We had to leave them behind."

"You left them with the fuckin' Apaches?"

"It's a long story, Big Wade."

"Yeah, well, I want to hear the whole damn thing," Big Wade said. "But first, you know what my next question is, don't you, kid?"

"Sure I do, Big Wade: Did I get the shot?"

"Well?"

"Not only did I not get the shot," I said, "but I lost your camera."

"You lost the Leica? You can't be serious, kid?"

"Well, I didn't exactly lose it," I said. "I think Margaret has it."

"You *think* Margaret has it? Oh well, this is just dandy," Big Wade said. "Because I imagine the Apaches will be taking real good care of my equipment . . . considering that they are, after all, *Stone Age people*. I can't believe you lost your *fuckin'* camera. Kid, you do know what a photographer is without his camera, don't you?"

"Yeah, yeah, I know, Big Wade, a photographer without his camera is like a man without a dick."

"In the lad's defense, Big Wade," Tolley said, "we ran into a spot of trouble among the bronco Apaches. Young Ned here was busy with such niggling matters as saving our lives and entering the state of unholy matrimony."

"Oh, you got married while you were away, did you, kid?" Big Wade said. "Well, why didn't you say so? I guess congratulations are in order. Who's the lucky girl?" He shook his head, and muttered under his breath, *"Jesus Christ, I leave you alone for five fucking minutes . . ."*

"I'll get your camera back, Big Wade," I said. "I will. And if for any reason I can't, I'll buy you a new one."

"Ah, hell, kid," Big Wade said grinning, "I'm just giving you a hard time. I'm not really worried about the camera. I'm damn glad to see you. Now start at the beginning and tell us everything."

And so over dinner we told Wade and the others what had happened to us since we left them back in Bavispe, which seemed already like another lifetime ago. Afterward, we were summoned to Colonel Carrillo's tent to give our report. Chief Gatlin, Billy Flowers, and the rancher Fernando Huerta were also present.

"Did you see my son?" Señor Huerta asked us straightaway.

"Yes, sir, we did," I said.

"And he is well?"

"Yes, sir, he appears to be healthy."

"Thank God."

"We will move against them first thing tomorrow," Carrillo said. "Mr. Flowers assures us that he can locate the *ranchería*. We've got them cornered now. In two days, señor, you will hold your beloved son safe again in your arms."

"It's not going to be that easy, Colonel," Albert said. "Your troops will never be able to get through to the *ranchería*. Ask Mr. Flowers. Half a dozen of their warriors can hold off your entire army, just by raining rocks down on you from above."

"Albert is right, Colonel," said Tolley. "It would be a slaughter. All your fine horses will end up like mine, dead at the bottom of a canyon."

"Mr. Flowers?" the colonel asked.

"I'm afraid they're probably correct, Colonel," Billy Flowers said. "It is not by accident that the Apaches have made their *ranchería* in this place. It is nearly impregnable. The route there is treacherous and easily defended by a handful of men."

"And there is no other route?" Carrillo asked.

"None from this side," Flowers said. "Possibly if we descended and circled the sierra and came up from the south. But that could take weeks."

"With the monsoons beginning," Carrillo said, "perhaps even longer. Assuming we could even cross the river."

"We do not have that much time," Señor Huerta said. "We are so close now."

"I say we go through the pass at night," Chief Gatlin said. "While there's still enough moon to light our way. The Apaches are superstitious and they won't attack in the dark."

"That's a crazy idea," I said. "It's hard enough negotiating the pass in broad daylight."

The little muscle in Gatlin's jaw twitched. "Mr. Giles, I think we can all agree that your plan has been a distinct failure," he said. "You've lost the Apache girl, who was supposed to be our bargaining chip, you've failed to recover the Huerta boy, and now you've lost three members of the expedition, including a woman who you abandoned in the clutches of the savages in order to save your own yellow-bellied skin. Suffice it to say that we are not seeking your advice in this matter."

"No, I don't suppose you would be, Chief."

"It wasn't Giles's fault," Tolley said. "I was in charge and I take full responsibility."

"There is one other thing you're all overlooking," said Albert.

"And what might that be, *scout?*" Gatlin asked.

"You should read your history of the Apache wars, Chief," Albert said. "Because then you would know that traditionally, when an Apache village is attacked, the first thing they do is kill the captives, women and children included. In this way they deny their enemies the satisfaction of a true victory."

Gatlin looked at Albert with contempt. "You don't have to lecture me about Apache atrocities, scout," he said. "I know as well as anyone what low-down scum they are. I know they have no sense of honor, no sense of a fair fight. If it were up to me, we'd have finished 'em off a long time ago."

It was the wrong thing to say to Albert, and I could see the blood rising in his face. "You White Eyes come into *our* country with your armies, your guns and cannons," he said. "You steal our land, you slaughter every native that stands in your way, you lock the survivors up on reservations. And you ask us to fight fair against you? How do you think a tribe of a few thousand souls has managed to survive three hundred years of persecution? How do you think we avoided being *finished off,* as you put it, Chief? By learning *not* to fight fair. The White Eyes and the Spaniards and the Mexicans taught us everything we know about atrocities."

"*We,* is it now?" Gatlin said, nodding. "I thought you were on our side, scout? Hell, I thought you were about half civilized. But now I see that after only twenty-four hours among your own kind, you're all set to put the loincloth back on and take to the warpath. Your old granddad went native again, did he?"

Albert regarded Gatlin with loathing and addressed Carrillo. "Colonel, assuming that you can even get through the pass," he said, "if you invade the *ranchería,* you're going to find Margaret and Mr. Browning dead. And Señor Huerta's son, too. Their blood will be on your hands."

"We must listen to them, Colonel," said Fernando Huerta, standing. "We cannot risk my son's life by acting rashly."

"We have no other choice, señor," Carrillo said. "Our attempts to negotiate with the savages have clearly failed. We must take military action."

"No!" shouted Señor Huerta. "I will not allow it!"

"You are not in command of this operation, sir," Carrillo snapped.

"There's one other thing you should all know," I said.

"What's that, Mr. Giles?" said Gatlin.

"The leader of their band is a white man."

"What are you talking about?"

"Have you ever heard the name Charley McComas?" I asked.

"Of course," said Gatlin. "Everyone in the Southwest knows the story of little Charley McComas. Kidnapped by the Apaches in 1883."

"He's not so little anymore, Chief," Tolley said. "He's all grown up."

"Oh, hell," Gatlin scoffed. "We been hearing rumors for years in this country about Charley McComas. Old E. H. White, used to cowboy over on the Diamond A, always claimed that one time back in twenty-four when he was looking for strays up in the timber, he ran into a big red-headed white man leading a band of Apaches. He always claimed it was the McComas boy. 'Course, old E.H. was known to stretch the truth a bit in the interest of a good yarn."

"It wasn't a yarn," I said. "We've seen him."

Tolley, Albert, and I walked glumly back through the camp. The violent storm had passed earlier, but the faint rumblings of it still sounded in the distance, and lightning flashed on the far horizon.

"Well, that went well," Tolley remarked.

"We've really made a mess of things, haven't we?" I said.

"Not to worry, old sport," Tolley said. "Things will look brighter after a good night's sleep. I can hardly think straight I'm so tired."

We split up, off to our assigned tents, Tolley with the paying guests, Albert to the staff quarters, and I back to the "press" tent. Big Wade was already asleep, snoring as usual, and the boy Jesus, exhausted from the trials of the past days, slept curled on a mat on the floor. It was strange being back with the expedition, as if we'd never left, as if our brief time among the bronco Apaches had been nothing more than a dream, a nightmare. How I wish that it had been. How I wish that I could wake up in the morning and have everything be as before, with Margaret and Mr. Browning and Joseph safe with us. I don't know if I've ever been so completely bone-weary tired in my life. Or so discouraged. I hope Tolley is right and that things look brighter by the light of day and after a good night's sleep. Because right now they look pretty damn hopeless. Good night, Margaret; good night, Mr. Browning; good night, Joseph; I hope you're all safely sleeping. Good night, Chideh.

23 JUNE, 1932

Yet another disaster has befallen us . . . This morning at dawn Colonel Carrillo rode out of camp with a small detachment of Mexican soldiers and half a dozen volunteers, with Billy Flowers guiding them. Their purpose was to make a short scouting expedition so that the colonel could himself get the lay of the land.

Less than six hours after their departure, Carrillo, Flowers, and five other survivors, two of them wounded, straggled back into camp. Only Flowers still had his mule, bearing the most seriously wounded man. All else were afoot. All told, eight Mexican soldiers and four of the volunteers had been killed in the ambush, and all the other horses and mules were either dead or captured by the Apaches. Without any explanation for what had happened, Carrillo and Flowers went immediately into conference with Chief Gatlin. One of the American survivors of the ambush was the steel magnate's son Winston Hughes, the Yale boy who so enjoys tormenting Tolley. With none of his customary fraternity-boy cockiness in evidence, Winty described to us the terrible events of the day.

They never even reached the pass but had been ambushed only an hour out of camp, at another spot where the trail narrows along an arroyo. Above the trail on the one side was a series of low bluffs, and it was here among the rocks that the Apaches lay in wait. The party was riding single file, with Colonel Carrillo in the lead, when a single shot was fired and the colonel's horse went down beneath him. Two more shots followed in quick succession and the man bringing up the rear, a volunteer named Larkin from upper state New York, fell dead out of the saddle, his horse collapsing with the next shot. Now the trail was blocked at both ends by the floundering, dying horses, and the other animals began to panic, rearing and whinnying, wheeling in circles, slipping on the rocks, stumbling and falling to their knees. In the ensuing chaos some of the riders were unseated, others were picked cleanly off by the steady, methodical gunfire. Colonel Carrillo shouted orders for everyone to dismount and take cover. Some of the soldiers had managed to unsheathe their rifles and began to return fire, but they had no idea where the shots were coming from and all they could do was shoot wildly in the general direction of the bluffs. The steady, almost leisurely gunfire continued with deadly accuracy, one man after the next falling dead or wounded.

"We were like the tin ducks in a carnival shooting gallery," Winston

Hughes said in a low voice, close to tears. "We couldn't get off the trail and we couldn't even tell where the shots were coming from."

Only Billy Flowers, on his big white mule, sure-footed as a mountain goat, managed to get off the trail and ride almost vertically down into the arroyo, where he left his mule out of the line of fire and worked his way around on foot to give himself a clear vantage point of the bluffs above. Flowers took his time, scanning the rocks with his eagle-eyed hunter's eyes until he had identified the shooters and then he began to return fire himself, just as methodically. He picked off two of the Apaches before they realized that their position had been discovered, and as they were relocating, and trying to determine where the returning gunfire was coming from, Flowers hollered up to Carrillo and the others to leave their mounts and drop down into the arroyo on foot. In this way, Billy Flowers had saved the lives of the remaining men, though they lost all their horses.

Dinner tonight in the mess tent was subdued, to say the least. Now that some of the volunteers have actually died at the hands of the Apaches, the expedition has taken on a sober new tone. No longer is this simply a hunting and fishing excursion into interesting virgin country, with the vague, though highly unlikely possibility that the volunteers might add a wild Apache to their trophy bags. Suddenly the Apaches are not only shooting back, but actually hunting the sports. Some of those who have never seen real military service (i.e., the vast majority of volunteers) have announced their intention to resign from the expedition, and a contingent of them has already approached Colonel Carrillo to demand safe escort back to Douglas. "I'm out," said Winston Hughes. "This is no fun anymore," he added in gross understatement. Even a few of the veterans and retired military men among them seem to have lost heart. The notion of fighting an elusive guerrilla army in this impossibly rugged country in order to rescue a single Mexican boy suddenly seems less romantic and a great deal more dangerous.

"Well, hell," said a fellow named Kent Sanders, a young banker from Greenwich, Connecticut, and one of the biggest blowhards of the bunch. "It's just a Mexican kid. He's hardly worth dying for."

"Yeah, but what about the woman and Phillips's butler?" said another man. "Are we just going to abandon them to the savages?"

"They're staff members," said a third. "It's a personnel problem. Let Chief Gatlin deal with that."

"That's what the Mexican army is here for," said another man. "It's their country, let them solve their own Indian problem. We took care of ours fifty years ago."

And so the sports debated the level of their responsibility and their dwindling commitment. The fact that they're each paying thirty dollars a day to participate made it an easy decision for some. Clearly, the Great Apache Expedition has ceased to seem like such a good value for their money.

After dinner, Tolley came to see me in my tent. He seemed somehow sheepish and uncomfortable. "You know, old sport," he said, unable to look me in the eye, "I've given it a great deal of thought and I really feel that I should be getting home. Fall semester is right around the corner, you know."

"Fall semester?" I said, stunned. "No, I don't know. What are you talking about, Tolley? You're not thinking about leaving?"

"Senior year and all that rot . . ."

"Fuck senior year!" I hollered, incensed. "You can't just quit. We can't just abandon Margaret and Mr. Browning up there."

"Yes, well, we've already done that, haven't we, old sport?"

"Only to go get help."

"And so we have done, Giles. You heard what Stewart said. It's really a personnel problem. Very little I can do about it personally. Up to Carrillo and the army now really, isn't it?"

"A personnel problem? Jesus, Tolley, those are our friends up there. We promised them we'd come back for them."

"Just a bit over two months before classes begin," he said. "I've got a monstrous number of things to do . . ."

"What kind of things, Tolley? You have to pop into New York and get your new fall wardrobe at Brooks Brothers?"

"Well, yes, as a matter of fact, that is among the things on my list. Wouldn't do a bit to appear at Princeton in last year's frayed collars."

"Who cares about Princeton and your fucking frayed collars?" I asked. "If you quit now, you're just going to prove your father right about you. It'll just give him another opportunity to say you're not a man, you're just a sissy."

"Well, actually, old sport, I am a sissy."

"I think you like disappointing your father, Tolley," I said. "Look, I know you were scared up there. Who wouldn't have been? I was scared, too. So was Albert."

"Let me tell you something about scared, Giles," said Tolley. "When they hung me upside down off that spit, I pissed my pants I was so scared. And when they built the fire under my head, I shat myself. Upside down. That's how scared I was. I realized that I'm not ready to die in order not to disappoint my father."

"Forget about your father, Tolley," I said. "If you go home now without seeing this through, you'll disappoint yourself for the rest of your life."

"I guess I'll just have to live with that, old sport," Tolley said. "Colonel Carrillo has already agreed to spare half a dozen soldiers to escort those of us who choose to leave back to Bavispe. We'll be met there by American representatives from Douglas, who will see us over the border. We're scheduled to depart first thing in the morning. I just wanted to pop in and say good-bye, Giles. Damn fine adventure we've had together, hasn't it been? Say, if you're ever on the East Coast . . ."

I refused Tolley's outstretched hand and turned away from him. "Get out of here, Tolley."

25 JUNE, 1932

I made my decision before I went to sleep that night of Tolley's defection, and I only slept for a few hours, getting up well before dawn, quietly leaving the tent and walking down to the corral. The same kid, Jimmy, had the night watch, and this time he wasn't asleep. On the contrary he was so jumpy that he almost shot me first and asked me to identify myself later. Obviously, the proximity of the Apaches had him on edge.

"Damn, Ned, you ought not to sneak up on a fella like that," he said. "That's a good way to get yourself shot."

"I wasn't sneaking, Jimmy," I said. "That's why I was whistling while I walked up. I didn't want to make too much noise and wake the others or spook the stock. So I whistled so you'd know I was a friendly party."

"Don't you know nothing, Ned?" Jimmy said. "That's just how the injuns communicate. By whistlin'."

"Yeah, well, they don't whistle 'I Got Rhythm,' Jimmy."

"What are you doing out in the middle of the night, anyway, Ned?"

"I need a mule."

"I got no orders to let you have a mule, Ned," Jimmy said.

"I know you don't, Jimmy," I said. "But I'm asking you to give me one anyway."

"I can't do that."

"Sure, you can."

"What do you need a mule for in the middle of the night, Ned?"

"I have to go back, Jimmy."

"Back where?"

"Back up the trail a ways," I said. "I accidentally left my camera bag sitting by a spring when we stopped to water the horses the other day. I don't want Big Wade to find out that I lost it. I just need to borrow a mule for a couple hours, Jimmy. That way I can be back here before sunrise. And no one will be the wiser."

"If you're just going for a couple hours, Ned, why you packing a bedroll and those saddlebags?"

"I just like to be prepared, Jimmy, that's all."

"Ain't you worried about runnin' into the Apaches?"

"They never attack at night, Jimmy," I said. "They're real superstitious about that. They might steal horses at night but they'll never kill a man, because at night his ghost will get lonely and attach itself to whoever killed him. And they'll never be able to shake it."

"*Damn,*" Jimmy said with a little shiver. "Is that so? How do you know about that, Ned?"

"Because I was with them, Jimmy, remember?"

"I give you a mule, you promise to bring him back before daylight?"

"Scout's honor. It won't take more than two hours to make the round-trip. You'd really be helping me out, Jimmy."

"Awright then, Ned, I guess I can let you have one," Jimmy said. "But you're gonna run into guards on the edge of camp. After all that's happened, the colonel's got the place buttoned up pretty tight."

"Yeah, well, they're trying to keep the Indians *out*, Jimmy," I said, "not keep me in."

The waning moon had been late rising, but still cast plenty of light. I led the mule out to the main trail, where I identified myself to the guard, a Mexican vaquero named Estevan. As I suspected, he didn't object to my leaving, although he, too, seemed to think I was loco to be riding into Apache country in the middle of the night.

And I have to admit it was a strange and somewhat eerie feeling to be headed back alone toward what we had been so anxiously fleeing a few days before. The air was dead calm, the high, razorback peaks of the sierra flat black against a pearly gray sky, and each tree and rock I passed seemed to stand out in bold relief and perfect focus in the moonlight.

Even for a city boy, it wasn't hard to follow the trail left by the soldiers the day before, the same trail we had ridden in on. Just over an hour out of camp my mule suddenly raised his head and flared his nostrils. He snorted and balked, stopping dead in his tracks, refusing to go farther. Something had spooked him. I dismounted and coaxed him along by the reins and he followed me nervously.

I saw first the dark outlines of the roosting buzzards; enormous hunched-backed creatures like a congregation of hooded black-robed monks praying, they squatted atop the corpses and on the backs of the dead horses. As I approached, they lifted their wings proprietarily, holding them out at their sides like unholy angels, their vile red beaks agape. One by one they sprang into the air, their wingbeats making a heavy nauseating *whoosh*. They did not fly far, just a short loop before setting back down, unwilling to give up their prize of carrion.

Obviously fearing another attack, Carrillo hadn't sent out a detachment yet to bury the dead. I counted thirteen of them altogether; twisted in grotesque postures, stripped and scalped, they glowed a ghostly alabaster white in the moonlight. They looked so inhuman, so abstract, even more so for the fact that the buzzards had been working on their eyes and mouths, their scalped heads. I remembered experiencing the same sense of unreality when I found Pop dead in the bathroom of our house, the back of his head blown out. And it occurred to me that our mind creates this sense of abstraction and unreality in order to protect us from the sheer horror. I was unable to imagine these men only a day before, as living, breathing human beings, and I tried not to look too closely at their faces for fear of recognizing those among them that I knew, and whom I had seen last time around the dining table at camp, joking, laughing, and boasting. All the tack had been stripped from the dead horses, so that they, too, looked naked, their tongues swollen and mouths locked in grotesque death masks. I imagined how I would have composed a photograph of the terrible scene if I'd had my camera; in this way, even without it, I hid behind it; I imagined that the image I would make might look something like Goya's *The Disasters of War*, which I had studied in a university art class. But my dead men and horses seemed considerably less epic, even more violated.

The trail was completely blocked by the carnage and I had no choice but to descend into the arroyo on foot, leading the mule, trying to pick our way through the rocks and around the boulders. The mule was patient and I let him choose his own way. It was a long way around and over three hours before we found a place to climb out again and regain the trail, or at least what I hoped was the trail. By then I was afraid that I was lost; nothing looked even remotely familiar to me any longer and it occurred to me how foolish I had been to attempt this passage alone. Maybe I should have asked Albert to come with me, after all; he would be furious when he discovered that I'd left without him. But I knew he was better off with the expedition. As the girl's "husband," I was staking my hopes on the belief that I might still have safe passage among the bronco Apaches, but clearly Albert would not. And so I had chosen to wander around out here alone, pretending to know the way, lost in this labyrinth of canyon and arroyo and impassable mountain trails, in the shadows of moonlight. Those had been real men back there, real dead men, their eyes plucked out by buzzards.

"Do you know the way?" I asked the mule suddenly, the sound of my own voice startling both of us. The mule seemed relieved to be back on the trail, or at least *a* trail, and he stepped along steadily now, almost briskly, as if trying to put distance between us and the corpses, fleeing death. "Why were you so afraid back there?" I asked him, because after the initial shock of hearing my voice, which seemed strangely disembodied, I decided that it was comforting to talk to the mule. *"Did you know those horses? Were you afraid of the smell of death? Or are you just afraid of your own death? Did it make you think that you might be next? That anyone of those dead horses could have been you? Did you think about how lucky you were that you hadn't been chosen to be ridden yesterday morning? Remember when they rode out? The soldiers on their eager, prancing horses, their coats glossy with currying, the sports a bit self-important with the gravity of their mission, having some trouble controlling their skittish polo ponies. Those horses probably thought they were better than you, a lowly mule, half donkey, half horse. And you probably thought so, too. Yet now they are nothing but carrion. Not that Colonel Carrillo or Billy Flowers would have asked me, but I'd have gone along if they had, and maybe Jimmy would have assigned you to be my mount, because my own mule, Buster, is pretty beat up. Maybe we would be lying back there right now with the others, buzzards roosting on us, feasting on our eyes and tongues. We would taste just as sweet as the rich men and their polo ponies. I'll bet that's what you're thinking about. What's your name anyway? Jimmy forgot to tell me."*

I understood now that I did not after all remember the way back to the *ranchería*, that I was just following the trail we were on, or rather letting the mule follow it. What else was there to do? We were gaining altitude, that much was true, and I kept looking for familiar landmarks, a particular tree or a specific rock formation that I might remember. The moonlight was already bleeding into dawn. I was lost. What a hopeless fool I was.

I saw the movement this time out of the corner of my eye and barely had time to be afraid in that flashing white moment of surprise to which I could do nothing but surrender, a kind of willing relinquishment. Had it come from behind or above? It hardly mattered. The mule, too, shied, his ears cocked back, undecided yet as to whether or not the situation warranted a full-fledged blowup. Then I knew, felt the light warmth of her like a wind enveloping me, leaping, vaulting behind me on the mule, just in the way that I always seemed to encounter her, never quite able to fix her in place. Had she come from behind or above? Floating, hovering like a bird. More than a different race, she was a different species than I. And her scent, like the smell of the mountains after the monsoons.

I felt her arms around my shoulders and one hand grasped me lightly by the throat. She laughed and I realized that it was a kind of practical joke, the memory fresh of the last time she had fallen upon me like this, with a knife at my throat.

She swung around in front of me, in the same way that she had cut capers on the burro, a litheness that seemed to defy gravity, so that she was facing me now, her slender brown legs over mine. She seemed to weigh nothing at all.

"I knew you would come back to me, my husband," she said.

"Did you kill those men back there?" I asked.

"No, it was Indio Juan's war party," she said.

"And you ride with him."

"They were coming to kill us," she said.

"They just want the boy back. And the others. *¿Mataste a esos hombres?*" I asked again.

"No, I was not there," she said. "But if I had been, I would have killed the Mexican soldiers. And the White Eyes, too. They are our enemies."

"Then so am I."

"No, with you it is different."

"How?"

"You are my husband."

"What are you doing here?" I asked.

"You are lost," she said. "I came to find you."

"How do you know I'm lost?"

She laughed. "Because you are going the wrong way."

"How did you know I was coming?"

"We know everything that takes place in these mountains," she said, "and all who pass. I knew you would come back to me."

"Is Margaret okay?" I asked.

She nodded.

"Mr. Browning?"

She averted her eyes.

"What's the matter?"

She shook her head.

"Tell me. Did something happen to Mr. Browning?"

"He went to the Happy Place," she said.

"Oh, no . . ."

The girl slipped around to ride behind me, her slender brown fingers light at my waist. We descended off the trail and through a dense pine forest and out into the valley of a small river. A trail ran along a low bluff above the river and we followed it for some time, twice coming down off the bluff to cross the river and follow the trail on the other side. The mule did not like these crossings because the river was swollen and muddy with the recent rains and he could not see the bottom, and also because mules, in general, though they are more sure-footed on the rocks than horses, do not like getting their feet wet. But the girl clucked to the mule and spoke to him in her tongue and they seemed to reach some kind of agreement, because he crossed, the muddy water lapping his stomach. I remembered that the girl had power over horses. And I suppose this extends to mules and burros as well.

After a while we came to a place where the river widened into a small meadow. On the bluffs on one end of the meadow were a series of ancient cave dwellings. It was a beautiful spot and you could see why the "first" people had chosen to live here. Beneath the bluff and the caves were several pools formed by a spring and here we dismounted. I unsaddled the mule and hobbled him, turning him out to graze contentedly in the meadow. The girl led me to one of the pools; I could smell the faint sulfurous odor of it and realized that it was a hot spring. She sat down on a rock and removed her high moccasins, her warrior's breechclout, and the loose gingham cloth shirt she wore, and without any trace of self-consciousness she stood naked before me, this perfect brown being with small feet and slender muscled legs, her mound of dark pubic hair, and the smooth taut breasts of a girl just become a woman. She entered the pool.

I suppose I'm a bit of a prude myself because I was shy about undressing in front of the girl and I turned my back and took off my own clothes, and when I stood, I covered myself with my hands. I must have looked ridiculous to her with my skin so pale beneath my brown neckline and above my arms where I rolled up my sleeves. But then I remembered that her own grandfather was a white man and so perhaps I didn't look so foreign to her after all. She looked quizzically at me as if she didn't altogether understand my shyness.

The water of the spring was warm and soft, oily with minerals, and I sank gratefully into it. People must have been bathing here for thousands of years and all along the edge of the pool there were well-worn rocks that looked like they had been placed to provide seating. These were sculpted smooth by time and the action of the minerals and perhaps the gentle friction of a millennium of naked buttocks. No wonder the first people had settled here in this little valley, with its river and hot springs, good grass for stock and rich soil for crops, protected on one end by the high bluffs with their network of caves to provide lodging. It was a paradise. What more could you want than this?

I lay back against the rocks beside the girl and fell almost instantly asleep, as if all the exhaustions and terrors of the last days had been suddenly released by the soothing waters. I don't know how long I slept, but I woke to a distant roll of thunder, and I felt truly rested for the first time since I could remember. It was late afternoon, and the sky was darkening with colossal storm clouds building to the south. The girl was gone. I looked into the meadow to see that the mule still grazed placidly and then I scanned the bluffs and saw smoke rising above one of the caves. I got out of the pool and sat on the still sun-warmed rocks to let myself dry for a moment. I dressed and picked up my saddlebags and followed the path up the bluff.

The girl had made a campsite in the cave, with a sleeping place of pine needles and grass, covered with blankets and deer hides. She had a fire burning and meat roasting, a tin pot of beans bubbling and another with what looked like some kind of corn mush. She had an iron skillet on which a stack of fresh-made tortillas were warming. And she had a tin coffeepot.

"Where did you get all this?" I asked.

"We cache provisions in this place," she said.

It occurred to me that this was the same place I had flown over with Spider King, and now I wondered if some of the gear had come from the raid on Colonel Carrillo's party. "Did you kill those men back there?" I asked her again. I wonder why it even matters to me. Am I trying to civilize the girl, who sees nothing morally wrong in the butchery of her enemy? Do I need to be reassured that she is somehow incapable of such an act, this slender fierce warrior girl, even though she clearly is not? And what difference does it make, finally? The elegant, beautifully educated Colonel Carrillo, with his fine dress uniform and pomaded black hair, would certainly kill her given the chance, would take her scalp as verification in order to collect the bounty. Both my own people and the Mexicans have been butchering our natives for centuries. How many Apache babies have been slaughtered by our soldiers? Yet only the atrocities of the conquered are referred to as criminal acts; those of the conqueror are justified as necessary, heroic, and, even worse, as the fulfillment of God's will. What difference, finally, between the civilized man and the savage?

"It was Indio Juan's raid," the girl repeated, not defensively but as a simple statement of fact.

"Okay," I said, and I did not ask her again.

We ate our meal sitting in the entrance of the cave, looking out over the valley as the blue-black storm clouds, lit by sustained flashes of lightning, moved across the mountains, pushing gray undulating curtains of rain ahead of them, the deep rumbling closer and louder, sounding as if it issued from the belly of the earth itself. I had the strangest sense then that we were the last human beings on earth, that the others all lay dead back there on the trail, consumed by buzzards, and we were all that was left, the last and the first people, Adam and Eve in the Garden of Eden, an Indian girl and a white boy. We would stay right here and begin our own race of man. We would do better this time.

But then someone would come along and try to take away our poor possessions, or our home, and we would have to defend it and ourselves; we would have to kill them or be killed and the wars would begin all over again. What had become of the "first" people who lived here thousands of years ago? I had once asked Margaret. She said that scientists didn't know exactly, but indications were that for some reason or other their economy and social structure had broken down, possibly as a result of some sort of climatological shift or event, until they descended into chaos and internal strife, and finally self-destructed. But it was also quite possible that their land had simply been invaded by a more powerful race of man, and they had been killed off or absorbed by the invaders.

The sky went black and the rain came all at once with a thunderous crash of lightning. We moved farther back in the cave to lie together on the sleeping place. I took the girl's clothes off, and my own, and covered us with a blanket, and put my arms around her and held her, breathing deeply of her scent, the scent of the mountains and the rain and the faint ozone scent of the storm. We were warm, dry, and snug here with the roaring deluge outside. Every few moments a flash of lightning illuminated the inside of the cave.

There was no sense of urgency this time and we took our time exploring each other, sometimes shyly, sometimes wantonly. I don't know if she'd ever been kissed before as a woman, because she didn't seem to even know how to do it. And maybe this is how it begins, this is how new races are born, a couple of kids together, touching each other, putting their hands and their mouths on each other, learning to love all over again, with no memory of the carnage of yesterday, and no thoughts of tomorrow.

We lay together like that all night. We slept and woke to love again and fell asleep holding each other. And we talked a little in our new language, part Apache, part Spanish, part English, a language of our own creation that only we would understand.

We rose at dawn this morning and bathed again in the hot spring and built a small fire to warm some food from the night before. We don't have to talk about it; we both know that we have to go back to the *ranchería* today. Last night existed in that perfect all-consuming limbo time, the pure uncomplicated space carved out by love and desire when there is nothing else on earth. I wish we could live forever in that moment, or at least just a little longer. But in the real world, I have Margaret to worry about. And, in any case, neither of us can walk away from our old races just like that, not just yet. It is far too complicated by the light of morning; we have friends and family and responsibilities to attend to. Our respective armies prepare to march against each other, and though we are powerless to prevent this, neither can we ignore it.

We packed some food for the trail and cached the cooking utensils and the staples, the dried beans, some dried corn and jerky, the flour and coffee in a niche in the rear of the cave. We covered it carefully with rocks so that animals couldn't dig it up and you'd have to know where to look for it. Maybe we will come back here when everything is over, or someone else who knows where to look will stop here for the night, uncover the cache and appreciate it for giving them sustenance, treat it respectfully and perhaps even add to it. In this way the girl tells me the People have lived for a long time.

In a few minutes we will saddle the mule and ride up out of the valley. We both have the sense that things are coming to an end and will have to begin again.

28 JUNE, 1932

We rode into the *ranchería* at midday yesterday. Of course, the Apaches had been alerted by the scouts and all knew we were coming. Some of the children had run out to meet us on the trail and escort us in, and as we entered, others came out of their wickiups to watch us pass. I saw that some of the men wore new Mexican army hats and coats, others the hats and clothes of our dead volunteers, the spoils of war. No one molested me; for the time being anyway, it seemed that I could come and go among worlds with impunity.

I wanted first to see Margaret, and the girl led me directly to the white Apache's wickiup. Before we had even dismounted, Margaret herself came out of the wickiup. She was dressed in Apache fashion, in moccasins and a brightly patterned, loose-fitting blouse and skirt of Mexican fabric. We looked at each other for a long time before speaking.

Finally I said: "I came back to get my camera."

"I figured you would," she said, smiling. "Why do you think I hung on to it? I knew you weren't going to come back just for me."

I slid off my mule and we embraced.

"Are you okay, Mag?"

"I'm alive, little brother."

"That's not what I asked."

"I'm alive and I'm not living in Indio Juan's wickiup," Margaret said. "In this world, that's okay."

"What happened to your face?" I asked.

"A little unpleasantness early on." She shrugged.

"What does that mean?"

"It means that once I accepted the fact that I'm a slave, things have been better. Mostly I do chores, fetch water, gather firewood, that sort of thing. And as long as I do what I'm told, they pretty much leave me alone."

"A slave?"

"They're just like us that way, Neddy," she said. "Despite all the vast cultural differences, it seems to be common human nature to turn the weaker sexes and races, not to mention conquered peoples, into servants." She laughed bitterly. "That's been one of my great anthropological discoveries of the past week."

"Tell me about Mr. Browning, Mag."

Margaret looked away from me. She shook her head and tears began to well up in her eyes. "I tried, little brother," she said. "I tried to keep him alive."

"I know, Mag," I said. "I know you did."

"He was so brave and strong, Neddy."

"Joseph?"

"Joseph is okay," she said. "Thank God he's been here with me. Without him I'd certainly be dead."

"We never should have left you here, Mag," I said. "I'm so sorry. I thought the girl would be able to look after you."

"She did, Neddy," Margaret said. "She did everything she could. It was my choice to stay. I couldn't have lived with myself if we'd left Mr. Browning to die here alone. I'm glad I was with him at the end. I think I brought him a little comfort. And I'm okay, really I am. And to answer the big question that's on your mind, and that you're too damn polite to ask, no, I have not been ravished by the savages."

"That's a good thing, Mag," I said. "Where's Charley?"

"He left here this morning with Joseph," she said. "I don't know where they went."

"Carrillo and some of his men were attacked," I said.

"I know, believe me," she said. "They danced all night over the scalps. I couldn't stop myself from trying to identify the hair they were waving."

"Was Charley involved?"

"No, he was against it," Margaret said. "It was Indio Juan. All Charley wants to do is keep away from the whites and the Mexicans. That's how he's survived here for fifty years. Through avoidance and nonengagement. It's Indio Juan who's causing all the trouble now."

"I'm going to get you out of here this time, Mag," I said. "I promise. I won't leave you again."

"Well, you'll have to discuss that with the big guy, little brother," she said. "The Apaches are quite possessive of their slaves. You know, it's so hard these days to find good domestic help."

"Carrillo and his soldiers are going to get here one way or another," I said. "Flowers knows the way up."

"Where's Albert, Ned?"

"With the expedition. He'd have come, but I left without telling him."

"And Tolley?"

"Tolley quit, Mag. He had some important shopping to do to get ready for fall semester at Princeton."

Margaret smiled forgivingly. "Yeah, it's always such a crunch to get everything done before the end of summer vacation, isn't it?"

"After the attack on Carrillo, the rich boys fled like rats from a sinking ship," I said.

"Who can blame them?"

"I can blame Tolley for bailing out on you and Mr. Browning."

"I can't," Margaret said. "What was he supposed to do, come back here and let them dangle his head over the fire again?"

"I didn't expect him to come back here with me," I said. "But he could have stayed with the expedition and seen this through to the end. By the way, Mag, I love the new getup."

"Becomes me, doesn't it?" she said. "God, if only my colleagues at the university could see me now . . . Oh, where are my manners . . . won't you come into my humble abode?"

The inside of the wickiup was covered in hides and blankets and wasn't at all uncomfortable. We sat down and Margaret handed me my camera bag. "I made a few entries in your notebook, little brother," she said smiling. "Just to keep you up on what's been was going on around here . . ." And then suddenly she began to weep, great inconsolable sobs, her body convulsing. I took her in my arms and held her, and when her tears had subsided a bit, she pushed away. "God, I'm sorry, I don't know where that came from, it just snuck up on me. I've been okay, really, I have. I've been strong, Neddy."

"You're a rock, Mag," I said. "You have nothing to apologize for. I don't know any man who's stronger."

"I thought I would never see you again," she said. "I thought this was going to be my life. And who knows, maybe it still is. The thing I've learned is, I can survive. You know what's most terrifying, Neddy? Is what we're willing to endure to do that. How adaptable we are. I'm a professional, I nearly have a doctorate degree, for Christ sake. And yet after a little over a week here, I'm getting rather accustomed to living with these people, to being their slave. And it's not really that bad. They treat me pretty well . . . I even catch myself being grateful to them for that, for not treating me worse, you know, or even killing me. Do you understand what I'm trying to say?"

"I think so, Mag."

"I danced with them over the scalps, Neddy."

"What choice did you have, Mag?" I asked.

"It's more than that," she said. "I started to identify with them, I got caught up in the celebration of their success. I *liked* it."

"Well, then maybe we'd better just stay right here," I said jokingly.

"You think we have any choice in the matter, Neddy?" Margaret asked, dead serious. "They're not going to let us go again. You understand that, don't you?"

"The expedition will come for us, Mag," I said. "You'll see."

"Oh Christ, Ned!" she snapped. "Are you just trying to cheer me up, or are you really so damn naive? You saw yourself what happened to Carrillo's men. You think these people are going to just sit here and wait for the Mexican army to show up in their camp and then dutifully hand us over and surrender?"

"What do you think is going to happen?"

"I think Indio Juan will ambush them again . . . and again," she said. "I think he'll kill every Mexican soldier and every gringo he can before they even get here. *If* they even get here. And in the meantime, I think Charley will take his band somewhere else, farther south, deeper yet into the mountains. He has other *rancherías,* even more remote and just as inaccessible as this one. And the thing is, Neddy, they're going to take me with them. I'm a captive, I'm their property now."

"I came back for you, didn't I, Mag?" I asked. "Just like I said I would. And one way or another, I'm not going to let that happen."

8 July, 1932

I have been over a week now at the *ranchería.* Maybe it's just the lull before the storm, but it's been a quiet, peaceful time. Indio Juan has been gone since before my arrival. His scouts have reported back that the expedition has not moved from its base camp; rather than risking the loss of more men, Carrillo is clearly taking his time to formulate a new plan. Also it's likely that the monsoon weather has kept them pinned down, as travel in the mountains this time of year is problematic.

Due to the heavy rains, many of the people have moved out of their wickiups, which are impossible to keep dry, and taken up lodging in the elaborate network of ancient cave dwellings on the bluffs above the valley. Chideh and I are settled in one of these. It is a crude habitation by any modern standards, but warm, dry, and cozy inside. Life among these people strikes me a bit like a perpetual camping trip and I can see how seductive it could be, especially to a young boy taken captive from the civilized world. When I was a kid growing up in Chicago, I read all the books and periodicals about the Old West I could get my hands on. I read about the Indians and trappers and mountain men, and I dreamed of this wild life. Little did I imagine . . .

For the most part the people have been guardedly friendly to me, though I seem to occupy an uncertain role in their minds. While they're quite used to the men taking wives from other tribes and races, clearly an adult White Eyes moving into the band as the "husband" of one of their young women is without precedent. I've started exposing some film again, having "borrowed" some additional rolls from Big Wade when I was back in camp. It's a great relief and I think that I've made some startling images here. I don't care what Margaret says, wasn't it Confucius who said "A picture is worth a thousand words"? But when I pointed this out to Margaret, she answered. "Yeah, but didn't Franz Kafka say: 'Nothing is so deceiving as a photograph'?"

Charley and Joseph returned to the *rancheria* two days after the girl and I arrived here. The old man came directly to see me.

"My grandson is well?" was the first thing he asked.

"He's fine," I said. "Where have you been?"

"I took Charley to show him the Mexican soldiers and the White Eyes of the expedition," he said.

"You went down there?" I asked. "What for?"

"So that Charley could see how many of them there are," he said.

"Did you tell him that he should give himself up?"

"I told him to take his People and hide."

"Is that what you wish you had done, Joseph, all those years ago?" I asked. "Instead of surrendering?"

"It is too late for me," said the old man.

"It's too late for Charley, as well," I said.

"What would you wish for him to do?" Joseph asked. "Return to the White Eyes world? They would put him in a circus."

"It's the twentieth century, Joseph," I said. "Wild Indians don't get to live in the White Eyes world anymore."

"That is so," Joseph said. He opened his arm out to take in the country. "But this is not the White Eyes world."

"You, of all people, know better than that, old man," I said. "Everything is the White Eyes world now. Even this."

Since we have been here, the girl has been showing me her home country. I carry my camera on these outings, which we often make on foot in the vicinity of the *ranchería*. Sometimes, if we're going farther afield, we ride my mule. Either way we try to return before the afternoon rains begin, but if we get caught out, she always seems to know another cave in which to take shelter, and sometimes we'll spend the night there. We are like a couple of kids exploring, and somehow we manage to exist in this time together in that same spirit of childlike innocence and wonder. We have managed to create our own private world and we let nothing else in to violate or spoil it. And yet we are both aware of the fact that this world we have made does not exist outside itself.

I've never been a big believer in signs or portents, but the Apaches are a deeply superstitious people and yesterday during one of our explorations something very disturbing occurred that seems to have shaken the girl to her core.

We had lost track of time and wandered on foot several hours away from the *ranchería*. The afternoon storm clouds had begun to build over the mountains, but not until we saw the first distant flash of lightning and heard the accompanying rumble of thunder did we realize that we were too far afield to make it back before the rains came. The entire region is pocked with caves and as usual we had little trouble finding one in which to take refuge. Obviously because the caves also provide shelter to a variety of wildlife, including mountain lions and bears, we always investigate them thoroughly before seeking lodging inside. On these outings, we carry a rawhide bag with fire-making materials—a juniper stick about the length and thickness of a pencil, a flat piece of wood made of sotol stalk and dried bark or grass to use as tinder. I'm much less adept at the process than the girl; by twirling the stick in a notch on the wood, she can start a fire in a matter of minutes. When we had some larger sticks burning, we made a torch using a piece of cloth saturated with pine pitch. We had to crouch down in order to fit through the opening of the cave, but once inside we were able to stand up. It had obviously once been inhabited, for in the center was an old fire ring and the roof of the cave was blackened with smoke. The side walls were decorated with a number of prehistoric drawings—odd representational figures of birds, animals, and men, and various symbols, the meaning of which it was impossible to decipher. We had come upon similar rock drawings in other caves and on some of the canyon walls in the area. The cave seemed like a perfect place to wait out the storm, and as we had brought a blanket and a little food, we could easily spend the night here if we had to.

While the girl got a fire burning in the fire ring, I explored the cave further, just to make certain that we were its only residents. It was maybe fifteen feet deep and had two more passages in the rear. I crawled through one of these, which opened up into another smaller chamber. When I raised my torch, I saw the outline of the figure lying on the floor and I nearly jumped out of my skin. It was clearly a human form, but covered in a mound of silty white dust. I knelt down and began to carefully brush away the dust. As I did so, I began to expose the mummified remains of a woman. She was lying on her side, with her knees drawn up. Although desiccated and shrunken, her skin was nearly unbroken, stretched taut against her bones, and her features were perfectly intact. She had light, wavy hair, nearly flaxen, not at all like Indian hair, and as I uncovered more of her body I saw that she cradled an infant in her arms, and that the child was also perfectly preserved. Both of them wore oddly serene expressions on their faces, as if they had just lain down for an afternoon nap.

I sat there for a while as my torch burned down, watching the mother and child, and when I finally spoke to the girl it was in a whisper, as if afraid of waking them from their centuries-long slumber.

"*Chideh,*" I said, "come here. Bring my bag and another torch."

I wish now that I had left the burial chamber and never called to the girl, never even told her what I had seen there. It was a secret better kept to myself.

She came in through the passage, holding the torch ahead of her and dragging my camera bag. When she saw the woman and child, her expression went from incomprehension to disbelief and finally to horror. She shrank back against the wall of the cave. "What have you done?" she asked. "*¿Qué has hecho?*"

"I have done nothing," I said. "What's the matter with you?"

"It is a very bad thing to disturb the dead."

"I only brushed the dust off them. That's all."

"Why are they not bones?" she asked.

I did not have the words to explain that some substance in the dust must have preserved the bodies. So I just said, "I don't know."

"You dug them up," she said. "You let their ghosts loose. Look how they smile."

"That's nonsense. There's no such thing as ghosts."

"They will haunt us now," said the girl, not to be assuaged. "We cannot stay here."

The rain had already begun and fell in loud, driving sheets.

"Look, I'll cover them up again," I said. "Just like I found them. Then I'll close the opening of the passageway with rocks. They won't be able to get out."

The girl looked at the woman and child, but there was something like compassion now in her gaze, the tenderness with which another woman looks upon a mother and her child. She put her hand on her own belly. "It is too late," she said. "They are already out."

She went back into the main cave, and I made some time exposures of the bodies using what dim light I had from the torches. I was not superstitious about it and, unlike the girl, had no sense that I was violating the peace of the dead. I knew that later, when I looked at the images themselves, I would see them differently; I would see then the poignancy of a mother holding her baby for eternity, at least, that was the image I hoped I was making. I hoped that my camera might breathe life back into their human remains.

When I had finished shooting, I carefully re-covered the bodies with the white dust. I touched a little to my tongue; it was some kind of mineral which must have preserved them so perfectly. I hoped that it would be another thousand years before they were disturbed again.

With the torrential downpour, we had little choice but to stay in the cave. The girl was sullen and withdrawn, did not speak or eat, and curled up with her back to me when we lay down, in much the same posture, it occurred to me, as the woman with the child. I fell asleep with my arm around her, holding her, trying to reassure her that everything was all right, that the ghosts would not harm us. But during the night I dreamed that I woke and rolled the girl over toward me, and she had become the desiccated corpse of the ancient woman. I was not afraid of the corpse in my dream, just enormously sad for her death and that of her child, and I held them, weeping. In the morning I did not tell the girl of my dream.

9 JULY, 1932

The *ranchería* was quiet and seemed largely deserted by the time we returned this morning. The girl went immediately to seek one of the old woman *di-yins* so that she might be cleansed of her contact with the dead, so that she and our unborn child would not be stricken with the "ghost sickness," as the Apaches call it.

For my part, I went to find Margaret in order to tell her about my discovery of the mummified bodies. Charley and the old man were sitting in front of the wickiup when I got there. Margaret and Charley's wife were grinding corn on a stone metate nearby.

"I'd love to chat, little brother," Margaret said. "But as you can see, a woman's work is never done around here."

"What happens if you refuse, Mag?" I asked.

"Trust me, Neddy, it's easier just to do the work."

"Joseph," I said to the old man, "would you ask Charley if I might speak with Margaret for a few minutes?"

Joseph spoke to the white Apache. "Charley says it is a good thing that the White Eyes are finally learning some manners," he said. "Although you should make this request of his wife, Ishton, rather than of him."

"Go ahead and ask her then, will you?" I said.

In his most florid oratorical manner, Joseph spoke for what seemed like forever to the woman. But after all that, it was clear that when the woman,

Ishton, answered him, she did so in the negative. In exasperation, Margaret dropped her grinding stone and said something in what sounded to me like surprisingly fluent Apache. Then she stood defiantly, wiped her hands on her dress, and began to walk toward me. Ishton grabbed hold of Margaret's arm to stop her, squawking at her like an angry hen. Without hesitating, Margaret turned and threw a roundhouse punch that caught the woman behind the ear and knocked her to the ground.

"I've had all I'm going to take from you, you *fucking bitch*!" Margaret screamed, standing over her, her fist cocked. "Do you hear me? I quit as your slave. And if you lay another hand on me, I'll fucking kill you. Do you understand me?"

Surprisingly, Charley began to roar with laughter, sitting cross-legged and rocking back and forth in a state of utter hilarity. Even more surprising was that his wife did not fight back, but like a submissive dog who knows it's outmatched by an alpha dog, she assumed a kind of cowering posture.

Margaret rubbed her knuckles and turned toward me. "*Damn*, that felt good," she said. "I don't know why I didn't do that a long time ago." And to Charley, she raised her fist and said something in Apache that made him laugh even louder.

"What did you just say, Mag?" I asked.

"I told him that I did not mean any disrespect to the chief, but that if he ever hits me again, I'll give him a little of the same medicine." Margaret sat down next to me as if she owned the place.

"Wow, I didn't know you threw such a mean haymaker, Mag," I said. "What brought that on anyway?"

"I don't know," she said. "I guess I just couldn't bear for you to see them treat me like that. It's one thing to submit to being a slave when you're all alone, and another thing for your friends to witness the indignity. I guess I kind of snapped."

"That is a good thing you did," Joseph said. "My Mexican captive, La Luna, was also very strong and proud. She, too, did not wish to be a slave. She wished to be treated like the other women. After a time she became my wife and the others all respected her just as if she was one of them because she had Power. The Apaches treat people as they deserve to be treated. You submitted to Charley's authority, and now you have shown him that you deserve his respect."

"So why didn't you tell me that story when we first got here, Joseph?" Margaret asked.

"Because it is something that you must learn yourself," he said, "and prove to them by your own behavior."

Charley's hilarity had finally subsided and we all sat cross-legged in front of the wickiup. The girl joined us, quiet as a spirit, and took a seat beside me. Another woman with two preadolescent boys came over and requested permission to sit. I had noticed that the *ranchería* was even quieter than usual, and although women and children had already outnumbered the men here, now there seemed to be virtually no men about at all.

Charley's wife prepared food to eat and served everyone, including Margaret. Ishton's ear had swollen like a cauliflower and a little blood ran from it. When Margaret noticed this, she rose and wet a piece of cloth from the water jug, went to her, and gently dabbed her wounded ear. *"Lo siento,"* she whispered. "I didn't mean to hit you so hard." The woman smiled gratefully.

Now Charley began speaking, and Joseph translated for us. He explained that one of the boys with Indio Juan's band had returned to the *ranchería* last night with news that the expedition was on the move again and that Indio Juan was trailing them, waiting for another chance to attack.

"I myself have seen the Mexican soldiers and the White Eyes," Charley said. "As always, there are too many of them for us to fight. We will let our brother, Juan, fight them if he wishes, and while he keeps the soldiers occupied, we will leave here and travel to a new home, deeper in the mountains, where no one will find us."

One of the boys spoke up then, with a kind of bravado that was almost amusing given his young age.

"We let the warrior Juan fight for us," he said, "while we slip away like women. Why do we not fight like men?"

Charley looked at the boy for some time before answering. "Why do we not fight like men?" he asked finally. "Because you are not a man, you are a boy. And these"—he gestured with his arm—"are women."

"All the warriors have joined Indio Juan," said the boy. And though he was clearly losing his courage for challenging Charley, he managed to screw up the last of it to say, "All but the old men and the boys . . . and . . . and you . . . Why does our chief not fight the soldiers?"

Charley smiled wryly at the boy's impudence. "Because it is my duty to see that the People survive," he said. "And to do that I must protect the women and children. We have learned that it is useless to fight the Mexicans or the White Eyes because even when we win a battle and we kill the soldiers, they only come back with more soldiers. They are like ants, there is no end of them. Ask this old man," he said, indicating Joseph, "how many White Eyes and Mexicans there are on earth."

The boy looked questioningly at Joseph.

"There are so many White Eyes and Mexicans on earth," said Joseph, "that if they were all lined up in front of you and you started walking past them, you would walk your whole life and grow as old as I am, and you would still not reach the end of the line."

The boy looked puzzled. It occurred to me that he had probably never seen more than thirty people assembled in one place in his life. How could he possibly imagine how many White Eyes and Mexicans there were on earth?

"We will pack our belongings tonight and leave in the morning," Charley said.

"May I speak?" I asked. "*¿Puedo hablar?*"

Charley looked at me approvingly. He nodded and answered in Apache.

"Charley says that this White Eyes has good manners," Joseph translated.

"They don't really want to fight," I said. "They just want the Huerta boy back. And they want this woman, too." I indicated Margaret. "If you give them up, no one will even follow you. You can disappear in the mountains, and if you stay away from the ranches and settlements, you can continue to live up here forever."

"Charley wishes to know if you are coming with them?" Joseph asked. "With your wife."

"You're on the spot now, little brother," Margaret said. "Are you going to do the right thing?"

"Is there a right thing to do, Margaret?"

"Well, you can tell them that you're planning to abandon your wife," she said. "In which case they'll probably kill you before they leave here in the morning. Or you can go with them. In which case, they'll never let you leave once you get there. And Neddy, it's going to be really tough to find film for your camera where they're headed."

"That's what I'm asking, Mag," I said. "Is there a right thing to do?"

"The right thing to do around here," she said, "is to avoid dying. Live one more day. That's my position. And on the bright side, at least we'll have each other."

"Tell Charley I'll go with them," I said to Joseph. "But that they must leave the woman and the boy here."

"Don't try to be noble, Neddy," Margaret said. "You don't have that kind of bargaining power."

"Charley says that everyone comes," Joseph said. "That there are not enough People left to leave any behind. He says that you will take more Apache wives and make more Apache babies. He approves of you."

"Sounds like you're going to have to get a *real* job, sweetheart," Margaret said. "To support your extended family."

"That's real funny, Mag."

"Just remember what I said, Neddy. One more day. Whatever it takes."

It was then that an extraordinary thing occurred, something that I expect I'll remember until the day I die. We heard a commotion on the edge of the *ranchería*, a cry of alarm from the boy who had been posted as lookout there. Everyone leaped up and Charley scrambled for his rifle as we heard the pounding of horses' hooves, and three mounted figures rode into view up the valley, riding hard. The lead man held a rifle aloft and issued a kind of high-pitched war cry that was immediately and unmistakably identifiable. *"Chaaaaaarrrrgggge!"*

"Oh, *good God*," Margaret said under her breath.

Yes, it was none other than Tolbert Phillips Jr., galloping another of his polo ponies up the river bottom, whooping like a madman, waving a rifle overhead; he was dressed in a preposterous white-fringed buckskin outfit that I'd never seen before, and that made him look like he'd ridden right out of Buffalo Bill's Wild West Show. Behind him came Albert Valor on a running mule, and bringing up the rear on a burro, trotting as fast as its little legs would take it, came the boy Jesus.

"What in the hell does he think he's doing?" I muttered.

Charley calmly jacked a shell into his Winchester and raised it to his shoulder; in his hands the weapon looked as small as a child's toy. Stupidly, I stood there frozen, watching him as if in a dream. But Margaret had more presence of mind, and before he could squeeze off a shot, she leaped onto Charley's back, wrapping her arm around his neck and her legs around his waist. The rifle discharged and Charley dropped it. Although he was not a young man, a lifetime in the wild has given him a physique as lean and hard as a mountain lion, and although Margaret hung on for dear life, he shook her off easily and flung her to the ground. But by now I had recovered my senses and I picked up the rifle and held it on him.

Still whooping, Tolley rode into the *ranchería*, slowing slightly when he saw that the place was virtually deserted. A couple dozen women, children, and old people faded into the trees along the river bottom, where they had instinctively run as soon as they heard the young guard's warning cries. It was a lesson well learned over centuries of attacks upon their villages. Tolley spotted us and spurred his horse anew, covering the last fifty yards at a dead run and pulling up short in front of the wickiup, his horse lathered, snorting and prancing.

"What's with the getup, Tolley?" I asked, still holding the rifle on Charley, who remained stoically silent.

"I liberate you from the fiendish clutches of the savages," Tolley said. "And that's how you greet me, Giles? . . . I had it made by my tailor in New York, if you must know. I've been saving it for a special occasion." He raised his arm, from which the fringe dangled at least eight inches long. "Not a bad look for me, don't you agree, old sport?"

"You do know how to make an entrance, darling," Margaret said, laughing. "And your timing is impeccable."

"What the hell are you doing here, Tolley?" I asked. "I thought you went home. How did you get through?"

"All of that in good time, old sport," Tolley said, dismounting and looking around like a conquering general.

By now Albert had reached us. He dismounted and embraced Margaret, and they held each other for a moment without speaking. Finally, Jesus trotted up on his burro. "Señor Tolley, why do you leave me behind like that?" he complained. "I cannot keep up to your fast horse on this little donkey."

"Sorry, young lad," Tolley said. "But I had to make an impression, and you and your burro don't exactly strike terror into the hearts of men. You appear to have been correct, Albert, when you said that the Apaches are inordinately impressed by displays of personal courage. I seem to have taken the village single-handedly and without firing a shot."

"I came back to rescue you, Señor Ned," the boy said proudly.

"And a fine job you did of it, too, kid."

The question of what to do with Charley presented itself, and for now we bound his arms and legs and left him on the ground in front of the wickiup. He did not utter a sound. The girl had disappeared, as had Charley's wife, Ishton, with her baby, presumably all of them fleeing into the river bottom with the others as soon as the commotion began. We had to assume that they might have weapons cached there, but we suspected that they would be less likely to try to attack us if they saw that we held their chief.

"Where is my good man, Mr. Browning?" Tolley asked.

Neither Margaret nor I wanted to be the one to break the news to Tolley, but it must have been clear in our faces.

"Oh, no . . ." Tolley said, stricken.

"I'm sorry, Tolley," Margaret said finally. "I did everything I could."

"You mean to say that I've come all this way," said Tolley in a low voice, "to prove to him that I wasn't the same kind of cad as his former employer, to show him that Tolbert Phillips Jr. stands by his people through thick or thin . . ."

"I think Mr. Browning knew that, sweetheart," Margaret said. "In any case, there's nothing you could have done. He died of his head wound that first night."

"Trying to be the big hero, weren't you, White Eyes?" Albert asked me. "Coming back here all alone. Why didn't you tell me? I'd have come with you."

"That's exactly why I didn't," I said. "I wasn't trying to be a hero. And don't worry, Albert, Margaret knows you would have come, too. What about you, Tolley, why the sudden change of heart?"

"You never gave me a chance to come to my senses, Giles," said Tolley. "I got to thinking about everything you said that night, and damned if I wasn't ashamed of myself. The next morning I couldn't bring myself to leave with the others. At the same time, the prospect of a long journey home in the company of that insufferable moron Winston Hughes was more than I could bear. The fact is, I missed you, old sport. However, when I came looking for you, you had already sneaked off."

"Carrillo just let you go like that?" I asked.

"No. In fact, at first the colonel forbade us from leaving," Tolley said. "Which is why our rescue of you was delayed. But with the American-Mexican alliance already unraveling with the defection of so many volunteers, and the fact that Carrillo had no clear plan of action of his own, he was finally powerless to stop us."

"And Gatlin encouraged him to let us go," Albert added. "I think the chief figures he's seen the last of the city boy, the fairy, and the injun now."

"How did you get past Indio Juan and his men?" I asked.

"Providence, old sport," Tolley said. "Or as some might say, pure dumb luck. By the time we reached the scene of the ambush . . ." Tolley paused here. "You must have seen it yourself, Giles. Well, you can just imagine it a week later . . ."

Tolley hesitated for a long time, quite overcome with the memory, and finally Albert continued for him. "We had dropped down into the canyon to get past the scene of the ambush," he said, "as you must have done. We had just stopped to rest in the shade of the rocks, when we spotted Indio Juan and his band on the trail above us. Tolley's right, we were just damn lucky. If we'd been moving, they'd have seen us or heard us. And if we'd been a moment earlier or a moment later, we'd have run directly into them on the trail. As it was, we were well concealed by the rocks."

"We kept our hands clamped over the mouths of our mounts as the Apaches passed above us," Tolley said, "for we were close enough that had one of them so much as nickered, we'd have been given away. It was the longest five minutes of our lives, I can tell you. We waited over two hours before we dared move again. We had expected that they might have posted a lookout at the pass, and when we reached it, Jesus and I hung back while Albert climbed into the rocks above on foot to investigate. It appeared to be unguarded. And so we crossed one at a time. And miraculously, we passed unmolested. Evidently, every able-bodied man among them, with the exception of Charley here, was in Indio Juan's war party and he must have been focused on the expedition, not expecting a mere three people to try to slip by. And voilà," said Tolley, opening his arms wide, "we have taken the *rancheria*."

"So you see," added Albert, with a sly smile, "Tolley knew there were no warriors here *before* he made his heroic charge."

We all laughed.

"Well, it was still damned effective," Tolley protested.

"You scared the hell out of the women and children, darling," Margaret said. "Sent them scurrying into the river bottom. They must have thought an entire army was attacking."

"And you don't know how close you came to getting your head shot off by Charley," I said.

"Don't tell me you saved my life again, Giles, just when I thought I had repaid the favor?"

"I had nothing to do with it, Tolley," I admitted. "Margaret saved your ass this time. I'd say we're all even."

"Which, of course, begs the next question," Tolley said. "What do we do now?"

It was a good question. We looked at Charley, lying hog-tied on the ground. He had still not spoken a word, would not even look at us.

"If we give him up to Carrillo," Albert said, "the Mexicans will certainly execute him."

"Why not return him to his own people?" Tolley suggested. "Take him back across the border."

"That would be worse for him than execution," said Joseph, who had remained silent up to now. He had not tried to speak to Charley, either, and it occurred to me that his loyalties must be divided at this point.

"I agree," Margaret said. "What are you going to do, Tolley, get him a haircut and a shave, dress him in a suit, find him an apartment and a job in the bank?"

"Yes, he could be rehabilitated," Tolley said. "Look at Joseph, he's a civilized man."

"We can't take him back to the United States, Tolley," I said. "Imagine when the newspapers get hold of the poor bastard. Little Charley McComas found alive fifty years later. We might as well put him in a zoo. And as Albert says, we can't give him up to the Mexicans, either."

"Then what do you suggest we do with him, Giles?" Tolley asked.

"Let's make a trade with him," I suggested. "His own freedom in return for the Huerta boy."

"He will never agree to such a trade," Joseph said, "without some assurance from the Mexicans that if he lets the boy go, they will stop hunting the People."

"Okay, then we take Charley and the Huerta boy back down with us until we locate the expedition," I said, "and we let him make that deal with Carrillo: They get Geraldo back, Charley and his people go free and unmolested. Everybody goes home happy."

"In the long, bloody history of the Indian wars," Albert said, "has that ever happened, White Eyes?"

"You got a better idea, Albert?"

"Your plan overlooks one other, not-so-minor detail, old sport," Tolley pointed out. "The wild card."

"Yeah, I know. Indio Juan."

Tonight we have moved back up into the caves above the valley, where I make these entries. The evening monsoons have come and gone. We feel relatively safe here, protected both from the elements and from the women and children, who have not yet come out of hiding, although it's possible that they've slipped back into the *ranchería* without our knowing it. We built a fire and ate our dinner, and afterward Tolley and I sat smoking in front of the entrance to the cave. We will all take turns guarding Charley through the night. Chideh still hasn't come back, either. She must be trying to sort out who the enemy is now; I am her husband and I hold her grandfather prisoner. I'm not so naive as to believe that her loyalties will lie with me, and perhaps by staying away, she avoids having to make that choice.

10 JULY, 1932

This morning just before daybreak, I slipped away from the cave without waking the others and walked down to the *ranchería* with my camera. The place felt like a ghost town and I had the sense that the others had come in the night to gather their possessions, for it seemed somehow even emptier and more deserted than it had yesterday. Through my lens, the wickiups had the dead look of archaeological relics, long abandoned, as if the people who once inhabited them could only be imagined. I looked down the valley where it fell away and rose again to a series of impassable rock pinnacles, wrapped in morning mist, the earth lying so silent and calm beneath, patient and unhurried and timeless as it always seems by first light. I wished that I had my large-format view camera with me, as it is impossible to capture the enormity and grandeur of this landscape with the Leica. I wondered how it is that such a vast, wild land stretching away farther than the lens can reach, or the eye can see, how is it that even still it is not large enough to accommodate this tiny band of people. Even here, civilization intrudes on wildness; even here the bears and mountain lions cannot escape the relentless pursuit of Billy Flowers, any more than the Apaches can avoid that of General George Crook or Colonel Hermenegildo Carrillo.

I walked down to the river, which was high and muddy with runoff from the monsoons, the trees heavy with summer foliage, their leaves motionless in the dead calm of dawn. I found a pool where the current did not run so strongly, set my camera bag down on a rock, stripped and waded into the water. The rocks were slick under my feet, the water ice-cold so that my breath caught in my chest. I submerged myself quickly in the pool until the initial shock had turned to a tingling numbness, and when it began to hurt I got out. The air raised gooseflesh on my body.

I was sitting on the rock, putting my clothes back on when the girl appeared beside me. I say it that way because that's just how it seems; she moves so lightly and silently that it's as if she is just suddenly there. I wasn't startled or even surprised when she put her hand lightly on my shoulder.

"I've been waiting for you," I said. "Why did you run away?"

"From the time that we are very small children," she said, "we are taught to run and hide when the village is under attack."

"Yes, but couldn't you see that it was just Tolley?" I asked.

She smiled. "Yes."

"Why didn't you come back?"

"You have tied my grandfather up."

"We had to. Listen, Chideh, you have to bring the boy Geraldo back to us. We're not going to hurt Charley, or anyone else. Don't you see by now that we don't want to hurt your people?"

"The soldiers hurt the People," she said. "The Mexicans hurt the People. The White Eyes hurt the People. This is why we hide from them."

"Yes, I know. And as soon as you give Geraldo back, you can hide again. That's all we've ever wanted from you. The boy."

"And you will release my grandfather?"

"Yes. Tell the others to come back in. You have to trust me."

We brought Charley back down from the caves to the *ranchería* later that morning, and shortly thereafter the girl brought Geraldo Huerta in. An old woman from his Apache family came in with them. She is protective of Geraldo and kept him close to her; he is such a slight, ethereal boy, and there is something nearly fey about him; he hardly seems suited to this hearty life in the wilds.

The others, too, began to trickle back in until little by little the *ranchería* took on life again as if they had never left. Soon fires were burning, and the smells of wood smoke and food cooking filled the air. Joseph negotiated the boy's return with Charley and convinced us that it was safe to release the big man from his bonds, for a true Apache's word is never broken.

"What about Geronimo?" Tolley asked. "Wasn't he a notorious liar?"

"That is so," Joseph admitted. "Geronimo was not a truthful man."

"And how do you know we can trust Charley?" Tolley asked.

"How does he know he can trust you?" Joseph answered.

So we untied the white Apache, and in that simple act of trust every-thing was suddenly equalized, leveled, so that no one holds any advantage over anyone else. Just as Charley is no longer our prisoner, so, with his free-dom, is Margaret no longer his slave. And in this new democratic arrange-ment, the tension has been greatly relieved. Margaret and Charley's wife, Ishton, seem to have grown quite fond of each other and putter around the wickiup like equals now. (Clearly that well-placed roundhouse punch also helped level the playing field.) Margaret, who has always professed to have no interest whatsoever in children, even dotes on Ishton's baby, cooing and gurgling at it. We all continue to be astonished by Margaret's command of the Apache language; although I've learned a few words and phrases that I use when I communicate with the girl in our particular patois, Margaret, on the other hand, chatters away almost like a native.

Tomorrow we head out to find the expedition. I don't know about the others, but I am filled with dread.

11 JULY, 1932

Charley has elected to bring the rest of the band with us. We rather expected that he would leave the women and children at the *ranchería* rather than risk exposing them to the soldiers. But evidently he wishes to keep them close at hand. All that stayed behind were two old women too feeble to travel, one of whom is the blind old woman Siki. The Apaches are so private that Joseph has barely spoken to us of her, and in their own stoic fashion, there were no sentimental good-byes. The two old women were simply left sitting outside the wickiup. They had provisions and firewood.

"I don't understand," I said as we were preparing to ride out. "Are they coming back for them?"

"Siki and the other are too old to travel," Albert explained. "It is the

Apache way for the old, the injured, and the sick to step aside for the good of the tribe. Everyone's time comes. This is understood."

"Just like that?" Tolley asked. "Don't they even say good-bye?"

"Good-bye is a White Eyes concept," Albert said. "They have said all that needs to be said."

And without a look back, the white Apache, astride a small dappled gray horse that looks like a child's pony beneath his giant frame, rode out of the *ranchería,* his red hair and beard long and wild, his skin sun- and wind-burned the color of old mottled rust. Behind him followed his ragtag band of mixed-blood women and children, some mounted, others on foot, trotting to keep up; they put me in mind of Lilliputians following Gulliver. Old Joseph Valor rode with them on his quickstepping donkey, his long gray braids bouncing, his ancient wizened face cut as deeply by time as the canyons and arroyos of this strange wild country.

I had ridden on ahead so that I could expose some film of Charley and his people as they approached. No one in America will believe that such a race of man exists, and when Big Wade asks me the inevitable question— "Did you get the shot, kid?"—I want to be able to say with certainty that I did. *The Last Wild Apaches,* I've decided I'm going to call it.

I rejoined the others, and we rode spread out along the trail behind the Apaches: Margaret, Albert, Jesus, Tolley, and I; sometimes Chideh rode beside me, sometimes she joined her people; we rode abreast in twos or threes whenever the trail opened up to allow it but mostly keeping single file, down the rocky, winding slopes, traversing the canyon and arroyos, through the solemn pine forests, across the lush creek bottoms. The summer rains have brought out the season's brief, intense flash of color, so that the formerly sere slopes of the Sierra Madre are a bright green, tufts of grass sprouting even from the rocks themselves.

Without our even being aware of it at first, Charley has led us on a different route than that which we have taken from the *ranchería* before. Tonight we are camped for the night in a spectacular setting, on a high plateau at the head of a waterfall. We arrived just as the sun was setting, lighting the mountaintops purple all around. Here the stream has cut a deep channel into the hard conglomerate rock, before falling off into a nearly straight-walled canyon, perhaps a hundred feet to the bottom. It's a spectacular sight and we crept to the edge of the chasm and watched as the water dropped in silent sheets through the air, gathering itself again at the bottom to rush down a narrow gorge with a faint distant roar. I didn't have enough light left to find my way down to the base of the canyon, but I intend to rise early and do so in the morning.

We pitched camp some distance back from the canyon at the edge of the pine forest, built fires, and made our dinner. The Apaches camped a bit off by themselves, and after dinner, Tolley, Albert, Margaret, and I went to speak with Charley, to see if we could get a sense of why we had taken this route and where we were headed tomorrow.

"Charley sent two boys ahead this morning to scout," Joseph explained as we sat around their fire. "They report that the lion hunter has led the soldiers a different way, and so Charley has taken this trail in order to intercept them."

"And did the boys see Indio Juan?" Albert asked.

"Yes, they report that Indio Juan and his men are following the expedition," Joseph said. "At night they steal stock and whatever provisions they can from the Mexicans and the White Eyes. They have killed two guards so far."

"How long before we reach them?" Margaret asked.

"They are less than a day's ride from us," Joseph said. "We will find them tomorrow."

Chideh and I have camped a little away from the others. Some have hung blankets or pieces of oilcloth between the trees or bushes to make rough shelters for the night. But we are sleeping in the open. The night sky is clear and moonless with so many stars visible that it's difficult to identify the constellations, vast masses and dizzying swirls of them. We lie on our backs, huddled under a blanket, looking up at the stars. We don't have enough language between us to have much of a conversation about astronomy, and I don't know what her people think about the stars, or what myths and superstitions they have devised to explain the heavens. I wonder if they make her feel as small and as insignificant as they do me; I sense by the way she holds on to me that the sheer enormity of the universe, the cold indifference of the stars, frightens her . . . as it does me. I wonder if they give her the same sense of vertigo, the same hollow pit in her stomach, as if the night sky threatens to suck us off the earth and absorb us like specks of dust.

A shooting star blazed across the sky, its long tail burning bright, and just as suddenly extinguished. The girl raised her hand and traced the trajectory of it with her finger, running it all the way down to earth.

"There," she whispered, pointing. "The enemy is there."

"What do you mean?"

"This is why the stars fall at night," she said. "To show the People in what direction our enemies lie."

Undated entry

In fact, the shooting star did point to the location of the expedition. We departed our campsite by the waterfall at dawn and traveled hard all day, keeping up a punishing pace, mostly downhill through increasingly rough country. By late afternoon we had reached the eastern foothills of the sierra, which looked out over a broad plain. Down below we saw them, moving along the edge of the plain like tiny toy soldiers, their passage marked by a small raising of dust. Billy Flowers and Colonel Carrillo must have thought that they would make better progress in the flats than they could in the mountains and had elected to go the long way around, to approach the *rancheria* from the south. They had obviously not bargained on the Apaches coming to them.

Shortly after we spotted the expedition, Indio Juan met us on the trail with his small band. The Apaches all dismounted for a tense conference. Juan swaggered and postured in his maniacal way, proudly displaying two fresh scalps he claimed to have taken off soldiers. He remained intractable about giving up Geraldo Huerta and he and Charley exchanged heated words. We stood some distance off and kept silent, trying not to even look at Indio Juan. He is so crazy and volatile that just a glance can set him off.

At one point he walked over to Margaret and put his face up close to hers and whispered something the rest of us couldn't hear. Margaret colored and clenched her teeth. Albert immediately stepped toward her to intervene, and Indio Juan whirled on him with his knife drawn, smiling wickedly, as if he had just been looking for this excuse. Charley spoke sharply, and in that same moment Tolley, who was still mounted, drew his rifle from the scabbard and cocked it. Only then did Indio Juan back down. He spoke derisively to Charley.

"What did he say?" I asked Albert.

"He said now that Charley rides with White Eyes, he has grown weak."

Indio Juan remounted and wheeled his horse around, and he and his people galloped off.

It was decided that Tolley, Margaret, and I would ride down to make contact with the expedition. We would take Jesus with us and leave Albert and Joseph with the Apaches. We asked Charley if we could take little Geraldo, in order to show his good faith.

"You bring back six strong horses," he said, "and the word of their chief that in return for giving up the boy, the soldiers will leave our country. Only then will we give them the boy." Charley doesn't seem to understand that the Mexicans don't think of this as the Apaches' country.

And so we rode down out of the foothills to the plain below, which lay like a great undulating sea at dusk, the shadows of clouds scudding in dark patches across the pale green summer desert. The expedition had pitched camp for the night out in the open, rather than up against the foothills, which seemed odd to us at first. But then we realized that they had probably done so in order to be able to see all who approached from any direction. We carried a white flag of surrender to alert the guards that we were friendly. Anyway, who could mistake Tolley's white buckskin getup.

"You were a regular gunslinger back there, Tolley," I said to him. "The way you pulled that rifle on Indio Juan."

"My hero," Margaret added.

"You know, when you wear the clothes," said Tolley, "you have to fill them. That's what I love about fashion. It can make a new man out of you. I thought to myself, 'Now what would the old injun fighter Buffalo Bill do in this situation?' And, of course, the answer was instantly apparent."

As we approached, we called out to identify ourselves to the guards, who recognized us and called back, waving us in.

The Great Apache Expedition has clearly lost a considerable amount of its luster and is a far more spartan affair out here in the middle of the Chihuahuan desert. All but a handful of the American volunteers have dropped out by now, and those who remain are no longer the polo crowd but a few of the more hard-core retired military men. Gone, too, are the days of catered dinners and full bars; everyone has the lean, grizzled, dusty look of subsistence about them. Morale is low, and the fear level high. Besides the nearly nightly pilfering and theft of stock by Indio Juan and his warriors, no matter what precautions are taken, two soldiers, whose scalps Indio Juan so proudly displays, have been murdered, and the constant harassment is clearly taking its toll on everyone. The enemy has come to seem like a ghost who strikes in the twilight of dawn and against whom there is no defense.

We were taken directly to see Colonel Carrillo in his tent, and moments later were joined there by Chief Gatlin, Billy Flowers, and Señor Huerta. Gatlin was unshaven and hollow-eyed; the expedition has hardly turned out to be the promotional bonanza for the city of Douglas that the Chamber of Commerce had envisioned, and as its chief architect, he will certainly be held responsible for the fiasco. Even the resplendent peacock Colonel Carrillo, so generally elegant and immaculately attired, appears frayed and harried. Only Billy Flowers looks unchanged, his bright blue eyes undimmed. A man clearly accustomed to a life of hardship and deprivation, he seems, within the hard shell of his severe biblical stoicism, entirely impervious to the reduced circumstances of the expedition.

Fernando Huerta wept and thanked us profusely when we told him that his son was nearby, alive and well, and that the Apaches were willing to trade for him.

"You will bring the renegades here tomorrow morning," Carrillo said.

"Unarmed. They will give up the boy and at that time we will accept their unconditional surrender."

"That's not exactly the arrangement, Colonel," I explained. "They want six good horses and assurances that you won't pursue them. And they want the bounty on Apache scalps lifted."

Carrillo took this in for a moment, and then in a very low voice he said: "Young man, after all this, do you think that I am going to allow the Apache devils to dictate the terms of the boy's release to me?"

"Yes, sir, if you want the boy back, I think you would do that."

"Why risk the boy's life," Margaret asked, "when the Apaches are willing to give him up for six horses?"

"For God's sake, Colonel," Señor Huerta said angrily, "I will give them the horses myself."

Carrillo wheeled on Señor Huerta. "No, señor, you will *not*," he snapped. "May I remind you that you came to the *presidente* for his assistance after your own efforts to rescue your son failed. This is a Mexican federal military campaign. And our government does not negotiate with criminals. They return the boy and surrender unconditionally. Those are *my* terms."

Tolley surprised everyone by laughing at that moment, his high whinnying laugh. "Have you lost your mind, Colonel?" he said. "Why in the world would they give the boy up and surrender themselves to you now? You remind me of Custer's famous last words at the Little Bighorn: 'We've got them now, boys!'"

Carrillo's face darkened in rage. "Your father's money may allow you to address people in this manner in your own country, Señor Phillips," he said in a low threatening voice. "But you are in Mexico now, and you are here at the pleasure of the *presidente*. I will have you stood before a firing squad and shipped home to your father in a box before I will tolerate your disrespect."

"Let's all calm down," Chief Gatlin said in a conciliatory tone. "It's been a long campaign for everyone. We've lost men. Everyone is tired. Everyone wants to go home. Toward that end, Colonel, may I respectfully suggest a compromise?"

Carrillo looked at him, his dark eyes shining with an unnatural fervor.

Tolley had clearly touched a nerve, and the colonel's own military career was probably at stake with the success or failure of the Great Apache Expedition.

"Is the white man you claim to be Charley McComas still with the Apaches?" Gatlin asked us.

"Yes," Margaret answered. "He's their leader. But it's the Apache called Indio Juan who is killing your men, Colonel, not Charley."

"Charley, is it now?" Gatlin said with an amused smile. "How nice that you're on a first-name basis, Margaret. I'm beginning to wonder whose side you folks are on."

"We're on the side of all those," said Margaret, "—white men, Mexicans, and Apaches—who won't die if we negotiate a fair and peaceful conclusion to this."

"Which will be exactly the result of my compromise," Gatlin said. "I understand your reluctance to negotiate with the savages, Colonel. But why not accede to their demand for the horses in return for the boy, on condition that their leader, the white man, comes in alone and unarmed for the exchange? I want Charley McComas alive. I want to take him back across the border to his own people. That's two kidnap victims saved from the clutches of the savages—one American boy and one Mexican boy. What more fitting conclusion than that to our noble mission?"

"Charley McComas hasn't survived up there for fifty years by being stupid," Margaret said. "Why would he agree to come in with the boy to get the horses alone and unarmed?"

"Because you're going to convince him to come in, Margaret," Gatlin said with a small thin-lipped smile. "That's why."

"Fuck you, Leslie," Margaret said. "I'm not participating in your little plot."

"Yes, Margaret, you are," Gatlin said. "As you clearly enjoy Charley McComas's confidence, both you and Mr. Giles are going to participate. And as your own loyalty seems to have been somewhat compromised, Colonel Carrillo has given me an excellent idea to ensure that participation. The colonel is going to put all three of you—you, Mr. Giles, and Mr. Phillips—under house arrest. The charge will be collaborating with the enemy, a charge of which, under the circumstances, you are clearly guilty. In any case, you will be tried by a Mexican military tribunal, without access to an attorney, or to our own system of due process. Indeed, as the colonel points out, he has absolute authority in the field, and even without a trial, can order your execution by firing squad."

"Oh, nonsense," said Tolley with a slightly uncertain bravado. "You can't execute Tolbert Phillips Jr. My father has connections all the way to the White House. It would cause an international incident."

"You would be surprised, Mr. Phillips," said Gatlin, "at how little influence your father has in a Mexican military court. At the very least you'd be facing a long prison sentence . . . ummm, ten, maybe twenty years, is that about right, Colonel?"

"At the bare minimum," Carrillo said. "And that is only if I decide not to have you stood up in front of the firing squad instead."

"Ten years in a Mexican prison taking it up the ass every day from half a dozen hardened criminals," Gatlin said, shaking his head. "Even for a faggot like yourself, Mr. Phillips, I should think that might feel like a long way from home."

Tolley had gone quite white.

"And so, Margaret, and Mr. Giles," Gatlin continued, "I believe that the colonel might consider dropping all charges against you and your friend if you were to agree to bring Charley McComas in with the Huerta boy. It would be a way to negotiate a fair and peaceful conclusion, as you yourself put it, Margaret, a way to save your own skins, and to avoid a great deal of bloodshed in the process."

"Tomorrow morning, Mr. Giles," Colonel Carrillo said, pivoting on his toes like a bullfighter, "you and Miss Hawkins will lead us to the Apaches. You will enter their camp alone, bearing a white flag. You will tell them that we have agreed to their demands and you will escort the boy and the white man out to us, under whatever pretext is necessary. Mr. Phillips will be waiting here for word of the successful completion of your mission."

As the sergeant led us from Carrillo's tent, we looked at one another in stunned silence. Tolley spoke first.

"If I hadn't listened to you, Giles," he whispered, "I would be in New York right now, staying in Father's suite at the Waldorf and being fitted at Brooks Brothers for my fall wardrobe. Instead I'm going to be stood in front of a firing squad in the middle of the Mexican desert."

"Carrillo is not going to execute you, Tolley," Margaret said. "It's a bluff. He wouldn't dare."

"Yes, well, the alternative does not sound much more attractive, does it, darling? And by the way, old sport," he said to me, "I might just remind you that you're rather an adorable little white boy yourself, and your own charms will certainly not be lost on the Mexican prison population. My father may be able to pull some strings to get me out, but who's going to come to the poor orphan boy's aid?"

We were split up then, Margaret and Tolley taken to their separate quarters, and I back to Big Wade's "press" tent, where I make these entries by the light of a lantern. A soldier stands guard by the entrance.

Jackson himself has lost a great deal of weight in the weeks since the expedition departed Douglas, and actually looks healthier than I've ever seen him.

"It's not easy to get a drink out here, kid," he said. "I've had to ration myself to whatever rotgut I can lay my hands on in the villages we pass through. And just try finding a decent cigar." He held out the unlit butt he was chewing. "Look at this piece of shit. I swear the Mexicans roll cow shit up in cornstalks and call it a cigar."

"You look good, Big Wade," I said.

"What's with the guard, kid?" he asked. "What kind of mess have you gotten yourself into this time?"

I told Big Wade everything. And when I had finished, he shook his head. "Didn't I tell you not to get involved?" he said. "Didn't I tell you just to do your work? That your only concern is to get the shot?"

"Hey, look," I said, holding out the camera bag. "I got the Leica back. And I *got* the shot. Wait'll you see this film, Big Wade, you'll be proud of me."

"What are you going to do, kid?"

"I don't know," I said. "You don't think Carrillo would really execute Tolley, do you?"

"I don't think so," Big Wade said. "But, hell, this is Mexico, anything can happen. And as Gatlin said, whether they execute him or not, they can make a world of trouble for you kids. Look, everyone's tired and frazzled, nerves are on edge. Carrillo has lost men, and every night it seems like the Apaches manage to sneak into camp, pilfer supplies, steal horses and mules. They already slit two guards' throats. And scalped them. It's spooky as shit, they're like fuckin' ghosts the way they got the run of the place."

"That's just how they are, Big Wade," I said. "Like ghosts. Even when you're among them, they come and go like ghosts. They're not like us."

"No shit."

"It's how they've survived all these years up here," I said.

"What about Charley McComas?"

"He's just as Apache as they are," I said. "It's strange because he's a huge man, maybe six-four, six-five, with long hair and a beard . . . Tolley says he looks like an Irish cop in need of a haircut and a shave . . . but he's just like one of them, and after a while you don't even think of him as a white man, or see him as being any different from the others. And they don't see him any differently, either. He's not going to surrender to Carrillo, Big Wade. That much I know for sure."

"Then I'd say you're fucked, kid," said Big Wade. "Right now Gatlin and Carrillo are both just trying to save their own asses from this fucking disaster. Unless he produces the Huerta boy, dead or alive, Carrillo loses face. And if Gatlin goes home with nothing to show for all of this but half a dozen dead volunteers, his own career is finished. Their backs are against the wall, and that's when men like them are most dangerous. If I were you, kid, I would figure out a way to bring Charley McComas in. That's the only solution that lets everyone off the hook."

"Are you coming with them tomorrow, Big Wade?" I asked.

"Hey, you think I'm going to let you hog the limelight again, kid?" he said. "And miss a story like this? Besides, you're going to be way too busy to cover it yourself."

. . .

I wish I could talk to Margaret tonight. I don't see what choice we have other than to betray Charley. And in so doing, of course, I will betray Chideh. The band can survive without him, as they have for several centuries, and indeed, without Geraldo to draw the Mexicans—or Charley, the Americans—it's possible that the survivors might simply fade away again into the mountains to live as they always have. I know I'm making excuses now for giving Charley up, but I just can't see any other way around it. Even if Carrillo is bluffing, I can't take that risk. My father always taught me that in every situation there is a right thing to do, and all you need is to figure out what that right thing is and everything will be okay. But then my father killed himself, and I wonder where he found the right thing in that . . . I'm beginning to realize that Pop was wrong about many things. As Margaret has pointed out to me, sometimes there is no right thing to do. And sometimes the right thing doesn't reveal itself until it's too late. And right now, everything about tomorrow feels wrong to me.

NOTEBOOK VIII:
The Aftermath

Albuquerque, New Mexico

Almost three months have passed since I left Mexico and only now can I begin to try to set down the terrible events of our final days there. I have to laugh when I read my last entry . . . for the right thing proved to be even more elusive than I had expected . . . and, indeed, it never did reveal itself.

We rode out of camp at dawn the next morning, a clear, windless day in the plains of Chihuahua, the mountains still black against the horizon, the pale sky cloudless, darkened only by Mexico's ubiquitous circling buzzards, for whom, before the day was out, we would make fresh carrion. Despite all the precautions and the fact that Carrillo had bivouacked out in the open, Indio Juan and his renegades had still managed to penetrate the camp in the night; that morning they found the young wrangler, Jimmy, murdered, his throat slit ear to ear, his scalp taken. I knew how jumpy Jimmy had been in his night-guard duties, and I imagined his terror when the Apaches had set upon him. I'll bet it happened just before dawn in that pearly twilight, when he was feeling relieved at last that another night was over. Everyone had liked Jimmy, and the mood as we set out that morning was particularly glum and vengeful.

In a show of force obviously intended to intimidate the Apaches, Carrillo had mounted his entire company, except for less than a dozen soldiers, wranglers, and volunteers who had been left behind to guard the base camp. They moved out in perfect formation, their bright dress uniforms seeming gaudy and clownish against the muted earth tones of the desert. It was a solemn procession and the only sounds to be heard were the metallic rasp of spurs and clank of sabers, and the dry moans of saddle leather before it has been lubricated by sweat and the heat of day.

We civilians rode alongside them: Chief Gatlin, Señor Huerta, Billy

Flowers, Wade Jackson, Albert, Margaret, and I. We had left Jesus back at camp to look after Tolley, who had been confined to his quarters, and whom we had not been allowed to see before our departure. Because of the proximity of the others, Margaret and I were unable to talk privately as we rode, and we had not formed any kind of plan. The Apaches would surely already know that we were on the way, and I knew that they must be watching us even now as we made our way across the desert. By now, a keen-eyed scout would have identified the herd of six unsaddled horses that were being driven between us and the soldiers, and Charley would have concluded that the Mexican colonel had agreed to the trade. As Tolley had pointed out, Indio Juan was the wild card in this whole game, and there was no telling where he might be or when he might launch another of his strikes.

From the desert flats of sparse creosote bushes, prickly pear, and cholla cactus, we soon gained the foothills, lightly timbered in scrub oak and cedar. The sun was up now and the mountains had turned the copper color of tarnished pennies. As we gained altitude, we looked back to see the camp lying below in the plains, so peaceful looking, smoke still curling from the morning cook fires.

By midday we had reached the general area in which the Apaches had been camped the day before. After some deliberation with Billy Flowers and Chief Gatlin, Carrillo found a place to hold the rendezvous, an opening on the edge of the pine forest, protected on one side by a low ridge, upon which he stationed some of his men to stand guard.

"Mr. Flowers will lead you on to the Apaches' camp," Carrillo said. "We will wait for you here. You will bring the white man and the boy to us. You will tell the white man that we will give him the horses as soon as the boy has been released to us. There is to be no deviation in the plan."

"What if he won't come?" I asked.

"Then your friend, Mr. Phillips, is in grave danger," Carrillo answered.

"Why should Tolley be held accountable?" Margaret asked. "What if Charley agrees to give up the boy but refuses to come in himself?"

"You know the terms," said Gatlin. "We want both of them. You're very persuasive, Margaret. I feel certain that you can convince Mr. McComas that we wish only to meet him. A powwow, isn't that what the savages call it? Tell him we're inviting him to have a smoke and a powwow. And then he can have his horses and be on his way."

Big Wade was already setting up his camera gear, taking a light reading with his meter. "Knock 'em dead, kid," he said to me, cigar butt between his teeth, half distracted by his work. "We're counting on you. I got things covered on this end."

"Just make sure you get the shot, Big Wade," I said.

Billy Flowers, Margaret, and I rode through the tall pine forest, silent and shadowed from the sun. As I always did in Apache country, I had the eerie sense that we were being watched. And I think Flowers and Margaret felt it, too.

"What will you do when this is all over, Mr. Flowers?" Margaret asked, her voice sounding hollow and unnatural in the stillness of the forest.

"I will do what I have always done, Miss Hawkins," Flowers said. "I will go back to hunting the lions and bears. I am told that some Mormon ranchers in Colonia Juarez wish to contract my services."

"Don't you ever tire of killing things?"

"The killing is a necessary part of it. But it is only the end result. It is the hunt of which I never tire."

"Don't you ever get lonely?"

"I have my dogs."

"Didn't you ever want to settle down with a family?"

"I have a family," Flowers said. "A wife and three children back in Louisiana. I still send money home but I haven't seen them in almost thirty years."

"What happened?"

"I had to leave them when the Voice summoned me," he said, "and I've been on the move ever since."

"What kind of Voice would send you away from your family?" Margaret asked.

"The Voice from on High," Flowers said, "the Voice of our Lord Jesus, the Voice of our beloved Creator."

"You believe that God told you to abandon your wife and children so that you could spend your life killing grizzly bears and mountain lions?" Margaret asked. "That's the saddest thing I've ever heard."

"'As it is written, the just shall live by faith,'" Flowers said.

Before we had even reached the Apaches' camp, one of the boys, afoot, faded out of the trees in front of us, and without a word turned and began trotting through the timber. We followed him and a short distance later came upon Charley, Joseph, Albert, and Chideh, all mounted. Neither little Geraldo nor any of the others in the band were anywhere in sight, but I knew that they were close by, hidden in the trees and rocks, as only the Apaches can hide. The girl looked shyly at me and smiled.

Charley and Flowers regarded each other, two large bearded white men, one a heathen, the other a Christian, and it occurred to me that in an odd way, they were more similar than they might have known.

"Why do you bring this White Eyes with you?" Charley asked. "Why did you not bring the horses?"

"Did you think they were going to give you the horses before you turned over the boy?" Margaret asked. "You must come with us. They wish to speak with you first. Then you can have the horses."

Albert looked searchingly at Margaret, sensing that something was wrong.

"For what reason do they wish to speak with me?" Charley asked her, himself suspicious.

"Because they know who you are," she said, her gaze not wavering from his. "And they wish to see Charley McComas in person."

"The only way they're going to give you the horses," I added, "is if you come in and make the exchange for the boy yourself."

Charley considered this for a moment. "I will speak with them," he said finally. "Chideh will ride behind me with the boy. She will come just far enough so that all can see her. When they have given me the horses and I am safely away from the soldiers' guns, only then will she release the boy. But if they betray us, she will kill him. This is how the trade will be made."

Charley whistled once, a piercing sound like the shriek of a hawk, and from the trees behind us, little Geraldo Huerta appeared. He trotted up to

Chideh's horse, and with her assistance, deftly swung up in front of her. He moved just like an Apache.

Now I looked at the girl, this girl with whom I had shared intimacies, tried to see into her dark inscrutable eyes. Did I still know so little about her that I didn't know whether or not she was capable of killing a child, a child of whom she was clearly fond, whom she held now on her horse, her arm lightly and affectionately around him? I realized that not only did I not have the answer to this question, I wasn't even sure that I wanted to have it.

"That's not going to work," I said, with an edge of desperation in my voice. "Mag, Charley has to ride in with the boy, no one else. You heard Carrillo, there can be no deviations."

Charley studied me for a long moment, and then he reined his horse around. "We will keep the boy," he said. "They can keep their horses."

"No, wait," Margaret said. "It will be as you wish." And to me she said, firmly: "Neddy, keep your mouth shut now before you queer the whole deal. A small deviation is better than nothing. Charley has agreed to speak with them and they'll see that he brought the boy. That's the important thing. We're fulfilling our end as best we can; that's all we can do."

"I have to speak a moment with my wife," I said. I rode over alongside her, and our horses standing head to tail, we faced each other. "Don't do this, Chideh," I whispered. "Take the women and children and ride into the mountains and hide. I'll find you."

"I cannot," she said. "I must do what my grandfather asks of me."

"I'm your husband," I said. "You should do what I tell you."

She smiled sadly. "He is my family."

"You couldn't kill that boy, could you?" I asked.

"I must do what my grandfather asks of me," she repeated, tears filling her eyes. "If the soldiers betray us, I must kill the boy."

"*I* have betrayed you," I said, tears coming to my own eyes. "Please, take the others, run and hide."

A slight breeze came up as we rode back toward the rendezvous, swaying the tops of the tall pines, a faint whispering sound like a warning. Flowers rode in the lead, Margaret and I behind him, followed by Joseph and Albert, then Charley and the girl with little Geraldo on the saddle in front of her, this thin, delicate boy whose abduction had launched this entire expedition, who had brought us to this place at this time. At last he was going home to his father.

We approached the clearing where Carrillo and the others waited, and I wondered if everyone else felt the same sense of doom as I, the sense of things set irrevocably in motion, and already gone wrong. And then Billy Flowers intoned in his deep Old Testament voice: "'The time is fulfilled, and the Kingdom of God is at hand,'" and Margaret whispered under her breath: "Yeah, that's exactly what I'm afraid of."

I turned in the saddle to look back at the girl. She smiled again at me, an oddly hopeful, even innocent smile.

We stopped at the edge of the clearing. When Fernando Huerta recognized his son, he cried out: *"Geraldo, mi chico, mi chico pequeño!"* He spurred his horse forward but two soldiers cut him off, one of them taking hold of his bridle.

Colonel Carrillo spoke sharply to him. "You will wait, señor, until we have conducted our business as planned." The colonel waved us in.

The girl hung back on the edge of the trees as the rest of us rode into the clearing. She still held her arm lightly around Geraldo, in a kind of sisterly embrace, except that now she held a knife in her hand for all to see. The boy did not appear frightened, only a bit confused by these proceedings. He had been only three years old when he was abducted, and he did not seem to recognize his real father.

Carrillo and Gatlin sat their horses in the middle of the clearing, behind them a dozen or so mounted soldiers. Big Wade stood on the ground to the side of them with his Graflex set up on a tripod in order to capture this historic moment.

Charley looked around as we rode in, checking the lay of the land, identifying the soldiers on the ridge. Carrillo held his arm up in the universal sign of greeting as we came to a halt in front of them.

Gatlin spoke first, in a low voice of wonder: "Well . . . I'll . . . be . . . *goddamned.*" And of us he asked: "Does he understand English?"

"I don't know, but he speaks Spanish," I said.

"Is your name Charley McComas?" Gatlin asked.

Charley looked at the chief but did not answer. He addressed Colonel Carrillo. "*Tomaré los caballos.* I will take the horses now." He glanced up at the sun. "You and your soldiers will stay where you are until the shadows of the trees strike this place." He gestured with a slash of his arm. "At that time, the girl will release the boy to you. If you move before then, she will kill him."

"Why, you dirty *son of a bitch*," said Gatlin with venom in his voice. "You think you can dictate to us? Look at you, a traitor to your own race. Well, we've come to take you home, *little* Charley McComas, back to your own people." I realized in that moment that Gatlin hated Charley more for being a white man who had gone over to the Apaches than he would have had Charley been a full-blooded Indian.

Everything fell apart right then, in such rapid succession and in such utter chaos that as I look back it's hard to reconstruct the exact chain of events, what was remembered and what was only perceived. Clearly aware that things were going wrong, Charley turned to signal the girl, wheeling his horse, as Carrillo barked an order to his troops. In that same instant, Indio Juan came riding hard out of the timber, headed directly for the girl. I called out to warn her. The sound of gunfire came from the ridge above. At first I thought it must be the soldiers stationed there who were firing; but then two of the soldiers mounted behind Gatlin and Carrillo fell from their horses, and I realized that Indio Juan's men must have taken the ridge. The rest of Carrillo's mounted troops broke ranks in disarray.

Indio Juan slowed briefly when he reached the girl, snatching the boy roughly from her. Geraldo cried out, terrified, and his father answered him in an anguished bellow, spurring his horse toward his son. But Indio Juan was already disappearing into the timber with the boy. Three more soldiers fell from their saddles, and several others had their horses shot out from under them in the deadly cross fire from the ridge. It was all the rest of us could do to control our panicked, bolting mounts. Some of the soldiers tried to return fire but they weren't even sure where the shots were coming from.

Charley had broken away and now rode for the girl, who was herself retreating into the trees. Carrillo was still shouting orders, trying desperately to rally his confused troops. I didn't know in that moment who or where my enemy was, but like everyone else, my first instinct was to flee, and yet I seemed paralyzed as if in a nightmare, stuck there in the clearing with the deadly bullets flying, trying desperately to control my wild-eyed mule as horses and men fell screaming around me. In the chaos, I lost track of Margaret and the others.

The shooting stopped as suddenly as it had begun as Indio Juan's men fell back from the ridge. Only then did Carrillo manage to bring what remained of his soldiers under control, and they galloped off in the direction Charley had taken. I looked around desperately for Margaret but could not find her. Wounded men and horses floundered on the ground. The Mexican army doctor attached to Carrillo's company was trying to minister to the wounded soldiers. It was then that I saw Big Wade lying on the ground next to his shattered camera and tripod. I dismounted and ran to him, kneeling beside him. He was covered in dirt and blood but he was still alive.

I hollered for the doctor. "Aw, Jesus Christ, Big Wade. What happened, are you shot? Oh, *goddammit*, please." Tears welled up in my eyes.

"I'm okay, kid," he answered, clearly in great pain. "Don't be a *fuckin'* crybaby. Where's my camera?" He tried to sit up, but fell heavily back to the ground.

"It's right here. Your camera's fine," I lied.

"Hey, cut the crap," he said. "The camera's fucked. A fuckin' horse ran over it. See if you can't save some of the film, will you, kid?"

"Yeah, sure, of course I will," I said. "But you're going to be okay, Big Wade."

"Fuck, what a bonehead I am," he said. "You'd think I'd have learned by now, wouldn't you?"

"Learned what?" I asked.

"I made the same mistake I warned you about, kid," Big Wade said. "I got to thinking that my camera was a shield, that it would protect me . . ." His voice went suddenly quiet and distant, as if coming from a very long way away. "But you know, kid, when you work for the *Dog-ass Daily Dispatch* and your most exciting assignment in three years is covering traffic court, you don't really expect to die in the line of duty."

"Who said anything about dying?"

"But what the fuck," he went on as if he hadn't heard me, "getting shot by the bronco Apaches makes a lot more interesting obituary than chronic liver failure. You get what I mean? Write it yourself, will you, kid? Pump it up a bit, like I taught you. Make me sound heroic."

"I'm not writing your obituary, Big Wade," I said, "because you're not dying."

He nodded and smiled. "I got the shot, kid," he said. *"I got the shot."* And with that, just as the doctor finally made his way to us, Big Wade stopped breathing.

I did not have time to mourn. That would come later. Right now I had to find Margaret and the others, I had to find Chideh. I remounted. In the distance, I heard the haunting tones of Billy Flowers's hunting horn, a deep, resonant trumpeting that wafted above the trees like a strange and soothing music.

I assumed that Flowers was blowing his horn as a signal to Carrillo, and I followed the sound myself, knowing that Carrillo would be, as well. I soon caught up to the tattered remnants of the Great Apache Expedition, Colonel Carrillo and Chief Gatlin with a handful of soldiers, as well as Señor Huerta who had rejoined them. Unsuccessful in his pursuit of Indio Juan and his son, who had disappeared once again, the man was utterly beside himself with grief and frustration. After three years of hardship and self-denial and fruitless searching through these mountains, he had been at last so close to recovering his son; Geraldo had been right there, almost within reach, only to be snatched away again, as if in a cruel prank. Now he cried out for the boy, shouting his name, alternately begging and cursing his Apache captors.

I followed them up a short incline on the trail, which opened up onto a small grassy bench. Here the summer grasses were green and lush from the monsoons, the trees and bushes heavy with new growth, sunlight filtering through the leaves. It was the kind of little oasis where, on another day, you might want to stop and rest in the shade. Then I heard Señor Huerta's anguished bellow, a sound of such utter despair that it made my skin prickle. Just off the trail ahead, his son Geraldo dangled from a tree limb, hanged, his slight body still twirling at the end of the rope. Indio Juan had killed the boy rather than give him up, to leave a wound so deep that it would render any other victory hollow.

As Carrillo and his men cut down Geraldo's body and occupied themselves with the inconsolable, grief-stricken father, I slipped past them and rode as hard as I could up the trail, following the sound of Billy Flowers's hunting horn. I knew that he must be tracking the Apaches. Before I had gone a hundred yards, the girl appeared on the trail ahead of me. She did not speak, only motioned for me to follow her, leaving the trail and riding up a steep slope.

On the far side of the slope, hidden in a small, rocky bowl, I found Margaret, Joseph, and Albert, all dismounted. "What the hell happened back there?" I asked them. "I lost track of you. I didn't know where you'd gone."

"We didn't wait around to find out what was happening," Margaret said. "When the shooting started, we followed Charley."

"Why Charley?" I asked. "Why didn't you stay with the expedition?"

"Because there were bullets flying around there, little brother," she answered. "It just didn't seem like a healthy place to be."

"Where is Charley now?" I asked. "Where are all the others?"

"They've scattered out," said Albert. "They'll come together later."

"Flowers is trailing some of them," I said. "Do you hear his horn? Carrillo and his men are not far behind."

"We know," Margaret said. "We don't have much time. We have to get moving again. I just wanted to see you before we go, Neddy."

"What do you mean *we*, Mag?" I asked. "Go where?"

"I'm going with them."

"What are you talking about? When did you decide this?"

"Just now," Margaret said. "It's my chance, Ned. I'd kick myself later if I gave it up now."

"Are you fucking insane, Margaret? Chance for what? To be a slave?"

"To write the definitive anthropological study of the bronco Apaches," she said. "I'm not a slave if I go of my own free will."

"But doesn't Charley know that we deceived him?" I asked. "Aren't you worried that he'll kill you for it?"

"He doesn't know that," she said. "And who's going to tell him, sweetheart?"

"Do you know what Indio Juan did to Geraldo?" I asked.

It was clear that they did not.

"He hanged him," I said. "Right back there off the trail for his father to find."

"Oh my God . . ." Margaret said. "Oh, no . . ."

"Carrillo and the Mexican ranchers are never going to give up, Mag," I said. "They'll hunt down every single member of this band and kill them all—men, women, and children. There will be no mercy for anyone."

"They'll have to catch us first, won't they?"

"Aw, Christ, Mag, is this really how you want to live the rest of your life?" I pleaded. "With a band of renegade Apaches, running from the Mexican army?"

"It's not the rest of my life, little brother," she said. "It's just for a little while. I'll come back. You'll see. And when I do, I'll prove to the bastards that a woman can do fieldwork."

"You remember what Charley said, don't you, Mag?" I asked. "Nobody is ever allowed to leave."

"I'll find a way."

I looked at Albert, and didn't even need to ask; I knew he wouldn't leave Margaret or his grandfather.

"I promised my mother that I would take care of my grandfather," he said, reading my look.

Old Joseph Valor smiled. "My grandson believes that because I am an old man he must take care of me," he said, "but really it is I who takes care of him. I must teach him to be an Apache."

"You're a civilized man, Albert," I said. "You grew up on the reservation. It's too late for you to lead the life your grandfather led. It's even too late for you, Joseph."

"I do not wish to live that life again," Joseph said. "I am an old man, and I only wish to die in the place where I was born. And before I do, I have things to teach the People."

"What kind of things?"

Albert smiled at me. "You don't know much, do you, White Eyes?" he said.

"No, I guess I don't," I said. "I'm from Chicago."

"We must leave now," said Joseph. "The soldiers are coming." He remounted.

I looked then at Chideh, meeting her eyes, gazing deep into the bottomless depths of her dark irises. We had saved each other's life, we had lain together and loved each other. And yet I realized in that moment more surely than I ever had before that I knew nothing more about her now than I did the first time I set eyes upon her in that Mexican jail cell. As she knew nothing more about me.

"Let her go, Neddy," Margaret said. "Even if he allowed you to, why would you want to take her away from the only world she knows?"

"She's just a kid, Mag," I said. "She could have a whole new life ahead of her. We could have a whole new life together."

"Do you really believe that, sweetheart?" Margaret asked. "Don't you know that there are some species that simply can't be domesticated, that die in captivity?"

"She's going to have my baby, Mag."

"All the more reason to let her go, sweetheart," said Margaret. "Children belong to the mother's tribe, and these people need all the babies they can get."

"Why, so they can be slaughtered by the Mexicans?"

"We have to go," Margaret said. She gave me a quick, awkward hug, but she wouldn't look me in the eye and I knew that she was fighting back tears.

"How will you find me when you come back, Mag?" I asked. "I don't have a home, I don't even know where I'll be."

"Don't worry, little brother," she said. "I'll find you. Big Wade will know where you are, won't he?" She swung back onto her horse, agile herself as one of them. "Will you say good-bye to him for me, and to Tolley, too? I know you'll take care of things, Neddy."

I decided in that moment that Margaret didn't need to know about Big Wade. There had been enough death for one day, and she had enough to worry about. "Okay, sure I will, Mag."

"Good-bye, Neddy," she said, and she reined her horse around to follow the others.

I watched her ride away. "Don't forget to write, Mag!" I called after her. And she laughed and waved back at me without turning.

Now only the girl remained, looking uncertainly at me, and then at the others as they rode away from us.

"*Vete,*" I said. "*Vete con ellos.* Go with them."

"*¿No vienes conmigo, marida mio?* You are not coming with me, my husband?"

"I cannot."

"Why?"

"Come with me," I said.

We heard an exchange of gunfire behind us; Indio Juan must have engaged the soldiers again, which would at least slow them down.

The girl looked in the direction of the gunfire and then back toward me. She shook her head sadly. "*Puedo no,*" she said. "I cannot." She reached out and touched my arm lightly, just the slightest touch; I can still feel her fingers grazing my arm. "*Te quiero,*" she whispered. "I love you."

"You weren't going to kill that boy, were you, Chideh?" I asked.

She smiled softly. "I loved that boy like a brother," she said. "I could not hurt him."

I reached out for her but she was already gone, as in a dream, and in that specific, otherworldly way she had of moving, lithe as a spirit, she swung onto the back of her horse, touched his flanks lightly with her heels, and galloped up the slope without another glance back. "*Te quiero,*" I whispered back.

I had nowhere else to go now but to find Carrillo and his men, and with the others gone, my last responsibility was to try to protect Tolley, and myself. The fact was that we had fulfilled our end of the deal: We had brought Charley to them. That things had fallen apart and they had failed to capture him, and failed to rescue little Geraldo Huerta, was hardly our fault.

I rode up over the saddle and back down the steep slope on the other side to regain the main trail. But it was not Carrillo whom I encountered first, it was Indio Juan, riding hard down the trail toward me with two of his warriors. I knew that he had already spotted me and that there was no sense in trying to flee. I reined up and waited for them. It had not occurred to me until this very moment that I did not have a weapon on my person, not even a knife.

At their approach I saw that the warriors were only boys and that one of them was badly wounded. He rode slumped over on his horse, holding on to its neck, and as they came to a halt in front of me, he slipped off and fell to the ground. Indio Juan sat his horse and made no move to go to the boy's aid. *"Cabalga sólo ahora, ojos blancos,"* he said to me, smiling malignantly. The boy was moaning on the ground, and I dismounted and went to him. He had been shot through the stomach and was bleeding profusely; I could do nothing for him. Now Indio Juan also slid off his horse and approached me where I knelt beside the boy. I knew that he intended to kill me. He held a rifle in his hand but I saw as he swaggered toward me that he was not going to waste a precious bullet; rather, he was turning the rifle in his hands and was preparing to bludgeon me in the head with the butt of it. I could do nothing but cower and raise one arm defensively over my head and say, *"Por favor no me mate,"* which made Indio Juan laugh, for nothing amused him more than watching his enemies cower and beg before their death. *"Duu nk' echiida,"* he said with contempt, repeating, *"eres débil,* you are weak, White Eyes." But the truth is I was no longer afraid of Indio Juan; my heart was too filled with hatred of him to be afraid; I would rather die myself than allow him to return to the People, to violate Margaret or Chideh, or, even more unthinkable, to harm my unborn child. It was not so much a question of courage on my part, I was just plain angry, filled with outrage and indignation; I could not bring Mr. Browning or Big Wade or little Geraldo Huerta back, but I could avenge their brutal, senseless deaths at the hands of this strutting little madman. At the same time that I cowered with my arm held in front of my face, an impotent defense against the rifle butt that Indio Juan now raised overhead, laughing as he did so at the cowardice of the White Eyes, I slipped the blood-soaked knife from the sheath at the dying boy's waist, and I lunged at Indio Juan as if trying to tackle him, plunging the knife into his stomach, driving it as hard and as deep as I could. I pulled it out and drove it in again, and a third time. With each thrust of my knife, Indio Juan staggered backward, finally dropping his rifle and falling to his knees, before collapsing over onto his back. I do not believe that I am a violent man by nature, but my rage had become a kind of cold vengeance, and within it I did not feel yet that Indio Juan had sufficiently paid for his crimes. And so before the light had faded completely from his eyes, so that perhaps he would know he was going to the Happy Place without his hair, I grabbed a handful in my fist and lifted his scalp and hacked it from his head, holding it aloft and uttering a terrible cry of triumph.

I sat on the ground, breathing heavily, Indio Juan's bloody scalp in hand, his dead body lying beside me. My rage drained away quickly, my sense of vengeance soon replaced by a vague queasiness, a sense of anticlimax. I guess you have to kill a man to know this feeling.

The second boy still sat his horse, paralyzed, staring at me, terrified now, certain that he would be next to die. "Go on," I said, waving him away. "*Vamonos.* Get the hell away from here." And the boy smiled at me with relief and gratitude, pressed his heels to his horse's flanks, and galloped away.

Later, I presented Indio Juan's scalp to Señor Huerta, scant consolation to be sure for the death of a man's son . . . Besides the wounded Apache boy, who died moments later on the ground beside me, Carrillo's soldiers had managed to kill several of Indio Juan's men in the running skirmish. The other Apaches, whom Billy Flowers had been tracking, largely women and children, had dispersed into the mountains, leaving a dozen separate trails.

The chase was finally called off and we bivouacked that night in the mountains, burying the dead and attending to the wounded. No one slept much for their moans and cries in the night. The next morning, we headed back down to base camp in the plains, a trip that took us most of the day, our progress greatly slowed by the transport of the wounded.

We made a ragged procession riding back into camp, and from our greatly reduced numbers and those who were carried, or dragged in on travois, it was clear to all there that our mission had been a disaster. They had brought Tolley out of his tent for our arrival and he stood between two soldiers as we rode in. Of course, I knew even more surely now that Carrillo had no intention of executing him, or me, or of putting us in prison. Having lost little Geraldo and so many of his own soldiers and volunteers, the colonel had enough professional troubles without now causing an international incident. Ironically, the single success he could claim was the death of the notorious Indio Juan. I heard later that they put his (scalpless) head on display in the town square in Casas Grandes and that people came from all around to see it.

The Great Apache Expedition was officially disbanded a few days later, though Colonel Carrillo sent to Mexico City for reinforcements and resupply, and he and his soldiers spent several more weeks in the mountains, searching in vain for the remaining Apaches. But as is their way, they seemed to have once again vanished off the face of the earth, absorbed like the spirits of the dead in the canyons and arroyos and the hidden valleys of the Sierra Madre.

The old predator hunter Billy Flowers took his dogs down to the American Mormon settlement of Colonia Juarez, near Casas Grandes, where he contracted to hunt mountain lions for the ranchers there. And the rest of us followed Chief of Police Leslie Gatlin back across the border to Douglas, Arizona. Gatlin may not have brought little Charley McComas back to show off, but the very act of contact with the mythical white Apache has saved his reputation and given the Greater Douglas Chamber of Commerce the fodder to organize yet another expedition next spring. Now instead of using little Geraldo Huerta as the bait, they tell everyone that a poor defenseless young woman anthropologist by the name of Margaret Hawkins, from the University of Arizona, has been kidnapped by the bronco Apaches; it makes a better story that way, despite my repeated insistence that Margaret went with them voluntarily and did not wish to be rescued.

Most of Wade Jackson's film had been exposed that morning when his camera was trampled under the horse's hooves, but I managed to salvage a few frames. One of them was "the shot" Big Wade had referred to in his dying words—an image of Charley himself, riding in to meet with Carrillo and Gatlin just before things went wrong. The *Douglas Daily Dispatch* ran it on the front page the following week, under the banner headline: WILD MAN CHARLEY MCCOMAS FOUND! Both the story, which I wrote myself, and the photograph were picked up by the national press services and have run in newspapers all across the country. Big Wade would have been pleased with our final collaboration. On the strength of it, and because of my other work on the expedition, I was offered a job here on the *Albuquerque Journal*. Bill Curry asked me to stay on at the *Daily Dispatch*, but I took Big Wade's advice and got the hell out of Dog-ass.

I said good-bye to Tolley at the train station in Douglas. Like all of us, he had been subdued by the terrible attrition of those past weeks and months. "Christ, Giles," he said before boarding the train, "you and me and the kid are all that's left, aren't we?"

"It looks that way, doesn't it, Tolley?"

"You think we'll ever see Margaret and Albert again?" he asked.

"I don't know, what do you think?"

He looked south toward the Sierra Madre and shook his head. He held his hand out to me. "I wish I had something amusing to say in parting."

"Me, too."

"Adios, old sport."

"So long, Tolley."

As to Jesus, I left him back in Agua Prieta, where presumably he has resumed his career as a street hustler, guide, and "facilitator."

"I will come to America with you, Señor Ned," he offered. "I will carry your camera."

"I don't think so, kid," I said. "I think I'd better carry my own camera for a while. I'll come back and look you up sometime, though."

And he nodded sadly, because we both knew that I probably wouldn't.

I went to see the Mexican girl, Magdalena, the last time I was in Agua Prieta. They had taken her back at Las Primorosas, after all, and in those few months she seemed to have settled into her profession. She seemed coarser and more predatory, flirting with the men, one eye always out for her next trick. We danced together, but it held none of the innocent romance that it had before. We had both changed; neither one of us was any longer a kid, and it seemed like those days were another lifetime ago.

"Come to my room now," she said at the end of the dance. "I will make you very happy."

"No, I don't think so," I answered. "I just wanted to see that you were doing okay, Magdalena."

But she was already looking around for another mark.

The next day, I recovered the Roadster from the parking lot at the Gadsden, where I had left it those many weeks ago, and headed out of Douglas. It has been a strange adjustment returning to the world of automobiles and trains, and to the cities and the economies that the White Eyes have built. The Depression, which we more or less forgot all about during our time in Mexico, has deepened even further. But Roosevelt just won the election, and everyone has high hopes that he can turn things around.

I've rented a little adobe casita in the barrio neighborhood of downtown Albuquerque, and I've set up a darkroom in the shed behind it to process my own work whenever I have time off from the newspaper. On weekends I sometimes drive down to the Mescalero Apache reservation to shoot film. As Albert used to say, on the reservation there's always a depression going on, and I can see why he didn't want to come back here. I've been to see his mother, to tell her what became of her son and her father, and to give her some photographs of them. I like to visit with the Apaches at Mescalero, to make images of them, and to practice the language with some of the old-timers who still speak it, though sadly, not many do anymore. Even though I'm a White Eyes, the people there have more or less come to accept me. I tell them stories of my time in the Sierra Madre. I don't know if they really believe me or not, but they listen quietly and politely as is the Apache way. I tell them that I have an *In'deh* wife, and a son or a daughter, up there somewhere in the Blue Mountains, still living in the old way, and that someday I plan to join them.

LA NIÑA BRONCA

When the end of the earth is coming, all the water will begin to dry up. For a long time there will be no rain. There will only be three springs left. At those three springs the water will be dammed up and all the people will come there and start fighting over the water. In this way most of the people will kill each other off.

When the new world comes after that, the white people will be Indians and the Indians will be white people.

MORRIS OPLER, "THE END OF THE WORLD," *Myths and Tales of the Chiricahua Apache Indians*

THE GIRL KNELT WITH HER LEGS APART, HOLDING ON TO AN OAK post set in the ground, as the midwife, the old woman Dahteste, massaged her abdomen downward. The girl was silent, did not utter a sound as the head of her baby emerged, then its shoulders, and as it slipped from her body and out into this world, the old woman caught the falling infant in her sure hands. It was a boy and he took a deep, lusty breath, hungry for life. But he did not cry.

"That is good," said the old woman. "A baby who does not cry at birth grows to be strong."

Old Dahteste cut the umbilical cord with a piece of black flint and knotted it, bathed the baby in warm water, and laid him on a soft robe. She rubbed his body with a mixture of grease and red ocher, strewed a pinch of pollen to each of the four directions, clockwise beginning with the east, and then she held the baby up and in the same order presented him to the four directions so that he would always know his way. She wrapped the afterbirth and the umbilical cord in a piece of the blanket upon which the girl had knelt during the birth. Later the old woman would place this bundle in the branches of a lemon tree and bless it by saying: "May this child live and grow up to see you bear fruit many times."

The years passed. Her son grew to be a strong, healthy boy. He was brown-skinned like his mother but he had fair hair for an Apache, and the sclera of his eyes was pale, so that when he was a child the People called him White Eyes Boy. Eventually the girl remarried a young man named Bishi and had two more children by him. Together with the others in the small band, they lived quietly back in the secret hidden recesses of the Blue Mountains, country so rugged and so remote that no Mexicans and no White Eyes dared venture there. She never forgot the boy who had been so kind to her, the White Eyes boy who had bathed her and covered her with a blanket in the Mexican jail cell, who had taken her away to release her back into the wilds as one releases a caged bird; this boy who had saved her and loved her once. She told her son the stories of his father and of the other unknown world in which his father lived, and from which his father would surely one day return.

Now the Mexicans claim that *la niña bronca*, the wild girl whom the American lion hunter Billy Flowers trailed into Bavispe, Sonora, hobbled and tethered to a dog chain on that spring day in 1932, was the last of the bronco Apaches in the Sierra Madre. They say she was so wild that she bit anyone who tried to touch her, and because they didn't know what else to do with her, they put her in the town jail. They say she curled up in a fetal position on the cold stone floor of the jail cell and refused food and water, and starved herself to death in five days. They say they buried her in an unmarked grave on the edge of the town cemetery, just outside the fence, because, of course, she was not a Christian. But that's just what they say, and none of it is true. She curled up on the cold stone floor and lay perfectly still, closing up into herself, and she dreamed this life of the People from beginning to end. *Daalk'ida 'aguudzaa. It happened long ago. Five thousand years and two hundred generations ago, she had already been among them as both man and woman, child and elder, hunter and suckler of babies, dressed in the heavy skins of mastodons as they made their way in a blizzard across the frozen Siberian plains. White-Painted-Woman, mother of all Apaches.*

Author's Note

IN THE WINTER OF 1998, while traveling in the Mexican states of Sonora and Chihuahua, I met an elderly gentleman in the village of Casas Grandes, Chihuahua. We sat on a bench in the town plaza, and he told me the story of the young Apache girl they called *la niña bronca*, who had been treed in the mountains by the hound dogs of an American mountain-lion hunter, in the spring of the year 1932. The lion hunter did not know what to do with the girl and so he brought her into town. And because she was so wild and tried to bite anyone who touched her, they put her in the local jail. The Apaches still occupied a kind of mythic role in the folk (and actual) history of northern Mexico, and everyone in town and in the surrounding villages wanted to see this wild girl for themselves. And so the sheriff charged a small admission fee and allowed people to come into the jail to view her. The old man who told me this story had been only a boy himself at the time, and like so many other curious townspeople, he paid his fee and saw the Apache girl in her jail cell. Looking back on it, all those years later, he was still ashamed about this, and he did not wish to discuss it further. "I was just a boy," he said in a low voice, "I didn't know any better." And when I asked the old man what had happened to this girl, he shook his head and refused to say.

I couldn't get the story of *la niña bronca* out of my mind, and I knew I had to find out for myself what had happened to her. In this way was this novel born.

Although certain actual historical events are recounted in this book, it is entirely a work of fiction. Similarly, although some actual historical characters appear in this book, they are entirely fictional creations. The Great Apache Expedition, for example, was organized out of Douglas, Arizona, under the name the "Fimbres Apache Expedition." This was to be a joint Mexican-American operation, ostensibly to rescue the six-year-old son of a Mexican rancher by the name Francisco Fimbres. The boy had been kidnapped three years earlier by the Apaches and was reported to be still alive with the renegade band in the Sierra Madre Mountains. However, because the Mexican government was understandably nervous about a vigilante force of armed Americans entering their country, the expedition was canceled before it ever crossed the border. The boy's father, Francisco Fimbres, then launched his own posse of ranchers and vaqueros, who finally cornered the Apaches in the Sierra Madre. But when they closed in, Fimbres found his son hanged by a rope from a tree limb.

The boy Charley McComas, who was kidnapped on the Lordsburg to Silver City road in 1883 by an Apache band led by the warrior Chato (who later became a prominent scout for the U.S. Army), was never recovered. Differing accounts of little Charley's fate were told by the Apaches of the era. Some said that he had died as a boy when General George Crook's soldiers attacked his captors' camp in the Sierra Madre later that same year, though the boy's body was never found. Still others said that Charley McComas had lived and grown to manhood among the bronco Apaches, and that he eventually became an important leader of his own band. This account was lent some credence over the years when generally reliable witnesses on both sides of the border reported sightings or encounters with a band of Apache raiders led by a tall, fair-haired white man with a nearly waist-length beard.

In all other respects this book is a work of fiction. Names, characters, places, dates, and geographical descriptions are all either the product of the author's imagination or are used fictitiously. At the same time, while a genuine effort was made to accurately interpret and portray the history and culture of the Apache people here represented, these, too, are rendered entirely as fiction and are not intended as either anthropological or historical fact. It is, finally, impossible for a "White Eyes" to fully comprehend, let alone represent, the Native American experience and life-way. For the presumptuousness of that effort, and all its inherent shortcomings and failures, the author offers his sincerest apologies to the Apache people.

BIBLIOGRAPHICAL NOTE

IN RESEARCHING AND WRITING THIS novel, the author gratefully acknowledges valuable insights and information gained from the following works:

Eve Ball. *In the Days of Victoria* (1970).
———. *An Apache Odyssey: Indeh* (1980).

Keith H. Basso. *Western Apache Language and Culture: Essays in Linguistic Anthropology* (1990).
———. *Wisdom Sits in Places: Landscape and Language Among the Western Apache* (1996).

John G. Bourke. *An Apache Campaign* (1886).
———. *On the Border with Crook* (1891).
———. *Apache Medicine Men* (1892).

Ruth McDonald Boyer and Narcissus Duffy Gayton. *Apache Mothers and Daughters* (1992).

Evelyn Breuninger, Elbys Hugar, and Ellen Ann Lathan. *Mescalero Apache Dictionary* (1982).

Terry A. Cooney. *Balancing Acts: American Thought and Culture in the 1930s* (1995).

Angie Debo. *Geronimo* (1976).

J. Frank Dobie. *The Ben Lilly Legend* (1950).

Grenville Goodwin. *Western Apache Raiding and Warfare* (1971).
———. *Among the Western Apaches: Letters from the Field* (1973).

Akhil Gupta and James Ferguson. *Anthropological Locations: Boundaries and Grounds of a Field Science* (1997).

James L. Haley. *Apaches: A History and Cultural Portrait* (1981).

Nelle Spilsbury Hatch. *Colonia Juarez* (1954).

Shelley Bowen Hatfield. *Chasing Shadows: Apaches and Yaquis Along the United States–Mexico Border, 1876–1911* (1998).

George Hilliard. *A Hundred Years of Horse Tracks: The Story of the Gray Ranch* (1996).

Herman Lehmann. *Nine Years Among the Indians 1870–1879* (1927).

Carl Lumholtz. *Unknown Mexico: A Record of Five Years' Exploration Among the Tribes of the Western Sierra Madre; in the Tierra Caliente of Tepic and Jalisco; and Among the Tarascos of Michoacan, vol. I–II* (1902).

Douglas V. Meed. *They Never Surrendered: Bronco Apaches of the Sierra Madres, 1890–1935* (1993).

Morris Edward Opler. *An Apache Life-Way: The Economic, Social, & Religious Institutions of the Chiricahua Indians* (1941).
————. *Myths and Tales of the Chiricahua Apache Indians* (1942).

Henry Bamford Parkes. *A History of Mexico* (1960).

Marc Simmons. *Massacre on the Lordsburg Road: A Tragedy of the Apache Wars* (1997).

Bernard Sternsher. *Hitting Home: The Great Depression in Town and Country* (1970).

H. Henrietta Stockel. *Women of the Apache Nation: Voices of Truth* (1991).

Edward Weston. *The Daybooks of Edward Weston, vol. I. Mexico* (1961).

Donald E. Worchester. *The Apaches: Eagles of the Southwest* (1979).

READING GROUP GUIDE

1. The title of the novel is *The Wild Girl*, and yet much of the novel is narrated from the perspective of Ned Giles. Which character did you respond to more? Why?

2. Do you consider Billy Flowers a moral person? What were his varying attitudes toward whites, Mexicans, Native Americans, and animals?

3. What do you think of the portrayals of women in the novel? Did you find the wild girl and Margaret to be believable? Did you think the author accurately imagined the way women in these situations might think and feel?

4. The novel takes place during the Depression, and Ned is very conscious of class. What are his attitudes toward the privileged, and how justified do you think his attitudes are?

5. Wealthy and homosexual, Tolley is at once privileged and an outcast in society. Which do you think affects his life in a greater way—his wealth or his sexuality? Did you find his character's flamboyance believable from a historical perspective?

6. Did anything surprise you about the history of the time period depicted by Jim Fergus?

7. Did anything surprise you about the depiction of the Apaches or their relationship with the Mexicans? Did you feel that the author was making any judgments in his depiction of the Apaches, Mexicans, and whites?

8. How did you feel in reading the story about the murder of Charlie McComas's parents and Charlie's kidnapping? Did it surprise you that a boy would embrace the people who murdered his parents?

9. Consider the choices made by Goso over the course of his life. Do you understand those choices? Did you find him sympathetic?

10. In much of twentieth-century filmmaking and writing, continuing to the present, Native American cultures have been represented in black-and-white terms. Do you think Jim Fergus's depictions of the wild Apaches, Mexicans, whites, and their interactions differ from other depictions?

11. Do you think that the Apaches and the whites and the Mexicans could have coexisted peacefully, or was a violent outcome inevitable?

12. What did you think of the love story between Ned and the wild girl? Did his choice to go back to the white world surprise you? Do you think he should have made a different choice?

13. Consider the course of Ned's life after his experiences with the Apaches. Why do you think his life took the turn it did? Is it due to what happened to him and his relationship with the wild girl, or does it stem more from the losses he experienced prior to meeting the wild girl?

14. How does Ned use photography to express himself? What do you think this says about how artists deal with emotion and human suffering?

15. In what ways is *The Wild Girl* similar to the author's first novel, *One Thousand White Women*? In what ways is it different? Which did you like best, and why?

A Conversation with Jim Fergus, Author of *The Wild Girl*

⁓

Q: You were a nonfiction writer for most of your career—primarily about hunting and fishing. What inspired you to write fiction?

A: To clarify the first part of that question: I got sort of typecast as a "hook & bullet" writer later in my journalism career, but I actually started out doing general-interest journalism—essays, literary and celebrity profiles, interviews, environmental writing, etc. From the very beginning, from the time I was about twelve years old, I had always intended to become a novelist. All my role models were fiction writers, and after I got out of college I wrote a bunch of short stories and shipped them off to the magazines, certain that I was going to get discovered. And I wrote an unpublished (and unpublishable) novel. It did not take long for me to figure out that I wasn't going to be able to make a living doing this, and so I became a teaching tennis pro, which was the only other thing I knew how to do. I worked in that profession for a full decade, during which time I wrote yet another unpublishable novel. Finally at age thirty, I had put together a little stake, about $8,000 dollars, which in those days still seemed like a lot of money. I retired from tennis and started freelance writing full-time. Of course, the Catch-22 of that business is that in order to make even a modest living at it you have to work all the time; when you're not working on an assignment you're trying to drum up new assignments. It's a very hand-to-mouth existence, not unlike being an itinerant farm laborer, and simply did not allow me any free time for fiction writing. So that old childhood dream was relegated very much to the back burner. Suddenly I found myself in my mid-forties, and it occurred to me that I wasn't any closer to being a novelist than I had been in my twenties. I came upon the idea for *1000WW* while researching what I thought was going to be a nonfiction book about the Northern Cheyenne Indians. An old friend of mine who had some money loaned me enough to take a year away from journalism and write the novel.

Q: You seem to have a great deal of familiarity with the landscapes as well as the cultures you write about. What kind of research have you done for your novels?

A: Well, I always start with the landscape, and the research there is simply a kind of accrual of experience in a place. I need to have a certain familial sense of the land in order to situate a novel in it. In the case of *1000WW*, I had traveled extensively in the northern Great Plains in the course of my magazine work, and I really knew and loved that country. With *The Wild Girl* I was less familiar with the landscape of southern Arizona and northern Mexico. But I had recently moved to the Southwest and had already spent enough time down there to know that I would come to love that country too. The northern Sierra Madre Mountains are incredibly rugged and spectacular, and I made several trips down there, traveling through the Mexican states of Sonora and Chihuahua. I took a horse pack trip up into the mountains with a Mormon outfitter out of Colonia Juarez, Chihuahua, just to get the lay of the land. And in order to be able to write the scene in which the wild girl is captured, I also went on a mountain lion hunt on muleback with a rancher who hunts lions with a pack of hound dogs. Because of my background in journalism, I tend to be very hands-on that way; I really need to see and experience these things before I can write about them. As for the cultural research, I felt a tremendous responsibility to know as much as I possibly could about the respective cultures and histories of the Northern Cheyenne and the Apaches in order to be able to write as truly and accurately as I could about them. For me the research takes as long as the actual writing of the novel.

Q: Some of your most memorable characters are female—May Dodd in *1,000WW;* the wild girl and Margaret in *The Wild Girl.* Do you enjoy writing from a female perspective? What kind of challenges does it present you as a writer?

A: Yes, I do enjoy writing from the female perspective. As a male writer, I find that it takes you completely outside of yourself, offering a kind of clean canvas, a completely fresh point of view, free of your own ego, opinions, and prejudices. It's quite liberating in that way. I've never been particularly interested in writing fiction about myself or in having myself as the protagonist of my novels, and I find that anytime a male writer writes from a male perspective, the author's own point of view inevitably bleeds through the character—which is not necessarily a bad thing, either. The challenge, of course, in writing from the perspective of the opposite sex, is to try to do so credibly.

Q: When westerns first became popular, Native Americans were frequently portrayed as savage villains. Then the tide turned and Native Americans were often depicted as noble and victimized. You depict Native American cultures with a great deal of texture and complexity. The Cheyenne in *1,000WW,* for instance, are being decimated by the U.S. government, but they also commit terrible acts of violence against other tribes. Do you think about the politics of the way Native Americans have been treated when you write, or do you try to put that aside and just tell the story? Do you set out to make a point in your novels?

A: One of the things I've heard from Native Americans who have read my novels is that they appreciate the fact that I try to avoid portraying them as one or the other of those one-dimensional stereotypes—either as the villain, or the noble savage. Of course, the truth is that they're human beings like the rest of us, capable of tremendous savagery as well as great beauty and spirituality. The revisionist notion of Native American history has it that all the tribes were living together in harmony, each in its own inviolable region, until the evil white man came along to steal their land and disrupt their perfect way of life. But the reality is that long before we showed up, these native tribes were, with some exceptions, warrior societies who had fought one another for centuries. As always in nature, the stronger had pushed the weaker out; they had enslaved one another and committed terrible atrocities. Which is not to forgive, or excuse, our treatment of Native Americans. As for the politics of this, it's hard to write about the subject, even fictionally, without touching on it, but I certainly don't set out to write political manifestos or polemics. My main goal as a novelist is simply to tell a good tale, and if readers also find a point in my novels, that's fine too.

Q: You write a great deal about morals. For instance, in *1,000WW* May Dodd is judged to be an immoral woman; the Cheyenne are judged as immoral savages. In *The Wild Girl*, Billy Flowers is depicted as having a very clear moral code, for better or worse, in great contrast with those around him. What is it about morality that fascinates you?

A: I'm interested in the sort of quicksilver, subjective nature of morality, the idea that virtually every culture, every religion, and even each era, has its own rather specific set of rules for it. And I also find fascinating the nearly desperate need that human beings have to impose their own particular version of morality upon others, to the point that we're willing to slaughter one another in the name of our own moral codes. At the same time, we have a tremendous capacity to rationalize our own behavior as moral, no matter how despicable it might be. What is more grotesque, for instance, than the killing of babies and children? And yet every nation does it under the banner of morality.

Q: What do you most enjoy about writing novels? What do you find the most difficult?

A: The first part of that question I'm going to answer with a quote from Gustave Flaubert that I have thumbtacked on the wall beside my writing desk:

> *"It is a delicious thing to write, to be no longer yourself but to move in an entire universe of your own creating. Today, for instance, as man and woman, both lover and mistress, I rode in a forest on an autumn afternoon under the yellow leaves, and I was also the horse, the leaves, the wind, the words that my people uttered, even the red sun that made them almost close their love-drowned eyes."*

How could I say it any better that? What I find most difficult is creating that universe.

Q: What do you read when you're not writing? Who are your favorite authors?

A: Like many novelists, I'm unable to read fiction when I'm writing it, as we're so easily influenced by other voices. And because I'm almost always writing I'm afraid I've gotten way behind on my reading, particularly of contemporary fiction. While I was writing *The Wild Girl*, I actually re-read *Anna Karenina*, because I was pretty sure that I wouldn't start writing in Tolstoy's voice. And I was struck once again by what an enormous novel that is (and I don't mean just in terms of page length, though it is a doorstopper). What a truly omniscient performance; the characters of all ages, sexes, classes, professions are all such individuals, so vivid and perfectly rendered, such complete and "real" human beings. I was humbled and stunned all over again by Tolstoy's greatness. Right now I'm in the middle of writing a new novel, and I recently decided to re-read Flaubert's (whom I also revere) *Madame Bovary*. I also love Knut Hamsun. And in terms of living authors, who's greater than Gabriel García-Márquez? Although I don't dare read him when I'm writing. My other favorites are too numerous to mention.

Q: Can you recommend some books for fans of your novels who would like to get even more perspective and historical background on the time period, cultures, and events that you depict in your novels?

A: Partly for that purpose, I've included extensive bibliographies at the end of both novels. But if I had to recommend just one book to provide historical background about the Indian wars in both the Great Plains and the Southwest, it would have to be Captain John G. Bourke's, *On the Border with Crook*. Bourke was General George Crook's aide-de-camp and a fine amateur ethnographer in his own right. He participated in almost all of the important events and military campaigns, against both the Cheyenne and the Apaches. It's an absolutely fascinating true account of that era.

JIM FERGUS is a freelance journalist whose work has appeared over the years in a variety of national magazines and newspapers. He is the author of two nonfiction books, and his first novel, *One Thousand White Women*, remains a bestselling epic of the American West. He lives in Montana and southern Arizona.